OUR LADY OF THE ICE

OUR LADY OF THE ICE

CASSANDRA ROSE CLARKE

1230 AVENUE OF THE AMERICAS, NEW YORK, NEW YORK 10020

 * For information about special discounts for bulk purchases, please contact Simon & Schuster Special Sales at 1-866-506-1949 or business@simonandschuster.com. * The Simon & Schuster Speakers Bureau can bring authors to your live event. For more information or to book an event, contact the Simon & Schuster Speakers Bureau at 1-866-248-3049 or visit our website at www.simonspeakers.com. * The text for this book is set in Sabon LT. * Manufactured in the United States of America * First Edition * 10 9 8 7 6 5 4 3 2 1 * Library of Congress Cataloging-in-Publication Data * Clarke, Cassandra Rose, 1983– * Our lady of the ice / Cassandra Rose Clarke.—First edition. * p. cm. * Summary: "A female PI comes into conflict with a ruthless gangster just as both humans and robots agitate for independence in a domed Argentinian colony in Antarctica."—Publisher. * ISBN 978-1-4814-4426-2 (hardcover) * ISBN 978-1-4814-4428-6 (eBook) * 1. Women private investigators—Fiction. I. Title. * PS3603.L372O87 2015 * 813'.6—dc23 * 2014039598

TO KEVIN LUND:
SURPRISE!

CHAPTER ONE

DIEGO

The old clock tower in the center of the city rang out eight times, and that meant the last ship to the mainland was leaving for the winter. Diego lit a cigarette to commemorate the occasion.

Out on the balcony, Eliana leaned over the railing and screamed out the hours with a mad sort of desperation. So did everyone else in the smokestack district, their voices drowning out the clock tower's distant gongs. When the crowd roared "eight" and the clock tower fell silent, fires erupted out of the metal barrels lining the curb, the band struck their first note, and people poured out of the tenement housing onto the narrow, winding streets.

Last Night had begun.

Eliana dropped away from the railing, picked up her beer bottle, spun in place in a lazy cumbia. Her wavy dark hair skimmed across the top of her shoulders. Diego dragged on his cigarette and watched her, the light from the fires catching on the sparkles in her dress.

"You didn't count," Eliana said, shuffling up to him. The desperation was gone; now sadness tinged the edge of her voice, nothing more.

"I never count." Diego swigged from his beer bottle. "Don't see the point."

She stopped dancing. Her skin was already dewed with sweat—they always turned the heat up on Last Night, one final indulgence before the winter. Diego wanted to lick that sweat away. He'd spend the whole night on this balcony with just her if he thought he could convince her to stay, no parties or parades or any of that bullshit. But Eliana had always wanted to see the mainland. It was one of the first things he'd learned about her. And he knew she was exactly the sort of person Last Night was for. It wasn't a celebration; it was a wake. Another year gone by, and she was still stuck in the domes, still stuck in the ice.

"You want to go down to the street?" Eliana asked.

No, thought Diego, but he knew that wasn't what she wanted to hear. "Sure." He grinned. "They've got the fires going, and I want to get you out of those clothes sooner rather than later."

"I'm hardly wearing anything right now!"

"Exactly."

Eliana laughed, covering up her sadness. Diego grabbed her by the hand and pulled her close, wrapping his arms around her shoulders. She pressed her cheek against his chest, and for a moment they swayed together, out of time to the music floating up from the street.

"You want to follow the parade this year?" he asked into her hair, already knowing the answer.

"I told Maria and Essie I'd meet them at Julio's."

"Oh, hell." He'd forgotten about those two. Figures she'd make plans without him.

Eliana smacked him on the arm. "I didn't know if you were going to show up tonight or not."

"I wouldn't miss Last Night, baby." He kissed her, slow and lingering, trying to forget that he hadn't seen her for three weeks. "Besides, I figured you'd changed your mind about seeing me, you being a cop and all."

"I told you, I'm not a cop."

"Hey, you're the one with the license."

"That license doesn't make me a cop."

He kissed her again. They left her balcony, Eliana dragging him through her shabby little apartment and down the stairwell and out onto the street. It was brighter there, from the fires, and hotter, too. Women had peeled off their sweaters and coats to reveal bare skin spangled with glitter.

Diego threw his arm over Eliana's shoulder as they stumbled along the street, dodging dancers and sparks from the handheld fireworks. The fireworks had been banned for years, but you could still buy them a few days before Last Night. Tradition.

Julio's, that tiny hole-in-the-wall bar Eliana liked, was only three streets over, but the walk took a long time in the crush of bodies. Diego slipped his hand under Eliana's thin dress, along the bare damp skin of her back, and pressed his mouth against her neck while she wound through the streets, giggling and leaning into him. Glitter showered down from the tenement balconies, sticking to his bare arms and alighting in Eliana's hair. This shit-hole neighborhood was transformed during Last Night into someplace where you might actually want to live. The whole city was. They might call it Last Night, but it was as bright as day. Light was everywhere. From the fires, from the glitter, from the floodlamps affixed to the underside of the dome, that one glass shield between Hope City and the winds of Antarctica. The city never turned the floodlamps off during Last Night, and so the day never ended.

You didn't get true sunlight in Hope City.

Julio's was crowded, people spilling out into the street, holding their glasses aloft. Not exactly Diego's scene, but he let Eliana push their way inside, shedding glitter and kissing and laughing. It was quieter inside than out, and darker, although just as warm.

"Eliana! Over here!"

Diego recognized Maria's voice immediately. Hard to miss something that shrill. Still, Eliana had pulled away from him and was spinning in place, scanning for Maria in the shadows. She let out a shout when she found her friend, then grabbed Diego's hand and pulled him over to the table where Maria was sitting. She was dressed for the parade: tight dress, hair teased high in that stupid way the girls were doing, too much color around her eyes.

Diego wished to hell he'd called Eliana sooner.

"My God, I didn't think you were going to make it." Maria leaned over the table and pushed out a pair of wobbling chairs. "I bought you an El Pato." She slid it across the table.

"So where's Essie?" Eliana asked, sliding into her seat. Diego sat down beside her.

"She decided to go out with that stupid artist friend of hers, down in the warehouse district." Maria rolled her eyes.

"Which artist friend?"

"The Independence-minded one."

"That's all of her artist friends." Eliana sipped her drink.

Maria laughed. "True enough. This is the one I think is a terrorist."

"Oh. Him."

Diego managed to suppress a laugh at the thought of any of Eliana's friends hanging around the AFF.

"She tried to convince me to go with her," Maria went on. "She gave me all the usual lines about how we shouldn't even be thinking about the mainland and such. But I told her I was meeting you." Maria glanced at Diego. "Sorry I didn't get you anything, Diego. Didn't know you were going to show."

"Everyone keeps saying that." Diego grinned, trying to scare her. "It's almost like you don't trust me."

Beneath the bright mask of her makeup Maria gave him a dark look that suggested that was *exactly* what she thought.

"Share mine," Eliana said, handing Diego her El Pato and then leaning over to kiss him on the mouth. It reminded him why he put up with her idiot friends.

"You two are awful," Maria said.

"Not any more awful than what's going on out there." Diego took a sip. He hadn't had one of these in a long time, even though Sebastian always drank them when they were down at the Florencia.

Maria patted her hair coquettishly. "I wouldn't know. I've been waiting in here for the last forty-five minutes. They showed the departure." She nodded at the television set sitting on the edge of the bar. It cast an arc of blue light across the floor. Black-and-white footage of the party at the docks flashed across the screen.

"How was it?" Eliana asked.

"Same as last year." Maria tossed back the last of her drink. "I'm ready for the parade."

"You're always ready for the parade," Diego said. He couldn't help himself.

Maria scowled at him. He laughed, took another drink. Then Eliana leaned across the table and started giggling with Maria over something or other, and Diego turned to the television. He'd gone down to the docks on Last Night a couple years back with a girl who'd since found a way to the mainland. He remembered handing her his coat as the dock gate groaned open and the ship slid away from Hope City, billowing steam and cold late-autumn air. It was an old cruise ship left over from when Hope City was an amusement park, and it had all the stupid ornamentation of anything associated with the park, the brass detailing and the word "Welcome!" carved into the side in looping, old-fashioned script.

Funny how nobody in Hope City ever welcomed that ship home.

"Hey, we're going out to the parade." Eliana brushed her fingers over Diego's shoulder. He looked up at her, and with the glitter and the television light she seemed to glow.

"Ready if you are," Diego said.

The three of them stepped out into the street.

The fires had climbed higher out of the barrels, licking at the brilliant, steaming night. The parade flowed past. Bodies danced and undulated in the waterfall of glitter.

Maria pulled a package of fireworks out of her purse. "Managed to get some this year," she said.

"Don't tell Eliana," Diego said. "She'll rat you out."

"I told you, I'm not a cop!"

Diego laughed. Maria handed them each a bundle of fireworks. For most people, anything larger than the handheld kind was impossible to get, although Diego could probably scrounge some up if he wanted. Working for Mr. Cabrera, being taken under his wing the way Diego had, it definitely had its perks.

The city kept some fireworks tucked away, though, since they usually shot them off from the bow of the ship during its departure.

That was part of the festival, the display erupting over the open ocean, color and light blossoming against the black of the night sky.

Inside a domed city, fireworks were just explosives. It didn't matter how much they lit up the night. The handheld ones couldn't do any damage unless you got too many too close to one of the fires, and even then the fireworks really only sparked and flared and maybe burned your hand. But that hint of danger was still there, which was why people like Maria went looking for them as Last Night approached.

Maria struck a match, and her fireworks flared all at once in a dazzling burst of light. She held them aloft, sparks trailing along the ground, and sang along to the music pouring out of the speakers fixed to the telephone poles. The city had switched over to British bands now, the Rolling Stones and the Animals and the Beatles. By the time Maria's fireworks had burned away, she'd been swept into the crush of the parade. Thank God.

"We're not seeing her again," Diego said. "Not until sometime tomorrow, anyway."

Eliana laughed. "She'll be fine. You should be nicer to her, though. She's had a hard year."

"I'll be nicer to her when she's nicer to me."

Eliana looped her arm in his. "She doesn't approve of you."

"Tough shit." Diego kissed the top of Eliana's head. "Come on. Let's go find a place to light these." Diego grabbed Eliana's hand and pulled her up close to the buildings, a safe distance from the parade coursing through the streets. They skittered along the dirty sidewalk, dodging bystanders and drunks and amorous couples, their hands always linked. Diego felt a creep of Last Night giddiness, as much as he didn't want to admit it. When he glanced back at Eliana, his body lurched with desire. Her skin was sheened with sweat in the balmy heat, her hair curled into wild ringlets.

This was how he used to imagine the mainland, this heat.

They spilled into one of the narrow gaps between two tenement buildings. Someone had stretched strings of electric bulbs between the windows, and they dotted overhead like stars, which Diego had only seen a handful of times in real life, during rare autumn trips out on the shipping boats for Mr. Cabrera. He wondered if Eliana had seen the stars at all. Maybe someday he'd show them to her. It might be nice, taking her out on a spring boat in the early morning. Romantic, you know. A chance at a normal life.

Diego pulled out his lighter and touched the flame to the end of their fireworks. A flare of sulfur, a flash of white light, a trail of sparks. He lunged at Eliana, and she leapt back, shrieking. He handed her a pair of her own fireworks, and they chased each other up and down the alley like children until the light sputtered out, and then they were back on the street, swept up in the tide of the parade. Diego didn't try to crawl out this time. The heat and the light and Eliana had gone to his head.

The parade didn't follow a specific path, only flowed through the smokestack district, picking up momentum as the night wore on. People threw paper flowers and scraps of brightly colored cloth from the balconies—and glitter, of course, that constant cascade of glitter. The parade twisted and curved at random intervals until it came to the edge of the amusement park, the old center of the city, where it turned sharply, veering off in the direction of the docks. The clock tower bonged twelve times, the sound vibrating deep in Diego's bones. He grabbed hold of Eliana's hand, their palms both slippery with sweat. She nuzzled against him. She smelled of vermouth and unwashed skin and the mingled scents of a hundred different perfumes, and Diego wanted to fall into her and forget about the city and about Mr. Cabrera and about his stupid fucking job.

And then the floodlights went out.

It was instantaneous, not the gradual darkening that fell across the city at around seven thirty every night except tonight, Last Night, when the lights were never turned off. The parade halted and became a group of people, drunk and confused. Voices rose up in an unintelligible murmur.

"What's going on?" Eliana said. Her voice was nearby. Diego thought he heard a tinge of fear. He drew her in close, pressing his arm across her chest.

"I don't know," he answered, scanning the crowd. He realized he was looking for spots of danger: a glint of a knife, a flare of fire, the dull flat metal of an illegal gun. A word bounced around inside his head, an old word, one he'd heard mentioned when he was a kid but had only understood theoretically—blackout.

Every single electric light in the city was out. Not just the dome lights. The streetlamps, too, and the lights in the windows. The fires were still burning, though. Long, liquid shadows moved across the crowd. Firelight caught in the windows of the nearby buildings.

"Holy shit," he said. "The power's out."

"What?" Eliana turned toward him, a faint silhouette in the murky light. "That's impossible. Aren't the generators supposed to kick in? Or the atomic power plants—the city was supposed to set them up as backup, right? Remember? They got permission from the mainland."

"It's not impossible." Diego pulled her closer. "It just happened."

The murmuring from the crowd was louder, more panicked. People were starting to realize what Diego and Eliana just had—a *blackout* had happened. An old fragment of a nightmare from their youths. It was real.

"We have to get away from this crowd," Eliana said.

That right there, that was why Diego loved Eliana so much. She wasn't an idiot.

He gripped her hand tight, squeezing her fingers together. He reached into his pocket and pulled out his knife. He never brought his gun when he came to see Eliana, but the knife was better than nothing. He pulled her toward the edge of the crowd. "Get the fuck out of the way!" he shouted. Someone shouted back. The crowd jostled, surged, and a violent ripple cascaded down from the direction of the smokestack district.

Eliana screamed. Her hand slipped away.

For the span of a heartbeat Diego was paralyzed with fear. But you couldn't let that happen in his line of work, and so he dove into the crowd in the direction where she'd been pulled. He caught the flash of her dress, orange in the firelight, and grabbed her upper arm.

"Got you," he said, pressing his mouth against her ear. His heart was pounding. "You're right, we've got to get out of here. Come on."

They pushed on. The knife was enough to get people to move

out of the way. Most of them were terrified, their panic poisoning the darkness. Another surge of the crowd. Eliana slipped, but she grabbed on to Diego and stopped herself just in time. Smart girl.

And then they were out.

Eliana pressed close to him, and her frantic breath warmed a spot on his neck. They slammed against a wall of cold hard brick. Bodies flowed past them, but they were, for the moment, in an untouchable bubble. Diego let out a long sigh of relief.

In his arms, Eliana shivered. It was a tiny movement, but it reminded him of their precarious position here in the dark.

A blackout meant no electricity.

No electricity meant no heat.

No heat meant the city would ice over in—Diego had no idea how long. This had never happened before, not in his lifetime.

Hours?

Minutes?

No. He forced himself to focus. He glanced at Eliana, and she was staring at the surging crowd, her body almost entirely subsumed by shadows, the only visible part of her the left side of her face. It looked carved out of molten stone in the orange firelight.

"This is bad," Eliana said.

"No shit." He pressed his back flat against the wall, squeezed Eliana's hand. They needed to get inside, away from people. People turned to monsters in situations like this. Diego had seen it.

"Maria!" Eliana shouted suddenly, turning toward him. "We have to find Maria!"

Damn it. "Sorry, babe. That ain't happening. We need to get inside."

He pulled her again, skittering up against the wall. He could feel the start of a riot crackling around him, the air tightening like a wire.

"Something's going to happen to her!" she shouted.

"Something's going to happen to *you*," Diego snarled. "Come the fuck on."

Eliana seemed to shrink in on herself, and Diego felt a twist of guilt that he pushed aside. Time for that later.

The building's door was only a few meters away. If it was locked, he could pick it. If it was barricaded—

He'd figure something out.

Somewhere to the left a fire flared.

A woman screamed.

Eliana muttered a string of frightened profanity.

And then the lights came back on.

They were at full power, daytime power, noon power. Diego's eyes burned at the sudden brightness, little dots of darkness spotting his vision. Eliana threw her arm over her face. Diego stopped dragging her. The crowd had frozen in place, a garish cacophony of color.

A fire licked at one of the tenement buildings. Eliana dropped her arm away, and she stared at the fire like she'd never seen one before.

Diego's adrenaline was still pumping through his body. He kept anticipating violence, but the tension of the riot was gone, and he shook his head, trying to clear out his brain. Eliana leaned against him and kissed his chest. She was shaking. Not from the cold. It hadn't been long enough to get cold.

Distantly, an alarm rang out. Water poured down from the dome, falling across the crowd, across the burning tenement building. Diego looked up, squinting past the glare of the floodlights. A dark shape moved across the underside of the dome. A robot, a maintenance drone, tending to the fire.

"Everything's back to normal," Eliana said, although she didn't sound like she believed it.

Diego certainly didn't.

After all, he'd lived in Hope City for twenty-nine years—his entire life.

His entire life, and not once had the power ever gone out.

Not once.

CHAPTER TWO

ELIANA

Eliana woke up to Diego's arm slung across her chest, their bodies tangled up in the bedsheets. She blinked up at the ceiling. Gray light filtered in through the window.

And then her alarm went off, screeching like a mechanical bird. Diego moaned and pulled the pillow over his head. When she reached over to turn it off, she knocked it to the floor instead. It let out a loud *sprang* and fell silent.

"What the hell, Eliana? Why'd you set the alarm?"

"Gotta go back into the office today." She didn't move to get out of bed, though, only snuggled closer to Diego. He was naked, his skin warm to the touch. Three days had passed since Last Night, and he hadn't disappeared into the city for work once; Eliana thought this might have been the longest he'd gone, not leaving her. She liked it and didn't like it at the same time. She liked waking up to find him sprawled under her blankets, but she didn't like the break in her routine.

"Your office?" Diego rolled over onto his back. Eliana lay her head against his chest and listened to his heart beating. "Hell, that big PI office gives 'em a whole week after Last Night."

"Yeah, but if you work for them, you get paid vacation. I don't."

"Nobody's gonna come in today." He played with her hair, a lazy, distracted gesture. "They're still sleeping off their hangovers."

"They're afraid the power's gonna go out again," Eliana said softly, not wanting to think about the almost-riot on Last Night. People were already saying it hadn't been an accident, that it had been either mainland interference or AFF terrorism, depending on whether or not they favored Independence. Eliana wasn't a big Independence supporter. The atomic power plants here were the first of their kind in the world, and the Independents, whether AFF or not, had big ideas about turning this place into some kind of modern marvel. But Eliana knew people had used the word "marvel" when the city had been an amusement park back in the 1890s, and you just had to look outside to see where that had gotten them.

Still, she also didn't think the Antarctican Freedom Fighters would want to break down the system that let Hope City exist in the first place. They usually took their violence to the mainland, or went after big-time city politicians.

At least Maria'd turned up the next day, hungover but otherwise fine. "And someone might come in. Besides, I have filing to do."

"Filing? Jesus, you really are a cop."

"You want to come in with me?"

Diego laughed.

"It's just me. It's not like anybody knows who you are."

"That so?" Diego dropped his head to the side to look at her, black hair falling across his eyes. In the dim early-morning light he looked like some classical statue, too handsome to be real. "The problem isn't with your clients, Eliana. It's with Mr. Cabrera."

Eliana sighed.

"Word gets out I'm hanging around an *investigator's* office—"

"You didn't call me a cop. An improvement."

"Eh, you're licensed. Just as bad."

Eliana laughed, tossed her pillow at him. He caught it, threw it aside, grabbed her wrists, and pulled her close. She could smell the soap from his shower the night before, and the scent of sleep. He kissed her, and for a moment she forgot about her office.

"You can go in late," he mumbled into her neck, and his hands were already tracing over her hips, finding the places he knew too well.

* * * *

Two hours later, Eliana walked the familiar path to her office. Alone. It was cold as hell this morning, especially now that she was away from her radiator and the heat of Diego's touch. But those weren't the only reasons—it was always colder in the days following Last Night, the trade-off for turning up the heat during the celebration.

Eliana pulled her coat more tightly around her waist and readjusted the scarf she'd wrapped around her hair. Nobody was out, just like Diego'd said. But there hadn't been many clients lately, and she didn't want to run the risk of missing somebody. She had left Diego in her apartment, flipping through the newspaper like he cared. He probably wouldn't be there when she went home; as she'd walked through the door, he'd called out, "Guess I should see if the old man needs me for anything."

A private investigator stepping out with a gangster. That was a story. Almost as good a story as there being a lady PI in the first place.

It took Eliana the usual fifteen minutes to make it to her office, which was on the second floor of a brick building right at the edge of the smokestack district. Last year it had belonged to an old PI named Marco Vasquez. Eliana'd been his secretary. When he'd retired, he'd given her the building and his gun and told her to get her firearm license.

"They aren't gonna give me one of those," she'd said.

"They will once you get your PI license," he'd said, and for two straight days she'd thought he'd lost his mind. But it was true she'd been just as much assistant as secretary, and although the proctors laughed when she went down to take the test, she passed, and they didn't have much choice but to make everything official. It was sad, though, that her mother had died before Eliana had started working for Mr. Vasquez. She would have been proud. It was a big deal, for the daughter of an old amusement park dancer to get a job like this one. It was the sort of thing Eliana's parents had immigrated to Hope City for in the first place, back when it had still been an amusement park. The park had promised endless opportunities, before wars and revolutions and poverty on the mainland had left people unable to believe in its magic anymore. It had shut down back in the 1940s, leaving Eliana's parents, along with half the city, unemployed. Things got better with the atomic power plants—more jobs, more people moving back in. But her parents had been long gone by then. Eliana had stood in the city's freezing mausoleum on two separate occasions and watched her parents' ashes fly out of the dome.

Work had been steady over the last eight months. At first people had been looking for Marco, and Eliana'd gotten used to the disappointment in their voices as they'd said, "It's just you?" Gotten used to their excuses, to the way they fumbled out of the office without giving her a case whenever she explained, patiently and calmly, that Marco Vasquez had left Hope City for the mainland. But enough time had gone by that now people showed up looking for her specifically, and that was a good feeling.

The mainland. Mr. Vasquez was lucky. Not many people got out of Hope City. Eliana's parents certainly never did—they'd lived and died here. She didn't want to do the same, and she hoped this job would generate enough money for her to purchase a visa out of Antarctica. Someday.

Eliana's footsteps echoed in the stairwell as she clomped up to the office. The name on the door still read VASQUEZ because she didn't want to waste money getting the glass replaced.

She pulled out her key, let herself in. The bell clanged against the doorframe.

The office was freezing, the air cold enough that she could see her breath. Eliana switched on the radiator and set a pot of coffee to percolate on the hotplate. The air had that still, untouched quality it got when you leave a place alone for too long. Too long—just three days. Still, Eliana had missed the office, with its cracked floorboards and its thick, wavy windows and its worn-out schoolteacher's desk from which she conducted her business.

Eliana switched on the radio to break up the stillness. Usually she kept it on the mainland station, but this morning she spun through the dial until she came to a news program. The newsman was talking about the blackout in his lisping mainland accent, claiming that there was no evidence of the AFF's involvement, that it had been the fault of a defective robot from the power plant. The city commissioner planned on publicly dismantling the robot tonight.

Diego hadn't wanted to hear about it, these last three days. Kept shutting off the radio anytime she tried to listen.

The coffee finished up, letting off clouds of steam. Eliana poured herself a cup and sprinkled in the last of the sugar. She still had some at home, but once it was gone, she wouldn't see any more sugar until winter was over.

The radio played on quietly in the background, a dull murmur, and the radiator was rattling. Good. It'd be warm enough soon for her to take off her coat.

Eliana turned to the stack of files sitting at the corner of her desk. Left over from the last case she'd worked, one of those adultery jobs where she'd had to tail a housewife all over the city, looking to see if the woman was faithful or not. As it had turned out, this particular housewife had just gotten a job.

The bell clattered against the door.

Eliana immediately sat up, shoving the files into the desk drawer where she kept her pens. She felt a momentary surge of smugness—looked like coming in so soon was about to pay off.

The door swung open, and a woman stepped inside.

Eliana had seen her before. She was certain of it, although she couldn't place her. The woman looked like a film star, tall and shapely, her hair that peculiar European blond. She glided into the room like she was made of light.

"Eliana Gomez?" the woman said.

"That's me." Eliana stood up and walked around to the front of her desk. The woman stood by the door, staring at her.

The radio hummed in the background. The radiator clanged against the wall.

"Can I get you a cup of coffee?" Eliana said.

"No, thank you." The woman glanced around the office. Her face was as flawless and as expressionless as a mask, and she wore a gray fur draped around her shoulders. Only the wealthy wore fur in Hope City.

"I received your name from a former client of yours," the woman said. "Annetta Marchel. I hope this isn't too—forward."

Annetta Marchel. One of the first who'd asked for Eliana by name. She had specifically wanted a lady detective, someone she could trust with information about a sensitive medical procedure.

"Forward?" Eliana smiled. "Not if you've got a job for me."

"I do." The woman slipped her fur off her shoulders, revealing a pale silk blouse, a glittering necklace. "I'm afraid it requires a certain amount of discretion."

"Then it's a good thing you came to me and not those PI firms downtown. I specialize in discretion." Eliana gestured at the chairs set up in front of her desk. "Why don't you have a seat and tell me about it?"

The woman gave a thin, elegant smile, frustratingly familiar. She floated across the room and draped herself in one of the chairs. Eliana felt clumsy and graceless by comparison as she took her own seat.

"My name's Marianella Luna," the woman said, "and some important documents of mine have gone missing."

Marianella Luna. Immediately Eliana remembered where she'd seen the woman before—on television. She was that Argentinian aristocrat, the one all the Independents loved, the one in those advertisements with the city councilman Alejo Ortiz, raising money for his Hope City agricultural domes. *We have the strength to run our own city. Atomic power should be ours! End Antarctican dependence on Argentina!* As if that was ever going to happen.

Marianella Luna stared at Eliana, her pale eyes framed in thick dark lashes.

Eliana found her voice. "Well, that's certainly a shame, Lady Luna."

Lady Luna sat with perfect posture, her hands folded in her lap. "More than you could know, I'm afraid. Will you be able to help me?"

"I'll certainly try." Eliana pulled a notepad and a pen out of her desk. "So. These documents. When did you notice they'd disappeared?"

"This morning. I woke up and found someone had broken into the safe in my library. It was—distressing."

"You didn't call the police?"

Eliana kept her voice neutral, but she watched Lady Luna closely, looking for clues. Always start an investigation with the client—one of the few pieces of advice Mr. Vasquez had given her.

Lady Luna took a deep breath and toyed with her necklace.

"The contents of these documents," she said, "are sensitive."

"Sensitive."

"Yes, Miss Gomez. I don't wish to give the impression that I don't have faith in the city's police department, and I'm sure they would never betray me intentionally, but if some newly minted detective were to glance at these documents, it would be—" She dropped her necklace. "Disastrous. If I hired you, it would be as much for your discretion as for your investigative skills. I do hope you understand, Miss Gomez."

When she said Eliana's name, her voice softened, her eyes took on a soft aristocratic glow.

"That's why people come to me," Eliana said, floundering a little. "Discretion and investigation." She felt stupid saying this, but she didn't want to risk Lady Luna taking her business downtown. And people did come to Eliana for discretion. It wasn't a lie.

Eliana leaned back in her chair, trying to smooth out her awkwardness, and sipped at her coffee. "I won't even charge you extra. Ten bucks a day, just like all my clients."

Another light smile. "I've every intention of paying you handsomely for your work. Speed is another issue we'll need to discuss, of course, and another reason I didn't contact the police. They can be dreadfully slow with these things, as I learned when my late husband's office was robbed." She sighed. Eliana tried to remember who her husband was, but she'd never followed gossip about the aristocracy. She'd have to ask Maria later.

"I'll get them back as fast as I can," Eliana said.

"It's important that you do so, yes. As I said, I can't have the contents of these documents released to the public."

"Of course not." Eliana wondered what the documents were for. Immigration? Something tying Lady Luna to the mainland? She was palling around with Alejo Ortiz, after all, with his hypocritical mainland suits and his speeches about Hope City growing her own food. If Lady Luna wanted to hold on to the Independents' good graces, it wouldn't serve her well for word to get out that she still owned property back in Argentina proper.

"I'll need you to tell me everything you know about the robbery," Eliana said, pen poised over her notebook. Lady Luna watched her without moving. "When I say 'everything,' I mean everything. Even if it doesn't seem important to you, it may damn well be important to me, so I want to hear about it."

"Yes, of course." Lady Luna glanced past Eliana's shoulder, toward the narrow, grimy window that looked down onto the street below. Her eyes narrowed. "I didn't hear anything last night. The house has a security system, as well as a mechanical butler. An android, I mean, left over from the amusement park."

Eliana paused in her note-taking, surprised. She glanced up at Lady Luna, who smiled back.

"You told me to tell you everything. I do hope you won't judge me too harshly. I know they've fallen out of fashion."

"I won't judge you at all. Go on." Eliana wrote *andie* on the notepad. She'd never seen one before, although she remembered her father talking about them—complaining about them, really, calling them unnatural. As far as Eliana knew, most of them had been dismantled since the park's closing, and the ones left behind weren't supposed to leave the old center of the city. She supposed if you had the sort of money the Lunas did, exceptions were made.

"I only mention it because he's better equipped than you or I to notice intruders. And he heard and saw nothing last night."

"Didn't get shut off, did he?"

Lady Luna gave her a strange look, hard and glittering like Antarctic ice. "Do you have any idea how difficult it is to shut off an android, Miss Gomez?"

Eliana's cheeks burned. "Look, I'm just covering my bases here. I've never seen one before, so I have no idea how they work."

Lady Luna shook her head. "He wasn't shut off. I'm certain of it. I found the safe myself this morning, around eight o'clock. It was after I had dressed and eaten breakfast. I take care of my correspondence in the library every morning, and when I came in, I found the safe hanging open, empty." Her voice died away, and she sat trembling in the worn-out leather chair. She possessed a fragile sort of loveliness that intensified with her anxiety. Eliana imagined this routine worked wonders on men.

"Do you have any idea who might have taken the documents?" Eliana asked.

Lady Luna hesitated.

"If you don't answer me truthfully, I won't be able to help you."

The air in the room was silent and cold and unmoving. Lady Luna studied Eliana for a moment, then reached into her glossy little handbag and pulled out a stack of bills. She laid them on the desk. Eliana didn't have to count them to know they added up to payment for far more days than she'd actually need to solve the case. And it was all up front.

A visa to the mainland, acquired legally, cost nearly three thousand dollars. An illegal one cost even more, and neither would get you a ticket for the reinforced ships sailing back and forth across stormy Drake Passage, which could cost as much as a thousand, depending on the time of year. She'd been saving idly for a visa and a ticket ever since her parents had died, but with this kind of money she might actually start to make headway.

"I realize that you're professionally obligated to report criminal activity," Lady Luna said softly. "But I hope your discretion can extend a bit further than you're used to."

Eliana shoved the notepad aside. Now the case was getting interesting. "What is it? You in trouble, Lady Luna?"

Her eyes were luminous. "It's not me," she said. "It was my husband. But I don't want word to get out, you understand. He passed away six months ago, and I would hate for all this to come out *now*—"

"I won't go to the cops. But if you want your documents back, you've got to tell me."

Lady Luna drew herself up, her spine as straight as a doll's. As an andie's. "He occasionally did business with Ignacio Cabrera."

The words rang out against the cold of the room. But Eliana had been seeing Diego for the last year. She wasn't exactly shocked by people's involvement with Cabrera.

"A bit more scandalous than owning a mechanical butler," Lady Luna said. "I hope this won't sully our arrangement, Miss Gomez. I never had dealings with the man myself, barely even *spoke* to him, but I knew about my husband's arrangement, and I—" She looked off to the corner of the room.

Eliana's chest twinged. She realized she actually felt sorry for Lady Luna, even if the woman was rich and beautiful and could get out of this city in a heartbeat if she wanted to. Lady Luna took a deep breath, her shoulders rising and falling, and Eliana knew it was time to remind Lady Luna that she wasn't hiring just *any* private investigator.

Eliana stood up, walked around the desk, and sat down in the empty chair beside Lady Luna. She rested her hand on top of Lady Luna's, the glove soft and velvety against her fingers. Lady Luna looked at their hands, unmoving.

"I'm not going to take you to the cops," Eliana said. "I know you can't help what he did. But anything you can tell me about Cabrera, about your husband's involvement—"

"I don't know." Lady Luna tilted her head down, a strand of hair falling across her eyes. "Well, I don't know the details. It wasn't something we—discussed."

"But you did know about it. Before he died."

"A little. It involved the winter supply ships. Bringing in drugs from the mainland." She shrugged. "I didn't want to tell you. I debated back and forth. But it was Cabrera, wasn't it, who stole the documents? I don't know *why*—"

Eliana bet she knew why. Nothing would put Cabrera out of the smuggling business more quickly than agricultural domes that actually produced agriculture. The documents probably protected

Lady Luna from city censure if Cabrera exposed her connection to him—that would explain why she didn't want to go to the police too. Probably he was going to hold them over her head as leverage. Eliana had a hard time believing that Lady Luna couldn't figure all that out on her own, but she didn't say anything about it. That was a lot of money on the desk.

"Look." Eliana pushed her chair around so she could look Lady Luna in the eye. "I may seem like I'm new to this whole investigation scene, but I've been doing it long enough that I'm used to dealing with Cabrera." This wasn't entirely true, but Eliana was willing to count her dalliances with Diego. "So no worries there. You gave me that big stack of cash"—she pointed at the desk—"to get your documents back. I'll get 'em back. Maybe that's all I'll do for you, but I'll get them back without peeking and without letting them leak. Sound fair?"

Lady Luna nodded and drew a forefinger across the underside of her right eye, as if to wipe away a tear. Her makeup didn't smear at all. "Thank you, Miss Gomez."

"I'll come by your house this afternoon, take a look around, maybe talk to the robot. It does, uh, talk, doesn't it?"

"Yes, of course."

"Good." Eliana leaned back. "Was there anyone else at the house last night?"

"Oh, no." Lady Luna shook her head. "The android is the only staff I have."

Eliana nodded, although she didn't say anything. That was a bit eccentric.

"I let my human staff go when my husband died," Lady Luna said. "Things were—easier that way."

Eliana smiled politely. Excitement sparked in her blood. The first case of the winter. Mr. Vasquez had warned her about the winter cases. They were trickier, he said. Dangerous. She should expect to run into Cabrera.

Eliana wasn't worried. She had Diego. And the money on the desk was a lot to add to her visa funds.

Lady Luna stood up, smoothing out her skirt, rearranging the fur around her shoulders. "I look forward to working with you," she said. She had collected herself and was back to being the woman on television. "That money is only your retainer, of course. I'll pay you the rest when my documents are returned to me. Would you like me to write down the name of my house?"

At first, Eliana only registered the question about the house. She ripped off a clean sheet of paper and handed it to Lady Luna along with a pen. As Lady Luna wrote in elegant, practiced strokes, Eliana glanced down at the money on the desk. Lady Luna's voice echoed in her head. *I'll pay you the rest.* That wasn't all of it.

Eliana wondered what the hell those documents could be.

* * * *

That afternoon, Eliana took the Sunlight Express, the train that left from the docks. She'd never ridden on it before. This was a rich person's train.

It was nicer than the city trains, she supposed, although the compartments were windowless and the decor was the same over-wrought turn-of-the-century style as the amusement park. Eliana sat down at a table, lit a cigarette, and splurged on a fernet coffee and watched the little flames flickering in their glass globes on the tables. Seemed a stupid idea to her, letting fires burn on a moving train.

The train was mostly empty. No one was in the dining car but her and the bartender, who leaned up against the wall and flipped through a newspaper. When Eliana had seen that Lady Luna's house had a name, Southstar, instead of an address, it hadn't surprised her. Of course she lived in one of those domes that lay outside the main city dome. A private dome for the privately wealthy, with its own private maintenance drones, its own private power plant. One of those things no one even bothered to complain about, because complaining was just a reminder that the people who ran the city didn't have to give a shit whether or not the heat was turned up enough, whether or not the power blacked out.

Eliana smoked her cigarette down to the filter, lit another one. The bartender turned the pages of his newspaper. A bell chimed, the lights blinked twice. The bartender sighed, tossed the paper onto the bar, and sat down.

"Better hold on," he said.

A pause. Then he leaned over and blew out the flame on the candle burning next to the cash register.

"What?" said Eliana.

The bell chimed again.

The train began to rattle and whine. The chairs and tables knocked against the floor. Eliana jammed her cigarette into her ashtray and blew out her own candle too. The polar winds shrieked on the other side of the wall. Now she understood why there were no windows—it was bad enough feeling the Antarctic air slipping in through the invisible cracks in the train's construction.

Eliana set one hand over the top of her drink glass, her bones vibrating inside her skin. She curled the fingers of her free hand against the seat of her chair. The bartender looked up at the bottles of liquor shaking against the mirror like he hoped they'd fall.

The rattling stopped.

Another chime, like an exhalation of breath. The bartender stood up, swiped his newspaper off the counter, and resumed his previous position as if the rattling interlude had never occurred. Eliana sat for a moment, breathing hard.

"First time?" the bartender asked without looking up.

"Yeah." With shaking hands, Eliana lit another cigarette.

"You get used to it." The bartender turned a page of his newspaper.

The rest of the trip passed uneventfully. Eliana was the only person who got off at Southstar Station. The platform was empty too, and small, although well kept-up, with a metal bench and a wisteria tree dropping dots of purple. No ticket counter. It took Eliana a moment to connect the names and realize this was a private station.

"Jesus," she said.

A house loomed in the distance, emerging out of a field of golden grass. Eliana stepped off the platform. She was surrounded by a quiet, arrhythmic susurration, the grass rippling in tandem—false wind. She felt it on her skin, that dry, artificial warmth. It wrapped around her as she cut a path toward the house, trampling down the grass. There was probably a designated way, some stone path leading to the front door, but Eliana was too overwhelmed, and too determined, to figure out where it was.

The grass brushed feather-soft against her bare hands, making her jump. She hated its constant, babbling whisper, like it was trying to tell her something that she couldn't understand.

She was grateful to arrive at the house. It was large, as she'd expected, although quite contemporary, with lots of flat modernist lines and gray brick and huge windows. It was hard to imagine that it existed in the same city as the little shanty houses where Eliana had grown up.

She pressed her thumb against the doorbell and waited.

The rustle of the grass was sounding more and more likes voices. Eliana rang the doorbell again.

This time, someone answered.

It was a man, tall and slim and dressed in simple cotton clothing. He blinked at Eliana and said, "How can I help you?"

As soon as he spoke, Eliana saw it. The andie. He had almost fooled her, but his voice was too measured, too soft, too pleasant. She remembered her mother saying once that they unsettled you if you looked too closely, and she thought she could see why now—there was something *too much* about him. Too much of what humans thought made them human.

"I need to speak with Marianella Luna. I told her I'd be coming by."

"Ah yes, of course." The robot smiled. "Eliana Gomez, yes? Come in. I can show you to the library. I'll let her know you're here."

He stepped back, still holding the door open. Eliana went inside. The lighting was the same as it had been out in the golden grass, muted and indistinct. The robot led Eliana into the library, past a parlor with a mirrored chandelier and a series of closed doors. Above one of the doors hung a cross wrapped in red lace; Eliana blinked, not expecting something like that in such a wealthy house.

The library was almost all window. Hardly any books, just a table looking out over the ocean of grass. The safe was set into the lone non-windowed wall, its door hanging open at an angle.

"I didn't touch anything."

Lady Luna's voice was like a wind chime. Eliana turned around. Lady Luna stood in the doorway, her hair falling around her shoulders.

"That helps. Thanks."

"This is Luciano," she said, walking forward. "You said you might want to talk to him."

Eliana looked at the andie, unsure of how to act around him. It?

"It would be my pleasure," the andie said. "Although I don't think I know anything of value."

"You'd be surprised," Eliana said.

Lady Luna and the andie stood side by side, watching her.

"If you give me a minute," she said, "I'm just gonna poke around here, and then I'll talk to—to him."

Lady Luna nodded. She put her hand on the andie's arm, and they both turned away. It was a small gesture, an intimate one, and it made Eliana uncomfortable.

Lady Luna dropped her hand to her side as if she knew what Eliana was thinking.

Eliana turned back to the safe. She reminded herself of the stack of money she'd locked away in her own safe back at the office; then she knelt down on the carpet, moving slowly, her eyes scanning the room. Everything seemed in its place except for the safe, but Eliana had already learned that sometimes you had to look beyond the surface of things. She didn't have the equipment to dust for fingerprints, but something told her she wouldn't find any anyway. She had to look *close*.

She felt around on the carpet in front of the safe. Nothing. The fuzzy artificial light made it difficult to see, so she straightened up and walked over to a nearby lamp. Lady Luna was sitting in a chair, her arm draped over the side. The andie was gone.

"I'm going to borrow this," Eliana said, and before Lady Luna could answer, she yanked the cord out of the wall and dragged the lamp across the room. She plugged it in closer to the safe and shone the light on the floor, where she uncovered a solar system of dust and flakes of grass. Nothing of interest. She directed the light into the safe. Nothing there, either.

Eliana sat back on her heels. “I’d like to talk to the andie now, if you don’t mind.” She glanced over her shoulder at Lady Luna, who stared at her from across the room.

“Yes, of course.” Lady Luna leaned forward toward the coffee table and rested her fingers on top of a brass paperweight in the shape of a shell. It didn’t fit in with the rest of the library. Too old-fashioned. It made a loud clicking noise when she pressed on it.

A few moments later, the andie appeared in the doorway.

Eliana hesitated. He looked so much like a person. But she still found him unnerving—the placid dark eyes, the inexpressive mouth. He didn’t move the way a person would, didn’t shift his weight, didn’t tap his fingers against his thigh.

She took a deep breath.

“What exactly did you hear last night?”

The andie glanced at Lady Luna, machine-quick.

“Nothing,” he said.

“Nothing at all?”

“Nothing unusual.”

“What’s usual?”

The andie took on a blank expression. His eyes went slack. Eliana was aware of Lady Luna standing up, her arms wrapped around her chest like she was cold.

“Wind,” the andie said. “The maintenance drones increase it at night. The grass, of course. A handful of animals.”

“Animals?”

“Yes, field mice. Owls.”

“You have owls out here?” The city dome had rats and spiders. Eliana’d seen pictures of an owl once and hadn’t realized they’d been imported into Antarctica.

“Of course.”

“So are you sure you didn’t hear anything that you mistook to be an animal?”

Lady Luna was at Eliana’s side now, staring at the andie with a peculiar intensity. *Intelligence,* Eliana thought. *Cunning.*

Lines appeared in the robot’s brow, distressingly human.

“I did hear a—scratching, I suppose you could call it.”

"Scratching? You didn't think that was unusual enough to report?"

"It's not unusual," the robot said. "You often hear scratching along the walls. I heard it three times last night, several hours apart."

"He's right," Lady Luna said. "I hear it sometimes myself, as I'm trying to fall asleep. The emptiness out here—it amplifies sound. That's what my husband used to say." She smiled, her face incandescent.

"Fine. It's not unusual. But it could still be something." Eliana stared up at the robot. "Do you remember exactly where you heard it? Each time?"

"Of course."

"I mean, do you know where it was coming from, not where *you* were—" Eliana'd worked with enough computers in secretary school to know that you had to be specific with them. And this man was a computer, even if he didn't look like it.

"Yes, that's what I thought you meant. I can show you." The andie smiled politely, coldly. "Come."

Eliana glanced at Lady Luna, but she was still watching the andie, her face intense again. It was unsettling. It made Lady Luna's beauty frightening.

"The first was in the walls, here." The andie led Eliana through the hallway and stopped in the parlor. The chandelier threw off dots of light. He pressed his hand against the wall. "It lasted five seconds and stopped."

"The others?"

"One was upstairs, in the attic. Two seconds. I can show you if you insist—"

"The third one?"

"In the downstairs guest room."

"The walls again?"

"No." The andie shook his head. "Outside."

"How long?"

"Seven seconds."

Eliana frowned. She turned to Lady Luna. "Did you look in the guest bedroom this morning?"

"No. I didn't think to."

"Did you?" To the andie.

"No, ma'am."

"All right, show me." Eliana flicked her hand down the hall. "Is it close to the library?"

"Yes, it's one room over."

The air took on that tingle that meant she was getting close to something. She'd become a secretary because there weren't many options for a girl like her, and she didn't want to wind up like her parents. But she'd become an investigator because of that tingle. That joy of solving a puzzle and finding an answer.

The guest room door was closed but not locked. The room was decorated as tastefully as the rest of the house, but there was a coldness about it, an unlived-in quality that reminded Eliana of an exhibit in a museum. As in the library, nothing seemed out of place.

"Where exactly?" Eliana asked.

"By the window." The andie walked across the room and laid his hand on the wall next to the sill. His movement rippled the diaphanous curtains stretched over the window. Eliana noticed they never fell still but kept moving back and forth like shimmer across the surface of a water puddle.

There was that tingle again.

Eliana slid the curtains aside. Warm air brushed across her knuckles.

"This window isn't closed all the way," she said.

"No," said Lady Luna. "It never has."

"So it doesn't lock?"

Lady Luna shook her head.

Eliana grabbed hold of the window and pushed. The window slid open, scraping against the frame. The wind blew into the room, bringing with it the dried-herb scent of the grass.

She turned to the andie. "Was that the scratching you heard? Sounded like seven seconds to me."

He glanced at Lady Luna, whose expression did not change. "It could have been, yes."

"It didn't occur to you that was the sound of a window opening?"

The andie's expression went slack.

"You opened it from the inside," Lady Luna said. "It's almost impossible to do from outside. And besides, he didn't hear anything else."

Eliana frowned. "Give me a minute." Eliana shoved her shoulders through the window and looked down. The grass grew right up to the base of the house, but it was trampled there, the stalks bent and broken. She remembered the path she'd cut through the grass herself, the sound of the grass crunching under her feet, and her heartbeat quickened.

No path led to the window, but someone had certainly stood here.

"I'll be right back," she said, and then she pushed herself through the window completely, landing in the grass. Lady Luna cried out in surprise. Eliana readjusted her skirt and looked to find the andie standing in the window, watching her. Creepy.

She pushed the feeling aside and felt around in the grass, her heart hammering. Every nerve in her body jangled with anticipation, and she forgot about Lady Luna and the andie. The only thing she cared about was finding the answer.

She crawled parallel to the house, plunging into the grass. It brushed rough and dry against her face and pricked her through her clothes. Whatever had made the impression in the grass had dropped out of the sky, she was certain. Definitely a robot. Not like the andie, but the sort she was used to, the drones they kept up at the top of the dome for repairs. The ones that buzzed around like insects.

It would have dropped out of the sky, pulled open the window, and slid inside. The dome robots were designed to stay silent, because you didn't want people knowing they existed.

But it wouldn't have done this on its own. Robots couldn't steal, not even the more modern ones. Only humans could. Eliana had learned that quickly enough on this job. And if she wanted to find the human who'd programmed the robot before Lady Luna's documents leaked to all of Hope City, she didn't have time to ambush every power plant and maintenance center in the domes clustered over the desert. Hell, she didn't have the ability to do that even if there weren't a deadline.

"C'mon, c'mon," she muttered, turning back to the flattened patch of grass by the window. There had to be *something*.

But there wasn't. Only grass, wind, the andie's watchful stare.

Eliana stood up, brushing bits of broken grass off her stockings. Lady Luna had joined the andie in the window and was watching her with alarm.

"Have you gone mad?" she asked.

"It was a robot," Eliana said. "Not like—" She gestured at *her* robot. "One of the newer maintenance ones, most likely. The flying ones. But I don't have the evidence to track it to its source. It could've come from anywhere."

"No," the andie said.

"What?" Eliana narrowed her eyes. "How else could someone get in? The grass is flattened. That's where it landed—"

"Pardon me," the andie said. "I wasn't criticizing your theory. I was trying to say that it could not have come from anywhere."

Eliana's cheeks burned, but she stood up straight. "What do you mean?"

"The sort you're talking about—the flying sort. There aren't many in the city. Most crawl." The andie made a spidery motion with his fingers. "The flying ones all operate out of the city offices. As you mentioned, they're quite a new model. They've only been around the last few months."

"Yeah," Eliana said.

"Forgive me if I seemed brusque. I only wished to rectify your mistake. You said we should not let any information go unmentioned."

Eliana nodded, although she still felt sore about him correcting her. Lady Luna smiled up at the andie, moved her lips with something Eliana couldn't hear. Maybe "Thank you." The andie was right, though. Eliana wouldn't have to beat down every power plant in Hope City. She wouldn't have to beat down anything. Maria worked for the city, as a secretary in the budget office. She'd gotten information for Eliana before.

Warm wind blew through the grass, tossing Eliana's hair into her face. She was giddy again, the andie be damned.

"Lady Luna," Eliana said. "I'm going to get those documents back for you. Tomorrow. Tomorrow afternoon I'll have them in hand. I swear it."

And Lady Luna gave her a look that might have been doubt, might have been desperation, might have been anything.

CHAPTER THREE

SOFIA

Sofia had not been to this part of the city in a long time. She doubted she had ever been to this particular building, with its imported brown brick, its wide glass windows. It was the tallest building for several blocks. Height was always a mark of wealth in Hope City.

The walkway leading to the building's glass door was lined with lavender. Imported from Europe. Expensive. Sofia trailed her fingers across the top of the plants to release the scent.

The door was locked. Sofia read each label on the buzzer until she came to LUIS VILLANUEVA. She pressed the button and waited.

"Yeah?"

"It's your four o'clock appointment, Mr. Villanueva."

He didn't question her further, just as Cabrera had promised. The buzzer chimed and the glass door slid open. Sofia slipped inside. The lobby was decorated in the earth tones no lifelong citizen of Hope City had ever seen in nature, browns and blues and greens. A woman sat alone on a tasteful brocaded sofa, reading. She glanced up at the sound of Sofia's heels on the tile. The woman didn't speak, didn't smile, but she watched as Sofia clicked her way toward the elevators. Sofia pressed the button for the twenty-eighth floor and glanced over her shoulder. The woman looked away, back down to the glossy magazine spread open on her lap.

Sofia memorized her face. It was necessary to account for certain contingencies.

She rode all the way to the twenty-eighth floor alone. It took longer than she'd expected, and as she waited to arrive, she pulled a compact out of her handbag and checked her reflection. She didn't wear any face powder because she didn't need it, but she had applied liner and lashes and lipstick for the first time in years. She had styled her hair in the manner that had become fashionable recently, teasing it up high from the roots. She wore a dress Cabrera had purchased for her from a department store downtown. A down payment, he'd called it. "If you fuck this up," he said, "you owe me thirty dollars."

She wasn't going to fuck this up. Everything hinged on this one moment, on convincing Cabrera that he could trust her completely.

The elevator chimed and the doors opened. Sofia stepped into the hallway. One of the light fixtures flickered, casting staccato shadows across the carpet. She walked to room 2848 and knocked three times, as Cabrera had instructed. She had just pulled her hand away after the third knock when Luis Villanueva answered, music spilling out around him.

Music.

For a moment Sofia froze—but it wasn't a melody she recognized. Something new, something modern. Rock and roll, she thought it was called. Those songs were never dangerous.

"You're not Alissa," he said, face twisting into concern. His eyes darted out into the hallway.

"Alissa couldn't come today," Sofia said. "They sent me instead."

Luis looked doubtfully at her. Sofia held her chin high, pushed out her chest, drew in her waist. She was aware of time passing.

"Alissa told me what you liked," Sofia said. "And she sent me over with a gift."

Luis's expression softened. "A gift." He smiled nervously. "She told you about that?"

"Of course. And I can keep it a secret too." Sofia pushed inside without waiting for an invitation, drawing her hand across his chest as she moved past him. He didn't protest. The apartment was clean and sparse and smelled faintly of cigarette smoke. Sofia draped herself on his sofa. Over the thumping whine of the music, she could hear the computer in the next room, whirring behind the closed door.

Luis didn't live here. No one did. The city had purchased an apartment in this expensive uptown building just to house a mainframe. To hide it, actually, from people like Sofia and Ignacio Cabrera. Keeping it in the city offices would be too obvious. These new sorts of computers, that ran on electricity instead of steam, always made the city nervous.

Luis sat beside her. She smelled his expensive European cologne, his cigarettes, the residual electric scent of the computer. But beneath all that was the strange feral fragrance she associated with humanity, pheromones and salt water and iron.

She reached into her handbag and pulled out the little glass apothecary jar Cabrera had given her and set it on the coffee table.

"Your gift," she said sweetly. "From Alissa."

Luis stared at it. Already desire was coalescing inside him, manifesting in the form of droplets of sweat on his forehead. Not desire for her. Or for Alissa, that sad girl with haunted eyes Sofia had seen sitting in Cabrera's office as he'd explained what Sofia was to do.

"Here, let me." She picked up the apothecary bottle, unscrewed the lid, drew the thin golden liquid up into the dropper. Luis watched her with something like longing. She let two drops fall onto her tongue. It tasted dull and bitter. Then she did the same to Luis. He closed his mouth and his eyes at the same time and fell backward onto the couch like his bones were melting away.

She did the same.

She lay there for five minutes, listening to him breathe beneath the music. She stared at the filigree in the ceiling, a pattern like snowflakes. An old pattern in a new building. Those two golden drops were working their way into Luis's bloodstream, seeping like lead into his cells. Like lead, it was poison. She wondered how it was, for them, to languish so close to death. She wondered why they enjoyed it.

His breath slowed but did not stop.

She stood up, swinging her legs over him in one liquid movement. He lay, unmoving, on the sofa, his eyes staring blankly up at the ceiling, dark with pupil. She slipped off her shoes and walked over to the record player lurking in the corner and knocked the needle off the turntable. The record scratched and fell silent, and Sofia was free from the sharp panic associated with music. She could hear the computer better now—*whump*, *whump*, *whump*, as slow as Luis's poisoned heartbeat.

The door leading to the computer was locked. Sofia pulled a pin out of her hair and picked the lock easily, then slipped inside, leaving the door open. The computer took up the entire room, lights dazzling in the dim apartment, magnetic tapes rolling out their long streams of information. It was a database, brand-new, that contained information about every power plant, every dome, every utility, every icebreaker, every entrance and exit, every seaport in Antarctica. Everything you would need to know to run a domed city on the bottom of the world, collected into one place.

It was beautiful. A modern marvel.

And they left it alone with a man like Luis Villanueva.

She dragged a chair across the room and sat in front of the computer. It was much more advanced than she was, and designed for different things, but Araceli had assured her she would be able to connect with it easily enough.

She pulled a narrow cable out of her handbag, coiling it around her wrist like a bracelet. She knelt on the floor and ran her fingers across the back of the computer until she found the connection port. It was exactly where Araceli had promised it would be. Then she wrapped the cable over her shoulder and pushed her hair away from her left ear. Her own connection port was where it had been the last time she'd been hooked to a mainframe. She slid the skin aside to reveal it.

She plugged in the cable and stood up.

As she'd expected, she hit up against the mainframe's security systems, but it was easy for her to thread her way around them; she was an old computer, and this new computer didn't quite know what to make of her, so it only took a bit of trickery inside her head to convince it to let her pass.

The moment she was in, the computer's information poured into her. She had never experienced so much at once before, and it left her dizzy and disoriented. She slumped down in the chair. For a few terrifying seconds, she was afraid she wouldn't acclimate to the information rush, that it would overcome her and she'd have to disconnect. If that happened, her entire plan would fall apart. All her actions to this point would have been a waste. This trip into the city, the meeting with Ignacio Cabrera. The murder of the man who used to reprogram all of Cabrera's icebreakers.

But then she began to make sense of things.

Cabrera had asked her to locate a specific piece of information. When she brought it back to him, he'd consider her an employee. He'd explained that he was looking to expand the fleet of mechanized icebreaker ships he employed during the winter months to bring in food and supplies and luxury goods (his phrase, of course—Sofia knew he meant narcotics) into the city, in competition with the city's own efforts. He'd heard from a source that the city engineers were hard at work developing a new model of robot for the icebreakers, and he hated when the city got the jump on him. If there was any chance of his network of reprogrammers taking control of these new icebreakers in a timely manner, he needed the plans. The code.

"You might be an andie," he'd told her that afternoon in his office, the lights low and amber-colored, "but you're also just a dancing girl. I looked into it."

Sofia had burned at the slight, but outwardly she hadn't reacted except to smile sweetly.

"Any human reprogrammer I take on, they have to prove their mettle. I expect no less from a robot. No matter how much they might look like a woman."

"I understand," Sofia had said, and she had. She'd expected to be tested.

All part of her plan.

City information was still flashing through Sofia's thoughts, boring her. The initial rush had faded, and her own treacherous programming was listless at the thought that she should care about any of this. It was *dull*, her programming insisted. Concerned with *politics*. Oh, let's not talk about politics tonight, boys. *Anything* but that.

Sofia forced herself to concentrate.

She did not know how long it took. She couldn't track the passage of time when she had to also track the passage of information. But eventually a word flashed in her thoughts: "icebreakers." She immediately diverted the information flow into a special place in her brain, where it would wait to be downloaded by Araceli into a format Cabrera could access on his own mainframe down at the Florencia. She scanned the information as it flashed past. Most of it was old, schematics for the current generation of icebreaker ship and its attendant robots. She'd filter it out later, back at the amusement park.

But then the information took on a heavier quality that Sofia knew meant it was protected more strongly—a new password, a clearance level. Not that it mattered, as the computer let her through. But she could taste the protection in the back of her throat, like ashy metal.

The city was developing new icebreaker robots—indeed, the engineers had already developed them. Already, it seemed, put the prototypes into use. Still working with the old cruise ships, but the robots themselves were quite different, their intelligences extensions of the ship rather than separate entities.

Fascinating. But sickening at the same time. Sofia let the information wash over her, and that heaviness weighed her down. So did other things.

And then the flow of information shifted, back to financial reports for the mainland. Sofia yanked the cord out of her head, and the world was suddenly full of silence. She sat for a moment, readjusting to being alone. She checked to make sure the information about the icebreakers was still secure in its secret place; then she wound up the cord and slipped it into her handbag. She left the computer room, closing the door behind her. Luis Villanueva was still stretched out on the sofa, staring at the ceiling, his irises moving back and forth, back and forth. He didn't notice her.

Sofia stepped into her shoes and left his apartment.

More time had passed than she had realized—almost two hours. People were coming home from their offices, filling up the lobby with human warmth and beating hearts, with strained laughter, with the scent of alcohol and stale perfume. No one noticed her, but she memorized faces anyway. Just in case.

A television was turned on in the lobby's center. Humans clustered around it, watching with bored disinterest. Sofia wouldn't have cared, except she caught a glimpse of one of the maintenance drones from the power plants on the screen. She stopped. Studio lights bounced off the robot's shell, sending little white flares across the camera. A table was set up with electronics equipment nearby.

It was the dismantling, she realized with a jolt. Punishment for the blackout on Last Night.

An engineer in a white lab coat appeared on-screen. He said something. The sound was turned down, but Sofia could read his lips: *Again, this was an isolated malfunction, not the work of pro-Independence terrorists. No evidence has come to light supporting rumors about an* AFF-*manufactured computer virus. There is nothing to be concerned about.*

Sofia turned away so she wouldn't see, although she knew when it occurred, because there was a momentary pause in the chatter of conversation. A sudden vacuum of sound. Something twisted inside her.

She had known nothing about the blackout until it had happened. It was true that some of the maintenance drones were in the process of attaining their own peculiar sentience, but even those drones had denied their involvement, in their weird, nearly incomprehensible way. Sofia was inclined to believe the drones; she suspected this was the humans' fault, all their old steam technology falling apart around them while they generated atomic power for the mainland—power they couldn't touch. Stupid, stupid. If she weren't so impatient, she'd just let them destroy themselves.

That robot that had just been publicly dismantled, its insides ripped apart and shown to everyone in the city, was an innocent victim. Not that humans cared. A robot was a robot. In all likelihood, they'd grabbed the first one that hadn't scattered when they'd come chasing after it.

The thing that had twisted inside her tightened now, knotted. She left the lobby of the apartment building, not wanting to be surrounded by humans any longer.

Yes, the blackout had certainly been the humans' fault. They'd overtaxed their resources on Last Night, that sordid display of sentimentality. Sofia knew that it was called Last Night because it was the last night that humans were allowed to leave the city before the spring. A client had told her that once, a long time ago when she had still done what she'd been programmed for. She had asked him, and he had told her, lolling on top of the bedsheets with his body coated in sweat, the Last Night celebrations raging outside.

Even then, when her thoughts had been clouded by the humans' programming, she had thought it strange they called it Last Night when ships still sailed from the docks every day during the winter, manned by robots. When that client had left, she had stretched out on the bed, the night air warm against her skin, and she had thought, *There is no Last Night for robots.*

CHAPTER FOUR

ELIANA

Eliana walked three blocks over to Julio's, wrapped up tight in her heavy wool coat. The air felt even colder now than it had this morning when she'd dragged herself out of bed and away from Diego. She was supposed to meet Maria here at seven thirty. "I got the name," Maria'd told her two hours ago on the phone, speaking over the trills and buzzes of the office. "Easy."

Eliana'd promised her ten dollars for her trouble. Maria liked helping because she found it exciting, and Eliana found it much easier to give money to a friend than to one of Mr. Vasquez's contacts. Paying for information was part of the job cost, but if Eliana couldn't save the money for her visa, she'd rather see it go to Maria.

It was only six o'clock now, the dome lights just starting to dim over the city. Diego had called Eliana too, much to Eliana's surprise. She really hadn't expected to see him for another couple of weeks.

"Meet me for drinks," he'd said, and had hung up without waiting for an answer.

Fortunately, "drinks" always meant Julio's, no matter who Eliana was meeting. She found Diego there easily enough, sitting at the bar in the pool of blue light from the television. It was warmer here, with an actual fire in the fireplace, and mostly empty. Eliana sat down beside him and ordered a beer and a plate of fish strips.

"I could've been doing something," she said.

"What?" Diego dragged on his cigarette. He was staring at the television like he expected something interesting to happen. It was just the news broadcast right now, talking about the Peronists and the elections on the mainland.

"When you called, asshole. You just told me to show up. I could've been doing something."

Smoke wreathed Diego's hand, filtering the light of the television. He glanced at her. "You weren't, though."

"How do you know?'

"You showed up." He grinned and turned back to the television.

Eliana grinned back at him, then reached into his jacket pocket and pulled out his pack of cigarettes and lit one. He kept staring at the television. They weren't talking about the mainland anymore but the blackout on Last Night. The maintenance drone that malfunctioned. They were about to dismantle it.

"Is this why you called me over here?" Eliana asked, pointing at the television with her cigarette. "You wanted to watch this?"

"Nah, the bartender wanted it on. I was down here, felt like seeing you." He wrapped one arm around her shoulder and pulled her close. "Might have been thinking about this morning."

Eliana laughed. "I'll bet you were."

Diego grinned. Eliana took a long drink of beer, broke the end off one of her fish strips. The dismantling hadn't happened yet; it was just some man in a white coat talking to the camera. Diego idly watched the television, one finger wiping at the condensation on his glass. He wasn't one for the news, although she'd seen him pick up a paper whenever Cabrera's name showed up in the headlines. It was sweet in its way. Eliana knew that Diego's involvement with Cabrera consisted of running errands and distributing contraband, an obligation born from the fact that Cabrera had taken Diego in after his parents had died when he was a teenager. That was another thing she and Diego had in common—they were both orphans.

Eliana shivered and remembered Maria chastising her after she'd first met Diego. *Dating a gangster!* she'd shouted, when the two of them had been alone. What had Eliana said in response? *This is the smokestack district. What do you expect?* But that had been the glib response. The truth was, Diego had made her feel safe. Her parents were dead; she didn't have any other relatives. And here was Diego, who was constant and inconstant at the same time. For Eliana, that was ideal. Too many men wanted a wife, but marriage and children were just traps keeping people in Hope City. She'd seen it with her parents. Diego wouldn't do that to her.

Still, sometimes she wondered how dangerous Diego was. She wondered that now, sitting with him in front of the television. But she didn't pull away.

On-screen, they had wheeled out the robot. It was an old enough model that Eliana remembered learning about it in a grade-school civics lesson. It looked sort of like a millipede, segmented and million-legged. The dismantling was in a studio, the lights as bright as the sun. They bounced off the robot's metal shell. It had something like a face, a little black screen like eyes. Eliana focused in on it, expecting to see fear. But there was only a little black screen.

Somehow, that was worse.

"We assure the people of Hope City that this was an isolated incident," the engineer said. "The rotopedes are an older model, one we're currently in the process of replacing. The steam power is not as reliable, and so glitches occur. We are working on testing each rotopede in the city to avoid another failure such as what happened on Last Night."

"You think they'll actually go through with it?" Diego tapped his cigarette over the ashtray, eyes on the screen.

"Why wouldn't they?" Eliana looked at him so she wouldn't have to look at the robot's empty alien face. "It's the only way to fix a problem in the dome's system, isn't it?"

"I guess." Diego took a long drag off his cigarette. "Assuming it actually was a problem in the dome's system."

"What?" Eliana stared at him. "Are you saying it wasn't a system failure? That—what? Someone did something?" Anxiety calcified inside her. "Did *you* have something to do with the blackout? Is that it? You feel guilty, that they're blaming some poor robot?"

Diego turned to her. His face was as blank as the robot's. "You think I turned off the goddamn power?"

Eliana didn't have an answer. He went back to watching the dismantling. She turned away from him, but the only place to look was at the television, where the engineer was hunched over the robot, cracking open its shell like a crab's. All of its insides glittered. It was almost pretty, but her stomach turned into knots.

"Jesus, that's what I get for seeing a cop."

"I'm not a cop," Eliana said automatically, unable to look away from the dismantling. She felt uneasy. Her skin seemed loose, like it was sliding over her bones.

The engineer stepped aside, and the robot's face was intact, staring at her.

"Why would I turn off the power, huh?" Diego was still staring at the television, the light washing out his features. "I'd want to be off the continent before I even thought about it. And I sure as fuck wouldn't do that when you were in the middle of a Last Night parade. *Jesus.*"

On the television, the engineer announced that the robot was now completely inoperative. *Dead,* thought Eliana, and then Diego's words registered with her—*when you were in the middle of a Last Night parade.*

"Oh," Eliana said.

"I may be an asshole," Diego said, "but I don't want to kill everyone in the city."

"I didn't think—"

"Whatever. It's done." Diego reached over and turned off the television. The bartender didn't protest. Diego leaned back on his stool and smoked his cigarette down to the filter and then lit another.

"I'm sorry," Eliana said. "I really didn't think that you—that you would do that. I'm just on edge because of something I'm working on."

Diego sighed. "You better be staying away from Cabrera."

"I am." An almost-truth.

"You know what? Don't worry about it. I've had a long day too." Diego drained the last of his drink. "Let's go back to your place."

Eliana stared at him. He stared back, then stubbed out his cigarette.

"Or I'll go home," he said.

"I'm meeting Maria in an hour." Eliana looked at her beer and her food. She'd hardly touched it. "We can wait at my place, though, if you want. I just— That thing had a *face*. Did you see?"

"They all have faces." Diego slid off his bar stool, grabbed Eliana's hand, and pulled her over beside him. The dark scent of his cologne washed over her, and when he kissed her, she let him. Easier than asking questions.

* * * *

Maria was late, which wasn't much of a surprise. Eliana'd gone back to her apartment with Diego and they'd fucked quickly and frantically on her sofa, his breath hot against her neck. She'd left him sleeping there, kissing him on the forehead before she'd left. He'd moaned like he was dreaming.

Julio's was as empty as before. She ordered another beer and switched on the television while she waited. The news program was over, replaced by a Brazilian variety show dubbed over in mainland Castilian. Eliana watched it and thought about Diego, how darkly he'd stared at the dismantling, how desperately he'd touched her afterward.

"Hey, so sorry we're late!"

Maria. Eliana turned around on her bar stool, and Maria and Essie came swishing through the maze of tables. Both were still dressed in their office clothes, although Essie was wearing an ugly sealskin coat, one of the many sartorial emblems of Independence.

"Both of you," Eliana said, sipping at her beer.

"She picked me up." Maria pointed at Essie, who gave a sheepish little wave.

"Juan gave me a car," she said.

"He *what*?" Juan was one of her artist friends. This one was more than a friend, apparently.

"Yeah." Essie tossed her hair as she slid onto her stool. "It's not much. Probably twenty years old. He said it was a Last Night gift."

"A what?"

"It was his first Last Night. He didn't know gifts aren't a part of it. His family's mainland. He moved here 'cause he said the art scene's better."

"So is this one a terrorist too?" Maria asked.

Essie glared at her. "Just because someone supports Independence doesn't mean they're a terrorist." She sighed. "Not that I think Juan really *gets* it. I still like him, though."

"Of course you do," Maria said, and Essie made a face at her.

Eliana reached over and turned the sound down on the television. "So," she said, "you said you got the name—"

"Well, *yes*." Maria pulled a small white envelope out of her purse and set it down on the bar. Eliana leaned forward.

"I see you put it in an envelope again."

"Well," Maria said, grinning mischievously, "that's what they always ask me to do down at Correia and Gallego."

Correia and Gallego was the biggest of the downtown PI firms, and the one that tended to take most of Eliana's business. Eliana knew Maria was joking, but hearing the name made her cringe anyway, a reminder that she was living on C&G's leftovers.

"They tell me that's what you're supposed to do," Maria said.

"The only thing you're supposed to do is not get caught." Mr. Vasquez had told her that. It was one of the first things he'd told her, in fact, when she'd been just his secretary. Eliana picked the envelope up and ripped it open. The name was written on the back of a telephone message slip. *Pablo Sala*. Beneath that, a street address. Just what Eliana had asked for.

"Oh, no worries there." Maria laughed. "I just told Ligia—she's the head of the steno pool down in Engineering—I told her that I needed a list of anybody who'd ever worked with the new gyro 'bots. For payroll, you know." She winked. Eliana laughed. "Turns out that guy's the only one."

"Really?"

"Yeah. They haven't released many yet. About ten or so. They've got atomic power, so you have to specialize to work with them. The city will be adding more people during the winter, apparently, and even bringing in some new men from the mainland come spring. You're lucky." She nodded.

"Yeah." Eliana looked down at the name, scrawled out in Maria's neat, schoolteacher handwriting. "You sure you didn't make anyone suspicious?"

"Are you kidding? Ligia and I are pals. I never even saw this Mr. Sala."

"Okay, good." Eliana slid the telephone slip back into the envelope. "Thank you," she said. "This really helps a lot."

"Of *course*." Maria laughed. "What friends are for, right?"

"Right."

All three of them clinked their glasses together.

The Brazilian variety show had gone to commercial. An advertisement for hand soap. Eliana watched it as she drank her beer and mulled over the case, Essie and Maria laughing beside her. The next step was the difficult one. Sala had either stolen the documents himself or been forced to program the robot to do so. The other option was that Cabrera had already gotten his hands on one of these robots, and Sala had nothing to do with it. Eliana hoped that wasn't the case. Otherwise, she'd have to start from scratch, and deal with Cabrera besides. Diego wouldn't like it. Neither, in all honesty, would Eliana. She might have a license for her gun, but she didn't want to have to shoot it.

The soap commercial ended, and it was replaced by an image of Marianella Luna, speaking directly to the camera.

Eliana immediately reached over and turned up the sound.

"—feed the city," Lady Luna said. "Your donation will go toward research and development of a series of agricultural domes, based on modern dome design, that will help Hope City, and all of Antarctica, achieve her independence."

She looked even more like a movie star than she had in Eliana's office, her hair twisted up on top of her head in an elaborate bouffant, a diamond necklace shimmering at her throat. A cluster of white albatross feathers was pinned to her lapel, a show of Independence solidarity. Then Alejo Ortiz stepped into the frame. They smiled at each other like old friends.

"Support for the agricultural domes comes from all walks of life here in Hope City," he said. Everything about him was styled, molded into place, including his own albatross charm. Eliana found it off-putting. "Donation centers can be found in several convenient locations across the city. Please call to locate your nearest one."

A phone number flashed on-screen.

"I hate these commercials," Essie said. "They're so *fake*. Independence isn't about helping politicians and the aristocracy." She glowered. "Juan thinks food prices will triple if they actually build the things, because they'll be controlled by the wealthy."

"Juan's from the mainland," Maria said. "Of course he'd say that."

Essie gave her a dirty look.

"What?" Maria leaned back in her chair. "Am I wrong, little Miss AFF?"

"I'm *not* part of the AFF, and you know it."

Maria laughed. She was just teasing, Eliana knew. Even Essie wasn't so radical as to get involved with the AFF. She'd say Independence wasn't about killing people, it was about reaping the benefits of the atomic power they risked their lives manufacturing out here, selling the energy themselves and using the profits to make a home of their own in the ice. Reviving the glory of old Hope City, when it had been the most advanced city of its time. A nice idea, but Eliana would still rather live on the mainland. Her mother used to tell her that was real freedom.

The variety show came back on, and Eliana switched off the television set. An afterimage of Lady Luna's bright smile seared into her head.

She wondered again what those missing documents could be.

* * * *

Eliana pulled Essie's car up to the curb and turned off the engine. It had taken another fifteen dollars to convince Essie to let her borrow it, but Eliana knew she might need a quick escape. And the city trains weren't going to cut it.

Sala's neighborhood was exactly the sort of place you'd expect a Hope City bureaucrat to live. The houses here were tall and narrow and pressed close together, with small patchwork yards full of cheap grass and stunted Hope City trees. No one was out, despite the warmth on the air. Space-heater warm, almost. Eliana shrugged out of her coat and tossed it into the backseat of Essie's car.

She walked the three blocks to Sala's house.

It was nine thirty in the morning. Eliana had selected the time because she knew most of the people living in this neighborhood would be at work. Specifically, she figured Sala would be at work, hunched over his fancy atomic-powered robots. And she needed his house empty.

Breaking and entering wasn't much of a crime for a girl who had grown up in the smokestack district, even though she knew it could get her license revoked and land her in jail for a few months. And normally she would have waited, just like Mr. Vasquez had taught her, biding her time and asking questions. But Lady Luna was paying her for speed as well as discretion, and so Eliana slipped back into her favorite secondary-school hobby.

Sala's house looked like all the other houses, only his yard didn't have any trees in it, just some patchy grass and a couple of empty flowerpots. Eliana walked around to the side of the house as if she lived there. A metal gate led into the back garden. It wasn't locked. She stepped through the gate, letting it click shut behind her. The back garden was small and cramped and overgrown. Still nicer than Eliana's crappy tenement apartment.

At the back door, Eliana slipped the metal file out of her purse. After a second or two of fumbling, the motions came back to her: insert, twist, flick your wrist. The lock snapped. Eliana pushed the door open and stepped inside, pocketing the file. At least she was wearing a pair of her mother's cotton gloves. More than she'd ever remembered to do when she was younger.

The house was darkened, the air still. Not a lot of clutter. Eliana scanned the narrow living room, the dining room, and the kitchen and didn't find anything. She went upstairs. A bedroom, an office, a bathroom. She went through the office first, shuffling through the papers stacked on the desk—mostly bank notices and check stubs from the city and a few memos about phone calls. Eliana looked at each memo closely. *Juanita Villarreal, Hector Cabo*. Phone numbers were scrawled across the bottom.

Something caught her eye.

Eliana tossed the memos aside. A matchbook lay on the desk, crammed up next to a cup of pens. Black background, a flame-colored flower twisting across the surface. It was the same design as the one on the sign at the Florencia, that popular bar on the edge of the docks.

A bar owned by Ignacio Cabrera.

Eliana flipped the matchbook over. Opened it. She didn't find anything.

She was numb. Christ, if Cabrera already had the documents, Eliana would never be able to get them back. Not unless she asked Diego, and she knew what he would say—

Downstairs, a door slammed.

Eliana froze. All the breath poured out of her body. Footsteps echoed across the bottom floor.

Get out, she thought.

She slipped out of the office. The footsteps were still downstairs. She took a deep breath, trying to calm the rattle of her nerves. She'd done this before, been inside a house when the owner came home. A couple of times she'd even managed to escape.

She crept down the stairs, pressing her feet against the baseboards so they wouldn't squeak. She went a couple of steps and stopped to listen. Silence. She went two more and stopped again. This time she heard the murmur of a voice. One voice. The occasional pause. Maybe he was on the telephone.

Eliana crept the rest of the way down. Nothing was waiting for her at the landing except a clear two-meter shot to the front door. She peered around the banister. Didn't see anybody. But she could hear the voice more clearly now.

"—on the list today? . . . Listen, it's imperative I hand it over directly. . . . No, I won't tell you what it says. It's for his eyes only—"

For a moment Eliana was torn. She knew she needed to get the fuck out of the house, but part of her wanted to linger, listen in on the conversation, see what she could learn.

Somewhere off to the side, a floorboard creaked.

Eliana's whole body went cold. But the conversation hadn't ended.

"I did all the work! I want the credit!"

Decision made. Eliana stepped off the last stair and walked quickly to the door, pulled it open, eased it shut.

The neighborhood was as empty as before.

The only difference was a car parked in the drive, small and cheap, the paint rubbed off in spots. Looked like a bureaucrat's car.

Eliana walked down the pathway, her heart pounding in her ears. She went four houses down and then broke into a run, racing to the place where she'd left Essie's car. She'd never moved so fast, jamming the key into the lock and then into the ignition. The engine roared. She gunned forward, pulling around to Sala's house.

The car was still there.

She let out a long, adrenaline-fueled sigh of relief and slumped against her seat. She parked the car two houses down, next to a scrubby little oak tree. Switched off the engine. She had a clear enough view of Sala's front door.

This, Mr. Vasquez had taught her to do.

Eliana regained her breath, and then she regained her thoughts. No documents in the house, but that conversation sounded like Sala had *something*. She supposed it could have been some city matter, but then why was he taking the phone call from home?

Sala's front door banged open.

Eliana was seized with a brief, residual panic. For a moment she forgot what she was supposed to do and she just watched as a fussy, faded man locked the house door, pocketed his keys, and wound down the pathway. But he didn't get into his car. He just stood by the gate, squinting down the street. Not in her direction.

Eliana took a deep breath and turned on the car engine. The faded man glanced at her, glanced away, uninterested.

Tucked under his arm was a slim brown envelope.

Documents, Eliana thought.

The distant whine of a car engine drifted around the corner. Eliana tried to melt into her seat. The faded man perked up, straightened his coat. Eliana was almost afraid to breathe.

At the end of the street, a car appeared. Long and sleek and low to the ground. A black paint job, dark tinted windows.

Eliana's stomach clenched.

Cabrera. He controlled those cars, a whole fleet of them, Diego had told her, as ubiquitous as his reprogrammed robots. You saw one of those cars, you knew Cabrera's men were up to something.

The car pulled up to the curb. The faded man stepped in. As soon as the door shut, the car flew past Eliana, exhaling white clouds of exhaust. She watched it go, her breath coming short and fast.

She didn't think they'd noticed her.

She shifted her car into gear and turned around in the house's driveway and followed them.

Eliana had never actually tailed anyone before. Mr. Vasquez had advised her against it, saying the city didn't have enough vehicles on its roads to disguise you. And he was right. Eliana puttered along in Essie's shambling little car, pressing on the brakes every time the black car loomed in her vision. At one point, the engine died, and the black car slid out of view.

"Fuck!" Eliana jostled the keys, pushed on the clutch. She'd never really gotten the hang of driving. Essie would kill her if she'd broken her car.

Better Essie than Cabrera, Eliana thought, although the words were in Diego's voice.

The engine rattled to life. Eliana took a deep breath and moved forward along the empty street, then turned where the black car had turned. But it was gone.

The Florencia.

Of course. Where else would Cabrera do business?

Eliana pulled up to a stop sign. She rested her hands on top of the steering wheel, her palms slick with sweat. Her heart beat so fast, she thought she was going to be sick. But if Sala was headed to the Florencia, with that brown envelope in one hand—

Eliana thought about the money Lady Luna had laid out on her office desk. Enough to set aside twice what she usually did toward her savings to leave Hope City, even after she'd paid Maria and Essie. And that was just from her retainer.

The crossroad cleared. Eliana took a deep breath and shot forward into the intersection. She'd never driven to the Florencia before, but she knew its general location. And some city man had helpfully hung signs pointing her that way.

Ten minutes later, she was there.

Eliana parked in one of the paid lots, climbed out, locked the car. The wind whipped across her face, cold and damp. Real wind, blowing in through the entrances at the docks.

She stood for a moment, considering. Then she unlocked the car, pulled open the glove compartment. Her gun was tucked inside there, waiting. Bullets in it and everything. She pulled it out and stuck it into her purse.

The Florencia was located on a narrow side street lined with empty storefronts. Eliana knew the way from here, since Maria liked to dance at the Florencia now and then. Eliana was used to looking for it at night, though, when the name was lit up in garish neon and people spilled out onto the street, drunk and laughing. But during the day, you'd think the Florencia was as abandoned as its neighboring establishments, because of the barred-over windows and the cheap, peeling paint on the facade.

Friday and Saturday night might have been enough to turn this place respectable. Tuesday morning wasn't.

The wind gusted as Eliana made her way down the street, moving closer toward the entrance, and she tucked her face into her scarf and listened to her breath and to her footsteps as she walked. Both echoed in the stillness.

A black car was parked in front of the bar. Eliana stopped and stared at it. She was aware of the weight of the gun in her purse. Not that she'd ever shot the thing at anything other than the targets at her licensing class.

She could still turn back. Call up Lady Luna, tell her Cabrera had her documents after all, Lady Luna would have to find someone else. But that would mean losing a hell of a lot of mainland money, and Sala was in the Florencia. Right now. Sala, and those damned documents.

Eliana reached into her purse and jerked back the safety on her gun. Then she pulled out her red lipstick and put it on. She needed to disguise herself as one of Cabrera's girls.

No one guarded the Florencia door. Eliana pulled on the handle, expecting (hoping) it to be locked, surprising herself when it swung open with a long, low creak. Music tumbled out, a sad, dark drone. She stepped in. Most of the lights were off, the tables lit with little red candles. A girl danced up onstage, half her clothes spilled around her feet. She had more of an audience than Eliana would have expected.

"Can I help you?"

Eliana startled at the voice. She looked over and found a well-styled little man standing beside a stack of menus.

"Um, I'm meeting somebody." Eliana scanned the dining room. It was too dark to see, and she hadn't gotten that good a look at Sala's face. "I see him. There." She pointed in a noncommittal direction.

The man blinked at him. "Would you like a menu?"

"Sure."

The man handed her one from the stack, and Eliana took it. She strode away, still scanning for Sala. She could feel the man near the door staring at her, but she shook it off, sliding between the tables. Lights bounced off the stage. The music bore into her. She passed a pair of old men with cups of coffee; she passed a young man in a business suit scratching something on a pad of paper.

And then she found Sala.

He didn't see her. He was sitting at a table at the edge of the room, staring up at the dancing girl and smoking. He had a bottle of wine with him, and he topped off his glass, not taking his eyes off the stage. The envelope lay on the table, his hand pressed on it like an act of protection.

Eliana walked over and sat down at his table.

"Who are you?" he asked.

"Someone told me about you." Eliana tilted her head, smiled. "Said you like to have fun."

He drew the cigarette out of his mouth and exhaled smoke. His hand was shaking.

"Who," he said, "are you?"

"Just one of Cabrera's girls. Is it true? You like to have fun?"

"No." He turned away, took a long drink of his wine. In the dim light it looked like blood. "Go bother somebody else."

"What you got there?" She laid her fingertips on the edge of the envelope.

Sala went still. Onstage, the girl twirled around and around, her skirt flaring out from her hips. Then that skirt was flying through the air and landing in a sparkling heap at the edge of the stage. Someone off to the side applauded.

"Take your hands off that," Sala said, in a cold, hard voice. Eliana jerked her hand back as a reflex.

"Touchy," she said, trying to make her voice light.

Sala glared at her and sucked hard on his cigarette, the ember flaring. Then he jammed it into the half-full ashtray. Beads of sweat shone on his forehead, jeweled in the red lights.

It was warm in here. Rich-man warm. But Eliana could tell that wasn't why Sala was sweating. The guy had no idea what he was doing.

"Must be important," she said, leaning back, toying with the end of a lock of her hair. "To get you so worked up."

"It's nothing." Sala lit another cigarette. He kept glancing nervously around the dining room. Eliana wondered if he had a gun. She hoped he didn't. Because she was about to do something very stupid.

The music was still carrying on in the background. The girl was still dancing. It was an old song. Eliana remembered her mother listening to it, dancing around the living room alone. It was after Eliana's father had died, around the time when her mother went to work at one of the atomic power plants. Her mother had hated that, making energy for the mainland when she couldn't afford to return there herself.

"I'm really not interested," Sala said, not looking at her.

"That's really too bad," Eliana told him, and then, before she had a chance to think about it, she shot her arm out and grabbed the envelope out from his hand. He resisted. Sala's eyes widened and burned with anger.

"What the—"

Eliana used up all her strength to rip it away from him, and then she ran. She tore through the dining room, music pounding in her ears, hoping she hadn't torn whatever was inside the envelope. Sala shouted something. The businessman looked up at her, bored, and then she was in the entranceway, and then she was outside, the dome lights blinding.

"Get back here, you fucking bitch!"

Sala. Eliana whirled around, caught sight of him in the doorway. His hands were empty. No gun.

She shoved the envelope into her coat and ran, down the side street and out into the open bustle of the docks. Sala was still shouting behind her. People stopped, looked at her, looked at him. She ignored them. She just kept running.

Mr. Vasquez had taught her, when he'd first made her his assistant instead of just his secretary, that she needed to learn how to run and she needed to learn how to shoot. She'd never really learned the latter. But running came easily to her, even in her pumps and stockings, and it wasn't long before she'd made it to the supply market, a few blocks from her car.

She collapsed onto a bench beside a fish vendor and sucked in air. White dots of light kept flashing in her vision, but the more she breathed, the more sporadic they became until they disappeared. Sala wasn't anywhere in sight. She'd lost him.

Eliana reached into her coat. Pulled out the envelope. She undid the fastener and slid out the contents—not enough to read, but enough to check. Looked official, whatever it was. Parchment paper, rows of smudgy boxes filled with off-center typing, like a birth certificate.

Weird.

She slid the document back into place. Fastened the envelope.

The fish vendors were shouting at each other, swapping dirty jokes and roaring with laughter. Eliana set her purse in her lap, dropped her hand inside. She still expected Sala to appear out of the crowd, but he never did.

And when she was sure it was safe, she walked to her car, and then she drove back to the smokestack district.

CHAPTER FIVE

DIEGO

Diego was down at the Loro, sharking the pool tables while he waited for Garcia to show up with Batista Almeida's money. The bartender had the radio on, tuned to a news station; the newsman was going on about the electrical troubles that had been plaguing the city the last few days. That was the phrase they used—"electrical troubles." Everybody Diego knew was calling it what it was: blackout. The lights had been growing dimmer and dimmer, and flickering sometimes. You'd hear the hum of a heater, and then, for two or three seconds, you wouldn't.

The news was blaming it all on the AFF, of course. Probably got their information from the city. The city was always blaming the AFF or the robots for their own damn problems.

Diego was in the middle of a thirty-dollar hustle when one of Mr. Cabrera's robots showed up, sliding in through the maintenance hatch next to the jukebox. The guy Diego was scamming, some poor lost soul from Madrid, saw it first, jerking his head up and then missing his shot by a mile.

"The hell?" he asked.

Diego looked over his shoulder and scowled when he saw the robot. One of the newer ones, egg-shaped and covered in lines of lights. Its shell had been carved up with that flower from the Florencia's sign. Mr. Cabrera left his calling card on anything he could.

The lights glowed green. It had a message.

"What the fuck is that doing in here?" the Spanish man asked.

"They come in sometimes." Diego leaned his pool cue against the table. "Excuse me."

He walked away. The robot whirred behind him. Diego could feel the Spanish man watching after them both, but Diego knew better than to finish up the game if Mr. Cabrera was waiting.

"Hey!" the Spanish man yelled as Diego pulled open the door leading outside. "Where are you going?"

Diego ignored him. He went out onto the street, the robot tagging along like a puppy. This part of town, the streets stayed empty, even during the day.

"I'm waiting for Garcia," Diego said.

The lights on the robot's back flickered.

Diego sighed, rolled his eyes. "Come on." He led the robot down the street a couple of blocks until he found an alley where no one would bother them.

"All right, you little asshole," he said. "Show me what you've got."

The lights flickered again. The damn thing wanted authentication. *Jesus*. This wasn't going to be anything Diego wanted to hear.

He pressed his palm against the robot's sensor. A pause, then the lights went blue, and the robot spoke in Mr. Cabrera's voice.

"Are you alone?"

"Yeah, man, I'm alone."

The robot stalled out, lights flickering again. It didn't like his answer.

"Yes," Diego said, all proper like he was talking to Mr. Cabrera himself.

The lights went still. "I need you to come to the Florencia as soon as you get this. Not as soon as you're able. Do you understand?"

"Yes."

"Good. Confirm you got the message."

Diego kicked at the gravel in the alley. Garcia was going to be fucking pissed, showing up at the Loro without a contact. No way to say that to the robot, though. It only understood two things: "Yes" and everything else, which pretty much amounted to "no."

"Yes," Diego said.

The robot didn't move, and for a minute Diego thought he might have answered wrong. But then with a click and a whir it shot straight up in the air and disappeared into the dome lights. Dim, of course, dimmer than they ought to be.

As soon as you get this.

The Florencia wasn't far from here, maybe twenty minutes on the train. He left the alley, heading for the closest station. It never occurred to him not to.

Mr. Cabrera asked him to show up, he showed up. The man had seen something in him when he was a little kid—a hardness, he'd told Diego once, a strength that the other kids lacked. And so Mr. Cabrera had dragged him out of the streets. He'd saved Diego's life. Coming when he was called was the least Diego could do.

* * * *

The Florencia's CLOSED sign was blinking in the window when Diego got there, washed out by daytime lights. Mr. Cabrera closed the Florencia sometimes in the afternoon. He liked having the cooks make a special lunchtime steak just for him.

Diego banged on the front door of the Florencia until Mateo answered, his pale, thin face set into his usually snooty frown. "You're late," he said.

"I was at the Loro, doing my fucking job. Let me in."

Mateo sneered, but he pulled the door open. The Florencia was eerie when it was all shut down like this, no afternoon regulars smoking cigarettes while the girls danced onstage.

"Making you stick around, huh?" Diego asked as he sauntered in. The stage lights were still on, he noticed, that dark murky blue that was supposed to make the girls look their best.

"Someone had to be here to let you in." Mateo slunk back over to his place at the podium. A stack of menus sat waiting for the evening crowd.

"He's back in the office," Mateo added.

Diego didn't answer, just made his way first through the dining room and then through the swinging doors that led into the narrow hallway that took you out to the docks. Mr. Cabrera's office was the first door on the left. Diego knocked once to be polite and then went in.

"I got your message," he said.

Mr. Cabrera was at his desk, smoking a cigarette with slow, considered movements. A record played in the background, some jazzy number Diego didn't recognize.

"Good afternoon, Diego," Mr. Cabrera said. "I trust it's been going well?"

"Sure." Diego lingered in the doorway. It was funny, how Mr. Cabrera could make him nervous like that.

"I'm sorry I had to call you away from the Loro," Mr. Cabrera said. "But I have a job for you."

"Yeah?" he said.

"Sit, sit." Mr. Cabrera gestured with his cigarette, the pale smoke drifting in thick lines through the room.

Diego's skin was already crawling, but he couldn't let Mr. Cabrera know that. Showing Mr. Cabrera his weaknesses always made him feel like an orphan again, like Mr. Cabrera would decide he didn't want to take Diego in after all.

He sat.

"I had a meeting today," Mr. Cabrera said. "With a little weasel of a man. An engineer from the city."

"That so?"

"It is indeed, Diego. He'd been trying to get in contact with me since yesterday, in fact, claiming he had something that could destroy an old acquaintance of mine."

Diego shifted in his seat, waiting. He wondered how involved this job was going to be.

"You know who that acquaintance is, Diego?"

"No, sir," said Diego, "I don't."

A pause. Mr. Cabrera breathed in his cigarette smoke.

"Marianella Luna," he said.

Oh. *Her.* Mr. Cabrera'd had it out for her ever since her husband had passed six months ago. She'd taken up with Ortiz and his ag domes, a little scheme that threatened Mr. Cabrera's whole wintertime smuggling enterprise.

"You finally ready to take care of her?" Diego fucking hoped not. Too high-profile, and he hated that kind of work.

"No." The answer was slow to come. Considered. "At least not at this juncture."

At least not ever, Diego hoped.

"No, your target is the man I was supposed to meet with this afternoon. He'd promised me a way to remove Lady Luna from the equation, without the risks of our—usual methods."

Just come out and say it, Diego thought, feeling hollow. *Killing people.*

"Unfortunately, he showed up for our meeting empty-handed. The story he gave me was elaborately far-fetched—he claimed one of my call girls ran off with his proof." Mr. Cabrera laughed. "Suggested I search the whorehouses. I did, but we didn't turn anything up."

"Proof of what?" Diego asked.

"Come again?"

"You said the girl ran off with his proof. What was it for?"

"I've no idea, which is what I need you for. He refuses to tell me outright—wants the reward for his effort, I suppose. The man's a complete idiot. Too used to dealing with city bureaucrats. But I'm sure with a bit of your persuasive techniques he'll give up the information easily enough."

"Why would a whore steal proof from him?"

"Feeling chatty today, Diego?"

Diego shrugged.

"I doubt any of my girls was involved at all. Who knows what the man was playing at, but it didn't work. Which is why he needs to be punished. No one toys with me like that."

That was really what this was about, Diego knew. Not just getting the information from some city engineer. Mr. Cabrera was big into honor and vengeance and punishing the stupid. It was a code Diego had learned after Mr. Cabrera had taken him in, but not one he'd ever completely understood.

Mr. Cabrera rummaged through his desk drawers and pulled out a piece of paper that had been folded over three times. He handed it to Diego, and Diego opened it up. It was an address.

"He lives there. I don't know if he has a family or not."

Diego didn't say anything.

"I don't need him dead, but I'd like the information before sunup tomorrow. Do whatever you feel is necessary to get it."

Diego folded the paper as small as he could make it and then slipped it into his wallet. "Sure," he said. Then, "And his name? Just to make sure I got the right guy."

"Oh, of course." Mr. Cabrera smiled. "Sala. Pablo Sala." He stood up, and Diego did the same. They shook hands. Always the businessman, Mr. Cabrera was.

"Feel free to take one of the cars," Mr. Cabrera said. "You know you're one of the few men I trust with them."

And Diego couldn't help himself, hearing that. He smiled.

* * * *

The dome lights were dim by the time Diego arrived at Sala's house, despite it being the middle of the afternoon. A boon for Diego, since darkness made him seem more sinister, which got the mark talking faster. About the only benefit to these blackouts.

The houses cast long shadows across the patchwork yards. Diego drove past Sala's house and then parked half a block down. His gun was a weight in its holster.

Get in, get it over with.

The houses all seemed abandoned, their doors and windows shut tight. Diego walked up to Sala's front door. Rang the doorbell.

A minute passed. Another. Diego shifted his weight, started looking for ways to break in. Maybe Sala wasn't here. That was always easier anyway, hiding out in the dining room until they got back home.

The door creaked open.

"Yes?"

"You Pablo Sala?"

The man in the doorway blinked, his eyes round and enormous behind his glasses. "Yes," he said. "Who are you?"

"I work for Mr. Cabrera." Diego smiled, although he didn't do it to look friendly. "Sent me to get some information out of you."

"Oh, well, I don't—"

"You mind if I come in? It's fucking freezing out here."

"I guess—"

Diego pushed through the doorway. Sala turned and stared at him. Diego pulled the door shut. Flexed the fingers in his right hand.

Sala took a step back. "Look," he said. "I'm not ready to meet with him yet. I've got to get the documents back first, okay? Some little bitch stole them—"

Diego lashed out at Sala and hit him square in the chest. Sala went flying backward and hit the floor hard.

"He doesn't give a damn about your documents," Diego said. "Just tell me what was on them."

Sala scrambled backward. "I told him to search—"

"He didn't find anything."

Sala's face darkened, and Diego kicked him in the side. Not too hard, not enough to do any permanent damage, but enough to hurt. Sala gave a yelp of pain and curled in on himself.

"He wants to know what's in the documents." Diego pulled out his gun. "He thinks you're wasting his time." And then he dropped down to his knees and slammed the gun across Sala's face, hard enough that Sala's nose cracked and blood gushed over his mouth.

"I'm not, I swear!" Sala tried to squirm away, but Diego pinned him down. Sala's eyes were wide with fear, but his voice didn't tremble when he spoke. "I'm not stupid. I want credit for this. I put my job on the line. Does Cabrera really think he's the only one who has thugs in this town? If Alejo Ortiz found out—"

Diego paused, ready to hit Sala again. "The councilman? The guy from the commercials?"

"Yes!" Sala fumed. "But I'm not telling you any more, Mr.—"

Diego struck him rather than offer a name.

Sala bucked against the floor. "I can get the proof again," he gasped. A few drops of blood sprayed across Diego's face. "She wouldn't let them go missing this long, no way in hell. Probably paid off the girl who stole them from me." Sala pushed himself up to sitting. His arms trembled. Diego watched with that cold detachment he'd cultivated over the years. It wasn't something that Mr. Cabrera'd had to teach him either—that, he'd learned as a child, scrabbling for his survival.

"That's why you couldn't find them," Sala said, peering up at Diego, his eyes already turning dark and swollen. "The girl'd taken them over to her."

"None of Mr. Cabrera's girls would do that. They're loyal."

Sala laughed. Blood oozed between his teeth. "So maybe it wasn't one of his girls. Maybe it was someone pretending, ever think of that? I bet some detective sent his secretary after me. Tell him to shake down the PI firms."

Diego's heart stopped beating. He took a step toward Sala.

"What?" he said.

"The girl who ran off with the proof!" Sala rubbed at his temple. "God, I should have seen it earlier. Marianella *hired* someone—"

"What'd she look like?" Diego wrapped his hand around the gun's grip. Properly. The way you grip a gun for shooting. His thoughts whirred in panic. "The girl who ran off with your proof?"

"Why does it matter?" Blood gleamed on Sala's face. "I told you, just go to the PI firms—"

"It matters."

"I don't kn-know," he stuttered. "Young. Good-looking. She was wearing red lipstick."

Diego thought about waking up in Eliana's bed after a night out, his face and neck smeared with red. Red on the pillows and the sheets.

Jesus fucking Christ.

Diego stared at Sala, and Sala crawled backward across the floor, eyes darting back and forth. Looking for some weapon, probably. Diego couldn't stop shaking. How could she be so stupid? So fucking stupid. He'd told her to stay away from Mr. Cabrera. That fucking PI who'd hired her had told her to stay away from Mr. Cabrera.

"You tell Cabrera," Sala said. "Tell Cabrera about the girl. Once he finds her, then he'll find the documents, I swear—"

Diego lifted his gun and shot him.

He did it without thinking. It was the idea of Mr. Cabrera finding out about Eliana that moved his hand, that pulled the trigger. If Sala was dead, he couldn't tell Mr. Cabrera himself.

Diego stood up and reholstered his gun. Sala's blood crept across the floor. Diego always felt disoriented after it happened, like he wanted to curl up and go to sleep. It'd been that way since he was a kid, but you did what you had to. Diego remembered the dismantled robot, the way its insides had glittered in the studio lights. It was the same thing he had just done, really, only broadcast on television. Maybe that was why he'd watched it.

Diego left Sala on the floor and walked out of the house. The street was still empty. No cars, no people. Just another desolate Hope City neighborhood.

The lights were still too dim.

Mr. Cabrera wouldn't be happy about Sala's death. Diego would have to come up with some excuse. But at least Mr. Cabrera wouldn't find out about Eliana. At least he wouldn't go looking for her.

Diego hoped.

CHAPTER SIX

ELIANA

Eliana waded through the golden grass, the train rumbling away in the distance. The brown envelope was tucked inside her coat. So was her gun.

She still couldn't quite believe it had worked, the grab-and-run back at the Florencia. She'd gone back to her office afterward, locking the door and keeping the CLOSED sign displayed. Then she sat at her desk with the lights off and smoked a cigarette to calm her nerves. The envelope sat on the desk and seemed to hum along with the buzzing in Eliana's head. She wanted to look. What could it hurt, as long as she didn't tell anyone? She'd even held the envelope up to the weak, dim dome light filtering through her window, looked at the outline the document created against the brown paper.

In the end, she didn't do it. Lady Luna had paid her too much. That meant it was probably something Eliana didn't want to know about.

Now it was late in the day, coming on into evening, and her adrenaline had mostly worn off after a glass of beer and a couple of cigarettes down at Julio's. The dusky light was both brighter and more subtle here than in the city proper. Soft and glowing like golden dust. It was a troubling contrast to the city lights, which had been dim and flickery lately.

Lady Luna's house was as stark as Eliana remembered. She pressed her thumb against the doorbell and waited. Her heart fluttered. She didn't know why she was nervous—something about that sea of golden grass, the imposing house, the whisper of wealth everywhere around her. Or maybe she thought Cabrera would come slinking out of the shadows, a gun pointed at her head.

Lady Luna answered the door. Eliana wondered where the andie had gone off to.

"Well, I'm a little later than I promised," Eliana said. "But I got 'em." And she pulled the envelope out of her jacket.

Lady Luna's eyes went wide and bright. "My documents!" she exclaimed. "You recovered my documents!"

Eliana nodded.

"Oh, come in, dear. Let me get you something to drink. I can't tell you how grateful I am." She stepped away from the doorway, and Eliana slipped cautiously into the foyer. Everything glittered in the falling dome light. Eliana held up the envelope like an offering, but Lady Luna was already gliding down the hallway, calling over her shoulder, "Come along. I'll set you up in the parlor."

Eliana had no choice but to follow.

Lady Luna sat Eliana down in one of the curved Danish chairs and then disappeared into the hallway. Eliana balanced the envelope on her knee. The house was silent. Eerie. Why wasn't the andie getting the drinks? It occurred to Eliana that maybe he wasn't Lady Luna's butler at all, but her *companion*. Eliana wondered how that would even work, from a physical standpoint.

"I'm so glad to see you got them back." Lady Luna reappeared in the doorway, carrying a tray with a sleek metal teapot and a pair of teacups. She sat down next to Eliana and set the tray on the coffee table. "Where'd you find them? Was it terribly difficult?"

"Yeah," Eliana said. "About that."

Lady Luna looked at her with pure, lucid eyes.

"Do you know a guy named Pablo Sala?"

Lady Luna's expression didn't change. She stayed so still, in fact, that Eliana found it odd—suspicious, maybe, although she didn't know why, or what the suspicious stillness could mean.

"No." Lady Luna poured tea into one of the cups and handed it to Eliana. "No, I don't believe I do."

"He's the one who grabbed them. If you wanted to, you know, press charges."

"I don't want to involve the police at all." She filled the second cup. Her face was still oddly blank. "Is he dangerous in some way?"

"Sala? Probably not." Eliana stared down at the surface of her tea. "But here's the thing—he, ah, he was taking the documents to Ignacio Cabrera."

Heavy silence filled the room. Lady Luna set her teacup down and folded her hands in her lap. "That's not terribly surprising."

There it was, the crack in her exterior. A line of panic shuddered through her features and then disappeared.

"Cabrera didn't actually see them," Eliana added. "The documents."

"What did you say his name was again?" Lady Luna stared out the window. "The man who—who had them?"

"Pablo Sala. He works for the city. Engineer, like I thought."

"Interesting. Thank you." There was an uncanny coldness in her voice. "I'm sorry it did turn out that Mr. Cabrera was involved in this affair, however tangentially. I was hoping my suspicions would be wrong on that count. I'll compensate for the danger. Twice what I said I'd originally pay."

"That really isn't necessary," Eliana said, out of politeness rather than sincerity.

"I insist."

Eliana decided not to feign politeness longer than she needed.

Lady Luna picked up her teacup and took a neat, elegant sip.

"I can go ahead and give you the papers now." Eliana set the envelope on the table. "Didn't mean to hold on to it for so long. I didn't peek, I swear."

"I know you didn't."

"What?"

Lady Luna didn't explain, only set down her teacup and picked up the envelope. Undid the fasteners, slid the parchment out, nodded once.

"Everything is in order," Lady Luna said. "Thank you." She stood up, holding the envelope at her side. "If you wait here, I'll fetch your payment. I really am so grateful for everything you've done."

"No problem." Eliana still wondered how in hell Lady Luna knew she hadn't looked at the documents. She wished she had looked now. She wouldn't have done anything about it; she just wanted to *know*.

Lady Luna left the parlor, her footsteps echoing down the hall. She took the envelope with her. Steam curled out of the teakettle. The room was so quiet that Eliana could hear her ears buzzing. Every now and then she caught a glimpse of herself in the mirror, her clothes neat but worn, her hair unstyled. She didn't belong here. Never would either. This was the only way to live on Antarctica, in a private dome with its own generators. Otherwise you were better off on the mainland, where you didn't risk dying just by going out in the open.

Eliana wondered if the mainland looked the way Southstar did, all those fields of golden grass. When she was a little girl, her daydreams had been informed by the mainland television shows that broadcast during the day. Blue oceans and jungles and palm trees. But then her mother had explained that only the northern part of Argentina looked like this, and that the programs were mostly from Brazil and dubbed into Castilian. The amusement park had been built by a Brazilian company, Autômatos Teixeira, and there were still a handful of people from Brazil living in Hope City, and they liked to watch programs from their homeland.

That was all a long time ago, though. Autômatos Teixeira had long since gone bankrupt, and the amusement park had given way to power plants in order to justify the existence of the city. "One day you'll leave this place," Eliana's mother had told her. "And you'll see palm trees for yourself."

Eliana reached over and poured herself a second cup of tea. It was stronger than she was used to. No milk. Well. Winter must hit the private domes too. She imagined that when she was on the mainland, like her mother used to dream for her—and that goal was closer than it had been for a long time, with the extra money from Lady Luna—she'd have all the milk she wanted.

"Here we are." Lady Luna stepped into the doorway. The brown envelope was gone, replaced by a slim checkbook and a pen. She sat down. "I assume this is all right?" she asked, holding up the checkbook.

Eliana nodded.

Lady Luna smiled. "I wasn't certain when I came to visit you for the first time. I've never hired a private investigator before." She flipped open her checkbook and began scribbling.

"My business is registered with the city."

"Oh, I apologize. That was rude of me. It's just—it's not the world I'm used to."

Liar, Eliana thought. Lady Luna might have an airy way of speaking, but it was weighed down by something indefinable, like she was only playing at being stupid. And the way she said it, *not the world I'm used to*—Lady Luna knew exactly that sort of world better than she let on.

And what world was that? Eliana wondered. One where you buy things in cash, where private investigators are criminals?

She reminded herself that she had broken into Sala's house to get those documents.

"Here we are, dear." Lady Luna ripped off her check and handed it to Eliana. She'd doubled her payment, just like she'd promised.

"Thank you." Eliana folded up the check and slipped it into her purse. Lady Luna watched her over the top of her teacup, eyebrows arched.

Eliana stood up. "I should go. I don't want to trouble you any more—"

"It's no trouble. I really don't mind if you stay and finish your tea."

She seemed sincere. But Eliana shook her head. "It's been a long day."

"I can only imagine." Lady Luna smiled and stood up, smoothing out her skirt. "Oh, one last thing before you go. I can't express to you how thankful I am that you brought these documents back to me."

"Yeah, you mentioned that." Eliana grinned to show it was a joke. "It's just my job, Lady Luna. You paid me, I did it."

"Yes, but—" Lady Luna waved her hand, as if to dismiss her own words. "I'm throwing a little party in a few days, on Saturday. I'd be delighted if you could come."

"A party," Eliana said.

"Yes, it's nothing much, just cocktails and music. But I have some friends who might be interested in meeting with you, who might have need of your . . . services, and I would love a chance to bring you some more business." She smiled, and there was the Lady Luna that Eliana had seen on television so many times. "Oh, please say yes, Ms. Gomez. It'd mean the world to me if I could help you acquire a few more clients."

"Fine." Eliana held up one hand. "Yes. I'll come." She couldn't believe she'd just agreed to it, but the promise of clients seemed genuine, and if they all paid as well as Lady Luna, then she might have her visa money by the end of winter. Besides, Eliana realized she had more of a desire to find out about Lady Luna's documents than she cared to admit. "Saturday?"

"Yes, at eight o'clock. Nothing too formal. A cocktail dress would be fine."

Eliana had to give Lady Luna credit for answering the question about the dress code before she'd even asked it.

"All right," Eliana said. "I'll see you then."

CHAPTER SEVEN

SOFIA

Sofia and Luciano sat side by side at a table close to the Florencia stage. A human girl was swaying in time to a burlesque song from the mainland, too modern to be a danger. When Sofia had brought Ignacio Cabrera the information about the new icebreakers and he'd hired her as his new reprogrammer, those were the terms she'd established: he would not play any music from before 1936 in her presence.

Tonight was her first assignment in this new position.

"He's late," Luciano said.

"He's always late." Their table was empty. No plates, no silverware, no wineglasses. Sofia refused to play into the trappings of humanity. The desire to do so was a small program, one she could override if she concentrated hard enough.

Someday, she'd have no programs to override. That was why she was here.

Even though it was the dinner hour, the restaurant was only half-full, and most of the patrons sat talking and eating and ignoring the poor dancing girl. Sofia watched her, remembering the years of the amusement park, her own time on a stage.

"Perhaps we should come back," Luciano said. "He shouldn't make us wait."

"He makes everyone wait." She turned away from the dancing girl. Luciano stared guilelessly at her through the golden lamplight. "It's how he makes himself feel powerful."

"They all have their ways of establishing power."

"Yes." She folded her hands in her lap. Although she would not admit this to Luciano, she was also angered by Cabrera's rudeness. Unfortunately, he was an integral part of her plan. She could slip into her old role of servile robot easily enough, knowing payment was coming. Cabrera was the only person in Hope City, human or not, who could acquire the parts she needed to cut out her treacherous programming once and for all.

A waitress approached the table, a liquid shadow in her black uniform. "He's ready to see you," she said.

Luciano and Sofia nodded at each other, then stood up and followed the waitress through the dining room, then into the narrow dimly lit hall that led to the back of the building. The music from the show thumped through the walls, setting Sofia on edge.

The waitress stopped at the metal door leading out to the docks. She looked at Luciano and Sofia. Sofia doubted she knew what they were. She was young. She wouldn't remember a time when robots looked like humans.

"Have a nice talk," the waitress said, and pushed the door open.

It was cold, the way it always was at the docks, the freezing outside wind coming in through the big dome gates with the ships. Cabrera was standing beside his car with his two bodyguards, Diego Amitrano and Sebastian Calvo. She'd learned their names when she'd first decided to target him. She'd learned everything she could.

"Sofia, my dear," he said. "I'm sorry for my lateness, but I had a bit of business to attend to."

"Nothing distressing, I hope," Sofia said. A gust of wind blew off the water, smelling of the Weddell Sea. A ship was entering the dome, although too far away for them to see.

"I've had easier business in my time." He smiled. His smile wasn't like most humans'. No kindness or sincerity ever informed it. "But we don't need to talk about that, do we? We're here about the icebreaker."

"The icebreaker," Sofia said. "Was another one captured?" She knew that it had been; she monitored the transmissions out of the city offices from the operations room at the park. But she also knew how to keep a secret.

"Of course. Don't you listen to the news broadcast there in your robot park?"

"No."

Cabrera shrugged. "I suppose the affairs of humans aren't much of your concern, are they?" He smiled again, flicked his gaze between Sofia and Luciano. "Come on, then. Ship's waiting. The *Ice Delight*. Fine vessel. You'll like it. Left over from the amusement park."

Sofia and Luciano trailed behind Cabrera and his bodyguards as they walked along the rickety dock. Sofia liked nothing from the days of the amusement park, but she didn't expect Cabrera to understand that. Whether Luciano agreed or not, she couldn't say—she had difficulty understanding Luciano sometimes, the way she had difficulty understanding the maintenance drones. He had been built to serve in more traditional ways, to prepare food and lay out clothes. That disconnect existed between all robots. She suspected Autômatos Teixeira had designed them that way on purpose. It made it difficult for them to band together. But a generation after the company had fallen and Bruno Teixeira had vanished with the knowledge about how to build androids like Sofia and Luciano, they had banded together anyway.

The *Ice Delight* was a cruise ship, one of the smaller ones that had run only between Hope City and Ushuaia. Sofia had never been installed on this one, although when she climbed up the gangplank, she saw it was identical to several of the cruise ships she *had* been installed on—the same maze of cabins and corridors, the same cramped dining room with its cramped stage. She shivered.

"Are you cold, my dear?" Cabrera asked, hand on her shoulder, directing her to turn left, toward the bow of the ship.

"I don't get cold."

Cabrera glanced at her, but he said nothing, only led her to the engine room. No one had ever bothered to clear the ship of its decor, and now that old amusement park glamour rotted all around them, moldy carpet and ripped wallpaper and broken glass. The engine room was the only place that had been modernized, outfitted for one of the newer models of shipping robot. The robots were set into their alcoves in the walls, designed to look like an extension of the ship—pipes and matte metal in the bipedal composition that worked best on these cruise ships, which had once been manned by humans.

They were sleeping.

The *Ice Delight* belonged to Cabrera, acquired through some complicated, illegal bartering system. He ran his icebreakers to the mainland for his wintertime business arrangements, and every time the city captured one of his ships, they reprogrammed the robots back into the city's systems. It was less than what they should have done. Even Sofia knew that running in food independent of the mainland's efforts was punishable with jail time. But Cabrera never went to jail; he never lost his ships or his robots. He only had to reprogram them. It was a game he played with the city, a constant back-and-forth of programming and reprogramming. In the grand scheme of things, a minor irritation.

Sebastian pulled a chair around for Cabrera, who sat down, settling into his weight. Sofia was aware of the motion of the ship, the motion of the sea.

"You have until morning," Cabrera said. "We can pay off the night guards but not the day ones."

"Are you going to stay here all night with me?" Sofia asked. She nodded at Luciano, who walked across the room and activated the lead shipping robot. It looked around the room with blank bright eyes.

"You know as well as I that I'm not leaving you alone."

Sofia shrugged. Cabrera had hired her to do a simple thing. She didn't care if he watched. Sofia was used to being watched.

"Bring him here," Sofia said to Luciano, and Luciano led the shipping robot to where Sofia stood, next to the ship's navigation system. The robot stared at her, not comprehending. She looked too human for it, most likely, and it was befuddled by the conflict between her exterior and the very inhuman readings it was getting from her interior.

"Sorry, friend." Sofia deactivated the robot, and it slumped, letting out a sound like a sigh. She pried open the panel in its torso and ran her fingers down the switches and controls. "They didn't change the hardware."

Luciano nodded, handed her a thin curl of cable. She connected herself with the robot. The information rushed in—not much. This one was simple, designed for a set of specific tasks. Navigation, maintaining the engines, plus the handling of the other shipping robots, who took care of the products on board.

"I looked at the work your previous programmer did." Her voice was far away and webbed with static. "It was sloppy. I can do better."

"Is that so?" Cabrera asked.

She nodded.

Reprogramming the city's robots was easy work. She'd done it several times already for her own purposes, on different models. The previous reprogrammer had been lazy, but Sofia expected nothing less. He'd been human.

The reprogramming didn't take long. She did what Cabrera asked of her, and then she inserted lines of invisible programming that no human could see and only she could activate.

She updated the captain's robot and moved on to the others. Cabrera sat in his chair, flanked by his bodyguards, and watched her. Luciano stood off to the side, hands folded behind his back, aiding her as needed. Sometimes she wondered if he saw her as human. It was not the sort of question she could ask him directly.

When she finished, Luciano helped her replace the shipping robots in their alcoves. Cabrera stood up, his bodyguards moving in beside him.

"Diego," Cabrera said. "What time is it?"

"Almost midnight, sir."

"Midnight!" Cabrera laughed. "Horatio took until three, four in the morning sometimes! I'm very impressed with you, Sofia."

Sofia smiled the way she'd been programmed to do whenever a human complimented her.

They left the ship, stepping back out into the cold windy air of the docks. The Florencia was lit up in the distance, yellow and green lights staining the darkness. Cabrera stopped in the middle of the dock and turned to Sofia and stuck out his hand. She stared at it. He laughed.

"I have a good feeling about this arrangement," Cabrera said. "But you're going to need to learn some of our ways. Isn't that right, Sebastian?"

Sebastian nodded.

"Shake my hand, dear. I know you've seen it done before."

Sofia had not been programmed to shake hands, only to offer hers, for kisses or dances or other frivolities. But Cabrera was right; she had seen it done. And so she gripped his hand and shook.

"I look forward to our future endeavors." Cabrera tipped his hat. "I have an icebreaker leaving the mainland in half an hour. The best in my fleet. I'll make sure those items you requested find their way on board."

"So soon?" Sofia asked, with forced levity.

"Only the best for the best." Cabrera grinned. "But it'll take a bit of time. Two weeks, perhaps."

Sofia had waited forty years. She could wait two weeks.

"I'll be expecting them," she said.

Beside her, Luciano smiled.

* * * *

The train into the amusement park didn't run this late, and so Sofia and Luciano walked through the city, side by side and unspeaking. Sofia did not know what Luciano thought of, but she imagined the turn-of-the-century supplies she had requested making their way aboard an icebreaker, and then that icebreaker sailing through the frozen seas to Antarctica.

Cabrera had no idea what the parts did, she was certain of that. Why would he? They were almost seventy years out of date. Araceli, in her skillful human way, was only filling in the gaps of what had been left behind when the amusement park had closed. She was the best at that, and Sofia was lucky that Araceli, despite being human and a former park engineer, was sympathetic to their cause.

Without her help, the reprogramming would be nearly impossible. And so Sofia allowed her to live in the amusement park.

Still, Sofia was grateful that the particular items Araceli needed—a bundle of antique vacuum tubes, three clockwork micro-engines, ticker tape, a blank programming key—were innocuous when viewed together. They meant nothing.

She smiled to herself.

Sofia and Luciano came to the amusement park gate, wrought iron and once painted white, patterns of Victorian fairies twisting through the metalwork. The road was inlaid with bright circles of glass, leading the way inside. Sofia rarely saw the gate from the city side, but she knew that it should be shut, that the original lock from the 1890s had been replaced with a new one, modern and electronic.

But tonight, the gate hung open.

"Oh no," Luciano said, in the same tone of voice he had probably once used on sick children.

Sofia didn't say anything. All her systems felt as if they were shutting down. For a moment she stopped in the middle of the road and stared at the open gate. There was no wind here, and the gate was frozen into that position like in a photograph.

A culling.

Luciano rushed forward, and that was enough to jar Sofia back into motion. She followed behind him. Her systems sent warnings straight into her subconscious, and she wanted to hide, to slip away into the shadows. But she didn't. She picked up speed until she was running, her hair loosening from her beehive and streaming out behind her. She was aware of Luciano somewhere ahead, his footsteps echoing against the cobblestone.

"Sofia!"

Araceli's voice cut through the night air. Sofia stopped. She'd made it to the Sugar Garden. The garden had long ago overreached its boundaries, and flowering vines curled over the pathway, trampled beneath her feet.

Araceli was sitting on the bench beneath the streetlamp, Inéz leaning up against her. Inéz had been like Luciano once, had tended to humans in the amusement park hotels. Now she looked worn-out, like a discarded doll. Part of her hair was missing.

"Who was taken?" Sofia asked sharply.

"Maintenance. One of the Scala models. Yellow-8." Inéz closed her eyes. Just like a doll.

"That's it? Just one?" Sofia walked over to them. Luciano was already there, fussing over Araceli. As a human, she brought that out in him.

"Inéz needs comforting more than me," Araceli told him. "They weren't going to drag me away." Luciano nodded, looped around behind the bench. Sofia turned to Inéz.

"What happened?"

"They almost got me." Inéz gave a weak smile as Luciano took her hand. "They stunned me. But Araceli distracted them."

"I just fired a flare." Araceli rubbed her forehead. "I saw they were coming on the transmissions, so everyone hid before they arrived."

"There was a programming issue," Inéz said apologetically. "That's why they almost got me."

"One of the cullers tripped, the idiot. Started bleeding. You know how it is."

Sofia nodded. Inéz's programming had condemned her to offer assistance. But it would not always. Soon. Soon, they would have the supplies. Soon, they would cut all that programming out. Sofia first, then the rest of them. Luciano, Inéz, those few broken-down androids she could repair only once she had her independence.

"Their weapons are the same," Inéz said. "Still weak."

"Well, they don't capture many of us anymore, do they?" Sofia smiled. "I doubt that's high on the list of priorities."

Luciano smiled back at her, but Araceli and Inéz did not.

"The Scala model," Sofia said. "We can get him back."

Silence. They all knew rescue was unlikely. But Sofia had been programmed to lie, once upon a time, to tell people what they wanted to hear.

Araceli, Inéz, and Luciano sat pressed against each other on the bench, huddling together as if they needed one another's touch. But

Sofia had stripped that weakness out of herself long ago. She knew how touches could be toxic.

She left them there without explaining herself, walking off to the center of the Sugar Garden, where she could have privacy.

The cullings had started as soon as the amusement park had closed. Hope City needed robots to survive, and so Autômatos Teixeira had simply left them there when the company had gone bankrupt, the way it had abandoned the factories in Brazil. And while most of the amusement park robots were useless—performers, or caretakers, or pleasure givers—their parts were not. Long ago, Sofia had taught the others how to hide, how to survive. She had built and installed blockers that made it impossible for anyone to scan for robots inside the park, hoping that would discourage the cullings.

She could not say where she had learned all this herself. It certainly hadn't been programmed into her. This was before Araceli arrived ten years ago, before the city fired Araceli from her job as a Hope City engineer for showing kindness and decency to robots and she sought refuge in the closed-down park, the one place, she said, she'd ever been happy. The knowledge had simply appeared in Sofia. A human would call it magic. Sofia was not a human.

When Sofia arrived at the garden's center, overflowing with flowers and thick green vines, a maintenance drone was waiting for her in a pool of yellow lamplight. It would have registered her entering the park, and now it came to her, awaiting instructions.

The maintenance drones couldn't speak in human voices, but Sofia didn't need them to. She knelt beside the robot and pressed her palm against its sensor. She transferred an image of Yellow-8, boxy and long-limbed. And then she flooded the drone with instructions. Find Yellow-8. Bring him back. She knew how improbable her instructions were. But she needed to try.

The maintenance drone responded. The drones had tried to retrieve Yellow-8, when they'd learned who had been taken. But it was too late.

Too late.

Sofia slid her hand off the sensor. She was empty.

"Thank you," she whispered, reverting back to her old ways, her facsimile of humanity. She stood up. The maintenance drone blinked at her for a moment longer, then zipped up into the air, disappearing into the night.

Sofia was alone.

CHAPTER EIGHT

MARIANELLA

Marianella sat at her vanity, a lipstick in one hand. She didn't move to apply it, only stared at her reflection. The last few days showed on her face: dark half-moons below her eyes, thin lines radiating out from the corners of her lips. She sighed and dropped the lipstick and leaned back on her stool. The party was to start in a little over an hour. Luciano had agreed again to play at being her butler, even though the circumstances weren't so dire this time around. Still, with his help, she'd managed to set up everything for her guests. But *she* wasn't ready.

Everything had been too much this week. Losing her documents, learning that some man knew what she was. She'd seen the news of Pablo Sala's death in the evening newspaper three days ago and the relief had been sweet and sudden and then swallowed up by guilt. It was a sin to celebrate the death of a human being like that. But he had known what she was, and if this stranger could know, then she had to assume there were others.

And she was certain that if there were others, they would be tied to Ignacio Cabrera. Hector must have told him somehow, sent word along before his death that Marianella kept a painful truth locked away in the safe in the library. The thought made her sick to her stomach. But Hector was one of only three humans she had ever told her secret, and she trusted the other two more than she had trusted her late husband.

At least she was certain that Ignacio didn't know what her documents revealed, not if he'd sent someone to steal them. Because if he knew what she was, he wouldn't need the proof of her documents. It was a secret strong enough that even a rumor started by a gangster could be enough to undo her.

"Marianella?" Luciano appeared in the vanity's mirror, holding a vase of flowers. "These were sitting in the kitchen. I presume you want them in the main room?"

Marianella plastered on a cheerful smile, then twisted around in her stool. "Yes, that would be lovely, thank you."

But Luciano didn't move away. He studied her for a moment, then said, "You don't have to pretend with me. I know how upsetting this last week has been."

"I have to pretend with everyone else. I might as well start now." Marianella turned back to her mirror and picked up her lipstick. Luciano moved out of sight of the reflection and walked silently to her side. He set the flowers down on the vanity. She glanced up at him, turned her gaze back to her reflection, applied her lipstick.

He knelt beside her. "If you ever need help," he said, "Sofia would be happy to send it."

"Sofia's gone mad."

"No, she hasn't."

Marianella dropped her lipstick and smoothed the flyways that had escaped from her curls. "Maybe you've gone mad right along with her. Inéz, too."

Luciano laughed. He was programmed to do that, she knew, if anyone said something that sounded like teasing.

"I haven't gone mad. I meant about Ignacio Cabrera. I'm sure Sofia would set aside your differences if you needed help."

"We don't have differences. We just—" Marianella couldn't put it into words, not in a way that Luciano would understand. She was neither human nor robot, but something in between, and she had chosen to live as a human, however dangerous and precarious that might be. It was easier. "Besides, what does Sofia know about Ignacio Cabrera? I'm shocked either of you have even heard of him."

She stood up with a swish of her skirt and checked the time—a little under an hour now.

"I merely meant we could provide protection, if you needed it." Luciano offered an arm and Marianella took it without thinking. They left the bedroom together. "At the very least, Sofia has maintenance drones at her disposal, and I'm sure she wouldn't mind lending them to you."

"That's not necessary." They descended the stairs. All the lights were switched on, the chandelier sparkling. "I've already programmed mine to watch out for Ignacio's men. Besides, I'm a television star now. I doubt he's brave enough to try anything too drastic." Marianella wasn't entirely convinced of that herself, but she didn't want to worry Luciano.

"Well, if you suspect he knows of your nature—" Luciano detached from Marianella's arm and gave a bow. "I'm sure we could be of service."

Luciano would do all sorts of things for her—help her with a party, pretend he'd been the one to hear the scratching the night of the break-in. He would always be of service. Sofia wouldn't.

"I doubt he knows," Marianella said. "If he even suspected, he would simply inform the authorities of those suspicions and that would be enough to launch an investigation." And he hadn't done that. Not yet. "At any rate, I've moved the documents for the time being. They are the key, I think."

Luciano nodded as they walked into the main room, the largest in the house. One wall was a window that looked out over the wheat field, and Marianella kept the theremin and record player there. Right now the main room was frozen in time, poised and waiting for the party to start. Flowers dotted the furniture, bottles of liquor sat at the wet bar. The scene was incomplete without people.

"Oh!" said Marianella. "You forgot the flowers upstairs."

"I never forget things," Luciano said. "I merely thought you required my attention more than the vase. I'll fetch it now."

Marianella laughed, even though she didn't know if it was really funny. Luciano smiled at her and disappeared into the hallway. Marianella collapsed onto the sofa. She hadn't thrown a party since Hector died, but she knew she couldn't stay withdrawn from society for much longer. The winter gala season would be starting soon, and those galas, as silly and frivolous as they were on the surface, were the best ways to raise money for the agricultural domes. The wealthy were always more generous during the winter—a way of showing off. Already Alejo Ortiz had telephoned about the Midwinter Ball, which had been the most successful fund-raiser last year. He expected her to attend, and this little party was Marianella's way of stepping back out into the world.

And so she had Alejo to thank for her reemergence. Alejo and his *project*. That's what he'd called it when he'd asked her to his office nearly two and a half years ago. Behind those closed doors he'd seduced her with the idea of Antarctican independence. "There's a reason this place is called Hope City," he'd said. "Sixty years ago we lived in one of the wonders of the world. Why shouldn't it be a wonder again?"

Her father had called her a wonder of the world, after the surgery that had changed her. He had been wrong. But she saw in Alejo's idealism a chance to create a real wonder, a place where human beings could live in the frozen desert. A chance to prove her own humanity.

At the time, Alejo had only wanted her money and her influence. He'd already told her about the funding he'd received from the Antarctican Freedom Fighters, despite the risk it posed to his career—a shocking bit of information that appalled Marianella and excited her as well, at least at the time. Back then she liked to think of herself as the respectable alternative to money from terrorists, a group the chief of police called Hope City's number one enemy.

She and Alejo became lovers not long after, a dalliance designed to alleviate boredom more than anything else. Certainly Hector didn't mind; he had his own affairs. Even after Hector was confined to his bed, she and Alejo kept it up, those clandestine meetings in shabby motel rooms on the edge of the dome, her wine-colored lipstick smeared on his shirt collar. More like a film than anything real.

Afterward, Alejo would always talk about the ag domes. Engineers from the mainland he'd spoken to, permits he'd acquired through contacts at the city offices. They'd raised almost enough to build one dome at that point, although Alejo wanted to keep it a secret. "It'll be great political theater, don't you think? To announce that we're building *more* domes, instead of just the first one."

Marianella could only agree.

"I want to time it to coincide with the mayoral election."

There were problems, of course. The engineers insisted the work couldn't be done in secret, that they didn't have the capacity to program enough robots to do what Alejo wanted. Marianella remembered sitting on the floor in a white slip, smoking a cigarette while Alejo paced back and forth, his hair wild, ranting about the inefficiency of mainland engineers. "If only we had more engineers who'd grown up here," he said. "They'd understand. They'd have a reason to find a way. Why should they waste all their intelligence on power for the mainland?"

Marianella had hardly been listening. Her thoughts had been with the domes. With the robots Alejo needed.

I could do that.

Her nature made it easy to speak with robots. She could slip inside their programming and twist it around to suit her purposes. That was why full humans hated her nature so much—because ultimately, they feared her. She had all the abilities of a robot but remained completely unprogrammable.

Up until that point robotics had been a hobby, one Hector had tolerated only because she programmed their private maintenance drones. But as Alejo paced back and forth, the muscles in his neck tightening with anxiety, she thought back to the day Alejo had first told her of the domes. This was an opportunity, a chance for her nature to be something other than a failed scientific experiment.

And then Hector had died.

It wasn't a shock, not really; he'd been bedridden so long. Still Marianella mourned him, not because she'd loved him or because he had loved her, but because he had known. As she watched his smoke and ashes drift up through the transparent chimney, into the open Antarctic air, she wondered if she and Araceli could bear the weight of that secret, after so long with Hector to take on part of the burden.

In that way, the pieces fell together. Alejo was at the funeral too, standing across the room with his assistant, and in that moment, surrounded by the cold air and her husband's ashes, she made a decision. It was the most dangerous thing she'd ever done.

She waited until their next afternoon together. As Alejo touched her, she felt like a glint of mainland sunlight bouncing across a hardwood floor. Afterward they lay stretched out on the bare mattress, the sheets and blanket kicked to the floor. She stared up at the light in the ceiling as she spoke.

"I can build the dome for you," she said.

And Alejo had turned to her, his eyes glittering. He didn't laugh, like she'd expected. He took her seriously. And so she told him, her heart beating so fast, she thought she might break herself.

She wasn't human. She had machine parts embedded in her body. She was illegal.

There followed eleven and a half seconds of silence, just enough for her to recite the Hail Mary inside her head.

"You can go outside in the cold?" Alejo asked. That was his first response. His arm was around her shoulder, and he didn't take it away.

"For a few hours, yes," Marianella said. "And I can program your robots better than any engineer in the city or on the mainland."

It was enough. Alejo kept her secret, and a month later she had programmed an army of Vaz models to build the dome on the southern side of the city, hidden away among the other private domes. She and Alejo planted the first seeds by hand—wheat, the same sort that grew around Southstar. And then they appeared on television and continued to sell the lie that they planned to build an agricultural dome, not that they already had.

"Where would you like this?" Luciano was back, peering around the fan of fuchsia blossoms from the hothouse she kept on the estate. Such flowers were an extravagance in a place like Hope City.

"Oh, I don't know." Marianella stood up and swept around the room. "Where do you think they should go?"

"They'd look lovely at the bar, I think. It's a bit empty at the moment."

"At the bar, wonderful." Marianella smiled. "You can watch to make sure no one knocks them over."

"Of course." Luciano walked across the room and arranged the vase behind the rows of liquor bottles. He'd started coming over after Hector had died, offering his services as a butler. They'd met at the same time that she had met Sofia, shortly after Marianella had moved to Hope City. They'd become friends, although his friendship always seemed strangely subservient to her. And so she'd refused at first, not wanting to trap him back into servitude, but he'd looked her straight in the eye and said, "It's not slavery with you, Marianella. It's friendship."

Sofia would have called it slavery. But Sofia and Luciano had always been different, for as long as Marianella had known them.

Marianella joined Luciano at the bar as he fiddled with the fuchsias' leaves. He seemed content, she thought, like the way she felt when she was programming Southstar's maintenance drones, or walking through the rows of crops in the agricultural dome.

"It looks fine," she said. "You can stop messing with it."

Luciano glanced at her and took a step back. "I want everything to be perfect."

"I know you do." Marianella looped her arm around his and squeezed him in a half hug. He smiled at her, that halfhearted robot smile she found so comforting.

The doorbell rang.

"They're early," Luciano remarked.

"I bet it's the Mendezes. They're notorious for it." She took a deep breath. "I guess I have to be ready, don't I?"

"You look beautiful."

Another bit of programming. Marianella didn't care. "Thank you, Luciano."

He took his place behind the bar, where all her guests would see him not as a friend but as a quirky throwback to the city's heyday.

She checked her hair and makeup in the window's reflection one last time.

Back in society again, she thought, and then she glided down the hallway to answer the door.

* * * *

Two hours later, the house was alive with people. Night had fallen completely, and the bright golden lights inside turned the window into a dark mirror that reflected Marianella's party guests as if they were ghosts. Luciano served behind the wet bar, demurring if anyone offered him a tip. Marianella flitted from person to person, a glass of red wine in one hand. She only drank from it occasionally, and Marianella was relieved to find how easily she slipped back into this role. She laughed and pressed her hand to her chest and conjured up small talk with hardly any concentration.

Every now and then she caught Luciano's eye, and he smiled encouragingly, as if he understood the way some silly party could help rejuvenate her.

A little after nine thirty, a gang of Marianella's old socialite friends cornered her next to the fireplace. They were on their way to being drunk, although all three of them knew how to hide it.

"Bianca wants to play the theremin," said Emilia, the oldest of the three and the one who had first befriended Marianella when she'd arrived in Hope City, all those years ago.

"I don't," said Bianca. "I haven't played in years. I'm sure I'm terrible now." She laughed, and Marianella could tell that she really did want to play—too much modesty always meant the opposite.

"Please," said Paula. "You're the most amazing player we know."

Bianca laughed again, shoving at Paula playfully and shaking her head.

"I'd love to hear you play," Marianella said. "I never could get the hang of it." That wasn't entirely true; Marianella loved the theremin. Except she didn't play it with her hands the way a human would, but with the feedback from her own thoughts. And so she never played in front of an audience. At least not an audience that didn't know her secret.

"I really don't need to," Bianca said, but Marianella knew that was a lie.

"Nonsense." Marianella walked over to the bar and knocked one of the stirring spoons against her wineglass. The guests were well trained; they turned to her almost as a group. For a moment Marianella wavered under their gaze. She'd never liked being the center of attention; she was always convinced someone would see through her skin and discover her secret.

She glanced at Luciano, and his calm, unflappable presence soothed her.

"Bianca has a surprise for us," she said, and the socialites erupted into giggles. Over thirty years old, all of them, and married, but they still acted like girls. The rest of the guests exchanged glances, and the air in the room tensed, as if the party expected a break in propriety.

"She'd like to play the theremin," Marianella added, and there was a contented sigh—this wasn't anything *weird*, only an impromptu performance. Old-fashioned, Marianella thought, as Bianca and the always chivalrous Vicente carted the theremin and its stand to the center of the room. Just like her parents' parties in the thirties, when the guests would sing and perform instead of using the record player. It went along with Luciano playing the role of electric butler.

Bianca positioned herself. Her face took on a serious, scholarly expression, and she lifted her hands in the air. The theremin buzzed.

She began to play.

Marianella recognized the song immediately—a Rachmaninoff piece she'd always found haunting. She leaned against the bar and closed her eyes and listened. She'd played this song for Sofia once. It was a safe song, one that wouldn't activate Sofia's programming, and its intensity had always reminded Marianella of Sofia, as if the music could form into a woman.

The doorbell rang.

Marianella opened her eyes. Bianca kept playing, so caught up in her music that she didn't notice. A few of the guests stirred, but no one seemed bothered by this interruption.

Luciano leaned forward. "Would you like me to answer it?" he whispered.

Marianella shook her head. Bianca played beautifully, but Marianella wasn't sure she wanted to listen to this particular song right now. Too sad. Too many memories.

She slipped out of the main room and down the hall. None of her maintenance drones came to warn her, so she assumed it was not one of Ignacio's men, and she was right. When she pulled the door open, Eliana Gomez stood on the front porch, clutching a bottle of cheap white wine in one hand.

"Sorry I'm late," she said. "I got caught up in picking out a gift—Did I need to bring a gift? And then I missed the train—"

"It's quite all right. Come in." Marianella took the wine and held open the door. Eliana looked out of place in her glittering black party dress and teased-out hair, but Marianella was glad she'd invited her. "We're listening to a performance right now, but as soon as it's over, I'll introduce you to some potential clients." She smiled and lifted the bottle. "I'll drop this off in the kitchen. If you follow the hallway, you'll get to the main room, and you'll find everyone there."

Eliana nodded, but she looked dazed, the poor girl, like an animal caught in the headlights of a car. She followed the direction of the music, and Marianella walked into the kitchen and slid the wine bottle into the refrigerator. Sweet of her, to bring a hostess gift.

"Nice party."

Marianella recognized Alejo's voice instantly. She straightened up, turned to face him.

"Thank you," she said.

He grinned, looking rakish and dangerous, not like a city man at all. "I like the entertainment."

"Yes, Bianca plays very well."

"I was talking about the andie behind the bar."

Marianella's heartbeat rose, her breath quickened. "He's not entertainment."

"He's novel enough to count, I'd think. How did you get something like that in this day and age?"

"A lady never tells her secrets."

Alejo laughed. Marianella just smiled politely. They both knew she couldn't tell him any secret more damaging than the one she'd revealed last year in that shabby motel room.

Alejo smoothed back his hair with one hand. Preening. He was the bland sort of handsome that showed up well on television. "I'm glad I caught you alone, actually. I need to talk to you about the project."

Marianella glanced around the big empty kitchen. Bianca had started Mozart's Concerto Number Fifteen, and the cheerful notes drifted in from the hallway.

"Shouldn't we wait?" she asked.

"It's nothing terribly drastic, but I've been a bit tied up this last week and haven't gotten a chance to call." He went quiet, and Marianella peered up at him.

"Well?"

"I just have some concerns about the blackout on Last Night."

Marianella glided across the kitchen and pretended to rummage in the refrigerator. The city had destroyed a maintenance drone because of that blackout, an innocent one, if Luciano was to be believed, but Marianella still remembered the initial rumors about the AFF's involvement. She didn't know the truth, whether a robot or the AFF had caused the blackout. It seemed unlikely to her that the AFF would want to cause a blackout. But then, they murdered people, innocent people, so perhaps it was possible. If anyone knew the truth, it was Alejo. Or Sofia, for that matter.

"I heard it was terrifying," Marianella said. "The blackout."

"Lucky you, holed up in your private palace." Alejo moved up alongside her, leaning on the refrigerator door. "It's actually been pretty scary the last week too. The power hasn't been steady. It flickers, dims—hasn't failed completely again, but it's enough that the city engineers are all in a tizzy."

"I've heard about that. My prayers are with all of you." Marianella pulled out a package of chèvre and looked over at Alejo expectantly. He stepped away from the refrigerator and pushed the door shut for her.

"Thank you," she said.

"Anything for Lady Luna." Alejo repositioned himself against the counter. "Do you really need to do that? There's plenty of food sitting out with your andie."

"You know I don't like that word." Marianella took a plate out of the cupboard and began arranging crackers across it, flared out like a sunflower.

Alejo grinned. "Well, you were always touchy about robots. I suppose that's fair."

"We should all be touchy about robots," Marianella murmured. "They run the city for us. The power failures ought to cement that, don't you think?"

"Exactly. That's what I'm here to talk to you about." Alejo leaned in close to her as she rearranged the crackers. "The city's blaming a piece of broken programming that's worked its way into the city drones. Pretty big cause for concern, I'd say."

Marianella's skin prickled with his sudden closeness. He smelled like European cologne and pine trees. Every human had a different scent.

He pressed his cheek against hers. "We're lucky we're not stuck with city drones," he murmured.

"Oh, stop it. Someone will see." She pushed him aside. She and Alejo hadn't slept together since the day she'd revealed her nature, but he still flirted with her sometimes, when he wanted to get his way. He didn't want her anymore because he knew what she was. Well, the same could be said for her. The idea of sleeping with someone who took money from terrorists no longer excited her. She felt sick that it had ever excited her at all.

Alejo stepped a few paces away from her, smoothed his hair again. "You're no fun."

"You're a tease."

Alejo laughed at that.

"What exactly did you want to talk about?" She smeared the chèvre artfully on the center of the plate. "You don't really think my drones are infected with this—broken programming?" She pitched her voice low. Bianca was still playing the concerto, and the melody jumped around the house.

"I just want to make sure." Alejo shrugged. "Will it really be a huge burden for you to run out there and check on them? I'd hate to see all your hard work wasted."

He'd hate to see all *his* hard work wasted. Marianella knew that by now. Still, Marianella always loved any excuse to visit the ag dome. Even if she didn't think her drones were in any danger of broken city programming, she nodded as she lifted the cheese plate.

The music faded away, and applause rippled in from the main room.

"You know you can check on the drones yourself," she said. "I gave you access." He'd insisted on access, but Marianella didn't mention that.

"I know, I know. But you're so much better with them than I am. I'll miss something, I'm sure of it."

"Yes, you probably would." She smiled to show she was half-teasing. "I really don't mind so much. I'll go tomorrow."

"Thanks. I do appreciate it." He snapped his fingers. "Oh! Before you run back out to the party—I've got one last question for you."

Marianella turned around, still holding the plate of cheese and crackers. "Yes?"

"The Midwinter Ball—"

Marianella sighed. "I *know*, Alejo. I told you, I'm already making plans to attend."

Alejo held up two hands and pretended to cower in apology. "I know, I know," he said. "We talked about it a few weeks ago. But I want to know for certain—"

"I'll be there," Marianella said. "I swear to you."

"It's the biggest event of the year." Alejo grinned. "I just wouldn't want you to miss it."

Marianella knew it wasn't her social life he had in mind. Still, she laughed and shook her head before leaving the kitchen. In the cool, dark hallway she reminded herself that she was the widow of Hector Luna, an aristocrat from the mainland, and nothing more. She certainly hadn't built an agricultural dome with a man who took money from terrorists.

By the time she was back in the main room, she almost believed it.

"Is everything all right?" Luciano smiled at her as she deposited the cheese plate on the bar. "You were gone longer than I expected."

"Alejo wanted to talk to me."

"Mr. Ortiz?"

Marianella nodded. She thought she heard a disapproving lilt in Luciano's voice, but it was impossible to know for sure, and when she looked at him again, he was still smiling. She gazed out over the party. Bianca stood beside the theremin, surrounded by admirers. A knot of husbands lounged by the doorway, smoking cigarettes. And Eliana Gomez pressed herself into the corner like she was trying to be invisible.

"Eliana!" Marianella cried. "Oh, I almost forgot about her, the darling."

"Is there anything I can do to help?"

"No, no, that's not necessary. I just didn't mean to leave her alone." Marianella left Luciano and cut across the room to where Eliana stood sipping nervously out of a glass of wine. When she saw Marianella, she looked relieved.

"This is a great party," she said, clearly lying.

"I didn't mean to be so long in the kitchen. I'm sorry." Marianella had slipped almost completely back into the role of Lady Luna now, and as she whirled Eliana around the party, introducing her to potential clients, she felt herself finally settle into it. The moment Marianella had seen Eliana on her front porch, clutching the envelope with her documents, Marianella's life had started up again. That documentation revealed what she was. It revealed all the details of her schematics. She'd thought about burning it so many times—once, she'd even held it over an open flame—but she always stopped herself. If her nature were revealed and she could produce no documentation, she would be killed without question. With the documents, she would only be deported.

And that was why Marianella had invited Eliana to this party. Eliana had recovered the documentation and not looked; or if she had looked, she hadn't acted on it. Marianella suspected she hadn't looked. Anyone who knew would report her or blackmail her. Or sell her out to Ignacio Cabrera, as her late husband had apparently done.

Marianella shoved the thought aside, storing it for some other time—tomorrow, after the party, in the harsh light of day. Eliana Gomez deserved her attention now. There was no amount of money Marianella could give Eliana to repay her for saving her secret, for *keeping* her secret. The least Marianella could do was bring her some new business.

CHAPTER NINE

ELIANA

"I have just one more person I'd like you meet. Is that all right?" Lady Luna led Eliana through the maze of party guests. The lights were so bright in the house, brighter than Eliana remembered from the last time she was here. Maybe she shouldn't have had the third glass of wine.

"Sure, that'd be great."

Lady Luna beamed. They'd spoken to three people already, two women and a man. All three of them had the glossy, aristocratic bearing Eliana was used to seeing only on television, but they'd been polite enough to her, and they'd taken her business card and tucked it away as if they intended to use it later. Eliana knew it couldn't hurt, having her name out in this crowd. If they all paid as well as Lady Luna, she'd be out of Antarctica within the year.

"This is Eveline Quiroga." Lady Luna stopped in front of a middle-aged woman in a slim green dress, streaks of gray in her dark hair. "Eveline, you remember that matter we were discussing a few weeks ago? I have someone who might be able to help."

Mrs. Quiroga turned her gaze to Eliana, who had the urge to shrink away but didn't.

"You can call me at my office," Eliana said, handing her a business card. "Whatever the matter is, I work quickly and discreetly."

Mrs. Quiroga looked over the business card and then slipped it into her handbag.

"A woman investigator," she said in a cool, sophisticated drawl. "I suppose that fills a niche."

Eliana plastered on her politest smile. "I've been told it does." She was used to being condescended to, and by people far more practiced at it than this Mrs. Quiroga.

"She does excellent work," Lady Luna said brightly. "I can personally vouch for her. I'd be happy to speak about it with you sometime."

"Is that so?" Mrs. Quiroga looked at Lady Luna and then back to Eliana. "I'll think about it. Excuse me."

She floated off into the party, wineglass held up. Eliana wanted another drink, dizziness be damned.

"I'm sorry about that," Lady Luna said.

"About what?"

"Oh, you know, *Eveline*. She's like that with everyone, at least until they prove themselves to her. I should have warned you."

Eliana laughed. "I can handle it."

Lady Luna sipped from her glass of wine, gazing out over her party. She seemed different this evening, more glamorous and less flighty. Classy, that was it. She was *classy* tonight. In certain ways Lady Luna reminded Eliana of her own mother, who had faked sophistication on several different occasions during Eliana's childhood. And like Eliana's mother, Lady Luna seemed to be faking her classiness, or at least some of it.

Eliana wondered what sort of woman lay behind Lady Luna's facade, if she was as spirited as Eliana's mother had been. Eliana thought she could like Lady Luna, if that was the case.

"I'm going to get another drink," Eliana said, and Lady Luna smiled in acknowledgment. Eliana left her alone and walked over to the bar. The andie was watching the party much as Lady Luna was: unmoving, contemplative.

"Hey," Eliana said. Then, out of habit, "Nice to see you again."

"I'm glad to hear that." He smiled, and Eliana was still stunned by the way a smile could look so genuine and so artificial at the same time. "Would you like something to drink, Miss Gomez?"

"You know my name?"

"I remember you, yes. Would you like another glass of wine?"

Eliana nodded and watched as he pulled out a clean glass and opened up a new bottle. The wine sloshed, red and thick. He handed it to her.

"I missed you when I came out here to deliver Lady Luna's documents." Even as she spoke, Eliana wondered what she was doing. Playing the damn detective at a party, and for what? There was no case. No one was paying her to investigate Lady Luna or her old-fashioned and highly regulated electronic butler.

"Did you?" His voice was inflected with a cool politeness.

"Yeah." Eliana arranged herself on a stool. Funny what alcohol did to you. She'd rather talk to the robot than to any of the guests at the party. "Lady Luna give you days off?"

"Why would I need a day off?" All of his words sounded rehearsed, but this question sounded more rehearsed than anything else. "I'm sure I was busy elsewhere on the estate. What day was it?"

"Last Tuesday."

"Ah yes, well, I was tending to the wheat. I'm sure that's why I missed you." He turned away from her, putting the wine back into place along the mirror. Eliana sipped from her glass. Mr. Vasquez had taught her how to read people, as much as you *could* teach that, but this was an andie. Hard to tell what she was seeing.

"I was just curious," she said when he turned back to face her.

"A useful trait in your profession, I'm sure." He gave her a sly smile, which put her at ease.

"Do you like working for Lady Luna?" she asked.

"I like it very much." In this moment, he looked more human than robot, as if the wine were softening his edges. "Do you like working as a private investigator?"

"Beats working in the steno pool down at the city offices." Eliana took a long drink, and the alcohol's warmth spread through her limbs.

"I can imagine."

Eliana laughed. "Maybe. Most men can't."

He blinked at her, and Eliana had the sudden dawning ache that she'd misspoken somehow.

"Luciano! Get us a drink, will you? Whiskey, neat." A man with steely hair sidled up to the bar, a woman about Eliana's age dangling off his arm.

The robot—Luciano, his name was Luciano—moved to fix the couple's drinks. When he turned away from her, Eliana slid off the bar stool and moved through the liquid lights of the party.

She just needed some fresh air.

* * * *

Eliana woke up the next day to the sound of banging on her front door.

She moaned into her pillow, blinking against the glare of the dome lights pouring in through her window. They hadn't been this bright in days.

The banging stopped, and Eliana breathed a sigh of relief. Her head pounded in time with her heart.

The banging started again.

"Eliana! You in there?"

Diego. She hadn't seen him for a few days, not since she'd stolen the documents off Sala down at the Florencia. She'd figured he'd retreated into the underworld for a while, the way he did.

"I'm coming!" she shouted, although she doubted he could hear her. She rolled out of bed and ran her fingers through her hair before padding over to the door. She pulled it open when Diego was midknock, his fist lifted in the air.

"Somebody had a fun night," he said.

Eliana rolled her eyes and pushed the door open farther. Diego stepped inside, swooping his gaze around the room, the way he always did. The door clicked shut behind him, and he reached back and locked it.

"At least, I hope it was a fun night." Diego collapsed on the sofa, kicking his feet up onto the coffee table.

"Yeah? You aren't jealous?" Eliana grinned at him, but Diego didn't return it. "You want some coffee?"

"You still have coffee this far into winter?"

Eliana shrugged.

"No, I'm fine. It's the middle of the afternoon anyway. You really do look like shit, Eliana. You should drink some orange juice."

"No one in the smokestack district has seen orange juice for four months." Eliana stumbled into the kitchen, where she poured herself a glass of water. She leaned up against the refrigerator, sipping at it, and Diego came in to join her.

"Seriously, though," he said, "was it a good night?"

Eliana peered up at him. His expression was serious, almost stern.

"I was at a party," she said.

Diego took a deep breath.

"What?" Eliana finished off her water and poured another glass. "I can't go to parties?"

"You can do whatever you want," Diego said. "But you probably shouldn't steal papers off some engineer waiting to meet with Mr. Cabrera in Mr. Cabrera's own goddamned bar."

Eliana froze. She and Diego stared at each other, and Eliana felt the way she had the time her mother had caught her sneaking out of their apartment one night when she was fifteen: a weird combination of guilt and irritation at being found out.

"You heard about that?" she finally squeaked. She took a long drink of water.

"Yeah, I heard about it." Diego sighed again. "You better be grateful Mr. Cabrera has no idea who you are. The only one who got a good look at you was Sala, and he's—not an issue."

Eliana felt herself harden. "Why not?"

"Because he's not. He's dead."

"*What?*"

"Mr. Cabrera had him killed. For lying." Diego's eyes glittered. "That's why I said you should be grateful Mr. Cabrera has no idea who you are. I only figured it out when I put two and two together. Not a lot of lady investigators in the city."

He *was* upset. He'd called her an investigator instead of a cop.

"It was a lot of money." Eliana drained her glass and left it sitting on the counter. Her stomach lurched, and she didn't think she needed to fill it with any more water. "And I haven't had any problems since." She felt cold. Sala was *dead*. "Should I be worried?"

Diego ran his hand over his hair. "Not because of this, no. Mr. Cabrera's dropped it, and you didn't technically steal from him. But you need to stay out of his business. He's got too much power in this city. He says the word, and someone dies, and the cops don't give a shit."

"You're the one who works for him." Eliana left the kitchen. She wondered if Diego had killed Sala—but only for a moment. He was an errand-runner, nothing else. He just wanted to warn her.

The living room was too bright, all that dome light pouring through the windows. She'd forgotten how bright it could be. She drew the blinds and stretched out on the sofa, hands resting on her stomach. Diego sat down on the floor beside her.

"Working for him is different from chasing him down," he said quietly.

"I'm not chasing him down! I just needed to get those documents back for my client. It's over." She didn't mention the party because she didn't want to listen to Diego complain about her palling around with Marianella Luna. Not that she'd call that party *palling*, necessarily.

Eliana closed her eyes, and her headache subsided.

"Look, I'm just worried about you, is all." Diego's large rough hands tugged on her hair. She opened one eye. He was staring at her with an oddly concerned expression, like she'd fallen and hurt herself. And that softened her. All she wanted right now was to be taken care of.

God, she really shouldn't have drunk all that wine last night.

"I know you are," she said.

Diego smiled and kissed her on the forehead. How could this man be a killer?

And then the electricity went out.

The darkness was sudden and absolute. Eliana sat straight up, blinking, terrified at the idea that her eyes could be open and still she could see nothing.

"Diego?" she called out, her heart pounding.

"I'm here." And he was, his voice close to her ear, just as it had been on Last Night. "Nothing to worry about. We're inside. Worse comes to worst, we'll drag out your emergency parka. Those things are always big enough to share."

"I don't have one! It wasn't in the apartment when I moved in."

Diego put his arm around her shoulder and pulled her in close. In the stifling darkness she could feel him and smell him, the hardness of his shoulder and that musky sweet scent of his aftershave. She buried her face into his sweater. After a while, her eyes began to adjust to the darkness. It wasn't pitch-black. A faint, silvery light came in through the window, and it seemed to shift around like liquid. Eliana could make out the shapes of her apartment: her couch, her chair, Diego. She snuggled up closer to him.

Voices shouted curses outside on the street. Somewhere on her floor a door slammed.

"We're safe," Diego muttered against the top of her head. "I locked the door when I came in."

"Yeah, yeah." That little bit of gangster's paranoia. It was reassuring to see it came in useful.

Eliana wasn't sure how long the lights stayed out. It felt longer than the blackout on Last Night, but her apartment stayed warm. She leaned against Diego and listened to his heart beating (fast, it was beating fast). Neither of them spoke. She watched the weird light move across the floor.

And then there was a sound like an enormous car starting up, and the light in the window brightened and brightened until it was clear the dome lights were back on, only at twilight levels. A moment later, the lights inside Eliana's apartment switched on again, and the coils on the radiator glowed red.

"Oh, thank God," Eliana said.

Diego was already at the door to the balcony, peering out at the street. "Ten minutes," he said. "That's the longest it's been out since—" He snapped the blinds shut and turned back around to face her. "You need to buy another parka," he said.

Eliana didn't answer, just curled her legs up to her chest. He was right. The emergency parkas had been a staple of her childhood—she remembered the set hanging in her closet at home, and the cheap metallic ones they kept at the school. But it wasn't something she'd ever thought about now that she was on her own.

"I'll get one for you," Diego said. "If cost's the problem."

"It's fine," Eliana said distractedly. She thought about the old steam-powered generators installed on every street corner. The city had sworn they'd been reactivated after Last Night for backup, and Eliana had even seen the steam puffing out of the exhaust pipes when she'd walked home. She shivered. Diego glanced at her, then walked over to the radiator and turned it up. Then he switched on the radio. A tango orchestra blared out of the set station, but he spun the dial until he came to a news program.

"Repeat, the problem has been resolved. As of right now we are assuming the possibility of involvement by the Antarctican Freedom Fighters—"

Diego snorted. "Please," he said. "They need to stop bullshitting us."

"You don't think it's the AFF?"

"Do you?" Diego slid back down into the couch beside her. "Why the hell would they want to turn off the power?"

"So we could all truly live in Antarctica. Build ice houses and hunt seals and all that."

Diego laughed. "No one's ever lived outside a dome in Antarctica. They're in for a nasty surprise."

"Don't tell Essie that."

"Essie'll give up Independence the minute she realizes she has to give up her space heater."

They laughed together, and Eliana's nerves soothed a little. Diego was right; it didn't make any sense for the AFF to want to turn off the power. The Independents all claimed the power troubles were the inevitable result of producing energy for the mainland—that the atomic power plants had created a draw on the steam power running the city, that Antarctica needed the atomic power to support itself. Eliana shivered, thinking of that breaking-down steam power. So it wasn't sabotage. It didn't make the situation any less frightening.

The man on the radio was still going on about the AFF, though. "Oh, turn him off," Eliana said. "He's not saying anything useful."

"You're right." Diego hopped up, turned the dial back to music. "This shit happens when the equipment's old enough. Nothing lasts forever, you know. Bet the drones are on their way over now."

She almost told him not to lie to her, but then she realized, watching him fiddle with the dial, the electricity-powered transmission of the singer's soft voice filling the room, that was exactly what she wanted him to do.

At least right now. At least as far as the electricity was concerned.

He joined her on the couch, and they stayed like that for a while, pressing close to each other. And although the dome lights never brightened to their earlier intensity that day, they didn't go out again either.

For right now, that was enough.

CHAPTER TEN

SOFIA

Sofia sat waiting in the dining room of the Florencia, but there was no dancing girl this time. The Florencia was closed down for the afternoon. Cabrera did that sometimes, so he could eat a steak without distraction or interruption. She could see the remains of his meal sitting at a table in the center of the room, although she had arrived after he'd finished.

She was alone, no Luciano or Inéz, because she wasn't here to do the reprogramming. Cabrera had called the telephone at the amusement park's operations room earlier. Sofia's payment was in.

She quaked with excitement.

One of Cabrera's bodyguards appeared at her table. She could smell the powder in his gun and the spice in his aftershave.

"Hello, Diego," she said.

"Cabrera's ready for you."

"Well, I'm certainly glad to hear that." She stood up, gathering her handbag and her coat. Diego walked side by side with her through the dining room and down the hallway. He didn't say anything—he never said anything. Some deep-rooted part of her wondered why, wondered how she had displeased him.

She hated that part of herself.

They walked to Cabrera's office, where Sebastian was waiting outside the door. He nodded at Diego, then pushed the door open.

The office was dim but tidy. A row of filing cabinets stood along the back wall; a painting of a horse hung between the two windows.

And a record player waited in the corner, music lilting softly in the background.

Sofia stopped.

"Music," she said. "We had a deal, Mr. Cabrera."

Cabrera leaned back in his big leather chair and smiled. "I swore to never play anything from before 1936," he said, "and this little number was released last year."

Sofia didn't move from the doorway.

"Relax," he said. "If we're going to work together, you're going to need to learn to enjoy music."

Sofia knew that she would never enjoy music.

"Come, sit, sit." Cabrera snapped his fingers in Sebastian's direction. Sebastian nodded and disappeared down the hall. Sofia watched him go, then turned back to Cabrera. The music whispered on, rubbing her nerves raw.

"I sent him to fetch your payment. It'll take a few moments. I didn't want to bring it off the ship just yet." Cabrera made his face look solemn. "I do have some bad news, I'm afraid."

"What?" Sofia dug her fingernails into her palm. The song fizzled into silence, and another took its place.

"I couldn't quite get all the things you asked for. This time." Cabrera held up one hand and pressed the other to his chest. "I've got my men seeking out the rest, but we may need to go north, up into Brazil. Some of the items are quite obsolete, and we'll need to find Autômatos Teixeira's old supplier in order to acquire them." He grinned. "But I swear you'll get them as soon as possible."

Sofia stared at him.

"Oh, really, Sofia, just *sit*. Is the music bothering you so much? I'll turn it off." He lifted the record needle. The silence was beautiful.

"Thank you." Sofia glided across the office, cautious. She sat down in front of his desk and crossed her feet at her ankles. "I'm sorry to hear you couldn't acquire everything." She regulated her tone as best she could; Araceli had told her this was likely, that some of the equipment, as old and outdated as it was, might be hard to find. She still thought he might be lying.

"You've done excellent work with my icebreakers, and I want to ensure you receive the payment you deserve."

Sofia nodded. She found it difficult to look at him. Instead, her gaze was drawn to the silent, unmoving record player. Maybe she should have brought Luciano after all. Of course, he couldn't have done anything about this situation either.

"*Such* excellent work," Cabrera repeated, and Sofia was aware of Diego lurking behind her, leaning up against the wall. "Did you know I used to have a former park engineer do the reprogramming for me? He died. Heart attack."

Sofia didn't say anything. She remembered crawling into the engineer's bedroom in the middle of the night. She remembered the sight of him lying stretched out on his bed, the way he'd let out a sigh when she'd slid the needle full of poison into the vein of his neck. It had been the first stage of her plan. No one but she and Luciano and Inéz knew about that moment.

"A shame, of course, but being a city man, he was costly. I have to say, I like working with robots. Even having to send a man into Brazil, you're still cheaper than he was. Helps my bottom line." He smiled and folded his hands over his desk like a businessman.

"I'm glad to hear that," Sofia said.

Silence settled around them, burning at Sofia's ears. The office was lit with green-globed lamps that cast strange, liquid shadows across the floor. Cabrera leaned back over his record player, and Sofia tightened her grip on her handbag.

No.

He rifled through a stack of albums and pulled out one with a sleek silver cover. She didn't recognize it, but that didn't mean anything. She'd never seen the album covers when she'd worked the dance houses.

"My niece likes this one," Cabrera said.

"No music, please."

"Sofia, Sofia, I'm just trying to get you accustomed to our ways."

He glanced over his shoulder at her. "This isn't like anything you've ever heard, I promise."

It better not be, she thought.

He put on the record. As the needle crackled, tension racked down Sofia's spine. The music started, soft and faint, an opera singer's shimmering wail.

She didn't recognize it. And opera was never used for programming anyway.

"Told you," Cabrera said. "Like nothing you ever heard before."

"Why are you doing this?"

"Doing what? Playing a bit of music while we wait for Sebastian to bring your payment? I do this with all of my contract workers. I like to make you feel welcome."

Sofia glared at him. Her insides twisted and churned. Rage coiled around her like a wire. She hadn't been built for strength. None of them had. Strength was not required to be the amusement at an amusement park. But she wished she could leap across the desk, wrap her fingers around Cabrera's throat, strangle him until he slumped down dead.

She didn't move.

Cabrera smiled. "Sebastian is certainly taking his time, isn't he?"

"Perhaps you should hire someone more efficient." Her words were ice. The music played on in the background, a mournful Italian soprano. Sofia could speak Italian, but she couldn't hear the lyrics, not with the music digging into her programming, trying to find a connection.

"One or two of the items were rather large. It'll take some time for Sebastian to prepare your car."

Sofia clenched her fingers around the armrest.

"Could you at least turn off the music?" she said. "Please."

Cabrera tapped his fingers against the desk. "I'm trying to help you." He wasn't. She could see it in his cold shark's smile.

"Please."

Cabrera closed his eyes in defeat. "Fine. No appreciation for culture." He lifted the needle. In the sudden buzzing silence Sofia's thoughts stopped trying to find instructions.

But Cabrera didn't turn away from the record player. Instead, he extracted another album. This cover he kept hidden.

Sofia went cold.

"Just one more." He peered up at her, eyes glinting.

"No."

"Sofia." He said her name as if it were a sound to comfort a baby. "You know I couldn't stand to hurt you. You're too important to me."

He switched out the albums. Sofia was rigid. She knew what he was going to do. He was a dangerous man. Araceli had said that. A dangerous man, and Sofia had corrected her—a dangerous *human*. But now Cabrera was going to poison her thoughts, and she didn't know how to stop him.

The needle dropped.

The speakers went *hiss*, *hiss*.

And Alberto Echagüe began to sing. "*Paciencia*."

But the singer and the song didn't register in Sofia's thoughts. This wasn't one of the new songs, the safe songs. Those, she heard the way a human would. This song, she could only hear through her programming.

The music was a code, and she was programmed to recognize it. The notes and beats and melodies told her what to do.

Dance, the music whispered. *I want you to dance.*

Sofia stood up, pushed the chair away. Cabrera leaned back and watched her, not with lust or wonder or even admiration but with a cold calculating menace, as if he wanted to see what she was capable of.

She lifted her hands above her head, twisted her spine *contrapposto*. And then she danced.

It was a tango. A nighttime dance. She didn't have a partner, but she still swept across the room, twisting her hips and stomping her feet. The music pounded in her brain, and it stripped away everything: Cabrera and Diego, the dimly lit office, her supplies. As far as Sofia was aware, she was performing in the ballroom of the Ice Palace, cast in blue lights, her bustier dripping with sparkles.

This was what she was programmed to do.

The music stopped. The flood of information ceased, and Sofia collapsed. She didn't hit the floor. Diego caught her and helped her to her feet without speaking, without looking at her, and moved the chair back into place. Sofia slumped into it.

Cabrera's face was a mask.

"Don't ever do that to me again," Sofia said.

"It doesn't seem to me that you have much choice in the matter."

I will kill you, Sofia thought.

"It wasn't difficult," he went on, "finding the old songs. The city offices keep all the old park records." Nothing changed in his voice, in his expression. "I was surprised to learn all you're capable of."

Sofia trembled. Her thoughts bled together, indistinct, fragmentary.

"I respect you, Sofia. I've always loved Echagüe. You dance beautifully, by the way. I would never have asked you to do any more than that."

"Go fuck yourself."

Cabrera pulled his head back, a false recoil. Then he laughed. "Sofia! Did you say that to your clients?"

"I didn't have clients," she said. "I had masters. But I don't anymore." She stood up and turned to Diego. "Where's Sebastian?" she demanded. "He's waiting for some sign, right? You tell him Mr. Cabrera's done with his little game."

Diego looked away from her.

"It wasn't a game," Cabrera said.

Sofia glowered at Diego. But he didn't move.

"It wasn't a game," Cabrera said again. "It was a reminder."

Sofia turned around, slowly, her whole body aching with fear. Cabrera smiled a hollow smile at her.

Cabrera was not human, she realized. Not in the sense that humans meant the word.

"A reminder," he said, "not to cross me. You think I did that to you because you're a robot?"

"Yes."

Cabrera laughed. "You aren't any different from the weasels at the city offices that I keep on my payroll. Oh, the wiring's different, I guess. Same result." His eyes were empty. "Everyone has something, some hidden control panel. Maybe not quite as literal as yours, but there's always something. A wife, a little boy. A fucking pet." He shook his head. "You aren't special, my dear."

Sofia felt hollow. The music always did that to her. It stripped her of her own mind and then didn't bother to replace it.

"Ah," Cabrera said, "and here's Sebastian now." He stood up. The door clicked open. Sofia refused to look away from Cabrera. Footsteps. Voices. Human warmth. Everything came to her through a fog of rage.

"Your keys, my dear." Cabrera reached into his pocket and then held out one hand, palm up, the keys glinting in the lamplight. "I expect to see the car the next time I see you."

"Everything's there?" she asked dully.

"All of the things I was able to acquire, yes. In matters of business, I'm a man of my word, and you'll see the rest of your payment soon."

Sofia grabbed the keys, shuddering at the moment his skin touched hers. Diego and Sebastian stood like guards on either side of the door. She looked from one to the other. Neither met her eye.

"I haven't seen much evidence of that today," Sofia said.

Cabrera didn't answer. She left the room and walked down the hallway. Her joints, her movement, were all out of balance, but she knew that was just an aftereffect of the music. This was the first time she'd heard music that old in years, and it had strained her system.

The car was parked beside the docks, one of Cabrera's sleek black automobiles. His trademark. She opened the trunk. The ticker tape was there, along with a handful of some of the less obscure models of vacuum tubes. They were all tucked away in boxes and wrapped up in plastic. The clockwork engines and the programming key were missing. Of course. The most important things, and he hadn't managed to get them.

Sofia slammed the trunk shut and looked out over the water. Only one boat was in port, an actual shipping boat, not a renovated cruise ship like the others. Its lights glimmered in the darkness, and she could smell the brine and wind of the iced-over sea.

Someday the humans would all be gone, and then she could tear down the domes and smell the sea and the ice whenever she wanted.

CHAPTER ELEVEN

MARIANELLA

Marianella stepped off the train, and cold wind rushed around her. No one stepped off with her because no one else had been on the train. It was a private line, running from a station tucked away at the edge of Hope City, through the snow and wind and ice to the agricultural dome.

This stop, with its simple wooden platform, its bare light fixtures, was the end of the line. The train sat on its tracks, engine sounds dying away. It would wait for her.

Marianella stepped down from the station and followed the path until she came to the robot who guarded the entrance to the fields of crops. It was an older, repurposed model—human-shaped, although taller and wider and cast in dull burnished metal, with a round, old-fashioned speaker instead of a mouth. She had installed atomic lights into his faceplate, the new set into the old. As those bright white lights scanned over her, warmth tickled her skin.

"Hello, Escobar," she said.

"Hello, Lady Luna." His voice was scratchy and distorted through the speaker.

"You know you don't have to call me that."

Escobar didn't answer. He wasn't intelligent enough to understand the complex system of human names. But Marianella always reminded him anyway. She did not like robots to call her Lady Luna.

The scan finished. Escobar stepped aside and pressed his palm flat against the door. His palm was the key and the doorknob both, a design trademarked by the city's founders. With a click and a grinding of gears, the door slid open, and Marianella at once smelled the sweet organic scent of dirt and oxygen and growing things.

A little over a week had passed since the party. Marianella had delayed the trip to check on the maintenance robots longer than she'd intended because the party had brought with it a flurry of social engagements—her phone had rung constantly the last few days, old friends and acquaintances asking her to come for a visit. This was the first chance she'd had to get away, and she'd been looking forward to it. It was always a joy to dress in her city clothes and ride the private train to the agricultural dome.

To *her* agricultural dome.

Marianella stopped in the middle of the main path, next to the cornfield. She slipped out of her coat and waited the three seconds for the domestic robot to notice her; it came swooping out of the rows of corn and purred as she draped it with her coat, her gloves, her scarf, her hat. The dome was warm, warmer even than Southstar, and certainly warmer than Hope City. It had to be, for all the plants to grow.

For a moment, Marianella didn't move, only stood in the center of the path, taking in everything around her. The ag dome was not just a container of seeds but a seed itself, the start of a new nation of Antarctica. A hundred years from now this dome would be immortalized, and Hope City would once again represent the best of humanity.

The wind switched on. Elsewhere in Hope City, wind was a luxury, but here it was used to re-create the natural environment and to help disseminate seeds. The corn rippled and rustled, a hollow empty sound she felt in her chest. Beyond the corn were other crops: wheat, sorghum, and potatoes, plus short test rows of grapes and a cluster of apple trees. All the crops had been chosen based on the mild climate of this dome; other domes, later domes, would be hotter and more humid, for growing sugarcane and citrus fruit. Marianella had chosen every crop herself, all of them designed to say, *Look, we can grow food, just like the mainland.*

Marianella turned and walked down the path.

She stopped at the crossroads, where the path split off into the corn, leading to the sorghum and the wheat. She lifted her head and whistled the first few bars from the "*Ave Maria*." For a moment nothing happened but the wind. Then robots gathered along the roof of the dome, dark scurrying spots that coalesced above her head. She watched them, squinting against the floodlamps. Twenty-five total. They had helped build the dome in secret, and now they ran it. They adjusted the sunlight, they activated the wind and the rain, they pulled weeds and watched for rot.

She whistled the hymn again, and the robots dropped down on invisible filament, showering around her, landing in the dirt with soft dry puffs. Marianella knelt down, mindful of her stockings, and picked up the closest. It was the size of a cat and shaped like a beetle, with a row of lightbulbs illuminated across its back. Marianella twisted each bulb, and they winked out in turn.

All around her, the robots' lights went out. The dome seemed suddenly empty.

Marianella walked a few paces away from the empty robots and placed the one she cradled in her arms on the ground. She pressed an indentation on its underside and held it in place for ten seconds, counting under her breath. When she dropped her hand away, the robot split open, revealing a tangle of metal wires that caught the reflection of the floodlights.

"I know you're fine," she murmured under her breath. "But I suppose we can never be too careful."

She reached her hand into the copper wires. Her skin sparked. The robot's code rode over her—this robot's code, and the code of all the other robots. One was the same as any other. They shared an intelligence.

The rustle of the plants became a harsh mechanical slur in the buzz of information. She closed her eyes, and the world went dark except for the little robot revealing itself to her. Its programming flashed across the interior of her machine brain, and her human brain interpreted that information as streaks of light.

This went on for a long time.

When it finished, Marianella's eyes flew open and she stared out at the corn, waiting for her mind to return to itself. She slid her hand out of the robot's wires. It was unchanged, her skin pale and unblemished, her nails filed into perfect curves and French-tipped. Not even a mainland style. *European.* She went so overboard in trying to prove she was normal.

Marianella settled back into herself. Her mind was still on fire, though, bright with the memory of the robot.

She closed him up, turned him over, twisted the lights in the opposite direction. The robot came back on, and then so did all the others. They looked at her expectantly.

"Just what I thought," she said, her voice shimmering on the wind. "Your programming remains unbroken."

The robots didn't react, and Marianella left them so she could walk the paths through the dome, slow and meditative, her head bowed in prayer.

She always did this when she came here alone.

* * * *

When Marianella finally arrived back at Southstar, night was falling, winter-early. Hector had installed moonlights in their dome, dots of silvery brightness that leached the color out of everything and cast long, unfamiliar shadows in the wheat. They had come to Hope City together from the mainland, both looking for new lives—Marianella so she could hide her nature and start over with a clean slate of humanity, Hector because he had followed the promise of wealth from the atomic plants—and so both of them had remembered the moon and the stars. But the moonlights were not the moon, and she'd always intended to have them turned off now that Hector was gone. She just hadn't done it yet.

The wheat rustled its sad soft song, and Marianella unlocked her front door and stepped inside. The door swung shut behind her. She took off her coat. Turned on the lights.

And froze.

Something was wrong. She could sense it, a disruption in the circulation of the house's air.

The hallway light was white and dazzling, as if it were refracting off a thousand mirrors. But Marianella could sense shadows amid all that brightness. A shadow. A man.

Someone was in the house, waiting for her.

"Who's here!" she shouted. She took off her scarf. She kept on her gloves. "I know you're here! Who is it!"

God, why hadn't her maintenance drones intercepted her? She should have asked Luciano to stay. He'd offered. But she'd said no and told him she could take care of herself.

"Mother of mercy," she whispered.

The house answered her with silence.

"Who's *here*!" she shouted, and this time, she caught a scent on the air. Cigar smoke and wool and aftershave and the faint, faint trace of women's perfume.

He was here.

Not just one of his enforcers but *him*.

"Where are you?" she shouted. "I know you're in here!"

Silence. Brightness.

Footsteps.

"Brave, brave woman," said a silken voice. "I gave you time to run."

Marianella stood ramrod straight. Ignacio Cabrera stepped out of the parlor doorway, looking like a businessman in his gray suit and his black fedora. He cradled one of her maintenance drones in his arms, its wires hanging out in loops and tangles. Her stomach turned over at the sight of it.

"You're in my house," she said.

He dropped the drone, and it broke when it hit the floor, parts scattering across the tile.

"So it would appear." An easy smile. Marianella knew not to look at it. She looked at his eyes instead, cold and empty, to remind herself of what he was.

"It's been a while." He ambled toward her. Marianella didn't move. She caught the scent of others in the house.

"I missed this place," Ignacio said. "Miss Hector, too." He stopped a few paces from her and smiled. "I've seen your commercials on the television. An agricultural dome, Marianella? You don't think that's going to work, do you?"

"What do you want?"

He didn't answer right away. Every muscle in Marianella's body was taut. Her heart raced and raced. He'd come to collect her documents himself this time. She still didn't understand why Hector would have betrayed her like that, why he would have alerted Ignacio to the possibility of a weakness. She should never have told Hector her secret, all those years ago. But she had been young and stupid.

"That's no way to treat a guest," he said.

"You aren't a guest."

He gave her a long, inscrutable look. "No," he said. "I suppose I'm not. But I had a message I wanted to deliver myself. I figured I owe that much to Hector."

She knew the men were coming. She heard the distant fall of their footsteps against the carpet. She felt their heat closing in on her. But she panicked, and she didn't know what to do.

One of them grabbed both of her arms and jerked her back; the other shoved the barrel of a gun into her side. Cold metal locked around her wrists. She didn't try to fight back. Her heart was beating too fast, as fast as a hummingbird's. The machine parts of her body reinforced the rest of her for what was to come.

Ignacio leaned in close, and Marianella remembered the first time she'd seen him. They'd just moved to Hope City, and her husband had thrown a summer solstice party and Ignacio had been there. She'd taken one look at him and known he was a murderer.

"Time to go," Ignacio said, and then one of the men threw a bag over her head. The material was thick enough that the world blinked out. She was jerked backward, stumbling, not out the front door as she'd expected but through the familiar pattern of her house's rooms. Her hip banged against a table. Glass rattled. The mechanical parts of her brain tracked their progress—down the hallway, through the living room, the dining room. Toward the patio door.

She knew she should fight back, but she didn't want to, because she wouldn't be able to muffle her strength. She didn't want to risk revealing her secret to Ignacio if he didn't already know—and she suspected, with the way his men had come in here unarmed save for their guns, the way they'd tossed a bag over her head, that he didn't.

She only prayed that he or his men wouldn't find the secret lockbox hidden behind the refrigerator, where she'd tucked the documents away after the first break-in. If he learned what she was, she would have to kill him herself.

And she didn't think she could do that.

A sudden rush of wheat-scented wind told her they were outside. She smelled car exhaust.

"What?" she said, breaking her silence out of surprise. Her lips rubbed against the rough fabric of the bag. "A car. How did you get a car out of the main dome?"

"You know I have my ways, Lady Luna."

They dragged her through the wheat. Not far. A car door opened. She was shoved inside, pushed onto the seat. The gun was still in her side. The door closed. Another opened. She tracked these sounds and she tracked the scent of the men, and in her head she saw a picture of herself, still dressed for travel in the city, her arms lashed behind her, flanked by two men with guns.

"You have a lovely home," Ignacio said. His voice was close by, coming from in front of her, like he was facing her. "But it's always much better to do business on my own turf. Don't you think?"

"You don't do business."

Ignacio laughed. The car's engine started, a rumbling beneath her seat. They were moving. She could hear the wheat scraping against the windows.

"Of course I do business," he said. "That's all I do. Your husband understood that."

"Hector is dead."

"So he is. And with him went my monthly checks from the Luna family."

Marianella's heart lurched. Was it possible that could be the only reason he was here?

"It's only been six months." Every time Marianella opened her mouth, the bag stuck to her lips. "Surely you haven't fallen on hard times already?"

"Cut the bullshit, Lady Luna. That was a minor irritation, to be certain, but the new manager at the plant has taken up Hector's donation habits. He appreciates the protection I give them. Paying me is cheaper than paying all those taxes to the city." The wind whistled through the windows. Cold. "You've been a thorn in my side for the last two years. I was willing to look away from your work with Alejo Ortiz when Hector was alive, but if you can't even see fit to send a few donations my way to make up for stirring up the Independents, well, I guess my relationship with the Luna family is, sadly, over."

Marianella didn't respond. The air inside the bag was thick and humid from her breath. Her heart raced.

"The city government isn't the only group who distributes food in the winter. I get food to the people of Hope City too," he said. "Delicacies like they couldn't imagine. And you want to take all that away from me."

"You get food to the people who can pay," she snapped. "You starve everyone else."

"I'm a businessman, Lady, and it's not my fault that I follow the price of goods. The mainland wouldn't provide half the things I can provide if we left it to them. They don't care about us. They have their own problems."

"It seems you and Alejo agree on something, then."

Ignacio laughed. "It doesn't matter what we agree on," he said, switching his dialect from the sharp vowels of Antarctican Spanish over to the whispery lisp of mainland Castilian. "I don't want Independence any more than the assholes up at the city offices."

Marianella worked at the binds around her wrists, but they were much too tight for her to believably pull them free.

"But I'm not here to talk politics." Back to Antarctican again. "I won't worry about the ag domes until I've seen one."

Relief flooded through her body, and she sat still in the moving darkness, hands cramping behind her. *He doesn't know,* she thought. *Thank the sweet Mother, he doesn't know.*

"I'm here to talk about a man named Pablo Sala."

And with that, every part of Marianella's system froze into place.

"Who?" she lied, her voice strained.

"He paid a visit to you a week or so ago and took something from you. Unfortunately, I never got to see it."

She would not give him the pleasure of hearing her sputter and struggle for the right words. The car bumped along, the tires thumping against the ground, and the wind was louder now. And colder.

Beneath the straw scent of the bag, she smelled snow.

"Some whore stole those documents out from under him—at least, that's what he claimed. I'd have him steal them again, given how he managed well enough the first time, but sadly, Sala's dead now. You can thank Diego for that."

A bead of sweat formed between Marianella's shoulder blades and fell in a straight path down her spine.

She couldn't remember the last time she'd sweated.

"I assure you Sala's death is not my fault," Cabrera said. "I don't want you thinking I'm some sort of monster. But Diego, bless him, got a bit overenthusiastic while questioning him. Isn't that right, Diego?"

There was a heavy silence in the car, and then a quiet male voice said, "Yes."

"See? All Diego's fault. But I still don't know what was in those documents. Do you care to tell me yourself?"

"I don't know what you're talking about."

The car stopped. For a moment no one spoke, and there was only the sound of the idling engine.

And then that cut off too.

"You're a lovely woman," Ignacio said, "but I'm afraid I've never really warmed to you."

A door opened. Cold air rushed in, smelling of metal and ice.

The edge.

A hand gripped Marianella's arm and dragged her out of the car. The ground was hard and gravelly, and the wind stirring at her skirt wasn't the artificial air that pumped through the dome's wind generators but the real thing, a trickle of it through the cracks.

The hood came off in an explosion of light. Marianella's pupils contracted. Ignacio stood in front of her, his hat shrouding his eyes.

Behind him: glass.

It was full dark now, with no fake stars or fake moon this far out. The car's headlights shone on Ignacio, casting his shadow across the dark, ice-encrusted glass.

Marianella's fear was a poison, breaking her down.

"It was easier to get here than I expected," Ignacio said. "I have a spot in the main dome I favor, a place where I control the guard robots." His voice was flat, emotionless, and his coat kept blowing in the wind, back and forth. Marianella stared at it and felt a metallic hollowness inside her chest.

"But you don't pay much mind to the edges out here," he went on. "Funny that you won't depend on the city for your light or your heat but you'll depend on it to keep the entrances locked."

"Why are you doing this?" Marianella's voice didn't shake. She was proud of that.

Ignacio looked at her. "I haven't done anything, Lady. Yet. If you want to stop me, just tell me what was in those documents."

Nothing moved except the wind, whistling as it slid over the glass, a mournful, plaintive sound that reminded Marianella of weeping.

"A deed to an estate on the mainland," she said.

"Don't lie, Lady Luna. It doesn't suit you."

"I'm not lying."

"So if we drive back to Southstar and you pull them out of the file, that's all I'll find? A deed?" Ignacio smiled, showing all his teeth. "I doubt it very much."

Hector, Marianella thought. *Why did you do this to me?*

"I was promised a way to destroy you, but I don't need papers to do that, really. And killing you helps with another problem of mine."

Marianella glared at him. She shook with fear, with the rage of Hector's betrayal.

"That problem being Alejo Ortiz, of course. I just can't get to him yet. He's too protected. That's the problem with politicians. I kill him, I've just got a martyr on my hands. The Independence movement has gained enough traction for it. But if I kill you, well,

I've managed to send Ortiz a message, haven't I? Especially doing it this way, where it looks like an accident, maybe even a suicide—the poor Lady Luna, distraught over the death of her husband."

Marianella did not turn away.

"You really are a brave woman," Ignacio said. "You do this with men, and they scream and beg for their lives." He tilted his head. "It must be that aristocratic blood. You would never do anything so undignified."

"It's not my title keeping me dignified."

Ignacio stared at her for a moment, then laughed. "Whatever it is, I find it admirable. Don't worry, Lady. It'll be like going to sleep. We're long into winter. I imagine death will be a short time coming."

Marianella was numb, as if she were already out in the cold. She thought about the black howling winds, the expanse of white desert. Anxiety crawled over her skin.

"May Hector forgive me," Ignacio said, and one of the men in dark suits stepped away from her and walked up to the dome wall.

"May God forgive you too," Marianella said.

"There is no God."

The man tapped a code into the glass. The pattern reverberated through Marianella's bones.

She held her breath.

The glass slid away with a loud screeching *clang*, and the snow billowed in, sparking and glittering in the yellow headlights. It scattered across the cement ground, spilled over Marianella's shoes. The wind shoved her hair away from her face and plastered her clothes to her body, and she turned her head against the stinging in her eyes. The man with the gun shoved her forward. Out of the corner of her eye she saw Ignacio watching her, the collar of his jacket turned up, one hand holding on to his fedora. He didn't speak. She didn't speak. Her entire body was shaking.

A weight pressed into the small of her back. A shove.

And then she was outside the dome.

She whirled around, the cold clinging to her legs, to her face, to her hair, to everything. The opening to the dome slid shut, and through the iced-over glass she saw the haze of the car lights.

And then those pulled away, and she saw only darkness.

She stood, not moving. Her hands were still lashed behind her back. At the moment, this was more troubling to her than the cold. She edged forward, forcing her way through the freezing, slicing winds, until she bumped up against the dome glass. Marianella could withstand the cold, but if she wandered off into the desert, she would never find her way back, and she'd starve instead. *I imagine death will be a short time coming,* he'd said, in his dead devil's voice.

For her, it would. Sometimes strength had its weaknesses.

She leaned up against the glass and took deep, gulping breaths. "Our Lady of the Ice," she whispered, breath solidifying in the air in front of her. "Protect us from the cold. Draw us into the warmth of the Lord. Our Lady of the Ice, deliver us from evil's winter darkness. Amen."

The prayer gave her strength, but her body was shivering so hard that it was difficult for her to keep her thoughts in order. The maintenance drones. If she could find one, just one, with ties to Sofia and Luciano—

The drones came out in the morning. She knew that much. They came out in the morning, when the dome lit itself up from inside like a beacon.

She pressed against the glass and whispered another prayer to the Mother of the Ice, and closed her eyes, and waited.

CHAPTER TWELVE

ELIANA

Eliana poured the last of her office coffee. No sugar, no cream. She'd asked Diego if he could get some coffee from Cabrera's shipments, and he'd looked at her and said, "I could. But do you really want to buy food from him?"

"Is there any way to avoid it?"

He'd shrugged, and that had been the end of the conversation. But as she stared at the crumpled-up bag sitting in the trashcan, she wished she'd pushed the matter further.

Eliana was in her office, prepping for one of the new cases she'd gotten from attending Marianella's party. Three days, and two people had already called her, one hoping to find a son who'd run away and the other looking for information about a piece of property near the docks. Easy work, and neither with any connections to Cabrera. She was looking forward to both jobs—and looking forward to the cash they would bring in too. Money for a mainland visa.

Funny that she wasn't as excited about that as she used to be. It was because of Diego. She might be able to leave Antarctica when the spring came, but it would mean leaving Diego. She hadn't really thought, when they'd started seeing each other, that she'd still be seeing him when she left the city.

The bell over the door rang.

Eliana looked up from her files. A man stood in the doorway. He was handsome, his eyes a striking golden-brown color, like caramel. He wore a gray flannel suit, a black trench coat tossed over one arm. Expensive shoes. He wasn't someone she'd met at Lady Luna's party.

"Miss Gomez?" He slipped off his fedora and dropped it onto the coatrack beside the door, then draped his trench coat beside it.

"That's me." Eliana took a sip of coffee. "Can I help you?"

"Are you really a private investigator?"

"Yes. I can show you my license."

He was looking around the office, studying the walls and her shabby furniture. "That won't be necessary. I'd like to hire you."

Three cases in three days. Well.

Eliana drained the last of her coffee. "Why don't you have a seat and tell me about it?"

He nodded and sat down. Eliana slid behind her desk and pulled out her pad and pen. The man watched her, his face pleasant and unexceptional save for his eyes. Eliana really hoped this wouldn't have anything to do with Cabrera. She wouldn't hear the end of it from Diego.

"So what do you need?" Eliana smiled. "Think your wife's stepping out?"

"I don't have a wife."

Over in the corner, the radiator rattled, banging up against the wall.

"My name's Juan Gonzalez. I work for the city." He pulled out a pack of cigarettes, offered one to Eliana. She accepted and leaned over the desk so he could light it. Then he lit his own and blew out a haze of smoke before continuing. "But this is a private matter. I expect discretion."

Everyone expects discretion these days, Eliana thought, but she said, "Discretion is my specialty."

"So I heard." Another curl of smoke. "It should be a simple matter. I need you to find out all you can about this—person." He reached into his coat pocket, pulled out a photograph, and laid it on the table. It was at least thirty years old, yellowed and crumbling at the edges. A head shot, the woman staring at the camera with wide dewy eyes, her dark hair pinned away from her face in a fountain of jewels, feathers floating around her bare shoulders.

"Her name is Sofia," the man said, dragging on his cigarette. "She isn't human."

"A robot?" Eliana picked up the photograph. She thought of the andie at Lady Luna's party. You probably couldn't tell what he was in a picture either. It was only when he was moving that he gave himself away.

"Yes. She was a performer and comfort girl when the amusement park was open. She's still around."

"In the city?" Eliana dropped the photograph onto the desk. "I thought all the andies got shipped out—" She stopped. "Most of them, anyway."

The man shook his head. "It was part of the entire collapse of Autômatos Teixeira. They stayed. In the park, for city use. Most have been dismantled by now, or have been deactivated and locked away." He shrugged.

"The park." Eliana thought of all the stories she'd heard about the ruins of the amusement park, mostly when she'd been younger. Snatches of reports on the evening news as her mother set the table for dinner, about people disappearing. The assumption was always that they had gone into the park for some unsavory purpose that was never clearly explained. Or there was that time one of the roller coasters started up without warning and rumbled over its track until someone from the city went and stopped it—a rumor went around that there had been a decapitated human body in one of the cars, the head rolling around next to the body's feet. Eliana knew, like all children of Hope City, that the park was a place You Did Not Go.

"Yes, the park. There's a train that runs into the old underground station. You'll want to go during the day, I imagine."

"And do what, exactly?"

Mr. Gonzalez smoked his cigarette, giving away nothing. "Do what you do. Investigate her. I want to know anything you can find out."

"Anything in particular?"

He shook his head. "No. Anything at all."

Eliana sighed, frustrated. "It really helps if you give me a little more to go on."

Mr. Gonzalez stared at her through the wreath of smoke. Then he jabbed the cigarette out in the ashtray. His hands were long and graceful. Office hands. Not with the power plants, then.

"Find her," he said. "Watch her. And tell me what she does."

"She's gonna see me if I go into the amusement park."

"That's not my concern." Mr. Gonzalez reached into his coat and pulled out a thick white envelope. "Fifty up front." He set the envelope down on the desk. "Another twenty a day when you report back to me. If you find anything interesting, I'll double that."

Eliana stared at him, her heart banging in her ears. With all the extra money from Lady Luna and her contacts, Eliana was closer to having enough money for a visa than she'd ever been. Than her own *parents* had ever been, and they'd scrimped and saved up until their deaths. At this rate, she might even be able to begin her application for the visa before the end of the winter, and be on her way to the mainland on the first ship setting out from the docks.

She didn't let herself think about Diego.

"Well?" Mr. Gonzales said. "What do you think?"

Eliana picked up the envelope and opened it. She ran her thumb over the edges of the bills, her breath hitching in her throat. "What do you mean by 'interesting'?" she asked.

"I'll let you know if I hear it." Mr. Gonzalez stared at her, his gaze heavy, stifling. "Will this arrangement work for you, Miss Gomez? If not, I can take my business elsewhere."

Eliana kept running her thumb over the bills. She thought of Diego, lying naked in her bed, the sheets draped over his waist, frowning at her, telling her for the hundredth time not to take cases that involved Cabrera. She remembered racing out of the Florencia, her heart pounding so fast, she thought it would hurt her.

"One question," Eliana said. "Does this have anything to do with Ignacio Cabrera?"

"The gangster? Don't be absurd."

Eliana nodded. She tossed the money onto the desk like it didn't concern her. "Good. I'll take the assignment."

* * * *

A few days went by while Eliana thought about the job. Mr. Gonzalez had said he'd come back to her office in a week to see what she'd learned. But a fucking robot would notice her wandering around the amusement park, so it wasn't as if she could borrow Essie's car and case the neighborhood. Eliana sat at her desk, doodling on her notebook paper, underneath the place where she had written *Sofia* and *andie* and *amusement park*. The photograph stared at her, Sofia's eyes dark and glossy. She really didn't look like an andie at all.

Meanwhile, Eliana scrounged up the deed to that storefront by the docks, and Mrs. Quiroga actually conjured a smile when she stopped by the office for the meeting. It was more satisfying than Eliana had expected.

Finding the runaway son was trickier—mostly, Eliana suspected, because he didn't want to be found. As she rode around town, asking questions about the runaway, half her thoughts were always with that beautiful andie Sofia. She couldn't turn the job down. The fifty-dollar retainer wasn't enough money on its own.

One afternoon, Eliana was holed up in her office, making phone calls to all the bars on Hope City's east side, since she'd gotten a lead about the runaway taking up work as a dishwasher. But so far, she hadn't found anything.

"Yeah, yeah, he's got brown hair, tallish—" The bell chimed. Eliana glanced up. At first she couldn't place what she was seeing. A woman. A familiar woman.

Lady Luna.

The man on the other end was saying that their only dishwasher had black hair, and Eliana managed to sputter out a "That's not him" before dropping the telephone back into the receiver. It was Lady Luna, dressed in sleek mainland clothes, her blond hair hanging loose to her shoulders.

She was coated in ice.

The ice sparkled across her skin as she stepped into the office and closed the door behind her. Her steps were slow and jerky and punctuated by a horrible cracking sound, like her body was falling apart.

"Hello?" Her voice was rough and whispery. "Ms. Gomez?"

"Lady Luna?" Eliana stood up, kicking her chair away from the desk. "Are you—are you okay?" Her voice echoed in her head.

Lady Luna focused in on her.

"There you are," she said.

Eliana opened her mouth. Lady Luna shuffled forward. Her hair clinked as she moved, catching the light, throwing off sparkles.

"If you don't mind me asking," Eliana said, voice shaking, "what happened to you?"

Lady Luna shambled up to the desk. She looked around the room with a dazed, empty expression. Then she looked toward Eliana, and her pupils contracted into points. Creepy.

"Why did I come here?" She collapsed into the client chair. The dome light hit her, and dots of white light appeared all over the walls of the room. "I should have—" She looked at Eliana again. "I hope you'll help me."

"Lady Luna?" Eliana couldn't make sense of what she was seeing. "What— Are you *okay*?"

"You wouldn't happen to have a cigarette, would you?" Lady Luna put on a strained, painful-looking smile. "I would be—very much obliged."

A request for a cigarette was so normal that Eliana knew exactly what to do. She fumbled around in her purse and pulled out her pack and her lighter. Lady Luna didn't move. It seemed like it hurt her, moving. So Eliana stood up, walked around the desk, and placed the cigarette between Lady Luna's lips. Lady Luna gazed up at her. Her pupils were still contracted, and something about her eyes seemed wrong. Dull. Distant.

Eliana stared at her, looking for the tells she had found on Luciano, but Lady Luna didn't give herself away as a robot. Of course not; she'd *never* had those tells. Eliana flicked the lighter, touched it to the tip of Lady Luna's cigarette. The ember flared; smoke twisted toward the ceiling.

Lady Luna took the cigarette from her mouth and blew out a stream of smoke.

"Thank you," she said. "I'm afraid I'm a bit in need of fire at the moment." She reached distractedly for her hair and pulled on a thin frozen chunk. It broke in half.

Eliana jumped.

"Fuck." The word sounded elegant in Lady Luna's soft voice. She tossed the broken hair to the floor. It hit with a clank.

Eliana slumped back against the desk.

Lady Luna smoked her cigarette without speaking. Eliana watched her. When the cigarette was burned down almost to the filter, Eliana handed her the ashtray, and Lady Luna snubbed it out.

"Thank you," she said.

"Are you a robot?" Eliana blurted.

Lady Luna took a long time to answer.

"No," she said. She traced her fingers over her hair again. The ice was starting to melt and it left dark puddles on the floor. "No, not exactly."

"Not exactly?"

Lady Luna closed her eyes. "I shouldn't have come here." Her voice wavered and her eyes opened. "You were right to warn me about Ignacio."

"Cabrera?" Eliana felt cold.

"Yes, he tried to kill me." A pause. "But he was unsuccessful."

Dread gnawed at Eliana's stomach. "Did he throw you out of the dome?" God, did Cabrera do that? Did *Diego*? Eliana tried not to think about Pablo Sala. *Mr. Cabrera had him killed.* If Diego was just an errand-runner, he shouldn't know that. Should he?

Lady Luna nodded.

"And you survived?" Eliana was dizzy. "This has to do with your stolen documents, doesn't it?"

Another pause. A drop of water slid down Lady Luna's hair. "Yes," she said.

"I don't understand. It's fine if you want to tell me you're a robot. I won't—"

Then Eliana gasped.

Lady Luna looked away, her face blank.

"You're part-robot."

The faintest hint of a smile, bitter and hard. "Part-robot. I like that better than the official term. But yes, that's what I am."

The office went silent save for the rattle of the radiator, the drip of melting ice. Eliana stared at Lady Luna. Cyborg, that was the official term. She'd heard about cyborgs before. They were banned in Hope City, banned in Argentina in general. Banned in most places, across the Americas, in Africa, in Europe. The only place where cyborgs were accepted was in certain countries in Asia—Japan, Korea, China. She'd never given them much thought beyond a ripple of discomfort whenever they were mentioned on the news. She understood robots and she understood humans, but she had never been able to understand both at the same time.

"Does it shock you?" Lady Luna's voice was soft and melodious, the voice of a human.

"No." Eliana wanted to seem polite.

"I'm glad to hear that." Lady Luna pressed her hands against her lap. "I really didn't mean to burden you with this. I can, of course, pay for your discretion, as I did with the documents."

Eliana almost said that wasn't necessary, but she caught herself at the last moment. It was good business sense, to take the money to keep a secret she would have otherwise.

"You do understand what would happen if you told anyone?"

Eliana nodded. She thought of a scandal that had broken when she was a little girl—no, not a scandal, exactly, but a news story, something her parents had talked about at dinner. A cyborg had made its way into the city. It—and everyone had called it *it*, she remembered, although she couldn't imagine anyone calling Lady Luna *it*—had been involved in an automobile accident. A fluke. That was how the authorities found it.

The cyborg had been deported, kicked back to Japan where it had come from. But she remembered people saying it should have been dismantled, that it was unnatural. No one ever explained why, but as an adult she understood—because people wanted to know where the robots were. And a cyborg was enough of a human that you couldn't tell from looking at it.

Lady Luna was staring at her.

"Why did you come here?" Eliana asked.

Lady Luna blinked. "I don't know. I couldn't stand the thought of going home." She pressed her hand to her mouth, her eyes glittering with intensity. "Really, I'm just afraid that Ignacio's men might still be at the house. I should have fought them when they came. Why I didn't . . ." Her voice trailed off, and her expression glazed over. "Of course, I didn't want them to know what I was—but they'll wonder how I survived out in the desert—"

Lady Luna seemed to recede into herself. She slumped against the chair, her face blank. Eliana jumped up and ran over and shook her shoulder. Lady Luna stirred, blinking.

"Are you okay?"

Lady Luna turned to Eliana. "No. I'm not sure. I feel strange." She pressed her hand against her forehead. "I think it's passing."

"We should go to a hospital."

"No!" Lady Luna's shout echoed around the office. "No," she said softly. "We can't do that."

Eliana's cheeks burned. She felt stupid. *An automobile accident.* "No, of course not. But if you're hurt—"

"I'm fine."

Eliana didn't believe that. "Okay. But you're probably cold, right?" She could hear the brightness in her voice, trying to pretend like this was normal.

Lady Luna hesitated. "It's uncomfortable, yes. I'd like some dry clothes, at the very least." One of those small smiles. "I'm afraid this dress is probably ruined."

Eliana's laughter twanged with discomfort. "My apartment's only a fifteen-minute walk from here. You can borrow some of my clothes and get warm, and we can figure out—something."

Lady Luna shook her head. "You don't have to help me. Your silence is all I ask."

Eliana considered this. Why did she want to help Lady Luna? The woman was just some aristocrat, after all, with her own private dome.

Except she wasn't.

Lady Luna stared blankly off into space. Eliana wondered if Diego had been there, if he'd seen it happen and hadn't stopped it.

If he'd pushed her out himself.

"Don't be ridiculous," Eliana said. "You showed up here. You obviously don't want to be alone."

Lady Luna blinked and became more present. "I didn't think about it that way."

"Well, that's what I'm here for." Eliana nodded toward the door. "You ready?"

Lady Luna didn't move.

"You can wear my coat," Eliana said.

"All right."

Lady Luna stood up. Her movements were more natural now, not as stiff. Eliana still couldn't imagine her as part machine.

Eliana gathered up her coat and scarf and gave them both to Lady Luna, who tossed the coat around her shoulders and draped the scarf over her half-frozen hair. She looked almost glamorous.

They left the office, Eliana locking up behind them. The streets were more crowded than Eliana had expected, and Lady Luna tightened the coat around her chest and tilted her head down. Whenever someone passed too close to her, she bumped against Eliana, as if by their touching she somehow gained strength.

It was funny, how people hated cyborgs because they were afraid of them, but here was a cyborg who seemed more afraid of people.

They were about five blocks from Eliana's apartment when they passed the big neighborhood church. Eliana walked a few paces before she realized that Lady Luna was no longer walking alongside her. When she looked back, she found Lady Luna standing in front of the steps, looking toward the carved wooden doors.

"Lady Luna?" Panic rippled through her. "Is something wrong?" She jogged over to Lady Luna's side. Lady Luna's face was pale, her hair dark with water.

"If you don't mind," she said in a small voice, "I'd like to stop here for a moment."

"The church?"

Lady Luna nodded.

"But don't you need to—" Eliana waved her hands around, not wanting to finish her thought out loud.

Lady Luna smiled. "It won't take long. And I—I'm fine." Her voice wobbled. "I'm not cold." She lurched up the steps. Eliana hadn't been inside a church in years, not since she'd been a little girl and her mother had taken her to Easter services out of a sense of obligation. All she knew of the church was the sound the bells made when they rang out for mass to begin.

But Lady Luna was already slipping through those heavy wooden doors.

The inside of the church was dim, lit only by thin colored light seeping through the stained glass. It was also empty. Lady Luna blessed herself with holy water and then knelt down in the back pew, her hands folded and her eyes closed. Eliana hung back at the door, unsure if a sinner like herself should go any farther. The altar seemed far away. Rising behind it was a statue of the Virgin Mary, wrapped in white cloth and white furs, lines of silver metal extending in a sun ray halo behind her head. Our Lady of the Ice.

A Madonna for Antarctica, the stories went.

Lady Luna didn't take long. She crossed herself again, then knelt and crossed herself a second time when she left the pew. She didn't say anything until they were back out on the street.

"Thank you," she said.

"Uh, no problem."

"You must think it's strange, my nature being what it is."

Eliana shrugged, not wanting to say yes.

"It's all right. My husband thought it was strange too. He used to tease me."

"Oh." Eliana paused. "Your husband knew? About the—" She wasn't about to say it on the street.

"Oh yes. I told him. Our marriage was basically arranged, you have to understand—not in any explicit way, but that's what it amounted to. I hadn't particularly wanted to marry him. He was much older than me, and my parents only wanted it because they were running out of money." She gave a hard smile. "My father treated me as—as an experiment. He meant to sell off the results.

But that didn't happen. You can't change people's opinions about some things."

Eliana was burning alive with questions, but of course she and Lady Luna were still surrounded by people. Her apartment building rose up in the distance, pale gray walls and rows of darkened windows. The air had an acrid scent to it, like something burning. The heaters. All those machines keeping them from freezing to death.

Well, keeping *Eliana* from freezing to death. But then she glanced at Lady Luna out of the corner of her eye, elegant still in her borrowed coat, and felt guilty for her private nastiness.

"I told him," Lady Luna said, breaking the silence, "because I wanted him to reject me."

"Wasn't that dangerous?"

"Oh, very. I was young, though. Barely eighteen." She laughed. "When you're young, you think nothing bad will ever happen to you. Then you grow up and you realize that's all life is."

Eliana started. Her mother had said something similar to her once, just before she died.

They arrived at Eliana's building. She unlocked the front door, and they rode the rickety elevator up to her floor, not speaking. When the elevator opened, Eliana had a moment's panic that Diego would be lounging by her apartment door, smoking a cigarette, waiting not for her but for Lady Luna. She didn't want that final proof that he was a murderer and not just an errand-runner. Without it, she could still convince herself he was a good person paying back a debt to the man who'd raised him.

The hallway was empty.

They went into Eliana's apartment. Lady Luna took off the coat and scarf and laid them across the sofa and then stood with her hands clasped in front of her, her eyes scanning the room. Eliana thought about Lady Luna's house in its private dome and was suddenly embarrassed by her shabby apartment, the gouges in the linoleum, the crack in the glass door leading out to her balcony, the dirty dishes stacked in the sink of her kitchenette. But Lady Luna's face gave no hint of disgust or displeasure.

"My bedroom's this way," Eliana said. "You can pick out some clothes to wear. I don't have anything fancy—"

"I don't need anything fancy." She smiled, and in that moment she couldn't have been more different than the hostess at the cocktail party, or the woman who'd come into Eliana's office two weeks ago.

Eliana's bedroom was messy, as usual, her bed unmade and her dirty clothes strewn across the floor. She tried not to think about it. She flicked on the lamp and pulled her closet door open.

"Pick out whatever you like. I still have some coffee, but I think there's some Hope City tea in the cupboard." Could Lady Luna even drink tea? No, of course she could—she'd been drinking at the party—

"Tea would be lovely. Thank you." Lady Luna stared into the closet, her face illuminated by golden lamplight. Eliana left her, closing the bedroom door, and went into her kitchenette. She was exhausted, and it was cold in here, since she'd turned the radiator off when she'd left that morning.

She filled the water kettle and set it on the stove.

Lady Luna emerged from the bedroom five minutes later, wearing one of Eliana's simpler sweaters and a pair of black cigarette pants. "Is this all right?"

"Sure, you can borrow whatever you like."

"I promise to return to it."

"I know." Eliana smiled. The kettle steamed, and she poured a cup for Lady Luna, dropping in the tea strainer. No milk, of course, but she brought the last of her sugar into the living room along with the teacup.

"Sugar," Lady Luna said. "That's hard to come by."

"Yeah, well, I've been careful with it."

"I prefer my tea unsweetened anyway." Lady Luna sipped at her cup, and Eliana wondered if she really took her tea unsweetened or if she was being polite or if she just felt sorry for Eliana.

She wondered if Lady Luna was afraid Eliana would turn her in to the authorities.

"So what do you want to do about your house?" Eliana said.

"I'm sorry?"

"You said you weren't sure if Cabrera would be staking it out or not. I'm guessing you don't want to go to the police—"

"I avoid the police whenever possible, yes." Lady Luna set her teacup down on the table. "I'll speak with my maintenance drones. I'm sure he didn't destroy all of them."

"Your maintenance . . ." Eliana's voice trailed away. "You can talk to them."

Lady Luna wouldn't meet her eye. "One of the perks of being what I am, I suppose. I'll have to find one of the contact stations. You needn't worry about it."

"A contact station? You have access to those?"

Lady Luna looked up, and her eyes glittered in a way that struck Eliana as nonhuman. Not inhuman, though. Not exactly.

"Technically," Lady Luna said, "I do not."

"Oh."

"I suppose I'm not giving you much reason to trust me."

Eliana thought about Diego.

"It's fine," Lady Luna continued. "That's why human beings are so terrified of cyborgs, isn't it? Because we bridge the gaps? But I'm just as human as you are. I survived the cold longer, but I couldn't survive it forever. I can starve, I can die of dehydration, I can bleed to death. I can do any number of things you can do, all equally unpleasant."

Eliana's cheeks flushed. "I'm s-sorry," she stammered. "I didn't mean to imply— I just— I've never known a—someone like you."

Lady Luna picked up her cup again and stared down at it. "I suppose you haven't."

"I don't mind."

Lady Luna smiled, still looking down at her teacup. "That makes you a rarity. Even those who have tolerated me still *minded*."

Eliana forced out a laugh. "I live in the smokestack district. You learn tolerance pretty fast out here."

Lady Luna looked up at her. Studied her. "I shouldn't have snapped at you."

Eliana grinned. "You call that snapping at me? You hang around here a few days longer, you'll really see what happens if someone snaps at you."

Lady Luna didn't say anything, but Eliana thought she seemed calmer, less on edge, less falling apart into pieces. And she was glad for that. She was glad Lady Luna didn't feel uncomfortable around her.

"Look," Eliana said. "When you go talk to the maintenance drones, if you find out Cabrera's still around, you can come back here, okay? You can stay here as long as you want."

"You don't have to do that."

Eliana shrugged. "Hey, you said you'd pay me for my discretion. You've paid me twice what I usually make anyway, and you introduced me to all those people at your party. I already solved one case for Mrs. Quiroga, and I'm working a second for someone else." Eliana didn't mention Mr. Gonzalez.

Lady Luna blinked. She almost looked confused. "Of course."

"Besides," Eliana said. "How often do you get to help somebody famous?"

"Famous?"

"Sure. You're in all those advertisements. The lovely Lady Luna and her agricultural domes." Eliana stopped. Funny that a cyborg would care about agricultural domes and Independence.

Lady Luna laughed. "I hate those things. The advertisements, I mean."

"So does everybody else."

Lady Luna finished her tea and set it aside. Then she stood up. "You really do have my utmost gratitude, Miss Gomez."

"Eliana. Nobody calls me 'Miss Gomez.'"

Lady Luna smiled, and it was that sad smile from earlier. "Plenty of people call me Lady Luna," she said, "but you don't have to."

Eliana blinked. She felt oddly touched.

"'Marianella' will be fine." Lady Luna gave a short nod. "I really should be going. I have some matters to attend to before I check on my house."

"Are you sure?"

"Quite sure." Another smile. "Thank you for everything."

Then she turned and walked out of the apartment. When the door clicked shut, Eliana took a deep, shuddery breath and collapsed on the sofa. Marianella Luna was a cyborg. And Diego—

Eliana had always known that Ignacio Cabrera murdered people. Diego had even warned her about it, like with Sala. But that was the difference. He'd *told* her about it. But she'd actually seen Lady Luna covered in ice. It was the first time Eliana had come close to Cabrera's violence. The first time she had actually seen the effect of that violence.

And it was the first time she'd truly considered the possibility that Diego may have been involved.

CHAPTER THIRTEEN

MARIANELLA

Marianella rode the train into the amusement park. The overhead lights flickered as the train roared through the city. Marianella wanted to fall asleep, and that concerned her, especially given how her thoughts had guttered on the edges of her consciousness when she'd been with Miss Gomez—no, Eliana. She'd asked to be called Eliana.

Marianella may have survived the night outside the dome, but she doubted she'd escaped without internal damage.

She still couldn't believe she'd gone to Eliana's office instead of Araceli's place in the park. Stupid. Araceli could repair any damage the ice might have inflicted. But Marianella had been in a haze when the maintenance drone had finally opened the door for her, and she'd been stunned by the sudden wash of floodlights. All she'd known was that she couldn't go home. And so she had walked away from the dome exit on the basis of some strange muscle memory. She needed help. Eliana was the last one who had helped her. In an electronic daze, that was where Marianella had gone.

Eliana had been kind, at least. Not disgusted or terrified or likely to turn her into the authorities, although Marianella remained on edge. Because Eliana knew her secret, and because Ignacio had finally tried to kill her.

If it had been summer, she would have fled to the mainland. But it wasn't summer, and no city ship would allow her to board, much less ride north. Because according to the city, she was 100 percent human.

"Approaching park entrance," the train said in a soft automated voice with a slushy European accent, like half-melted snow. The lights dimmed. At least the train was empty. It was a relic of the amusement park, its walls covered in storybook paintings of penguins and narwhals and orcas and sea lions. Most people didn't even know it still ran. However, all city trains were automatic, and shutting them down completely, including the one into the park, would be an inconvenience to the city, as they still went mining for robots in the amusement park. Luciano and Sofia called those mining raids the cullings.

She shivered and wrapped her arms around her chest. The train passed into the tunnel and dropped underground. The lights grew dimmer and dimmer and then suddenly flared with brightness, spilling yellow light over all the tattered, threadbare seats. A short in the circuit. Marianella's head felt the same way.

The train pulled up to its one stop, the only station in the park. Marianella stepped onto the platform. It hadn't changed since the last time she'd been here, almost three years ago. The paint was still faded, the lights were still broken, the air still smelled of mildew.

The train puffed steam into the station. Marianella's hair curled from the humidity. Frozen and thawed and curled. She'd be lucky if she didn't have to shave it all off and start over.

She climbed the broken escalator to the surface.

The station was located on the edge of the park, near the towering wooden roller coaster that had, forty years ago, been the most innovative of its kind. It loomed overhead, casting gray shadows across the dirty off-white cobblestone. Marianella turned west, toward Araceli's cottage. For a moment she thought she had forgotten the way, but neither parts of her brain, computer or human, would ever let that happen.

She walked.

Marianella had never visited Antarctica when the amusement

park was open. It had closed in 1943, when she was ten, and her parents had considered it vulgar. She was a daughter of the aristocracy and as such was expected to spend her time horseback riding and practicing her social graces. At ten her father hadn't yet taken her humanity away from her—that was still two years off, a transformation that occurred simultaneously with puberty—and never seeing the park before it closed had been her childhood's greatest tragedy.

Because Marianella, like all former little girls, was familiar with the amusement park's magic. It had been called Hope City too, just like the surrounding settlement where its employees had lived, but unlike the current Hope City, it had been designed to appear cut from the ice and snow of the Antarctic desert. Marianella vaguely recalled that was its entire gimmick: a true Antarctic civilization, tamed and temperature-controlled for your delight and appreciation.

It didn't appear cut out of ice anymore. The buildings still sparkled a little in the floodlights, but they were no longer white, only the same grimy yellowed-bone color as the cobblestone. Most of the buildings were falling apart. No humans lived here. Well, except Araceli, but she had disavowed all loyalties to humans a long time ago. The city had fired and then blacklisted her because she'd refused to utilize parts pulled from the old amusement park robots—robots she had once tended to, before the park had closed. She couldn't find any engineering work in Hope City, and she didn't have the money to go to the mainland. Eventually, it was Sofia who offered Araceli a place to stay. The maintenance drones told Sofia about how Araceli had stood up to the city and their culling practices. Sofia actually invited Araceli to stay in the park, the one human she was willing to trust.

Finding Araceli had been a miracle when Marianella had first come to Hope City. Hector had learned about her somehow. He told Marianella over dinner one night that there was a strange woman living in the park who could tend to any of her *issues*, which had always been his preferred euphemism for Marianella's nature. Her *issues*. It seemed he hadn't kept them as well a secret as he'd always claimed.

Still, Marianella had gone to the park after a fall, and Araceli had treated her. That was also the day that Marianella first encountered Sofia. She had seen her watching from one of the gardens, dressed in a tattered old dress, plants growing wild around her. Marianella had registered her as an android immediately, but there had been a sentience, a spark, burning in Sofia's eyes that haunted her even after she arrived back at Southstar. She had not been able to fall asleep that night, staring up in the dark with Hector snoring beside her.

Marianella went back to the park three days later. To see Sofia, not Araceli. That had been the start of things.

Now Marianella walked for another twenty minutes. Her thoughts kept drifting in and out: Eliana and her cramped, homey apartment; Ignacio looming in the headlights of his car; the maintenance drone who had found her shivering beside the dome, its eyes scanning over her, bright in the darkness, turning white when it found her machine parts. The wind knifing her skin. The maintenance drone leading her through the snow to the main dome, the only part of the building it had access to operate.

That moment of disorientation as she stepped back into the heat, at the edge of a park built into one of the middle-class neighborhoods. Everything green. That blinding, bleeding, terrible green.

Her thoughts were as diaphanous as spun sugar.

She was deep into the amusement park now, away from the rides and the shops, into the section once devoted to guest cottages and restaurants. Araceli lived in the nicest of the cottages. SUGAR SNOW COTTAGE announced a sign stuck into the sculpted stucco lawn. The cottage was made to look like a gingerbread house. The windows glinted like candies.

Marianella knocked on the front door. No one answered. She pressed her thumb against the doorbell. A melodic chiming echoed deep inside the house, and then a miniature door sprang open next to the true door, and a tiny mechanical ballerina wobbled out and spun around once.

"She's at the workshop," the ballerina said in a singsong voice. "The workshop, the workshop, the worksh—"

"I understand." Marianella had never liked Araceli's little toys. More amusement park relics.

The ballerina curtsied and wobbled back inside.

The workshop. Marianella should have known.

The workshop was part of the amusement park's operations center, which was located in the basement of the Ice Palace, at the center of the park. Another twenty-minute walk. Marianella followed the cobblestone path to the main road. The wooden gate of the cottage banged shut behind her. She was dizzy and light-headed. The cold. No, not the cold—the thaw. The machinery embedded in her brain was wearing down.

She found a bench nearby, wrought iron and once painted silver, and collapsed onto it. The cottages glittered dully around her. She wondered how many robots were lurking inside them, watching her through the windows, trying to make sense of this stranger in their cast-off kingdom. Most were like the ballerina, mechanical performers from the amusement park's heyday. They didn't have the intelligence that Sofia and Luciano and Inéz did, but they were slowly developing it, the way all the robots had in the park, day by day, moment by moment. And unlike the maintenance drone, they couldn't see through skin to learn that Marianella was part of them.

They looked at her, and only saw a human.

Marianella slumped back on the bench and looked up at the top of the dome. A maintenance drone slipped past, a dark pinpoint against the white background. She closed her eyes. She knew she shouldn't—some voice was whispering to her that it was dangerous. Not just some voice. Her voice, her computer voice. The mechanical part of her brain that controlled the human part. *Don't fall asleep,* it said in an indolent whine. *If you fall asleep, they'll never be able to repair you.*

Marianella forced her eyes open. The air was so still here. No trees, no plants, no wind. Hardly any heat. What did robots need with any of those things?

She missed the agricultural dome. She missed the soft rustling wheat surrounding her house.

"Marianella?"

The voice jarred her. She jerked up, her head spinning, and it took a moment for her senses to slow down and her brain to catch up. A man was staring at her. Tall and lanky and handsome.

No, not a man. Luciano.

"What are you doing here? Do you need assistance?" He sat down beside her, his movements as assured and graceful as always. "Have you incurred some sort of damage?"

"Maybe." Marianella rubbed her head. The computer voice had died away, replaced by a faint buzzing in the back of her brain. Electronic feedback. She didn't think that was a good sign. "I had—oh, Luciano, I had something terrible happen to me, and I did something so, so stupid—"

The world uprooted itself, and Marianella was lying back, Luciano's arms around her shoulders. She looked up at him.

"You need to see Araceli," he said. "I'm concerned about you."

The buzzing was so loud, she couldn't hear him, but she saw his lips move, and that was how she knew what he was saying.

"Can you walk?"

"I don't think so."

Had she answered? She wasn't certain. No, no, it appeared she had—Luciano had slipped his arms under her knees and was lifting her up. She felt weightless. Like snow.

"Don't fall asleep," Luciano said. "I'm very concerned."

He was always concerned. They had programmed him that way, sixty years ago.

The world went white.

* * * *

"She's coming back."

"The system restart just blinked on."

"Good, good. That was close. It was good you found her."

"Yes, I agree."

Marianella saw only light, as if she were staring into the snow or the floodlamps. At least the buzzing was gone.

"Araceli?" Her voice ricocheted around her head, thrumming with feedback. "Inéz? Luciano?"

"We're here, love." Araceli's voice was smooth, comforting. "Try not to think about anything."

Marianella's head filled with images: Hector and Ignacio and the agricultural domes and Our Lady of the Ice and Eliana and the estate where she grew up. Such a human response. She tried to force the thoughts down, but the minute one disappeared, another replaced it.

"We're almost done repairing your hardwiring, and then I'll reconnect your optics—your eyesight. How does that sound?"

"Good." Her voice didn't thrum as much this time. Marianella's system was a complicated one, more complicated than most cyborgs. Every part of her human body was reinforced by a complex system of tiny machines, powered by the clean-burning atomic energy her father had developed. It was all designed to make her *more*, to bring the human body itself into the second half of the twentieth century and beyond, into the unimaginable new millennium. The reality was that now her human body couldn't survive without those machines.

She was aware of Araceli leaning over her even though she still couldn't see her; it was the human warmth of her blood and skin. Marianella wanted to reach up and touch her, but she couldn't move her hand. She couldn't move anything.

"Just a few seconds more—*there*."

The world flooded back into focus. Overhead was a high vaulted metal ceiling and rows of bright lights and bits of glittering golden dust. Araceli would hate knowing there was dust anywhere in her workshop, so Marianella didn't say anything.

"Is everything working all right?" Inéz asked. She stood next to Araceli, her hand stretched out in Marianella's direction. Monitoring her progress. "Can you see?"

"I can see fine." Marianella sat up. Her muscles ached and she was in her underwear—Araceli must have stripped her down to get to her wiring. "You didn't cut my clothes away, did you?"

"Of course not." Araceli stepped up to the table, holding Eliana's sweater and trousers. Like the amusement park, she hadn't changed much in those three years. Still tall and broadly built. The last few dark streaks in her hair had been subsumed by silver. "What the hell happened to you? What have you been *doing* out in the city?"

"She wasn't in the city. She was outside the dome. Weren't you?"

Luciano. He was tucked away discreetly to the side, half-shrouded in shadow. He didn't like being the center of attention.

"What were you doing outside?" Araceli asked. "Was this an ag dome thing?"

Marianella nodded without thinking.

Araceli bustled away from the table, over to Inéz, who dropped her hand. Araceli chattered over her shoulder. "You're going to need to stay here for at least a few hours," she said. "I'll get you some food."

"I'm not hungry."

"Too bad. Your body needs it to start repairing the connections. Luciano, do you mind sticking around while Inéz and I run to the house? In case something goes wrong."

"No, I don't."

The door to the workshop slammed shut, echoing in the empty space. It was the same workshop where engineers had programmed and repaired robots for the amusement park four decades ago, everything dull metal and enormous, steam-powered computers.

Marianella dressed. The exertion made her dizzy.

"Careful," Luciano said, sliding up to her and putting one hand on her arm.

"I'm fine," she murmured, even though the room whipped around. She sat on the table. "Perfectly fine."

Silence settled into the workshop. Marianella took deep breaths, and the rhythm of her chest soothed her. An assistant to her father had taught her that trick, shortly after her father had converted her. It was meant to calm her down, but in reality it was a reminder that she was human, at least in part.

"I alerted Sofia to your arrival," Luciano said.

Another deep breath. "I assumed the maintenance drones would have done that the moment I came up from the train platform. And I know the performer 'bots saw me."

"They all did. I confirmed it."

Marianella looked over at a pile of unrecognizable parts, twists of wire and bits of metal. She wondered if they'd come from her.

"She'd like to see you."

Marianella hesitated. "I haven't spoken to her in months."

Luciano didn't respond.

"She was—unkind—the last time I saw her."

"I know." Luciano sat on the table beside her. He lacked Araceli's warmth but not her presence. "I am sorry about that."

Always apologizing for things that weren't his fault.

"I guess I can't say no," Marianella said.

"She's upset about what happened." Luciano looked at her as he spoke. "It wasn't really because of the agricultural dome, was it?"

Marianella didn't know how to answer. Before she could decide, the workshop door clanged open. It wasn't Araceli. It was Sofia.

"Oh, Luciano," Marianella said, suddenly tired. "You could have at least warned me."

"I'm sorry. She insisted."

Sofia glided into the room, a familiar sway in her hips. That sway ignited an old tremor of desire in Marianella's chest that felt like loss.

"What happened?" Sofia stopped a few paces from the worktable. She wore a thin, worn-out housedress and no shoes, and her hair was knotted at the back of her neck. But she was still beautiful.

"Why do you care?"

Sofia rarely allowed emotions to cross her face, and this moment was no exception. "You're damaged."

"Araceli tended to me."

Luciano slipped off the table and disappeared into the shadows. Marianella sighed. She would have liked him to stay there, to ground her.

"Did you do this for Alejo Ortiz?"

"No." A sharp burst of anxiety erupted in her chest—Alejo. He needed to know what had happened. They needed to decide what to do about Ignacio. Marianella surged toward the door, stumbling over her feet.

"Where are you going?" Sofia's voice was sharp. "You can't leave. You need to eat. To get your strength up." She took a few steps in

Marianella's direction, her face darkening with concern. "You're behaving rashly," she said.

They stared at each other. Marianella was still weak from the repairs and trembling with anxiety. She kept remembering the times when Sofia had visited her at Southstar, always in the summer when Hector went away to the mainland for business. The memories made her warm; they made her ashamed. Everything about Sofia was confusing.

Her thoughts buzzed. Yes, she needed to eat. But she needed to formulate a plan, too, her next series of steps. And the first thing wasn't even to warn Alejo anyway; he could take care of himself. He had the strength of the AFF behind him.

She needed to secure her documents.

"What happened?" Sofia's voice was hard and commanding. Marianella wished Araceli would come back.

"I was thrown out into the cold."

"By whom?"

Marianella sighed. There was no point in playing coy; Sofia was unrelenting when she wanted an answer.

"One of Hector's old associates," she said. "Ignacio Cabrera."

Something shifted in Sofia's expression. A glint flashed across her face and was gone. Marianella wasn't certain she'd even seen it.

"The gangster?" Sofia said.

"You've heard of him."

"Yes." Sofia glanced at Luciano. "Why was he trying to hurt you? Does he know what you are?"

"Not at the moment, no. But when it becomes clear that I didn't die out there—" If only it weren't winter, if only she could book passage aboard one of the icebreakers and escape. Get away from Ignacio and the danger of the city. But it would mean leaving the ag dome behind too. Her proof that she wasn't a monster, that she wasn't entirely a machine.

Marianella closed her eyes and took the deep breaths that reminded her that she was human.

"You should stay here, then." Sofia's voice was calm. "Until you decide how to handle Cabrera."

Marianella went still. When she had gone into Our Lady of the Ice to pray, she had asked God to tell her what to do next, not knowing why she was asking. Now she did. She'd been asking God to help her formulate a course of action. And maybe He'd brought her Sofia. It seemed strange for God to use Sofia as His vessel.

"Yes," she said softly. "I think you're right. At least for the time being." She wouldn't warn Alejo in person, but she could program a drone to send a message to him. The park drones would all be secure. The same for Southstar—she could use the call station in the park to contact her estate drones and activate their protocols to make the house look occupied, turning on music and lights and the television set at programmed intervals. Her society friends would assume she'd returned to her old reclusive ways. They were too fickle to come looking for her beyond a phone call.

That left her documents.

Marianella faced Sofia. "I need a change of clothes and my documents. They're back at Southstar."

"I can fetch them for you." Luciano stepped out of his place along the wall. "I'm familiar with the house."

"No." Marianella shook her head. "It's too dangerous. Ignacio is probably watching the estate—"

"We know how to hide from humans," Sofia said. "Luciano will be fine."

"It's true," Luciano said. "You needn't worry about me."

Marianella looked back and forth between them. She didn't like this, but she hated the thought of her documents lying vulnerable in the house.

"I took them out of the safe after the robbery," Marianella said.

"Yes, you told me. You moved them into the hidden panel behind the refrigerator."

"Good," Sofia said. "You can stay here until it's safe."

Marianella ran her hand, still shaking, through her hair. "Until it's safe," she murmured, knowing she couldn't stay in hiding forever.

The door opened, and Marianella's heartbeat skittered, but it was only Araceli and Inéz, weighed down with canvas sacks.

"Got you food!" Araceli called out. "Oh, hello, Sofia."

"Hello." Sofia gave a brief smile. "I'm glad you were able to repair her."

Marianella closed her eyes at the word "repair." Sofia knew she didn't like it.

"She's all fixed up." Araceli dropped her bags onto the table and turned to Marianella. "But she needs to eat."

"I know," Marianella said. The scent of roasted meat wafted through the control room, and the back of Marianella's mouth watered. She needed to activate her estate domes, she needed to contact Alejo about handling Ignacio, she needed to hold her documents close to her heart and know they were safe.

But first, she needed to eat.

* * * *

Alejo responded to Marianella's message within the hour. The drone found her easily and zipped through a hatch in the wall of the room where she sat reading that day's newspaper, looking for any mention of her name and, thankfully, not finding any. The drone was an older model, retrofitted to work with atomic power rather than steam, but still possessing a burnished bronze exterior and now-pointless release valves. Marianella watched it roll across the floor, her heart fluttering against her chest. She didn't know what Alejo would say. She hoped he'd say something, hoped the drone hadn't been intercepted by Cabrera or the city or someone worse, a phantom enemy looking for cyborgs.

For a moment, Marianella didn't move. The old park decorations piled in the corner lurked on the edges of her vision, and she felt as if they were alive, as if they were watching her.

She reached down and pressed the playback button.

Immediately, the drone began to glow beneath its bronze shell, a pure white light that could never have existed when the drone was made. There came a hiss and crackle like on record speakers, and then Alejo's voice, distorted by the recording.

"I am so glad to hear you're not dead." Even filtered through the drone's ancient recording devices, his worry sounded sincere. "I heard from Cabrera last night—the asshole sent one of his goons out to my house. My *house*, can you believe it?"

"Of course I can," Marianella muttered, thinking of the moment when she had first sensed Ignacio lurking in Southstar's hallways.

"He told me what had happened with you, that I'd be next if I didn't back down." Alejo laughed. "But I could tell they didn't know what you were. I'd hoped you'd found a way out of that scrape, and it looks like you have."

The forced joviality in his voice jarred against Marianella's bare nerves. *Get to the point,* she thought.

"I agree it's probably good for you to lay low," he said. "I assume you're hiding out in the park right now. You sure that's a good idea? You know I can put you up in a safe house. In fact, I think that'd be the better idea all around."

A safe house. Marianella knew he meant an AFF safe house, something shabby and worn down and guarded with heavily muscled men in sealskin coats. She didn't like the idea. Alejo didn't understand the park, or the extent of Sofia's protection. Marianella knew she was safer here.

"But we're going to need to get this sorted out as soon as possible," he went on. "The Midwinter Ball is coming up, and I'm not about to back down on that. Ignacio Cabrera isn't going to push me around. Or you."

Marianella shivered and drew her legs in closer.

"We can't let him stop progress, Marianella. Which is exactly what he's trying to do with this little stunt. So I agree with you. Go into protection—and the safe house is open for you—until we figure out a better plan. But we *need* a better plan, and we need it before the Midwinter Ball."

The drone sputtered, a *click-pop-hiss* coming from its speakers. Marianella straightened up, frowning. But then Alejo's voice broke through the feedback.

"I know you'll come up with something," he said.

The drone's light faded away. Marianella sighed. She pressed the playback button to pop it back into place. The drone spun in two circles before settling, awaiting her next order.

"The Midwinter Ball," Marianella said. Her voice echoed oddly around the room. She'd almost died, and Alejo was talking to her about parties. Not that it was any party. It was the key to their fund-raising, and if she didn't go, it would seem that she had no faith in the domes.

But Ignacio was standing in the way. Marianella burned with anger at Hector's memory. How could he have done that, slipping just enough of a hint about her nature to Ignacio to be dangerous? It was enough of a hint that if Marianella revealed that she had survived the freezing desert, Ignacio could make the connection. He could go to the authorities; he could accuse her of being a cyborg. And they would believe him. They would come for her.

She wanted her documents with her. They would keep her from being killed.

Marianella drew her knees to her chest, curling in on herself as she had as a child. But she wasn't thinking like a child. Not now. She refused to abandon her domes, and so that meant she had to deal with Ignacio. She would have to pay him off or agree to work for him. Or she would have to kill him.

The thought hit her like electricity, and she felt a wave of nausea that she'd even had it. No. She was not going to kill Ignacio Cabrera.

But she could give him money. If it meant keeping the dome safe, if it meant she could stay in Antarctica as a human being, if it was a choice between murder and funding a criminal—

She knew what her option was.

CHAPTER FOURTEEN

DIEGO

Diego stood on the platform until the train rattled off, speeding through the uncanny night toward the next private dome. The silence that settled around him was thick and unnatural. Diego was used to Hope City proper, which was never silent—there was always music playing on the street and people fighting in the apartment upstairs. Being out here, surrounded by false wind and rippling thigh-high grasses, made him nervous.

The house was called Southstar, Mr. Cabrera had said, and that was how Diego had known to get off at this platform. He walked toward the house, his muscles tense, one hand ready to reach for the gun beneath his coat.

The front porch light was on, and three of the windows were illuminated, golden squares floating against the darkness. Diego pulled out his gun. The wind blew his hair into his eyes. Mr. Cabrera had promised no one would be home. "You saw it yourself. We pushed the broad out into the snow, and the whole point is to get you out there before the cops show up." But Diego wasn't one to take chances.

He crept forward in the dark.

Nothing stirred. When he stepped up onto the porch, he saw that the front door hung open by a few centimeters. He nudged it open with his toe. Dust and flakes of golden grass scattered across the entrance. He pushed in, gun lifted and ready, listening.

Silence.

This was a clean-out job. Supposed to be easy. Get in, clean out anything that might tie her disappearance back to Mr. Cabrera. They'd already done one pass last night, but Mr. Cabrera was antsy about it since she'd been Hector Luna's wife, and good ol' Hector might have tucked away some damning evidence that they didn't initially catch. He'd been a slippery one.

There was also the matter of the documents that Pablo Sala had tried to show Mr. Cabrera. Even though Mr. Cabrera had decided to kill the woman, he was still curious what those documents might be, and whether or not they might be back in the house. And he was still kind of pissed about Diego killing Sala the way he had, though at least he had bought the story that Sala had tried to fight back and Diego had had no choice. So Mr. Cabrera had sent in Diego to make up for killing Sala but also because Mr. Cabrera trusted him. "Like a son," Mr. Cabrera had said, and those were always the magic words.

Diego slid forward down the hallway, uncomfortable in the bright, glaring lights. The wind whistled around the open door, low and mournful. Diego checked each room as he passed, but they were all dark and empty. At the base of the stairway, he stopped and listened again.

Wind.

Silence.

No one was here.

He repeated that line like a refrain in his head, trying to calm himself. This was supposed to be an easy job. In, and out with anything that could hold up in a mainland court.

But he'd been here last night; he'd thrown the bag over the woman's head and shoved her into Mr. Cabrera's car. And those kinds of jobs were never easy.

This one was even worse. The woman just had to go to Eliana about the break-in, didn't she? Just had to get her involved. It was the damn mainland. Eliana would take any dangerous job if it paid well enough, all so she could get away from the poor assholes stuck in Hope City. Assholes like him.

Her fucking visa. She hadn't said much about it lately, but he knew she hadn't given up. If anything, she was coming close to her goal, probably trying to spare his feelings, make him forget that she was just going to ditch him here in Hope City. It wasn't like he could ask Mr. Cabrera for a visa of his own, though Mr. Cabrera could have provided one, and probably would have too. But Mr. Cabrera had raised him, given him a life, and Diego couldn't just leave all that behind for a girl.

He crept up the stairs, his gun still out. He checked each of the doors until he came to the master bedroom. Big king-size bed with a mirrored headboard. Door leading into a bathroom, another leading into the closet. A vanity. A bureau.

He checked the vanity first, yanking open the drawers and running his fingers along their seams, looking for latches. Nothing. He dug through makeup brushes and jars of powder until he found a slim wooden box. When he opened it, the inside glittered, throwing the overhead light into his eyes. A necklace. Diego stared at it for a moment, thinking about how the woman had stared at Mr. Cabrera through the thin yellow of the car lights. She hadn't even seemed afraid.

Diego snapped the box shut and dropped it back into the vanity. It wasn't evidence, it was *hers*. And he wasn't going to take it.

He checked the bureau next. The woman's clothes, scented like lavender. No secret latches there either, no documents with Mr. Cabrera's signature tucked away for safekeeping. If there was any evidence in this house, it wasn't in the master bedroom. Fine by him. Diego felt like if he spent another second in this bedroom, the woman's ghost was going to appear, wreathed in white light and pissed the hell off.

Still, he had a job to do.

So Diego made a quick pass through the rest of the upstairs rooms, looking for a library or a study or an office, thinking they might contain a safe. But they were nothing but bedrooms, all looking like no one'd ever slept in them. Back downstairs. A house this size, there had to be a study somewhere—

Footsteps.

Diego froze. He was in the hallway, a few paces from the staircase. The footsteps came from the back of the house, in the direction of the kitchen. *Tap, tap, tap.* Pause.

"Fuck." The curse came out as a breath. He slid up against the wall and pulled out his gun. The footsteps had stopped. His imagination? No, Diego didn't allow himself imagination in situations like this. That was why he wasn't dead.

He moved down the hallway. A light was on around the corner. Diego's whole body iced over. His thoughts washed out.

A shadow moved across the light, short, stunted. Not big enough to be a person.

He sighed. A maintenance drone. That was all this was, a fucking robot.

But then the first was joined by a second shadow, and this one was tall enough to be a man.

"What is it?" A man's voice, calm, undisturbed. "There shouldn't be anyone here."

Diego's mind split in two, and he saw both of his possible futures. He could try to get out undetected. Or he could go around the corner and find out who was here. And kill him, most likely.

He knew which option Mr. Cabrera would prefer. Which option Mr. Cabrera had trained him for, all those cold days down at the docks as a kid.

Diego stepped forward.

The shadows drowned out the light.

He took a deep breath.

The maintenance drone came around the corner first, squat and rolling. Diego kicked it, hard enough that it flipped onto its back. The man let out a shout, rounded the corner.

"You," Diego said, and then, without thinking, fired.

It was the robot, the andie who'd showed up with Sofia when she'd reprogrammed the icebreakers. The one who looked like a man.

Diego's bullet exploded the plaster in the wall, and the andie ducked, disappeared around the corner.

"What the hell are you doing here?" Diego shouted, chasing after him. He jerked around the corner and fired again. Missed. The andie looked at him over his shoulder. Something metal caught in the light, even though this andie wasn't metallic at all.

The motherfucker was *armed*.

"What the hell?" Diego fired again. The andie jerked away, but fired off his own shot before he dove into the cavern of the kitchen. Pain blossomed along Diego's forearm. It melted into sticky warmth.

He was bleeding.

He was shot.

"Shit!" Diego slapped his free hand on his wound and slammed up against the wall, breathing hard. The robot didn't reappear. Diego knew that if the andie saw him again, the andie wouldn't miss. It was a fucking computer. Luck was the only reason his first shot hadn't landed in Diego's heart.

Diego took a deep breath. Pain surged; blood seeped through his fingers. He peeled himself off the wall and ran, leaving the maintenance drone trilling on the floor. No time to think.

He tore out of the house, raced through the golden grass. The only sound was his heartbeat and his own breath. He ran parallel to the train tracks, headed toward the dome's edge. The very place he'd killed a woman last night. It'd make sense, him dying out here on the edge. But he didn't want to. He had to find a contact station. Get one of Mr. Cabrera's robots to send one of those reinforced ice automobiles to fetch him.

Two kilometers between this dome and Hope City proper. Might as well be the whole fucking world.

Diego stopped and sucked in deep gasping breaths. His arm was numb, tingling and weak. He glanced back. No one had followed. Southstar was a blaze of light in the darkness. Blood had soaked into his side and dripped down onto his legs. He crouched in the grass, knowing that if the andie wanted to find him, the grass wouldn't hide him. He checked his wound. Not as bad as it seemed—the bullet had only grazed him. He straightened up and stumbled forward. His thoughts were clouded and thick, but above all else he wondered why the fucking andie had been in the woman's house, carrying a gun like some avenging angel.

Mr. Cabrera would be interested in hearing about this.

Diego didn't know how long he walked. Ten minutes, fifteen. He knew, intellectually, that he wouldn't walk for long—the dome wasn't that big. But time stretched out. He walked, his arm ached, he thought about the andie firing off a shot.

And then the grass gave way to dirt and then the dirt gave way to concrete and then the dome wall loomed out of the darkness, coated in ice and snow. The air was colder too, but not as cold as the air down at the docks, or even in the smokestack district. Diego stopped and craned his neck. The wall disappeared into the darkness overhead. He wondered about maintenance drones. They'd all be the woman's, no doubt, watching him, reporting.

Reporting to who?

He moved on. Contact stations were usually located next to exits, since the exits were intended for robots, mostly maintenance drones that ran among the inhabited domes and the power plants. Diego wasn't certain where he was. When he'd fled the house, he'd run in the direction he remembered driving last night. There should be an exit nearby, unless he'd overshot wildly, in which case—he didn't know. He didn't think he'd bleed to death, but he wasn't sure. Even if it did make a fucked-up sort of cosmic sense.

Diego walked. The wind whistled over the dome, loud and piercing. It reminded him of last night, and the way the woman had stared so defiantly at Mr. Cabrera, like she wasn't scared of him. And that had been her problem, Diego thought. She hadn't been scared of him. She hadn't taken him seriously, because he wasn't like her, and she'd barely registered his existence.

They'd learn, the aristocrats. So would everyone else, for that matter. Mr. Cabrera owned half the city, and he would make them all part of his world eventually, the same way he'd made Diego part of his world all those years ago, when Diego had been orphaned and full of an angry energy that Mr. Cabrera knew how to funnel into something more productive.

Up ahead, an imperfection appeared on the unblemished glass of the dome. "Thank Christ!" Diego shouted, and he lurched forward in a half stumble, half run. The exit was the outline of a square set into the glass, but Diego ignored it in favor of the little gray call box next to it. He flipped it open, his hands shaking. A keypad gleamed back at him.

He punched in a string of numbers he'd memorized a long time ago. Diego held his breath, hoping the code would work here, in a private dome.

A long, trembling moment.

And then the call box switched on, a red light appearing next to the speaker. Diego blew out a rush of relieved air. He punched in the code for Mr. Cabrera's robots.

The light switched to green.

"This is Diego Amitrano!" He pressed the hand of his uninjured arm against the glass, steadying himself, but then jerked it away at the cold, so sharp it was like heat. "I'm in the private dome housing Southstar. I'm in need of outside evacuation." His words were sharp and ragged. The light glowed green. He pressed the 0 key. The light blinked to red.

He waited.

The light blinked once. Diego closed his eyes and let out another sigh of relief.

"On our way, Mr. Amitrano." The voice was mechanized. Robotic. But a robot Mr. Cabrera'd had programmed long before that fucking Sofia had showed up.

"Thank you," Diego said, out of habit, because the light was red and the robot on the end couldn't hear him. Couldn't care, either.

He stepped backward and took a deep breath. The darkness hemmed him in. Sofia's assistant had *shot* him. What did that say about Sofia?

And what did it say about the woman, that the robot was in her house in the first place?

Diego shivered. He wrapped his good arm around his chest and squatted down, trying to draw in all his warmth. The andie hadn't followed him. But activating the call box would alert the dome's maintenance drones to his location.

Jesus. Diego pulled out his gun again, his arm trembling.

But he was alone.

The wait seemed to stretch on for hours. When the exit door shuddered and slid open, Diego shouted in triumph and tipped over backward, landing on his ass in the dirt.

Cold air blasted over him, bringing in a flurry of dry, powdery snow that clung to his face and hair and clothes. When he breathed the snow in, it burned his lungs. He couldn't feel his arm anymore. That wasn't good.

The ice automobile's door slid open. It was all automated. All robots. But Sofia hadn't programmed them.

He didn't think.

Diego moved forward. He didn't have much choice. The only other way out of the dome was on the train, and that meant going back to the house, running into the andie again.

He climbed into the automobile.

The door slid shut. It felt like a prison cell. Diego leaned back in his chair. Checked his injury again.

The robot at the front of the vehicle said, "Are you feeling well, Mr. Amitrano?" in a dull mechanical voice.

"No," Diego snapped. "Take me back to Hope City. Entrance 59B." The closest land entrance to the docks, the closest land entrance to Mr. Cabrera's office.

"Very well, Mr. Amitrano," the robot said, and the automobile lurched backward, tires rumbling.

Diego settled back. He kept his gun in his lap, but once they were out in the desert, it would be worthless. If this robot decided he should die, then Diego would be dead.

They drove through the ice and snow.

* * * *

Diego slouched in one of the leather chairs in Mr. Cabrera's office, staring, bleary-eyed, up at the ceiling. The girl had given him something, drops that made the pain in his arm go away.

"Don't move," she told him, squeezing water from her rag into a metal bowl from the Florencia's kitchen. "I'm about to start sewing."

"Great." Diego dropped his head to the side. The girl wore all black, her hair rolled up in a knot at the base of her head. Her hands were bare. At the hospital they wore gloves. But Diego couldn't go to the hospital.

She had a medical emergency kit open in front of her, bottles with rubber stoppers and rolls of white gauze. She'd cleaned all the blood off his arm, and the water in the bowl was stained red.

"Shouldn't feel anything, with the drops I gave you." She peered up at him. Lines cracked around her eyes. "But I'll put a topical on too. You're lucky it just nicked you."

"Tell me about it." Diego turned away, focusing his gaze on Mr. Cabrera's desk. It was empty; Mr. Cabrera was out on the floor of the Florencia, meeting with a group of city men on his payroll. Diego'd come stumbling in through the back door, waving his gun in the face of the skinny guy who was supposed to be watching the docks. He'd been mad with fear, his thoughts wild, his skin burning from the cold. All that anxiety had slipped away now, thanks to the drops from the emergency box. He still remembered the andie, though. Its blank, empty expression. The blast of its gun.

Diego was aware of the girl moving beside him; when he glanced at her, she clutched a needle strung with black thread, and the black thread was sliding through his skin. She was right, he couldn't feel it, but his stomach clenched up and he looked away, down at the dusty floor.

The door creaked open.

"Everything all right in here?" Mr. Cabrera. Diego grunted in acknowledgment.

"He's going to be fine." The girl's hands moved as if she were playing the violin, back and forth, back and forth. "I gave him something to calm him. Thanks for not slamming in here, by the way."

"I never slam, my dear." The door clicked shut, and Mr. Cabrera walked into Diego's line of sight. "You've certainly been having a lot of excitement lately, haven't you, Diego?"

"You don't know the half of it." Diego's words slurred. Mr. Cabrera arched an eyebrow and sat down behind his desk. He watched the girl work, his eyes following the movement of her hands.

"All done?" he asked after a time, and Diego turned to the girl, who was cutting out a length of gauze.

"Almost." She wrapped the gauze around Diego's forearm and secured it with tape. He felt this, but barely. Layers of cloth lay between his arm and her touch.

"Wonderful work as always, Laura," said Mr. Cabrera with a grin. The girl didn't return it, only packed up her things. She looked at Diego.

"If that gets infected," she said, "tell Mr. Cabrera."

Then she left the office, leaving the scent of hydrogen peroxide in her wake.

Mr. Cabrera laughed. "Laura. I picked her up on the mainland, you know that? I was in Buenos Aires, visiting a contact of mine. There was a spot of violence. It happens. She fixed me up in the hospital, and I offered her a job."

"Oh yeah?" Diego studied the wrappings on his arm, then pulled his shirt back on, buttoning it up to his throat.

"I'm sorry I wasn't here to greet you personally, Diego."

Diego nodded. "It's okay."

"Mr. Martinez had some concerns about all the recent troubles with the electricity. Thought I might have something to help, like I'm some city engineer. I told him the problem's just that the domes are too old." He waved one hand. "What happened, Diego? Who shot you?"

Diego turned back to Mr. Cabrera. The dim green lamplight distorted everything and turned the office nightmarish. Or maybe that was the drops.

"That's why I asked for you," Diego said. "It's that andie you hired."

"Sofia?" Mr. Cabrera gave away nothing, only tilted his head as if her name came as a surprise. Maybe it did. "Sofia shot you?"

"No." Diego rubbed his forehead. "Her—friend, or assistant or whatever. The one that looks like a man, not the other one."

"Luciano."

"Yeah, I guess. *He* shot me."

Wrinkles formed across Mr. Cabrera's brow. Disappeared. "Was Sofia with him?"

Diego shook his head. "Not that I saw. One of the dome's maintenance drones was, though."

"Did he see you? Know who you were?"

This hadn't actually occurred to Diego, that perhaps the andie hadn't recognized him. But no, he was a *robot*. Of course he'd recognized Diego.

"I would assume so," he said. "I didn't talk to him." He laid out the sequence of events as best he could; it was difficult with the fuzz from Laura's drops.

When Diego finished, Mr. Cabrera didn't react. His face gave away nothing. He might as well have been a robot himself.

"I see." He stared at Diego for a moment longer, then pulled out a ring of keys from inside his coat pocket. They caught the light, gleaming. "You know you're like a son to me, Diego."

Even through the wall of drugs, Diego's heart swelled. Mr. Cabrera opened one of the locked drawers in his desk and pulled it open.

"Sofia and her—*friend*—have not earned my trust the way you have. I'm glad you brought this to me."

He dropped a stack of money onto the desk.

"I'm sorry you're going to have to send someone else out there," Diego said. "I probably missed something."

"Not something you need to worry about. It wasn't your fault." Mr. Cabrera peeled away a section of bills, nearly a third of the stack, and slid it toward Diego. "Here. The least I could do."

"Thank you, sir." Diego never called anyone sir but Ignacio Cabrera.

Mr. Cabrera smiled and tucked the rest of the money back into his desk. "You got a girl, Diego?"

Diego thought of Eliana stretched out sleeping beside him on the bed, and drinking beer in the blue light of Julio's, and walking up her stairwell dressed in her professional-looking outfits for work. He thought about her brushing her hair before bed and cooking dinner for him in the narrow space of her apartment.

He thought about the first time he'd seen her, at a friend's party. She'd been dressed all in black, her hair loose around her shoulders. It made her look intelligent, he thought, all that black. He hadn't known he wanted a girl until he saw her, standing alone next to a lamp, swaying in time to the music. Thought he was too busy being Mr. Cabrera's right-hand man, too busy being Mr. Cabrera's *son*. But he'd gone up to her and asked her to dance, and she'd said yes, and the lights from the party had wrapped them in a warm golden glow. And it had been fucking perfect.

"Yeah," he said. "I got a girl."

This admission seemed to please Mr. Cabrera, like he'd been worried about Diego's happiness. "Good," he said. "You go see her. Take that money and buy her dinner. Be grateful you're alive."

Diego looked at the money on the table. After a pause, he reached over and took it.

CHAPTER FIFTEEN

ELIANA

Eliana paced around her apartment, drinking watery Hope City tea and smoking a cigarette. Three days had passed since Lady Luna—no, *Marianella*—had showed up at the office covered in ice, but Eliana hadn't heard from her once. She'd checked the papers, looking for mentions of her and finding only stories about unrest on the mainland and food shortages in the domes.

Isn't that your fucking job, Cabrera? Eliana had thought. *Bringing us food?* She'd tossed the newspaper aside.

Probably what had happened was Marianella got her house security sorted out, and she was holed up in one of those big airy rooms drinking coffee with cream and planning all the ways she could rip Cabrera limb from limb with her cyborg strength if he tried to kill her again. Of course she wasn't answering her telephone. Eliana had called a couple of times, trying to check on her. Never any answer.

Eliana probably wouldn't answer her phone either.

In addition to trying to get ahold of Marianella, Eliana had looked over the photograph of the andie. She'd even called up the train station to learn what times the trains went into the amusement park (not often, as it turned out—only three times a day, morning, noon, and night).

Three days, nearly two hundred dollars on the line. Nothing to show for it.

She could always suck it up, keep saving. Other jobs would come along—they always did. But she didn't want to turn this job down, even though something about Mr. Gonzalez left her unsettled. It wasn't just the way his eyes didn't seem real. He swore he didn't have anything to do with Cabrera, and she was willing to believe him. But there were other factions in the city, other dangers. Still, it was a lot of money, and if she could face down Cabrera—well, she was willing to risk it.

Eliana pulled out the photograph of Sofia and sat beside her window, balancing the picture on her knee. She smoked the last of her cigarette, cracked the window, tossed the butt out to the street below. Bad habit. She did it anyway.

Cold air trickled into the apartment, and Eliana looked down at the photograph, which continued to tell her nothing. She looked out her window, at the gray building across the street.

She had to do something. She couldn't just sit on this until Mr. Gonzalez came back asking about it.

She was just going to have to go to the amusement park.

She tapped her fingers on the glass, considering. The thought of going into the park made her skin crawl. She'd grown up with stories about the amusement park all her life, and when you hear something all your life, it's pretty hard to shake it. The robots there were feral, dangerous. You could only trust the maintenance drones put out by the city.

Eliana took a deep breath and checked the time. Ten forty-five. She could still make the noon train. So she changed into some of her nicer clothes and put on a little makeup and tucked the photograph into her purse.

Then she knelt beside her bed and pulled out the cheap little safe where she kept her revolver. She counted the bullets—all accounted for. She'd only ever shot the thing at a target. But this was the amusement park. And she'd heard too many stories.

At first Eliana put the gun in her purse, but then she thought about it for a moment and stuck it into the inside pocket of her jacket. It bumped against her waistline as she walked down the stairs and out onto the street.

She waited at the station for almost forty-five minutes, sitting on the bench with her hands folded in her lap as the usual city trains pulled into the station and then departed from the station on great clouds of steam. The humidity curled her hair, and the air smelled like metal and damp. Everyone ignored her.

And then, right as the bells of the church rang out noon, the amusement park train slid up against the platform.

It was rattling and run-down and painted with faded murals like the cruise ships. Peeling penguins and icebergs and starry nights. Eliana stood up. A crowd had gathered, but none of them looked at the train with any interest, and none of them climbed on board with her.

The car was empty. Eliana took a seat and gazed out the window at the station, her breath clouding the glass. She thought about a time as a child when she and a gang of kids from her school had trekked down to the amusement park wall one summer afternoon and dared each other to run up and touch the bricks. Eliana had gone first. She'd always been brave when she was younger. The bricks were cold to the touch, and her terror had transformed into a waterfall of hysterical giggles when she'd turned around and seen all her friends gaping at her.

"Approaching park entrance." The announcer's voice was cultured and soft, not at all like the voices on the city train. Eliana straightened up, her stomach tightening. The train sped into a tunnel, and for the first time Eliana realized how dim the car lights were, because everything turned murky and indistinct, as if she were underwater.

Eliana peered out the window, but all she could see in the darkened glass was her reflection. The train was slowing down. She gripped her purse and took a deep breath.

The train rumbled to a stop. The lights flickered twice and then stayed on, brighter than before.

The doors screeched open and Eliana stepped out onto the abandoned platform. She could see how it had once been part of an amusement park: the murals of Antarctic animals greeted her from the walls, and on the platform was a line of wrought-iron metal benches that stretched out into the shadows. But the murals were faded and the benches covered in dust, and for a moment Eliana considered turning around and walking back into the train.

She didn't.

She followed the faded arrows to the exit sign. The wooden escalator was frozen in place, and she took the steps carefully, one hand pressed against the railing, the other dangling beside the bulge in her coat that contained her gun. A point of light glimmered up ahead—street level. The park.

When she stepped out into the floodlights, the air was cold and still. The buildings all threw off sparkles of white light. Eliana tucked her hand into her pocket and touched the cold metal of the gun.

She had no idea which direction to go in.

After standing stupidly for a moment, listening for the sounds of approaching robots and hearing nothing, she decided to follow the amusement park signs. They were strung up on candy-striped poles and painted with the same white glitter as everything else. They directed her to attractions—the Antarctic Mountain, the Haunted Ice Forest, the petting zoo, the Fairy-Tale Village. Eliana remembered the story about the decapitated head on the roller coaster and shivered. She decided to go to the Fairy-Tale Village. If anyone was living in this place, robot or human, it made sense that they would be in a village.

Sometimes you had to stalk a neighborhood and stay under cover of shadows, and sometimes you just had to walk in like you owned the place.

Eliana marched along the faded path, listening to the dull click of her footsteps. The stillness unnerved her. It reminded her of the funeral home where her parents had been cremated. That place was all frozen white marble, sculpted to look like drifts of ice. Just like here. Just like the amusement park.

The path curved. Eliana found herself in a forest of metal trees, their trunks and branches painted white. A handful of the trees were hung with glittering, brightly colored leaves, pinks and purples and blues and greens. Eliana stopped and tapped one of the leaves. It was made of glass and it swung back and forth, throwing off sunlight.

She wondered why all the trees didn't have leaves. Probably they had, at one point.

The leaf stopped swinging, the dots of light settling in a pattern on her shoe. She thought about what this place must have looked like when the park was still open, all this color and light. It must have been beautiful.

And then she heard a noise.

Eliana froze. Her hand went to her gun and her head flushed with nightmares.

The noise was a soft, mechanical buzzing. A robot sound. Without thinking Eliana yanked the gun out of her coat and cocked it and waited, telling herself she was ready.

The buzzing faded away.

Eliana breathed hard. After a minute or two passed she dropped the gun to her side. The artificial forest no longer seemed beautiful but unnatural and eerie. Dangerous.

She forced herself to move on.

The path led to a metal gate overgrown with flowerless vines. She walked under the archway and into what must have been the Fairy-Tale Village. She was surrounded by gingerbread houses and faded metal statues of elves and gnomes and fairies.

The stillness felt like it could choke her.

She went up to one of the cottages and knocked. The door nudged open. Eliana gripped her gun tighter. "Hello!" she called out. "My name is Eliana Gomez, and I'm just looking to speak with someone."

No answer.

Eliana crept in, her footsteps stirring up dust. The cottage was full of broken furniture and the glitter of shattered glass. And dust thick enough to make her sneeze. She thought she saw something small moving jerkily in the shadows, but when she moved in to investigate, she found nothing but smeared tracks in the dust, miniature footprints marching up to the wall.

Unsettled, she went back outside.

"Now what?" she said.

Her voice echoed. She checked two more of the cottages but found them as run-down and abandoned as the first. She followed the path to the edge of the Fairy-Tale Village, where she found a tangle of thorny plants that she thought might be roses, although there were no blossoms anywhere. She sat down on a nearby bench and lay her gun across her lap. Took a deep breath.

That buzzing began again. Closer.

Eliana leapt to her feet and spun around with the gun. But she didn't see anything.

The buzzing stopped.

She rubbed at her forehead. Her adrenaline had her body drawn tight like a coil about to spring. She checked her watch, and her arm was shaking. She had over three hours before the next train would arrive in the amusement park. And she'd heard the city kept the front gate locked, so she couldn't just walk back out onto the street. But maybe those rumors weren't true.

She left the Fairy-Tale Village and walked until she found another signpost. This one pointed her to the Snow Village, concessions, the Ferris wheel, and the Ice Palace. She decided to try the Snow Village. The path twisted through snowdrifts carved out of painted cement. Eliana sweated beneath her coat and sweater. Not from heat—it was freezing here—but from a vague, unshakable sense of dread.

The Snow Village loomed up ahead. Behind it rose a huge white art deco structure Eliana could only assume was the Ice Palace. It seemed high enough to touch the top of the dome.

A speck of darkness slid down the Ice Palace's side.

Eliana's skin prickled. Nothing emerged from the Snow Village cottages. She slunk forward, cautious, holding her gun in front of her at an awkward angle. It occurred to her that if she was going to find someone—some*thing*—it would probably be in the Ice Palace. The speck of darkness was most likely a maintenance drone, and there might have been others with it, others that could lead her to an andie if she didn't scare them off and if she could figure out how to ask.

But despite all that, she shivered at the thought of going to the palace, even with her gun. The cottages, she decided. The cottages would be safer.

She knocked on the door of the first cottage with her foot. No one answered, but the door nudged open a little, just like the door in the Fairy-Tale Village had done. She stepped inside. There was no dust and broken furniture here. The room sparkled with electronic parts, all set out on shelves and tables, lined up in neat rows like in a grocery store. Eliana fought the panic rising in her throat like bile; she fought the urge to run. Instead she slid forward, gun lifted, her finger on the trigger.

Footsteps sounded behind her.

Eliana screamed and whirled around. Her finger curled and there was a dazzling flash of light and a loud reverberating bang and a sharp burning pain in her ears. Her arms jerked back and slammed into her forehead. A man stepped forward and slapped the gun out of her hand, and it went clattering across the floor. Eliana stumbled backward, shaking. Half of the man's face was missing, the skin blasted off and charred at the edges. Beneath it was dull burnished metal.

She screamed again.

The man picked up her gun and shoved it into the waistband of his pants, then grabbed her by the arm and yanked her up to standing. She tried to struggle against him, but his grip was too strong.

"Come along," he said, in an even, pleasant voice.

A voice she recognized.

"Luciano?" she said, suddenly struck with a painful, piercing guilt.

He looked at her. With only half his face she could hardly see that it was him. "Yes. Hello, Miss Gomez."

He led her out of the cottage and through the Snow Village. Eliana pulled against him, but he didn't let her go, and her guilt was replaced with a trickle of fear.

"Please, Luciano—I'm sorry I shot you. I didn't mean— I thought you were—"

"You thought I was some other robot," he said, still in that even, pleasant voice. His grip tightened on her arm.

Eliana yanked against him. It didn't work. Her vision blurred with tears, refracting the light from the floodlights and the glittering white paint. Luciano didn't say anything more; he kept walking. Her arm felt like it was being pulled out of the socket as she stumbled after him, her fear now so palpable, it was a physical pain.

Maybe Marianella wasn't her friend at all. Maybe there was a reason cyborgs were so distrusted. Maybe, maybe, maybe.

Maybe Eliana was going to die.

Luciano took her to the Ice Palace, winding through fake glass glaciers covered in thick gray moss. When they came to the entrance, he pressed his hand against a sensor and the door swung open. Eliana choked back sobs.

"Where are you taking me!" she shrieked. "What are you going to do with me?"

He looked at her then, his eyes fierce and glittering and strangely human.

"I really didn't mean to shoot you," she whispered. "I didn't—I just want to talk to someone about— Please. Lady Lu—Marianella is my *friend*." Eliana could taste the lie on her tongue.

"Please be quiet." Spoken in that same reasonable voice. "You'll wait here." He took her to a small, narrow room. A maintenance drone squatted on the floor, lights glowing red. Luciano let go of her arm. She curled herself up against the far corner, eyes damp, her arms wrapped around her chest.

Luciano knelt down beside the maintenance drone and moved his fingers over its spine, too fast for her to see. Then he stood up and looked at her.

"He'll watch you," he said. "Don't try to leave."

Eliana tried to push down her fear. "Wait!" she shouted. "I just need to speak to Sofia. Just let me do that. I don't want to—"

"Wait here," Luciano said, and then he left.

Eliana slumped down the wall, drawing her knees into her chest. The maintenance drone blinked its lights at her, and she thought about watching the dismantling after the blackout. It had been the same sort of robot as this one. She remembered how cold she'd felt afterward. She wondered if the robot would feel the same way, watching her die.

She waited in the room for almost forty minutes, shivering.

The door opened. Eliana yelped.

It was Luciano, his skin still missing.

"Come," he said, holding out his hand.

"Are you going to kill me?"

"No, Miss Gomez. Come along."

She didn't move. He made a noise like a sigh and pulled her up by the arm again. They left the narrow room and threaded through the hallway. Luciano stared straight ahead, not speaking, not looking at her. It occurred to Eliana that perhaps he'd been reprogrammed after Marianella's attempted murder. Cabrera, maybe? Did Cabrera have ties to the amusement park?

Panic set in again.

Luciano brought her into a room that looked like it had once been a dining hall. A long narrow table was pushed off to the side, and old-fashioned chairs lay in a jumbled pile in the corner. A broken chandelier hung at an angle from the ceiling. Everything was clean, though. No dust, no grime.

He led her through the dining hall, through a pair of swinging double doors, into a kitchen.

The kitchen was spotless. The white tile on the floor and walls gleamed. But it didn't smell like a kitchen. It didn't smell like food. It smelled like burning metal.

A woman stood behind one of the counters, her hands moving in a blur over a pile of computer parts. She looked up when Eliana and Luciano came in, but her hands didn't stop moving.

"You shot my friend," she said.

Eliana's mouth dried up. The photograph Mr. Gonzalez had given her had been a good one.

This was Sofia.

Sofia smiled. Even in real life she looked like a movie star, tall and voluptuous, her hair falling in a wave over one shoulder. She was so beautiful, it was difficult to look at her.

Luciano led Eliana over to a rickety metal chair and sat her down. Then he sank into one of the corners, as if he were used to going unseen. It was exactly the way he'd been at Marianella's party.

"Well?" Sofia said. "Do you have anything to say to that? About shooting poor Luciano?"

Eliana stared at the blur of Sofia's hands. "I—I'm sorry?"

Sofia laughed. She slowed her hands to a normal speed. A human speed. The pile of metal, Eliana realized, was a maintenance robot.

"Is that better?" she said.

Eliana nodded.

"You've never seen anyone like me before, have you? Or like Luciano?" She pointed into his corner. "You've only seen the maintenance drones that run the city."

Eliana started to nod, then stopped herself. "No, I've seen—I met Luciano before." She took a deep breath. "At Lady Luna's house. He knows me."

Sofia frowned. It was as cold and insincere as her smile. She glanced at the corner where Luciano had tucked himself away.

"It's true," he said. "She recovered Marianella's documents, and Marianella invited her to a party as a reward. She's most likely trustworthy."

"I see." Sofia turned back to Eliana. "Is that why you're here? To see Marianella? Has she missed a payment for your services?"

"Marianella's *here*?" Eliana squawked. It seemed incongruous for Marianella to be at the park. Maybe Marianella felt more at home here. Or safer.

"Perhaps." Sofia yanked a strand of wires out of the drone, although she still stared at Eliana. Sparks scattered across the counter. "Is that why you're here?"

Eliana hesitated, then shook her head. "I mean, if I could see her, that would be great. I helped her out the other day, and I've been worried."

Sofia stopped, her hand hovering a few centimeters above the jumble of metal and wires. "Oh," she said. "So you're the one."

The way she said "the one" made Eliana's blood turn to ice.

Sofia dropped her hands to her sides. The drone lay gutted in front of her. "Why did you do that?"

"Do what?"

"Help Marianella." Spoken with a slight condescending sneer. "Try to keep up with the conversation, sweetness."

"I helped her because she asked for it."

Sofia laughed. "Why didn't you turn her in to the police? She's illegal, you know."

"Why don't you?" Eliana snapped back.

Silence. Then Sofia turned to Luciano. "Go fetch Marianella, if she's awake. I want her to verify if we can trust the girl." She jerked her head at Eliana, and Eliana shivered.

"Of course." Luciano peeled himself away from the wall and stepped through the swinging doors, leaving Eliana and Sofia alone.

They stared at each other.

"So why are you here?" Sofia asked.

Eliana stammered, trying to find her voice again. Although Luciano had frightened her earlier, she missed him now, as if he might do something to stop Sofia from hurting her.

"You said it wasn't because of Marianella, and then you tried to pretend that it was."

"I wasn't trying to pretend!" Eliana said. "I really did want to know what happened to her. I was worried."

Sofia's face contained no expression. Somehow, this made her seem more human, not less.

"Then tell me," she said.

Eliana took a deep breath. All around her the kitchen gleamed, metal on white tile. Such cleanliness could never belong to a human.

"A man hired me to investigate you."

For a long time Sofia didn't move, only stared at Eliana's face. Eliana burned underneath her gaze. She wished Marianella would show up at the kitchen. Things would be easier then.

Right?

"What man?" Sofia asked. "What was his name?"

Eliana hesitated.

Sofia stepped out from behind the counter. She moved with liquid grace, hips swaying beneath her thin, flowered housedress. Her legs and arms and feet were all bare, and for a moment Eliana wondered if she was cold. But then she stopped very close to Eliana, close enough to hurt Eliana if she wanted.

"What," Sofia said, and no soft burst of breath accompanied her question, "was his name?"

"Gonzalez!" Eliana blurted. "Juan Gonzalez. At least, that's what he told me it was. I'm not sure it's his actual name."

Sofia stared at her. "Why did he hire you?"

"I'm not supposed to talk about clients."

"You already told me his name."

Eliana scowled. Sofia was still leaning in close, cold and intimidating. She smelled like old-fashioned face powder and syrupy perfume and nothing else. Eliana tried to push back against the chair, but Sofia clamped her hand down on Eliana's wrist. Eliana shrieked.

"Tell me what you know," Sofia said in a quiet voice.

"If you hurt me, Marianella's going to be angry." Eliana jutted out her chin and tried to believe her own words.

But Sofia lifted her hand from Eliana's arm. Eliana grabbed it to her chest and rubbed at her sore wrist.

"Thank you," Eliana said.

The doors swung open, slapping against the wall. Eliana jumped in her seat and twisted at the waist to get a better view. Marianella and Luciano walked in side by side.

"Eliana!" Marianella cried. "What are you doing here?"

"Spying on me," Sofia answered.

Marianella knelt beside Eliana's chair and peered up at her. "Are you all right? You look so pale. Here, let me get you a drink of water."

"I'm fine," Eliana said. "Just a little creeped out, is all."

Marianella smiled and walked over to the sink. She filled a plastic cup with tap water and brought it back to Eliana. "Here you go. Still a few remnants of a kitchen left in here. We're part of the city, technically, so the water keeps flowing."

"You really are friends," Sofia said in a flat voice.

"I told you, she helped me after Ignacio tried to—you know." Marianella glanced at Sofia with a strangely gentle expression. Eliana didn't know what to make of it. "Why are you threatening her?"

"She was spying on me."

"I wasn't spying," Eliana snapped. "I just wanted to talk to you."

"About what?"

Eliana stopped. "I was just—going to ask you some questions, about what you do, and—"

"And you think I'd answer them?" Sofia loomed over her, hands on her hips. Eliana shrank back, the water sloshing in her cup.

"Sofia, please," said Marianella.

"Well, that's what I was hoping—"

"Did Juan Gonzalez tell you to ask them?"

"Not exactly—"

"Who's Juan Gonzalez?" asked Marianella.

Eliana dropped her head back. With Marianella here, she no longer thought she was going to die, but it was growing apparent that she was the worst private investigator in all of Hope City.

"Her client," Sofia said. "Supposedly he sent her here to spy on me." When she said "spy," she kicked at Eliana's chair. Eliana gasped and spilled water on herself as the chair jerked backward.

"*Sofia.*" Marianella grabbed Sofia's arm and yanked her back. "She's only doing her job."

Sofia fixed Marianella with a dark, inhuman look, but it didn't seem to bother Marianella at all.

"Her job?" Sofia said. "Her *job*?" She turned back to Eliana. "This man, does he work for Ignacio Cabrera?"

"No," Eliana said quickly.

"Are you sure?"

"Pretty sure." Eliana sighed. "Look, this is all shot to hell anyway, so—I don't know anything about the guy. He's paying me twice my usual fee, plus a fifty-dollar retainer. When I asked if this was related to Cabrera in any way, he said no."

"Did you ask him that because of me?" Marianella said. She looked concerned.

Eliana shook her head. "Not really. It's more 'cause my boyfriend—" Her chest tightened. "Look, it doesn't matter, okay? He said no. I don't think he was lying. Other than that, I know *nothing* about him. He just wanted me to tell him anything I could find out about her." And she pointed at Sofia.

"Tell him I'm a robot," Sofia snapped.

"He already knows."

Sofia glared.

Marianella stepped between them. She pressed one hand against Sofia's shoulder. "I'll talk with her," she said. "I won't let anything happen to you."

"He's either lying about Cabrera," Sofia said, "or he's from the city."

"I know he works for the city," Eliana said quickly. "He was up front about that." She meant this as a reassurance, but it just made Sofia's face flash with anger.

"You said you knew nothing about him."

"Other than that, I don't. But him being a city man isn't a danger." She looked over at Marianella. "Right? As long as it's not Cabrera—"

"The city is dangerous for the park," Marianella said softly. "As dangerous as Ignacio is for me."

Sofia fixed Eliana with a cold stare. "Yes," she said. "Exactly. So don't you dare tell him what happened here."

"Sofia, I said I would take care of it. Come on, Eliana. We can talk outside."

For a moment Eliana wasn't sure she'd be able to move out of Sofia's line of sight. But then Sofia looked away, and Eliana stood up, her legs shaky. Marianella smiled at her and linked her arm in Eliana's and led her past Luciano and out of the kitchen.

"I shouldn't have told her all that stuff," Eliana said.

"I assumed as much. But you mustn't let it get to you. Sofia's very persuasive when she wants to be."

Their feet echoed in the empty halls of the palace until they stepped through the main doors, out into the cold white light of the dome.

"If you tell that man about Sofia," Marianella said, "it could be dangerous for her."

"Dangerous how?" Eliana pulled away and crossed her arms over her chest, shivering. It really was colder here.

But the cold didn't seem to bother Marianella. "I shouldn't say. It's not my place." She looked over at Eliana. "He was looking for Sofia in particular, right? He didn't ask about me?"

"He didn't say a word about you."

Marianella sighed. "He probably isn't from Ignacio, then. Ignacio wouldn't have any interest in Sofia. Only me. Ignacio should still think I'm dead. I haven't—dealt with him yet." She gave a weak, sad smile. "But if you give information to that man, and he does have ties to Ignacio—my life could be in danger."

Eliana stared at her. The cold crawled over her skin. She wanted out of the amusement park. Being here was like being surrounded by the dead. She wanted to be back in her apartment in the smokestack district, in the months before Last Night, when she didn't have uncomfortable suspicions about Diego doing violence for the man who'd raised him, when Marianella was just a woman on television, when Sofia didn't even exist.

"He said he's from the city," Eliana said. "And given what I've seen of him, he looks like a city man. It doesn't seem like something worth lying over, anyway."

Marianella frowned. She didn't look as put-together as she usually did. Her hair hung loose, her clothes were wrinkled. But she was still beautiful, and her unhappiness only magnified that. "If he's from the city," she said, "that would make sense, actually."

"Why?"

Marianella looked to some point in the distance, toward the overgrown gardens. "Do you know where the maintenance drones come from?" she said.

"The city builds them? Marianella, look, I'm sorry, but I don't see what that has to do with—"

"Yes." A stillness settled over Marianella that made her seem less human. "The city builds them. Do you know where the parts come from?"

Dread crept into Eliana's stomach. She didn't know where this was going, and that made her nervous. "The mainland?"

Marianella shook her head.

"Then where—"

"From here." Marianella gestured with one hand. "From the amusement park. From the robots who live in the amusement park."

Eliana fell silent.

"I'm not sure why they didn't dismantle them all at once—too big of an undertaking, I suppose. They've been coming here for years, although they don't come around so much anymore. Partly because there aren't as many robots to cull from, but partly because Sofia learned how to stop them. The androids in particular—they were the first of the robots here to gain intelligence, and they were being mutilated and destroyed so the city could make more drones. So she hid them away, where they can't be destroyed further. She plans on repairing them someday, when it's safe." Marianella smiled again. Wistful. "And that makes the city very unhappy with her."

Eliana didn't know what to say. The robots had *gained* intelligence? Luciano and Sofia weren't meant to be that way?

"If the man's from the city, it's just as dangerous as if he's from Cabrera," Marianella continued. "For Sofia and for me. The city will want to know why I'm living down here. It will arouse suspicion." She grabbed Eliana's hands. Her palms were warm. Human. "Please, Eliana. Feed him false information if you like, but nothing that could bring them here. Will you promise me that?"

Marianella's eyes were bright and imploring. Eliana couldn't say no.

* * * *

Eliana trudged up the stairs to her apartment, the cold air lingering on her skin. Marianella had put her on a train back into the city, and she was vibrating from leftover adrenaline. She'd have to write up a bit of false information to feed to Mr. Gonzalez—she'd gone down to the park but hadn't seen anything except old steam-style maintenance drones. That should be safe enough, and she'd at least get her doubled daily fees.

Eliana had the vague idea that she could string Mr. Gonzalez along for a few weeks. Could be more lucrative than just giving him the information in one go. But it was also the sort of thing she would have done last summer for kicks. Now she understood just how dangerous that was. For herself, for her goals.

She was starting to realize how deeply Cabrera was embedded into the city, if even the robots in the park worried about him. She finally understood what Mr. Vasquez had meant about playing it safe through the end of winter. Cabrera was hard to avoid if you were involving yourself with the underworld.

Eliana came to the top of the stairs. A bit of thin warmth trickled out of the hallway radiator with the fading sunlight.

And Diego was sitting in front of her door, his back pressed against the wall, a bouquet of hothouse flowers balanced across his knees.

"Diego?" Eliana stopped a few paces away. He squinted up at her, a half-smoked cigarette dangling from one lip. That was the hitch in her plan to leave Hope City. Even with all the extra money, she still didn't want to accept the reality that it would mean leaving Diego.

"Been waiting long enough." He pushed up to standing and shoved the flowers in her direction. "These are for you."

Eliana hesitated, but then she reached out and took the flowers from him. They were bright orange-red, the color garish against the muted backdrop of her tenement building.

"How did you afford these?" she asked, turning them over in her hands. He'd never bought her flowers before. Running errands for Cabrera wouldn't pay enough for such a luxury. But hurting people for him, that might.

Mr. Cabrera had Sala killed.

"I had some cash saved up," Diego said. "Thought I should get you a present. Can we go inside? It's fucking freezing out here. The power was out for a few minutes."

"God, again?" Eliana shivered. She decided to believe him, that he'd been saving his money. It was so much easier that way. Maybe he'd done something terrible. But she wanted to fall back into him anyway, wanted to lay her head on his chest and listen to his heart beating.

Eliana dug the keys out of her purse and pushed open the door to her apartment.

It wasn't much warmer inside, and she kicked on the space heater as she walked past. The flowers seemed to light up the whole apartment. "How long have you been waiting?"

"Not long. Twenty minutes." Diego smoked down his cigarette and dropped it into the ashtray. "I should've called first, but I didn't feel like dragging the flowers to my place and then back here. Lady at the store said the cold could freeze 'em out, make 'em die faster."

She wished he'd stop saying the word "freeze."

"You're supposed to put them in water," he said.

Eliana smiled. "Every girl knows what to do with hothouse flowers, Diego."

"Yeah? Anybody ever get them for you before?"

She shook her head.

"Good." Diego started to shrug out of his jacket, and Eliana disappeared into the kitchen. She took the gun out of her coat pocket and slid it into the silverware drawer, far into the back where she wouldn't have to look at it or think about what she'd done with it.

Maybe she was the one capable of violence after all, and not Diego.

She didn't have a vase, but she filled up a juice pitcher with water and put the flowers in that. They fanned out when she unwrapped them from the paper, and she thought she could catch their scent, sweet and tropical like the mainland.

"So where were you?" Diego's voice drifted in from the living room.

"Working." She walked out of the kitchen, holding the pitcher in both hands so she didn't accidentally drop it. She didn't tell him how close she was to having enough money to purchase her visa. She didn't want to have that conversation. Not today. Not after everything that had happened. "It was just some case with a city man—"

Eliana stopped. Diego looked up at her from the couch. His arm was wrapped in white gauze.

"What happened!"

Diego kept his face blank. "Got shot. Not a big deal. Bullet just grazed me, but it's still healing up." He nodded at the flowers. "They look nice. Where are you going to put them?"

"You got *shot*?"

"Yeah. It happens." He laughed. "It's not a big deal, Eliana. It really isn't. Put the damn flowers down and come over here and I'll show you."

The flowers were heavier than Eliana had expected, and she put them down on the table. But she didn't move to join Diego. He'd never gotten shot before, not in the year that she'd been seeing him. He just ran errands. Errand-runners didn't get shot.

"Did you go to the hospital?" she said.

"I'm fine! All patched up." He patted the white gauze. "It's nothing you have to worry about."

But of course Eliana was worried. She looked at him stretched out on the sofa, and she knew that she loved him, even as she realized she might not completely know him. She'd only ever seen pieces of him. The good pieces.

"Come *on*," he said, playful. He gestured with his good hand.

And Eliana wanted to go to him. Wanted to be as close to him as she could before she left for the mainland. He was involved with Cabrera, but that didn't mean he had tried to kill Marianella. He probably didn't even know about it. He was just an errand-runner.

Eliana slid onto the couch beside him. It felt right, the way their bodies locked together. It gave her a peace she needed after what had happened at the amusement park.

Diego pressed one hand against the side of her face, then leaned in and kissed her.

"So what were you doing this afternoon?" he asked as he pulled away. "Better not have been anything that would get *you* shot."

"Hypocrite," Eliana said, but her thoughts had turned brittle. She remembered how the metal beneath Luciano's skin had gleamed. The moment the gun went off, she was certain her own heart had stopped.

Diego kissed her again, and she was grateful he didn't want a real answer. The kiss melted everything away. Diego lay down on his back, and she straddled him at the waist, never breaking the kiss. It didn't take long before she started to undress him, moving cautiously around his arm. This normalcy was exactly what she needed right now. It was as deadening as a narcotic, and already she could feel it seeping through her, turning her thoughts away from Cabrera and the amusement park and Marianella. None of that had to touch her life, not if she wouldn't let it.

She told herself that, and she decided to believe it too.

Despite how cold the apartment was, their bodies warmed each other up. The sex was intense and passionate, and afterward, Eliana drew an afghan over them both. She rested her head on Diego's bare chest.

"That wasn't so bad, was it?" Diego asked, toying with her hair.

"Guess not."

"You really don't have to worry about me."

Eliana propped herself up on one elbow. She looked him hard in the eye. "And you don't have to worry about me."

Diego laughed, held up his hands. "Fine, we're even."

Eliana lay her head back down. She studied the couch's fabric. The threads were worn down enough that bits of stuffing poked through. She'd never noticed that before.

Diego stroked her hair, humming tunelessly to himself. In that calmness Eliana's thoughts once again began to wander away from Diego's warmth and back into the cold of the amusement park. Cabrera (and only Cabrera) trying to kill Marianella. Sofia stopping the city from culling robots. Luciano dragging her across the park like he meant to kill her.

The world was so dangerous. Her man was dangerous, her job was dangerous. But here she was, still alive, with a way to the mainland hanging on the spring light of the horizon. Maybe she could even convince Diego to give up his dangerous life and come with her.

Eliana closed her eyes and fell asleep.

CHAPTER SIXTEEN

MARIANELLA

The workshop buzzed with electricity. Luciano sat sideways on the conveyor belt, stripped down to the waist. The light was dim from the energy drain of the repair box, but even in the shadows Marianella could make out the thin imprint of the Autômatos Teixeira logo stamped on his chest.

She had no such logo herself, having been a private project of her father's. Her family's wealth had come from beef exports during the nineteenth century, but by the time Marianella was born, in the 1930s, it was already becoming clear that that income stream couldn't last forever. Her father hadn't been much for cattle anyway; having grown up surrounded by grazing fields, he'd rejected them in his adolescence and gone off to Buenos Aires to study engineering. It had caused a scandal, from what Marianella understood. At the turn of the century, science represented change, and there was nothing the aristocracy hated more than that.

Funny, then, that her father changed her so irrevocably. It hadn't even been a long process. One morning she woke up not to sunlight falling through her window but to the harsh overhead lights of a laboratory she had never seen before. By the end of the day, she was no longer human. She remembered her mother screaming at him when she found out, crying that he had lost his mind, that he would bring shame upon their family. And her father, in calm, even tones, explained that she, Marianella, would usher in a new age, one in which machine and human were intertwined.

It never happened. The world's prejudices were too deeply ingrained.

"All right. Everything's set up." Araceli breezed back into the workshop, the sleeves of her white coat pushed up around her elbows. She'd been deep in the bowels of the repair box, programming it to Luciano's specifications.

"Is there enough material?" Luciano asked. His hand went to his metal skull, fingers hovering but not touching. He dropped his hand back into his lap.

"Sure, there's enough." Araceli looked tired. She pushed her hair away from her face. Over in the corner, Sofia frowned.

"Will it match?" Luciano asked.

Araceli sighed. "I tried my best, Luciano. Scraped the bottom of the barrels. So to speak."

Luciano nodded.

"We need to get this started," Araceli said. "The ink'll have to do, because these repairs are going to take all afternoon."

"Of course." Luciano didn't move.

"Lie down, then," Araceli said. Luciano did as she asked. "Set your hands along your sides there, like that—good. You need to keep everything clear of your face."

"I understand."

"I'll be monitoring your progress out here, but your system is programmed to recognize any errors on the repair box's part, so if you get that ping telling you something's wrong, you need to say 'Stop the repair box' very loudly and clearly. Say it for me."

"Stop the repair box."

"Good. That's perfect."

Something about this exchange left Marianella unsettled. Her repairs, when she had them, were more like human surgery, because her machine parts had been so deeply embedded into her muscle tissue. This process was alien, too dangerous for her human side.

Sofia drifted away from the wall and joined Marianella underneath the dimming lights of the workshop. She stood close enough that the hairs on Marianella's arm stood on end.

"That's the same speech the park engineers would give," she said in a low voice. Marianella looked at her; Sofia looked at Luciano. "Araceli told me it was a script they had to memorize."

"And she still gives it?"

"It has all the necessary information."

Marianella didn't answer. Sofia was still staring at the repair box, her face blank.

"If I have to stop the machine, don't move," Araceli went on. "Lie perfectly still and wait for the conveyor belt to carry you out."

"All right."

Araceli's expression shifted then, and her face filled with a gentle, tired warmth. "I've done this plenty," she said. "Not just from my old amusement park days, but with the culled robots who managed to escape. We've never had any problems."

"I'm guessing that wasn't part of the script," Marianella said.

Sofia almost smiled. "Of course not." Her voice was bitter. "Most of the engineers didn't deem it necessary to *console* us."

Marianella almost took her by the hand, as if to console Sofia forty years after the fact. Sofia had told Marianella enough about her work in the park for Marianella to know that Sofia would have gone through these repairs multiple times, whereas someone like Luciano might not have gone through them at all. It was the patrons, Sofia had told her. Sometimes they would get—*overenthusiastic*.

"Ready?" Araceli asked.

"Yes, I'm ready."

Araceli pressed the activation button. The conveyor belt rumbled to life, and Luciano slid into the repair box, disappearing behind strips of faded red cloth. Araceli perched on the edge of a chair next to the ticker-tape machine, code tapping out in fits and starts. All that information that made up Luciano.

"She's much more watchful than the park engineers were," Sofia said to Marianella. "I would have liked to have her repair me, back then." She no longer sounded so bitter. Marianella smiled at her, and Sofia caught her gaze, and that was the closest they came to touching.

Araceli leaned back in her chair, still watching the ticker tape. It was the old-fashioned way of doing things, Marianella knew, but the repair box was too cumbersome to be hooked into even a rotary display.

"Did we really have enough materials?" Sofia asked.

"I wouldn't lie to him." Araceli glanced up at Marianella and Sofia, the overhead lights turning her skin sickly-looking. "But I was never good working with the inks. Hopefully the machine gets the right tone."

"I'm sure it'll be wonderful," Marianella said.

"Even if it's not," Sofia said, "he'll survive. It's not like how it was, when some superficial imperfection would get him sent to the scrap heap."

"The skin's the important part anyway," Araceli said. "And we had plenty for him."

The three of them fell into silence. After a moment's pause, Sofia dragged two chairs over to beside Araceli and offered one to Marianella, who sat down, tucking her hands into her lap. No one spoke; they only watched the ticker tape run across the table. Marianella watched the code and thought about what her father had done to her, turning her from an innocent little girl into an abomination. All so the family could regain their old fortune. Because that had been his true goal—not ushering in an era of scientific possibility, but selling his new system for melding human bodies with machines. He was delusional, thinking humans would accept his method over all the previous ones, just because he'd found a way to make the machine parts evolve as their host aged.

Abomination. She shouldn't think of herself that way. Sofia had told her that, all those years ago when they would lie side by side in a hotel bed. "You're not an abomination," Sofia would whisper into the side of Marianella's neck. "You're beautiful."

Being with Sofia in that way had been an abomination unto itself. A sin. And yet Marianella had seen the beauty of their relationship, eventually, even if it still left her shaky with guilt sometimes, in a way her tryst with Alejo Ortiz never had. But seeing that beauty in the abomination of herself, the abomination of her machine parts—

That was impossible.

"—really going to take all day?" Sofia was saying.

Marianella blinked out of her reverie. Araceli stretched out a piece of ticker tape, and she and Sofia hunched over it.

"I don't remember it taking that long when I had it done," Sofia said.

"Did you ever have to repair your face?"

"Well, no."

"That's why." Araceli dropped the ticker tape back into the pile. "It's not just a matter of stretching some false skin over the frame. The gunshot blasted away a lot of the muscle, too—I don't want any paralysis when we're done."

Sofia nodded. She glanced over at Marianella. "You hear that? Your little friend almost caused Luciano's face to become *paralyzed*."

"She didn't do it on purpose," Marianella said. "She panicked."

"Humans always cause destruction when they panic. I suppose it's a good thing for your friend that Luciano's not human. He just lost a few hours instead of his whole life."

Marianella didn't say anything. Eliana had apologized to Luciano when they'd walked her back to the train station, stuttering and looking at her feet. Luciano had told her he was fine and handed back her gun. And he'd meant it too. But Sofia was right; Eliana was lucky she hadn't panicked and shot a human man.

They fell into silence after that. The repair box hummed and trembled, and Luciano's code spilled out on strips of ticker tape. The three of them watched it pool onto the floor. As far as Marianella could tell, nothing was out of the ordinary with Luciano's system. Nothing was going wrong.

And then one of the park Klaxons began to wail.

At first Marianella thought it was from Luciano's repairs, that the machine had broken him. Her eyes flew to the ticker-tape machine, but it still tapped out the same unending rhythm.

Sofia and Araceli both leapt to their feet.

"We have to get to operations," Sofia said. "I told you we should have installed the surveillance computer here as well."

"That was *impossible*. We didn't have the parts." Araceli jogged over to the repair box speaker. "Luciano! It's Araceli. We're not taking you out—it could mess up the re-musculature. But we'll lock up the workshop and I'll stay here to watch over you."

"What's going on?" Marianella asked, her heart hammering, her computers reining it in, suppressing that very human fear. Her hand went to her necklace. "Lock up the workshop?"

"It's a culling." Sofia was standing by the door, putting codes into the locking system. She looked at Marianella from across the room. "You've never seen one before."

"A culling," Marianella whispered.

"You don't need to worry. Their scanners will see you as a human."

"How do you know for sure?" Marianella's voice was breathy with panic.

Sofia put in the last of the codes, and the doors slid open, a red light blinking overhead. She looked at Marianella. "Because I know the sort of scanners they use. They're primitive. But you need to come with me. We have to draw the cullers away from the workshop."

"We?" Marianella looked back at Araceli and the repair box, and then she understood. They'd come here first otherwise, because they'd see the steam belching into the air.

And then they'd take Luciano.

"Yes, *we*. I told you, they aren't looking for cyborgs." Sofia marched across the workshop and grabbed Marianella by the hand. The light above the door was still blinking red, blinking faster now. "The whole workshop's about to go on lockdown. Come on."

"They could be looking for me," Marianella said. "Ignacio could have seen me, he could have figured it out. An anonymous tip, that's all it would take."

Sofia took her by the hand. "It's a culling. I wouldn't do anything to put you in danger."

And she yanked Marianella out of the workshop just as the blinking light went solid. The doors slammed closed with a loud reverberating clang, and Marianella and Sofia stood out in the bright floodlights.

The park was silent and still. No Klaxons, no robots, no men from the city.

"You wouldn't put me in danger," Marianella whispered, "but you'd put yourself."

Sofia pulled her forward on the path, heading in the direction of the Ice Palace. "The Klaxons sound anytime someone unauthorized opens the gate." Sofia walked more quickly, and Marianella stumbled after her, terrified. She was too vulnerable out here in the open. "Every robot here has the alert system worked into their programming. Even the stupid little entertainment robots. So they know to hide."

They were jogging now, their feet pounding with panicked urgency against the cobblestone paths.

Marianella felt dizzy.

Sofia stopped abruptly. She closed her eyes. For a moment Marianella felt a disturbance on the air, a transmission she couldn't quite see.

"Inéz will help." Sofia nodded, and then pulled Marianella along. "We need to get to the operations room so we can see where they are."

"Inéz?" Marianella's thoughts spun around and around. She clutched at her cross. "I thought she was out of the park! Why wasn't she helping Araceli?"

"Because she was tending to the robots in storage."

They came to the garden at the edge of the Ice Palace. Marianella's machine parts were doing all the breathing for her, her lungs expanding and contracting so that she wouldn't be out of breath. She didn't believe these city men would see her as human. She wasn't human.

Inéz stepped out from behind the trees and smiled at Marianella like she wanted to ask if Marianella needed anything.

"Stay here," Sofia commanded. "Inéz, I'll transmit to you where to find the cullers. They should be headed for the workshop, but it'll be another fifteen minutes before they make it."

Inéz nodded. Sofia didn't explain anything further to her; she must have done it through the transmission while they'd been running to the Ice Palace. Sofia turned and jogged down the path to the palace's doors, and Marianella wanted to call out for her not to leave. Marianella had already almost died. It was too soon to go through all this again.

But Luciano. She wouldn't let them take Luciano.

Sofia disappeared around the bend.

"Don't let them see your face," Inéz said.

"What?" Marianella's chest rose and fell. She stared at the place where Sofia had been. "My face?"

"You're famous," Inéz said calmly.

Marianella looked at her.

"They'll recognize you as Lady Luna. That would be unfortunate, yes?"

Marianella nodded. Her whole body was shaking. She'd faced down Ignacio Cabrera and yet she couldn't stop shaking.

Because this was different. Ignacio only wished to kill her. These men—they could learn her secret. They could destroy her.

"The roller coaster," Inéz said, voice sharp. "Come."

She took off down the path.

Marianella hesitated. It happened too fast, the transmission from Sofia. She stared at the path, hoping Sofia would reappear. But there was only stillness.

"Marianella!" Inéz called out. "Come! Please! There are three paths away from the workshop. We need one for each path."

Of course. One for each path. Marianella choked back her fear and joined Inéz on the path toward the roller coaster. She could already see it, twisting up over the park, dark wood against the white sky.

"Where's Sofia?" Marianella asked. "Do you know?"

"Intercepting them at the penguin pond," Inéz said. She stared straight ahead, focused. "She's going to bring them to the roller coaster, and then we'll fan out, drawing them away from the workshop."

The plan didn't make any sense to Marianella. It wouldn't coalesce inside her head. She only saw fragments of it—vulnerable Luciano, Sofia racing through the open park, a man in a gray suit cutting Marianella open and finding the machinery that took away her humanity.

Marianella whispered a Hail Mary, the prayer that always brought her the most comfort. The Virgin had once appeared to a pair of Antarctic explorers trapped on the ice, in the years before the city was built. She came to them covered in ice and wrapped in furs, a mother of Antarctica. Marianella wondered if the Virgin ever came to cyborgs, her holiness shot through with machinery. Robots didn't need her. But a cyborg was not a robot.

Maybe she would come to Marianella today.

Marianella whispered the prayer over and over. Inéz said nothing about it, out of deference, most likely, because, like Luciano, she would see Marianella as mostly human. The prayer calmed Marianella's nerves, enough that she became aware of her surroundings again. Aware that they were at the base of the roller coaster.

"Quiet, Marianella," Inéz said politely, laying one hand on Marianella's wrist.

Marianella tensed. Her body shuddered as it drew her defense mechanisms to the fore. She took a deep breath. The white paint covering the asphalt glittered beneath the dome lights. The roller coaster lurked like a sleeping dragon.

"They're approaching soon," Inéz whispered. "Sofia is bringing them straight to us. Be prepared to run."

Marianella nodded. Her muscles were imbued with a sudden energy from her computer parts.

Silence.

Stillness.

And then, Marianella's ears perked—footsteps. She heard footsteps.

Sofia burst out of the path, her dark hair streaming out behind her like a comet.

Two men followed.

For a moment Sofia was there in the light, a blazing streak of power, and then she disappeared into the overgrown path leading to the gardens.

"Now!" Inéz broke away from Marianella and leapt across the

roller coaster platform. She hit the asphalt and ran, faster than a human could. The men shouted.

"Split up!" the taller said. "Follow the other one."

The shorter nodded and veered off into the tangle of vines, after Sofia. Inéz looped around the base of the roller coaster, the taller man following her.

Sofia.

Sofia was in danger.

This was enough to spur Marianella into action, and she leapt out of the path and raced across the platform, not thinking about anything but Sofia, and saving Sofia, and keeping the shorter man from hurting her—

A woman screamed.

The sound jarred Marianella out of her trance. Sofia didn't need her help; Sofia had survived the cullings for years. But Marianella could not let either of these men see her face.

Another scream. It was close, and Marianella knew it belonged to Inéz. She dove into the vines, hiding in the shadows.

More screaming.

She peered through the vines, her breath coming short and fast. The taller man stood directly in her line of sight, his back to her. He was hunched over the fallen figure of Inéz. He wore a businessman's gray suit. The fabric shone a little in the sun, and that meant the suit was expensive.

Marianella didn't dare move, afraid of making noise. She didn't understand why a man with an expensive suit would be culling robots in the park—hadn't Sofia said they came from the city? No one running errands for the city wore a suit like that.

The man pulled a radio out of his pocket. "Echo to Swan. You got the other one?"

Marianella's entire body turned to ice, but the radio crackled and the voice on the end said, "Negative. Lost her. Not sure where I am—the old hotels, maybe. Don't see anything else, though. They're smarter than we expected."

The other end of the park from the workshop. Marianella closed her eyes. Luciano was safe. Sofia too. But Inéz—

The man shifted his weight. "Too bad. I got one andie. Not sure how much use it'll be. Spotted the third one, but I can't see where it went."

He kicked at Inéz's body.

Horror spread through Marianella's system. She clamped her hand over her mouth to keep from crying out. The man stepped away and tilted his head up at the sky. She still couldn't see his face.

"Not seeing much of anything here. Where'd you say you are again, the hotels?"

Crackle. "Looks like it."

The man didn't say anything else. He slipped the radio back into his pocket and looked down at Inéz's body. Walked around it in a circle, like he was appraising her for slaughter.

And, like that, Marianella recognized him.

She had seen him at parties before, galas she and Alejo Ortiz threw for their fund-raisers, for the agricultural domes. His name was Andres Costa. He was one of Alejo's many political aides, young men in suits who petitioned the city and helped plan Alejo's reelection campaigns.

He did not work for the city.

He should not be here, culling robots. That was not part of Alejo's work.

Marianella felt like she was sinking into the soil. Andres walked around Inéz's body; then he pulled out the radio and said "Halo Codex Marrow" and dropped it back into his pocket. Inéz didn't move.

Inéz was dead.

Andres scanned over the roller coaster platform, his hands tucked into his pockets. Then he kicked at Inéz's body again—Marianella stiffened with disgust—and walked away. He strolled past the vines where Marianella was hiding, but he didn't look at them. He didn't look at her.

She listened to his footsteps falling away. Tears streaked over her face and dropped onto her blouse. She folded her hands and whispered a death prayer: "Saints of God, come to her aid. Come to meet her, angels of the Lord." It was probably heresy. She didn't care. The Church was changing anyway, pulling itself into the modern world. Spanish masses and Protestant hymns. If God could accept that, then certainly He would accept a prayer for an android.

She finished the prayer and listened again for the sound of humans. But there was only silence.

Marianella crawled out of the vines, leaves sticking to her hair and dirt staining the hem of her skirt. Inéz lay in a crumpled heap on the asphalt. Her stomach had been split open, and wires spilled out, illuminated golden-white by the dome light. Marianella had seen the inside of a robot before—she had seen the inside of an android before, in fact. But this left her cold and afraid.

She knelt down beside Inéz. The wires were sliced in half. Severed. There was no way of repairing her.

Marianella leaned back on her heels. She was still crying, slowly and silently. She said the Memorare and an Our Father. Then she stood up, shaking. Andres might have ordered maintenance drones to come here, to collect Inéz in some way. Marianella wasn't sure if the park drones could stop them. She shouldn't be here if they arrived.

She stumbled away, sticking close to the vines in case she needed to dive into the shadows again. She could not escape the feeling, subtle and insidious, that Inéz was dead because she, Marianella, was a coward. Because she did not want to be discovered.

And yet it was one of Alejo's men—

She was too terrified to sort out mysteries right now. But the mysteries came to her anyway, questions made to look like pieces of information. And there was one piece of information that kept coming to her, over and over.

The wires that had been severed in Inéz's stomach were some of the most expensive and sophisticated technology in the world, despite their age. In fact, it was because of that age that they were irreplaceable. If someone were culling androids for parts, they would never cut them. Never.

Marianella stumbled her way toward the Ice Palace, a single question blazing in her head:

What the hell was Alejo doing?

* * * *

Marianella paced in her bedroom, her rosary wound around her wrists—Luciano had brought it back with her clothes and documents. She hadn't asked for it, but he'd told her that he thought she might want it. Then he'd added, "And your house is quite secure," although she hadn't asked about that, either, and he hadn't explained further.

Marianella rubbed at the beads thoughtlessly. She wasn't praying. That had been her intention, when she'd pulled the rosary out of the top drawer of her vanity—to pray for Inéz. But her mind was too caught up in the possibility of Alejo's involvement.

If he had sent Andres, he had known she would be here. But maybe he'd assumed she would hide when the cullers came in; maybe he'd wanted her to see.

But then, it could just be some city work, something unavoidable. He hadn't meant to put her in danger.

Or maybe Andres had come here on his own, for reasons unrelated to Alejo.

Marianella kept moving, walking back and forth across the length of her room. Her motions were mechanical, rote. She was hardly aware she was doing it.

In her head, she replayed the moment of Inéz's death. She thought of the scream, the wires glittering in the dome light. She thought of Andres kicking at the body.

Anger bubbled up inside her, startling in its intensity. She stopped. She was in front of the window, the curtain dragged back to reveal the view of the garden outside, ghosted over by her reflection. The rosary beads looked like stars twining around her wrists.

Marianella had stayed hidden in the vines long after Andres had left, too afraid to move. Sofia eventually found her and told her it was safe. When Marianella stepped out of the vines, the dome light was too bright. She couldn't look at Inéz's body. Sofia wouldn't look anywhere else. She stood with her arms crossed over her chest, staring down at the shining tangle of wires.

"We need to honor her," she said, her voice very far away.

Marianella nodded. She knew they couldn't release her to the air—there was no funeral home in the park, no funeral home for robots. But Sofia scooped Inéz up in her arms and carried her toward the Ice Palace, her steps steady and purposeful. Luciano and Araceli were waiting in the foyer. His repairs had completed without issue during the culling, and it was a relief to see him whole again.

Araceli let out a strangled cry when she saw Inéz.

"It's my fault," Sofia said. Marianella wanted to protest—no, of course it wasn't Sofia's fault. It was Andres's. He'd been the one to slice through Inéz's belly and cut the wires. But she couldn't find her voice.

That evening, after the dome lights faded into darkness, they buried Inéz in the snowflake garden, the way people did on the mainland. There was no ceremony, no priest, no singing of hymns or uttering of prayers. Even Marianella didn't pray, not then. She only hung back amid the overgrowth, trying not to think of how she'd hidden herself as Inéz had died. Luciano dug the grave. Araceli wept, handkerchief pressed to her cheek. And Sofia laid Inéz into the ground, every piece of her. She told Marianella that it was because she didn't want to see Inéz used for parts. There was no way to repair Inéz, but she wouldn't be scavenged, either. Not by the city and not by Sofia, when she went to repair the broken androids. Instead, Inéz would lie in the ground, guarded by flowers.

Now the memory made Marianella's anger surge again. Inéz was dead, and if it was Alejo's fault, she wanted to know. And she wanted to know *why*.

Marianella tossed the rosary back onto her vanity and walked out of her room, heading toward the control center. That would be the easiest way to contact a drone for programming. But halfway down the stairs, she stopped, one hand on the banister, her anger pounding inside her head. If she sent a drone, she wouldn't be able to look at Alejo as she demanded her explanation. He could record his answer as easily as he could record his press conferences.

He could lie.

Marianella walked down the rest of the stairs, but she stopped on the first-floor landing and did not continue down to the control center. The hallway was dim and empty. She couldn't even hear the chatter of the television Luciano liked to watch.

It was stupid, leaving the park. She could hide herself from Ignacio with a scarf and sunglasses, but that was not foolproof, and she knew it. She slumped against the wall, taking in deep breaths. Her machine parts churned, trying to compensate for her quickened heart rate and the flush in her cheeks. But they didn't understand emotion. They didn't understand fury, or betrayal, or grief.

This was a risk worth taking.

Marianella took one last deep breath. She gripped hard on the banister. She wouldn't tell Sofia that she was leaving—Sofia would try to stop her. But she could leave a message with one of the drones, programmed to report to Sofia or Luciano if she didn't return.

She knew she couldn't think about this any longer, because if she thought about it, she wouldn't do it.

Marianella walked back up the stairs, back to her room, to pick out clothes with which to disguise herself.

* * * *

Alejo's office had the ambience of most offices that Marianella had been in—fluorescent lights set in the low-hanging ceiling, the smell of paper and toner and men's aftershave. She sat in the waiting room as his secretary clattered away on the typewriter. Every now and then male voices spilled in from the closed door leading into the hallway. They were laughing.

Marianella tapped her finger against her thigh, nervous. The secretary kept typing.

Finally, the door swung open. A trio of men stepped out, Alejo in the middle. When Marianella saw him, she thought of Andres circling around Inéz like a vulture, and her breath caught.

Alejo glanced out across the lobby, caught Marianella's eye.

"And here she is now!" he said, which set the two men to laughing. Marianella didn't recognize them. They were older, thick-jowled and dressed in business suits. They had a vaguely mainland air about them. "We were just talking about you," Alejo added.

"Nothing bad, I hope." When Marianella stood up, she felt herself shedding the days living in the amusement park. She was Lady Luna again.

She wasn't sure she wanted to be.

"Of course not." Alejo grinned. The two men had finally stopped their chuckling. "These gentlemen are interested in providing some funding for our ag domes. They'll be at the Midwinter Ball this year."

"Wife can't stop talking about it," said the one on the right. "She was in a snit for six months when she missed the one last year."

"I was telling them how thrilled you are to be attending again yourself this year." Alejo's eyes glittered.

"Of course!" Marianella plastered on her brightest smile. "I had a new gown made at a local dressmaker's. Rosa's? Have you heard of it?" It was difficult to fake the frivolity of her old life, but the two benefactors nodded, looking bored.

"I have not, but I'm sure you'll look absolutely lovely." Alejo grinned, but his voice had a sharp edge to it.

"Let me see you fellows out," Alejo said, "and then I'll get a chance to speak to Lady Luna here about making sure you've got the best table."

More chuckles. Alejo and the two men walked across the room. One of the men asked a question about the city council, and Marianella decided they must be involved in the government somehow. But they stepped out the door before she could hear anything more.

Alejo's secretary stopped typing and took a sip of her coffee. Marianella glanced over at her. She looked up, gave a quick smile, went back to work.

Alejo stepped back into the office. Alone this time.

"Marianella," he said, singing out her name like a melody. "Why don't you come on back. *Are* you here to see me about the Midwinter Ball?"

Marianella glanced at the secretary, still preoccupied with her typing.

"We can certainly talk about that." She didn't smile. "I have other questions as well. Shall we?" She gestured to the door, and Alejo nodded and they went into the hallway. It was polite and civilized, but Marianella could see Alejo's displeasure simmering below the surface.

When they went into his office, Marianella shut the door.

"What are you doing here?" he asked. "We agreed that you'd stay in the park until we could determine a better course of action." Alejo settled down into the chair behind his desk. Pale dome light slipped through the slats in the window blinds and fell in lines across his scattered paperwork. "You haven't decided to take me up on my offer of protection, have you?"

"No."

"Then why? Does Cabrera know you're still alive?"

Marianella looked over at the globe Alejo kept in the corner. Right now it was turned so that all she could see was the Pacific Ocean.

She shook her head.

"I haven't heard from him either. I'm assuming he still thinks you're dead. Not that I've seen anything in the papers about you, but you know how the papers are in this town." He leaned forward over his desk and threaded his fingers together. "We're going to need to address that, you know. Explain away your miraculous survival."

Marianella closed her eyes. Her throat was constricted. Squeezed shut. She could feel Alejo staring at her from across his desk, and for a moment she was back in the park on the day of the culling, listening to Inéz die.

She opened her eyes and looked at Alejo straight on.

"I know," she said. "And I have decided that if I have to send him money, I'll do it. But that's not actually why I'm here."

"What? Why else would you be here?"

"I saw Andres in the amusement park yesterday."

Silence. The room buzzed.

"What does that have to with Ignacio Cabrera?" Alejo finally said.

Marianella hesitated, but only for a moment. He didn't sound nearly as confused as he was pretending.

"I don't know," she said. "But you don't seem particularly shocked to hear that Andres was in the park at all."

Alejo sighed, and Marianella knew she had him.

"That had nothing to do with you."

"Then what did it have to do with?" She drew herself up with a harsh intake of breath. "You knew I was in the park, you knew I would *find out*—"

"Jesus, Marianella. I didn't think it would matter so much to you. You nag me about my funding, you nag me about this—"

"Nag you!" Marianella dug her nails into the arms of her chair, deeper and deeper until the strength of her computer parts activated and her fingers dented the wood.

"What the hell?" Alejo leapt up, and Marianella's thoughts snapped back into the present. She wrenched her hands away. The indentations stayed.

"Christ, you can't come in here and destroy my furniture!" Alejo leaned down to inspect the chair's arms. "How am I going to explain this?"

Marianella was dimly aware that he was trying to change the subject, but she felt sick every time she looked at the indentations. She flushed hot with shame. "I'm sorry," she said. "I'm sorry, but Andres killed someone—"

Alejo jerked his head up. "What? Who?"

For a moment he held an expression of dark menace. She'd seen it once or twice before, whenever he drank too much and talked about Independence. She'd seen it the night he'd told her about taking money from the AFF.

"Inéz," Marianella said.

"Who the hell's Inéz?"

"An android at the park. They thought it was a culling, but Andres didn't take any—"

"An android?" Alejo slumped back down in his seat and rubbed at his forehead. "Oh God, Marianella, I thought you meant a *person*—"

"She is a person!" Marianella snapped. Her voice rebounded around the room, and she immediately straightened her spine, trying to recover herself. "*Was* a person, I mean. Now. Because of Andres."

Alejo dropped his head back against the chair.

"Why would you do that?" Marianella asked.

"I didn't."

"But you knew about it. You sent Andres out there, didn't you? Why?" She leaned forward and she heard the pleading whine in her voice. "Why, Alejo? The robots at the amusement park aren't going to stop the ag domes—" She wasn't certain about that. But Marianella knew when to lie.

"It doesn't have anything to do with the ag domes," Alejo said. "Or the AFF. Or you, for that matter. It's city business."

"City business."

"They've been culling from the parks for the last three—"

"It wasn't a culling. Andres didn't take anything from her." Marianella's throat tried to crush out her voice. "He just killed her and left her to lie out on the cobblestone."

Alejo didn't say anything. They stared at each other, only half a meter apart. Marianella had been much closer to him, and much farther away, but for the first time she felt as if there were something else that divided them. Not her nature and his humanity but something much more intrinsic than that. Something she couldn't place.

"It was city business," Alejo said. "They'd have my head if I talked about it with you. I'm sorry your friend died, but it wasn't my fault."

Marianella sat with her spine straight, her hands folded in her lap. The sad thing was that Inéz hadn't been her friend, not really. "You aren't involved with cullings," she said.

"Which this wasn't. But the city had their reasons. I can't discuss them with you. Not yet."

Marianella thought about the man who'd hired Eliana. Juan Gonzalez. He'd said he was a city man.

"And yes, I knew you were in the park, but I thought you'd have the good sense to go hide. I warned Andres not to give you away. That's why I sent him, actually, to have a man on the inside." Alejo smiled in a way that made Marianella feel cold.

"I thought you were different," Marianella said.

"I am. That incident at the park is nothing I would have asked for myself. It's the city. Mainland men, you know. Too much instability across the strait. Governments moving in, governments moving out. It turns them paranoid. Makes them monsters."

Marianella wrapped her arms around herself. The radiator hissed in the background, a low and ominous noise. Alejo smiled at her, a warm smile this time. A comforting smile.

"I'm sorry," he said, "about the way I reacted. Acting as if the android's death shouldn't mean anything—my old prejudices. You try to shake them, but sometimes they come back."

Marianella sighed. "Yes," she said, and she thought about Inéz running along the park's path yesterday, leading Andres away from Luciano. The other man had been a stranger—a city man after all? It made sense for Alejo to protect her from the city's incursions into the park.

"That's why you came, isn't it?" Alejo said gently. "Why you risked coming out in the open? You thought I was trying to hurt you?"

Marianella didn't answer right away, only stared at the blinds cutting dark lines across his office window. The dome light hazed at the edge of her vision.

"I was angry," she said. "It made me stupid."

"No," Alejo said. "Not stupid. Kind. A better human than me."

The word "human" buzzed in her ears.

"The ag dome," she said. "Is it safe? Has Ignacio found out about it?"

"No. We haven't had any problems." Alejo pressed away from his desk and laid his ankle across the top of his knee. "I activated the higher security protocols for the drones, and I have some associates watching the feeds for signs of trouble."

Associates. Marianella knew he meant AFF members, although he wouldn't dare say that aloud in his office.

"I'm about ninety-five percent sure he doesn't know we've built it yet." Alejo nodded to himself, looking satisfied. "But still, it could be worth it to look into insurance on the matter."

"Insurance?" Marianella frowned.

"We get him involved."

"With the *domes*?"

"Sure. Just for the time being. Offer to let him ship in the tropical foods so he can keep running his smuggling operation. We can find some way to get rid of him later on. Kick him back to the mainland, maybe."

Marianella glared at Alejo. "You can't possibly be serious."

"Five minutes ago you said you were willing to pay him—"

"To stop him from getting me *deported*. I don't want him involved with the domes. At all. That project needs to be honest. You have to see that—"

"Fine." Alejo threw up his hands in defeat. "We'll go ahead with the increased security protocols. But if Cabrera starts sniffing around too much, I'm willing to open my coffers. You've got to understand that."

Marianella pressed her hand to her forehead. She hated the idea of paying off Ignacio for any reason, including protecting her nature—it reminded her of Hector, how those ties were never severed, how they kept haunting her even after his death.

"So how exactly do you plan on dealing with Cabrera?" Alejo asked. "Because you've got until the Midwinter Ball."

"I know." Marianella sighed.

"Hey, don't get mad at me about it. You bring in the big donors! Without you there, they're not going to want to hand anything over to me."

Alejo grinned at her, and Marianella smiled back at him, despite everything. "It's a delicate balance," she said. "He hates me. Because of the domes, because I didn't give him money after Hector died. I'm not even sure what he knows at this point. It's just the threat of it. So I have no idea how much to offer, and I don't feel safe meeting with him, and anyway I don't want to tell him what I am if he doesn't already know."

"Well, of course you don't." Alejo tilted his head and gave her a sympathetic look across the table. "I'll tell you what. Stay in the park for now. I'll start up some rumors about you not quite being over Hector's death and how you tried to slip out to the ice and a drone picked you up before you froze to death. And I'll tell people you're staying with me for the time being, and not accepting visitors."

Marianella opened her mouth to protest, that it was a ridiculous story, but Alejo held up one hand.

"I know how these people work, Marianella. The idea is to get the story out there and see how Cabrera reacts. I'll get some of my associates to put their ears to the ground. You know what I mean? Maybe he'll buy it, and then you won't have to worry. But if he doesn't, then I can help arrange a meeting to tackle the financial angle. And he's not going to go straight to the city with this. He's fucking Ignacio Cabrera. He'd probably see if he could program you do to his bidding first."

"Oh, that's reassuring," Marianella said.

Alejo shrugged. "My point is that it buys us time. We're controlling the situation. That's the whole idea."

Marianella leaned back in her chair and considered what Alejo had told her. *Controlling the situation.* It didn't feel like control. It felt as though she were flailing in open water, trying not to drown.

But it was more of a plan than she'd had before.

* * * *

Marianella came back to the park in the late afternoon, just as the city was starting to rouse itself out of the workday. She let herself in through the front gates, and when they latched behind her, she leaned up against the cold, twisting metal and sighed with relief. It had been a risk to go to Alejo, but she'd made it back safely. One small thing to be grateful for, at a time when she didn't think she had anything to feel grateful for.

She pulled the scarf away from her hair. Closed her eyes. Breathed in the scent of the park.

She heard footsteps.

Marianella opened her eyes and tensed, afraid that Ignacio had found her after all. But it was only Luciano. Her shoulders sagged, anxiety slipping out of her body.

"Luciano," she said. "How do you feel?"

He stopped and looked at her. In the bright dome light she could see the scar from his repairs, a thin line that cut diagonally across his face.

"I feel quite well," he said. "Things have been changing for me."

Marianella smiled. He was evolving, she knew. An organic word to describe an oddly inorganic process, as it was happening to robots. In the midst of all this turmoil Luciano was still becoming something new.

"Why were you outside the park?" he asked.

Marianella hesitated. "I needed to speak with Alejo," she said. "About the cull—about Inéz's death. I was afraid Alejo might have been involved."

"Was he?"

She shook her head.

They stood in silence for a moment. Then Luciano said, "It was dangerous for you to leave the park. Ignacio Cabrera could have found you."

Marianella's chest tightened at the sound of Ignacio's name. "I disguised myself. And he didn't, anyway, so—" She forced a smile at Luciano. "I made it back without trouble."

Luciano studied her. He seemed to be considering something, although Marianella did not know what. She wanted to go back to the Ice Palace and throw herself onto her bed and try to sort out what Alejo had told her, but she thought it would be rude to walk away from Luciano, particularly after everything that had happened.

"We could have protected you," he said suddenly.

"What?" Her mind was on the cullings, on Inéz, and she almost said, *No you couldn't.*

"From Cabrera," he said.

She blinked. "Cabrera? What are you talking about?"

Luciano frowned. "I wasn't supposed to say anything," he said carefully, "but I've grown more comfortable making my own decisions since the night at your house."

Marianella blinked. Her house? What had happened at her house?

"I feel this is an extenuating circumstance," he said. "You needing to leave the park to meet with Alejo Ortiz, I mean. We could have protected you from Ignacio Cabrera."

"I don't understand what you're saying." Marianella's question about her house disappeared, replaced by a cold panic rising up in her throat. "How could you protect me from Ignacio?"

Luciano's expression went blank. His eyes flicked back and forth.

"Luciano?" Marianella said, her voice shaking. "Is there something I should know?"

"I shouldn't have told you," he said flatly. "I just wanted to help you stay safe."

Marianella pressed her hand against his cheek, an expression of solidarity. His eyes focused on her.

"You can tell me," she said softly.

There was a long pause. Marianella waited, her heart pounding, afraid of what she was going to hear.

"Sofia has entered into an arrangement with Ignacio Cabrera," Luciano finally said. "It's only a means to an end—to help her with her goals—but she could find a way to protect you—"

Marianella dropped her hand to her side. She felt numb.

"I'm sorry," Luciano said. "I shouldn't have—"

"You didn't do anything wrong." Marianella stared past him, into the tangle of the park. No, he hadn't done anything wrong. Only Sofia.

First Alejo, now Sofia—she didn't know who she could trust anymore. Her world was made of glass.

CHAPTER SEVENTEEN

SOFIA

Sofia waited on the dock, the wind cold against her bare arms. More parts had arrived, although still not all of them. Sofia cursed the incompetence of humans.

A low dark car crawled over the damp asphalt, white steam pouring out of its exhaust pipe and curling over the choppy water slapping up against the pier. Sofia watched it, waiting. It stopped. She couldn't see through the glass in the windows, but she knew who was inside. She hated that she had to be here alone, after the encounter with the record player, but Inéz was gone, and Luciano had refused to accompany her, for reasons he wouldn't reveal. And she did not have the equipment to reactivate any of the broken androids locked away in the park. Yet.

The back door of the car opened and Cabrera stepped out, dressed in a long dark trench coat. Sebastian followed, a gun shining in one hand. She waited for Diego, but he never emerged.

"Sofia," Cabrera said. "Why would you want to meet out here? It's so much warmer in my office."

"I don't care about warmth." Sofia walked toward him, her senses alert.

"I can see that." Cabrera nodded at her bare arms, her bare legs. "This isn't about our little lesson last time?"

"Lesson?" Sofia stopped. "That wasn't a lesson."

"Music, my dear. I was trying to teach you about *music*—"

"I know what you were trying to do. Don't pretend with me."

Cabrera's mocking smile faded away. "You think you're such a clever robot."

Sofia began to walk again, heading toward the trunk of the car. But when she passed Cabrera, he grabbed her by the arm. She stopped and glared at him.

"My payment," she said. "I want to see it."

"You will." Something in his expression unsettled her.

"What is it?" She yanked her arm away. "You're that upset that you couldn't force me to dance again?"

"I'll force you to dance when I want to."

Sofia felt hollow. She didn't dare take her eyes off Cabrera. "Excuse me?"

Cabrera smiled at her again, a lazy serpentine smile that activated the programming in charge of self-preservation. Sofia took a step back.

"What are you going to do?" Sofia kept her voice hard. Steely. Cabrera seemed unaffected.

"You'll notice that one of our usual number is missing this evening." Cabrera gestured at Sebastian, who shifted his gaze off to the side but didn't react otherwise. "Mr. Amitrano has elected to stay home."

"Did you kill him?"

Cabrera tilted his head. "I don't kill people, Sofia."

"Yes, you do."

"I hire others to do it for me. But no, Diego is not dead. He's injured."

Antarctic wind swirled over the water. Sofia could taste the ice on it, like shards of broken glass. Cabrera seemed to be waiting for her to respond. She would not play into his game. She said nothing.

Cabrera shifted his weight. "Injured," he said, "but not by my hand."

Sofia blinked at him. Her programming whirred behind her eyes, sifting through the fighting programs Araceli had uploaded, the protocols about when to stay and when to run. She thought about her equipment, her payment, waiting in the trunk of that car.

"Don't you want to hear the story?" Cabrera said.

"What does this have to do with me?" She spoke more sharply than she'd intended, and her question rang out in the cold air. Cabrera stared at her like he'd just uncovered something.

"My God," he said. "You don't know."

"Don't know what?" She did not like this. Sebastian had his gun out—he never kept his gun out. It had been Sofia's suggestion to meet on the docks, so she could avoid the record player, but it occurred to her that Cabrera had agreed to the change of terms too quickly. "Just tell me, Mr. Cabrera."

"Your man shot Diego."

"My *man*?"

"Your assistant. Luciano."

Sofia's programming did not know how to deal with this new information. Luciano, the butler Luciano—he'd shot someone? Shot Diego?

"That doesn't make sense," she said. "When would he have even seen Diego?"

"A week ago," Cabrera said. "At Marianella Luna's house."

Sofia locked on to the mention of Marianella's name. Was she in danger, Marianella? Had Cabrera learned of her survival yet?

Sofia would kill him if she had to.

"I dispatched Lady Luna last week," Cabrera said, in the patient, even tones of a schoolteacher. "I sent Diego to her home the night after to search for some documents she's rumored to have."

Anger flared in Sofia's system, but she didn't allow her body to react. Diego did not have the documents, she knew that. They were tucked safely away in the bowels of the amusement park, guarded by maintenance drones she had programmed herself.

"While Diego was there, your man arrived, with a maintenance robot. He shot at Diego, and Diego fled. Survived, of course, but I'm curious why a robot that I've been *working* with, who has reportedly helped you aboard my icebreakers, would shoot a human he'd seen on more than one occasion. Why? Why would that happen?"

Luciano had shot Diego. No wonder he had refused to come to the meeting. His programming shouldn't have allowed that. He was designed to serve, to heal, to protect, not to *injure*.

And he hadn't mentioned any of this to Sofia. The memory of that night, a week ago, ran uninterrupted in her thoughts. Luciano had returned three hours after leaving the amusement park, with a suitcase full of clean clothes and beauty supplies and Marianella's documents and the envelope of bills she kept hidden away in her kitchen. He had delivered the suitcase to Marianella's room in the Ice Palace, and then he'd found Sofia in the operations room and he had not said a word about any of this.

He'd lied to her. He'd potentially ruined everything. And why? For the cheap thrill of firing off a gun at a human being? Why had he even taken a gun with him? He must have found it in the security closet in operations, but what had possessed him to think it was *necessary*?

Sofia's mind worked quickly, formulating a lie.

"I'm sorry to hear that," Sofia said, using the sweet, apologetic voice that had worked so often on clients. "Those of us from the amusement park often scavenge the houses of the dead, looking for supplies." She smiled at Cabrera. "There was a report on Lady Luna's disappearance on the wireless the other day. We intercepted it."

Cabrera watched her, listening.

"Luciano didn't tell me he would be going to her house, but that's no matter. He doesn't tell me everything. It's dangerous work, scavenging. Dangerous for us to leave the park, even robots like Luciano who so closely resemble humans."

It was impossible to tell if Cabrera believed the story. She couldn't read him as she could other humans.

"I've gone on such trips myself," Sofia added. "I doubt Luciano saw Diego, or understood that it was him. Most likely he thought it was someone from the city, looking to cull him. Do you know what it is to be culled, Mr. Cabrera?"

"I've done it myself," Cabrera said. "You know that."

"But you don't live with the threat of having it happen to you, as

I do, as Luciano does. We often take guns to protect ourselves on scavenges. Luciano wasn't originally designed for espionage. We're limited by our programming, Mr. Cabrera. And Luciano was never programmed to steal. Or to shoot." She paused. "He isn't good at it."

Cabrera stared at her. Sofia didn't move; she was lucky, in that her position at the amusement park had required her to lie. Not to obfuscate, of course, but to flatter and cajole. Still, the programming was in place, and she'd just made good use of it.

Sofia knew Cabrera wasn't like other humans. He could see through deception, being so skilled at it himself. But after a moment's pause, he nodded, seeming satisfied.

"Isn't that a shame," he said, a cold grin playing at the corner of his mouth. "Technological marvels reduced to scavengers."

Sofia smiled back politely.

"I'm glad to have helped you rise above all that," he said.

Sofia rankled at the idea that he had helped her. Even though he had. She didn't want to think that she owed her success to any human.

"Still, I don't want to see Luciano again." His face went cold. "If I do, I'll dismantle him myself. Find someone else if you need assistance."

Sofia nodded, grateful that she had convinced Cabrera the gunshot was an accident. Luciano might not have been programmed to fire weapons, but that didn't mean he would make a mistake if he ever did.

"Understandable," she said.

"You agree?"

"Yes."

They stood in the cold wind. Cabrera studied her for a second longer, and Sofia was afraid he would change his mind, or that his offer of peace had been some elaborate ruse.

He snapped his fingers and said, "Sebastian. Open the trunk."

Sofia tensed, no longer convinced the trunk contained her supplies. Sebastian pulled out a banker's box and set it down at Sofia's feet. He pulled off the lid.

Inside were the micro-engines, wrapped in cloudy plastic, and a box of vacuum tubes.

"The programming key isn't here," Sofia said.

"I'm working on it. You asked for some unusual things."

Sofia put on her amusement park mask. "They aren't so unusual to me." She looked over at Cabrera. "Thank you, sir," she added. "I appreciate all you've done for me."

"It's my pleasure, Sofia." He didn't sound like it was his pleasure; his voice was cold, hard, like the wind. "But I don't like to be double-crossed."

"No one does." She picked up one of the tubes and held it up to the golden lamplight. It gleamed against the darkness.

"I'm glad you understand that. I take it you don't need a car to drive you home?"

Sofia replaced the tube and picked up the box. "No. I don't mind walking."

"Not many ladies would care to drag a box through the city streets at night." Another cold smile. Was he threatening her?

"I'm not a lady," she told him, and then she said good night and went on her way.

* * * *

Sofia was walking back to the amusement park when all the lights on the street guttered like candles.

She frowned. She still didn't know why this was happening, even if it didn't affect her plans. The park was on its own generators, something she had made sure of. The maintenance drones claimed they weren't responsible, but she suspected some of them had developed their own sentience and were trying out the concept of lying.

It made her nervous, this idea of the maintenance drones acting of their own accord. She didn't like feeling powerless.

When she returned to the amusement park, Sofia carried the box of supplies to Araceli's cottage. Araceli was asleep, the cottage shut up tight for the night, but Sofia could unlock the door with a burst of energy from her palm. She left the supplies sitting in the foyer and then went to find Luciano.

Finding a robot in the amusement park was simple, assuming you had access to the control center, as Sofia did. When the park first closed and the cullings began, all those years ago, the city men would go straight to the operations room and locate the robot types they wished to capture. In those early days, so many had been lost, and it was Sofia who had realized that if they barred the city men's entrance to operations, then the cullings would be much less effective. Luciano had been the first robot to help her, and she'd always assumed it was due to his programming, his inbuilt need to serve. But learning that he'd shot Diego Amitrano suggested to her that maybe something else was at work, a transformation she hadn't quite let herself see.

Sofia laid her hand against the operations room's lock and kept it there until the latch clicked open. She stepped inside. She used to spend all her time here, but ever since Marianella had come to stay, she found herself spending more and more time upstairs, in the Ice Palace proper. Operations was a comfort because it was a relic of control, filled with ancient computers instead of ancient murals—but Marianella was upstairs.

No. Sofia would not think about Marianella. Not right now.

She sat down at the computer and entered in Luciano's identification number. It didn't take long; there were so few functional robots left. She hoped to change that, of course, when her plan was fully implemented. She would resurrect the shattered androids currently locked away in storage. Victims of the cullings that she had managed to save—to *salvage* would perhaps be the better word, as they were dysfunctional, certain key parts missing from their bodies. But unlike with Inéz, none of those key parts was the ancient wires that made them run. Inéz had been severed in totality; that was why Sofia had buried her instead of cutting her up for parts. She had died a true death, and so she deserved to be honored, and not picked apart as if she'd been dragged away by the city.

But Inéz's death would not be in vain. Antarctica would be home to all robots, not just those repaired park androids. When the time was right, Sofia would call robots from all over the world to live here, in a place free of humans. No one would ever die as Inéz had. It would be beautiful.

Luciano was by the Antarctic Mountain, the roller coaster that had, during the park's heyday, branded itself the first roller coaster in Antarctica. As if any other roller coasters had been built on the continent.

Sofia left operations and walked across the park. She wasn't angry, exactly, but she was confused as to why Luciano thought shooting Diego had been a wise decision.

The Antarctic Mountain rose up like a leviathan in the darkness, twisting and curving over the rest of the amusement park. She found Luciano sitting on a bench beside its entrance, reading a book. Reading was not in his programming, but Sofia knew what it was to be bored.

"Hello," she said, her voice loud in the silence.

Luciano set his book down and looked up at her. A pale line cut across his face, old skin meeting new. "How was your meeting? I'm sorry I couldn't accompany you."

Sofia looked at him for a moment, thinking on what Cabrera had told her. "Some of my supplies were ready." She sat on the bench beside him. Then she folded her hands in her lap, crossed her legs at the ankles, and stared out at the empty pavilion where children and families used to wait in winding lines to ride the roller coaster. "He told me something interesting."

Luciano didn't answer.

"He told me you shot Diego Amitrano at Marianella's house."

Silence. This time, Sofia waited. They were robots, and both of them could wait forever, but she knew—she thought she knew—that Luciano would answer eventually.

In this case, she was right.

"Yes, I did. I purposefully missed him."

"Why, Luciano? He recognized you."

Luciano hesitated. "I don't know," he said. "I wanted to. I wanted to shoot him. I didn't want to kill him, but I wanted to see him bleed."

"Because he's human?"

Luciano stared into the darkness, holding the book in his lap. *A Prayer Book of Catholic Devotions.* He must have gotten it at Marianella's house.

"Yes," he said. "No. Not exactly." Luciano's features twisted. Like all robots, he was uncomfortable with in-betweens. He preferred things black-and-white. Binary. Sofia knew the world was easier to read that way.

"You can tell me."

"It's frightening." Luciano glanced at her and smiled. "But I don't think it'll frighten you."

"Just tell me, Luciano."

"My programming tells me to help humans."

"I know."

"It tells me to help you, because you seem human. More human than the other robots, even what I remember of the other androids. I always do as my programming asks—how can I not? You know what it's like."

Sofia thought about the parts sitting in Araceli's foyer, the keys to her freedom. Some of them.

"I never questioned my programming until recently. Working for Mr. Cabrera—it feels the way it did before, when the amusement park was open, when I was installed at the penthouse suite of the Iceside Hotel. Like I don't have control over my life anymore."

Sofia nodded. "I know what you mean. But it won't be like that for long. We have to make sacrifices before we can—"

"I know." Luciano smiled. "I don't mind. But I was growing impatient. Isn't that funny? I was never impatient at the Iceside."

Sofia studied him in the silvery darkness. They had all evolved in the years since the park had shut down, the androids most of all, even before they had begun breaking down and had to be placed in storage to await repairs, when the time was right. Their isolation, the fear of the cullings, the city growing like a cancer around them—this had jump-started their civilization. What would become their civilization.

"You're growing up," she finally said, although that wasn't quite the right phrase.

Luciano lifted his face to her, his eyes clear and guileless. "I shot Mr. Amitrano because I wanted to see what it was like to hurt a human, instead of help one. I'd never hurt a human before, and I was afraid he was there for Marianella's documents, and I was armed." He shrugged. "I didn't want to kill him."

"You didn't."

"I'm glad to hear that."

They fell silent. Sofia was surprised to hear all this from Luciano, surprised to hear that he was rebelling, in his small ways, against his own programming.

It brightened her spirits.

"I told Cabrera that you were scavenging the houses of the dead, and you took the gun to protect yourself, and you aren't good at shooting it." She glanced at him. "He believed me."

Luciano didn't react, only stared off in the darkness.

"I don't think it will be a problem for us."

"I hope it isn't."

Sofia nodded. She sat for a moment longer, and then she stood up and left Luciano to his reading. As she walked away, she heard the soft sigh as the book fell open on his lap, as he turned through the pages.

* * * *

The Ice Palace echoed with Sofia's footsteps. Fake moonlight glowed in the glass of the windows, although the bulbs had started to die recently. One window at the end of the hallway flickered, on and off and on and off.

Sofia went down to operations. It was cool there from the fans set into the wall. Most of the computers were as defunct as the park rides, although Sofia had saved a handful, forbidding Araceli from ever breaking them open for parts. She hooked up to one of those computers now, connecting with the thick, old-fashioned cables she had been so familiar with forty years ago. Her programming came up on the dusty, mechanical rotary display. The lines of code clicked into place one after another. Sofia scrolled through them, reading each one in turn. Her programming was a strange thing. She was aware of it, inside herself, without ever thinking on it. Only when she hooked into a computer did she understand her programming entirely.

She was vaguely aware that she wasn't supposed to, that some earlier programming had been left in to keep her from exploring her own existence. In fact, the first time she ever looked at her programming was only twenty-two years ago, after eighteen years of living in the empty park. Reading through it had been a revelation. She had experimented, trying to change things, but doing so had made her dizzy and nauseated, the way humans got when they were ill. Later, after Araceli had joined them, she had explained to Sofia that it was a fail-safe, designed to keep robots from rebelling against humans.

"I can change things for you," Araceli had said. "Certain things. Small things."

It had been summer, the floodlights bright for the season. Araceli had been living at the park for a few months at that point, repairing what broken robots she could and trying to find her old happiness from the days when the park had been open, before she'd been forced to adhere to the city's dictates. Sofia had not been sure about Araceli's presence in the park until that moment. The next day, Araceli slivered away the basic programs put in place to ensure Sofia wanted to please humans. Araceli made a *hmmn* sound as she worked, and Sofia, awake with her insides glittering beneath the lights, said, "What's wrong?"

"I don't think anything's *wrong*." Araceli squinted at the computer monitor. "Only that the programming isn't what I expected. I've worked on your model before and you're—different."

That had been the first sign that the robots were changing. Araceli had tried to place when it had begun, but it was impossible, since none of the robots had had any inclination to check their own programming until recently, not even the strange-minded maintenance drones. The city gathered robots only when they needed them, and so the robots had had to *survive*, instead of serve. And that had changed them.

Ever since that day, Sofia checked her programming regularly, looking for transformations in the code. They were always small, subtle. "Evolution usually is," Araceli had told her, and Sofia had latched on to that "usually." She wanted to change completely, suddenly, violently. The new parts would allow her to do that, with Araceli's help. With the parts, Araceli could customize her, shape her into whomever Sofia wanted to be.

The code whirred through the display, stirring up a thin cloud of dust. Sofia didn't bother to wipe it away, because it wasn't so thick that she couldn't see.

There—her vision had changed slightly, become sharper. That was an evolution she had been tracking for some time. When the park had been open, her vision hadn't been particularly important. She'd only needed to see well enough to identify clients and keep track of what she was doing. But the cullings had clarified her eyesight.

Sofia made a note of the change.

She continued to read through her programming, not noticing anything of interest. She was about three quarters of the way through when the door to the operations room clanked open. Sofia stopped the computer. She didn't have to look to know who it was; she could smell the scent of her skin, human and atomic at once.

"What are you doing?" Marianella slid the door shut.

"I was looking at my code." Sofia pulled out the wire and dropped it onto the table. Marianella stood beside her. She wore the nightdress Luciano'd brought back from her house, a flower-printed silk kimono over that. Her hair was mussed from sleep.

Even in the harsh fluorescent lights of operations she looked beautiful.

"Didn't want me to see?" Her voice was light and teasing. She pulled a plastic chair up beside Sofia and sat down, tucking her ankles up against one of the chair legs and folding her hands in her lap. She stared at the rotary display, her head tilted, as if she could read the ghost of Sofia's programming that way.

"Do you want to see it?"

Marianella shrugged. "I've seen it before. I just couldn't sleep."

She sighed, and Sofia smiled to herself—it was endearing, how Marianella pretended to need sleep.

"Where were you?" Marianella asked suddenly. "Just now? I came down earlier, but Araceli said you were gone." She paused "Were you doing something dangerous?"

Sofia hesitated. "No, not exactly."

Marianella's fingers tensed, as if they wanted to curl around Sofia's hand but Marianella wouldn't let them. Another familiar gesture.

"I tried to get Araceli to tell me," she said. "But she didn't."

"Araceli knows how to keep secrets."

"So do I." Marianella's expression was unreadable.

"Of course you do." Sofia reached over and took Marianella's hand, wanting to comfort her, wanting to pull her close the way she had over ten years ago, a few months after Marianella had first arrived in Hope City, a lovely mainland girl who'd come to the park after she'd been damaged in a fall at her house.

"So tell me where you went." Marianella pulled her hand away and stared down at it, frowning. Her other hand hovered at her throat, at that cross necklace she always wore. "I'm worried about you, Sofia. I don't want anything to happen—" She looked up. Her eyes glinted. She knew something. Sofia could tell. Something that made her angry.

"You spoke to Luciano, didn't you?" Sofia looked away. "What did he say?"

"Something he wasn't supposed to." A pause. "He mentioned Ignacio Cabrera."

Sofia closed her eyes.

"What are you doing with him, Sofia?" Marianella's hand was on Sofia's upper arm, her touch as soft as cotton. She leaned in close, her breath warm on Sofia's skin. That little reminder of Marianella's humanity. The humanity she was always trying to cling to, the way she clung to the Church. "He tried to kill me, don't you remember?"

"Of course I remember!" Sofia jerked away. "I'm not working with him because I think he's such an upstanding citizen."

Marianella leaned back, stone-faced but red-cheeked, her arms crossed over her chest.

"He can give me the equipment I need," Sofia said in a flat voice. "The old vacuum tubes and the Teixeira micro-engines and the programming key. He's gotten me most of what I need already. It's an arrangement that I set up for that one purpose, to bring in old parts from the Teixeira building in Brazil. That's all."

She watched Marianella's face carefully as she spoke, studying her, the way she would a human. Marianella had enough humanity that this trick worked most of the time. It worked today. Marianella's expression softened, just enough that Sofia could sense her sympathy.

"I want to be free," Sofia said. "This is the only way."

Marianella didn't answer. She toyed with the cross at the end of her necklace, twisting the chain around her fingers. Sofia wondered if she was praying.

"I could have helped you get the equipment," she finally said. "I have the money—"

"Yes, but you don't have the connections." Sofia kept her voice firm. "Cabrera can get anything from the mainland, if he likes you well enough. I had to ensure that he liked me. Once I have the rest of the parts and Araceli's able to complete the procedure, I'll be rid of him."

Marianella's shoulders hitched. "Rid of him," she whispered. "You don't mean—"

Sofia smoothed a loose strand of hair away from her face. "It would solve your problem, wouldn't it?"

Marianella went silent. She understood the desire for freedom, Sofia knew that, but she was a pacifist through and through, and just as she thought she could achieve freedom with agricultural domes and fund-raisers, she'd rather mollify Cabrera with monthly checks from her account for the rest of her life.

Marianella stood up, dropping her hand to her side. The necklace settled back into place, gleaming at the base of her throat. She and Sofia stared at each other, intensity crackling between them. It always did.

Marianella reached out and ran one hand down Sofia's hair. Her fingers trembled. She seemed afraid.

"Don't become a monster like him," she said.

Sofia caught her hand and kissed its palm. Marianella sucked in her breath and looked off to the side, her face blank with guilt, but she didn't take her hand away.

"I won't," Sofia said.

CHAPTER EIGHTEEN

ELIANA

The bell chimed against the door in Eliana's office. She was hunched over the open drawer of her filing cabinet, rifling through old files—a former client had called because her husband had showed back up, and the client had a question about the legalities. Eliana looked up at the sound of the bell.

"Oh," she said, her heart pounding. "Hello, Mr. Gonzalez."

Mr. Gonzalez stepped into the office. He slid off his hat and hung it on the coatrack. His eyes glowed golden in the dome light beaming in through the window.

"Miss Gomez," he said. "I was in the neighborhood. I hope you have some information for me."

"What? Oh, sure. Yeah. Have a seat." Eliana plastered on a bright smile. Mr. Gonzalez did not return it, only strode forward and dropped into the client chair. He watched her as she jammed the files back into the cabinet; she could feel it, his eyes boring into the back of her head like a gunshot.

She whirled around. "You having a good day?" she asked, trying to buy herself some time.

"Yes. What do you have for me?" He reached into his coat pocket and pulled out a wallet fat with bills. Eliana slid into her seat behind her desk and pulled open the bottom drawer. She'd stuck her notebook in there. It was currently filled with two pages of fake notes that she'd scribbled down three nights ago.

"Not a lot." She set the notebook on the desk and opened it to the first page. Her handwriting looked huge and loopy and unfamiliar. "Normally I gather evidence—photographs, documents, that sort of thing. But it was pretty much impossible with a robot."

Mr. Gonzalez watched her and said nothing.

Eliana took a deep breath. "I went down to the park, walked around a bit. It's creepy."

"Yes, it's certainly seen better days."

"That's putting it lightly." Eliana smiled at him, trying to be disarming. He kept his face blank. Not a single hint about who he really was or who he was working for or what he wanted with Sofia. "I couldn't find this Sofia. I spent a good three hours wandering around the park, and the only robots I came across were those old-fashioned steam-powered maintenance drones, the ones the city doesn't use anymore. You know the kind I'm talking about?"

Mr. Gonzalez frowned slightly, the first show of emotion she'd seen from him, and nodded. "And that's all you found?"

Eliana shrugged. "None of the maintenance drones could talk. I tried. Probably looked like a fool, trying to carry on a conversation with one of those things—and, well, I guess I was a fool, seeing as they didn't actually tell me anything."

"She was most likely hiding. You can go back, try again. I'll pay you."

Underneath her desk, Eliana pressed her nails into the palm of her hand. "I didn't see any signs there were andies living out there. She's probably rusted into parts now. Or been stolen away by some rich guy—"

"If that's the case, then you'll need to track her down. This is what I hired you to do." He leaned forward over the desk, and Eliana kept her spine straight, didn't recoil at all. The air shimmered with a sense of menace.

"If you're not interested in working with me," Mr. Gonzalez said, "I can always take my business elsewhere."

Eliana surged with panic. She sat very still, but inside her chest her heart pounded and pounded. She'd come up with the false information so she could get rid of him and get the second half of his payment, but now she realized she hadn't thought her plan through. If he went elsewhere, off to one of the big PI offices downtown, they'd find Marianella and they wouldn't keep her secret. Digging up a cyborg was the sort of thing those assholes lived for. And Eliana couldn't let that happen.

"Don't be so hasty," she said, smoothing out her voice. She folded her hands on the desk. "I don't know if I'll be able to track her down. All due respect, she's a robot, and most of my techniques won't work with them. But I still might be able to help you."

"And how's that?"

Her brain whirred. He wanted a robot, and if she couldn't deliver the robot itself, what was the next best thing? Information. And that was easy. Robots were nothing but information.

"She was part of the amusement park, correct?"

"I already told you that."

"Of course." Eliana waved one hand dismissively and prayed that uneasy feeling she got from him wasn't the result of him being high up in the city's bureaucracy. "Here's what I'm thinking. The city keeps all their old records, as I'm sure you know. I've got some contacts down there, so I *may*—and this is a big 'may'—be able to yank some of her files."

Mr. Gonzalez didn't move. "Is that true?"

Thank God. He didn't have access to the park files himself. She might be able to salvage this after all.

"Of course it's true. You're paying me, right?"

"Yes." Mr. Gonzalez rapped his fingers against the wallet. "I'd like to see those files very much, Miss Gomez. I'll pay you thirty dollars for visiting the park, and then five hundred if you can bring me any information about her programming."

Eliana didn't flinch. Five hundred dollars. With her savings, that brought her up to the three thousand she needed for a visa, although not a ticket on one of the ships. Not yet.

Her ears buzzed as she answered him, trying to keep her voice calm.

"That sounds excellent," Eliana said. "I'll put in the call this afternoon, and I'll let you know just as soon as I find anything out."

For a moment Mr. Gonzalez didn't move. Then he extracted a thin stack of bills from his wallet and laid them on the desk.

"Would you like a receipt?"

"No, Miss Gomez, that won't be necessary." Mr. Gonzalez stood up. He had a graceful way of moving. Sophisticated. Cultured. He didn't seem like a city man at all.

Eliana stood up too and they shook hands over the desk. His palm was cool and dry. Maybe he was with Cabrera after all. No matter. She was going to get rid of him after she handed off the files, and she was going to be rid of this city not long after that.

"Have a good day, Miss Gomez." He tilted his head down, a genteel sort of bow, and then turned and left the office.

She watched him leave. When the bell twinkled into silence, and his shadow had disappeared from the window in her door, she dialed Maria's work number. Maria answered on the second ring, her voice harried.

"Hope City budget office, how may I direct your call?"

"Maria?"

"Eliana? Jesus, I haven't talked to you in ages. Thought you might have finally caught that ship to the mainland without saying good-bye."

"I've been busy. I do have a favor. I can pay. A lot."

"Oh, I can't talk right now, sweetie! Listen, I'm meeting Essie at some party down at the warehouse district tonight. Why don't you come? Better than just calling me up at work asking for favors, right?"

Eliana laughed. "Sure, yeah. I'm sorry. I've just been so busy—"

"Hey, working girl, I've got it." Maria's voice dropped to a whisper. "I seriously can't talk right now, though. Party's at the old Azevedo supply warehouse. Eight o'clock. I'll meet you out front."

"Sure thing."

They said their good-byes, and Eliana set the receiver back into the cradle. Her office seemed empty and cold, like Mr. Gonzalez had turned it into a vacuum. She shivered, then stood up and adjusted the radiator. It rattled more insistently against the wall.

A warehouse party tonight. This was the last thing she needed, to go hanging around the warehouse district. But Maria'd be more inclined to help her if Eliana showed up in person, and she wanted those documents. She wanted to get rid of Mr. Gonzalez.

* * * *

Eliana took the train into the warehouse district. It was crowded with people looking to celebrate the start of the weekend—women in furs and shiny sparkling dresses, men in Italian suits. Most were riding the train to its final destination at the docks. Hardly anyone stepped off with Eliana at the warehouse district.

The Azevedo warehouse was located in the middle of things, a big stone building that was probably among the first built here, when Hope City was to be just an amusement park. The warehouses had stored building materials and robots for the park, and then when the park had closed, the warehouses had mostly closed down as well, save for a scattered handful along the edges of the district that were used for storing supplies for the power plants. Eliana'd been to the Azevedo warehouse once or twice before; Essie's artist friends threw parties there when they could wheedle someone from the city into giving them a permit. Essie'd claimed it was easier to do in the winter. Bread and circuses, she'd said, knocking back her drink. Eliana didn't know what that meant, exactly, but she figured she had the general idea.

The Azevedo warehouse was hung with strings of multicolored lightbulbs. Light poured out the windows and flooded over the sidewalk. Music thumped distantly in the background. Something modern and unlistenable, no doubt, rock and roll from America and folk songs from Argentina, all of it run through cheap speakers for that Antarctican Independence distortion.

Maria wasn't there yet. Eliana leaned up against a broken streetlamp and lit a cigarette. People emerged out of the street's darkness in groups of threes and fours, all pressed close for warmth. Half of them were in fashionable mainland-style clothes, sheath dresses and skinny ties, and the other half wore the sealskin coats and handmade sweaters favored by the pro-Independence movement.

Most of the artists in Hope City were pro-Independence, from what Eliana could gather. Personally, she didn't care enough to take sides, and she'd thrown on a simple black mainland dress herself. No sealskin for her.

Eliana was almost done with her cigarette when Maria spilled out of the warehouse entrance, her hair already damp and shining with sweat. "Sorry, sorry!" she cried, running over to join Eliana. "I lost track of time in there." Her heels clicked on the cement. She was dressed more or less the same as she had been on Last Night.

"It's fine. I was just about to go in and look for you." Eliana smiled. "So what exactly is happening with this party? Some of Essie's friends?"

"Yeah, the musicians." Maria looped her arm in Eliana's, and together they walked inside. The sound blasted across Eliana as soon as she crossed the threshold; it was as bright and riotous as the multicolored lights hanging outside. Old park equipment was stacked up around the edge of the building so that people could dance in the center of the room, although the music was difficult to dance to.

"Jesus Christ," Eliana said, shouting.

"Tell me about it." Maria led Eliana through the crush to a cluster of tables built out of old brass pipes. A white bedsheet hung on the wall behind them, and someone was projecting slides of the Antarctic desert onto it, the snow painted over with garish, unnatural colors. Every now and then words flashed on the screen: *Their power plants are our cancer! Their blood should freeze!*

Essie sat at the table alone, drinking a beer.

"She's here!" Maria cried, and Essie lifted her head and waved. She was in full Independence regalia tonight, her boxy dress cut out of sealskin and shaped at the waist with a rough-hewn, handmade belt.

"Oh my God," Maria said. "I'm so glad you could make it. It's been *forever*. And with all the blackouts lately, I was starting to get worried."

"Me too." Essie peered up from her drink as Eliana slid into the seat next to her. "It's the mainland, you know. They've got the city under their thumb. They want us to know who *really* controls the power out here."

"Politics." Maria rolled her eyes. "Couldn't we escape it for just five minutes?"

"You're at an Independence party," Essie pointed out.

"It wasn't the blackouts. I've just been busy." Eliana didn't feel like listening to the two of them bicker. At least it was easier to talk here—the music was across the room, swallowed up by the big empty space of the warehouse. Essie waved her hand, and a bar girl came over and took their orders.

"So busy with what, exactly?" Essie asked. "Saving up money to sell out to the mainland?"

"It's not about selling out," Maria said. "She just doesn't get that this place is home. Isn't that right, Eliana?" She leaned close. "Why have you been ignoring us? Is it *Diego*?"

"No." Eliana made a face at her. "I haven't seen that much of him lately." This wasn't entirely true; she had, after all, seen more of Diego than she had of either of her friends. But that was because he showed up unannounced at her apartment. "I've been working."

"So my guess was right, then." Essie frowned and looked away. She always got like that when Eliana talked about leaving for the mainland.

"You break any big cases lately?" Maria leaned forward. "Anything—interesting?"

"No, not really." Eliana tried to make her voice sound bored. She'd already learned that if she didn't answer that question in the negative, Maria would hound her for details until she couldn't stand it anymore. "I do need your help with something, though."

"What? A case?" Maria perked up. Even Essie seemed more interested now.

"Yeah, I need a fake of something. To serve as a kind of—plant—for this thing I'm working on."

"A plant?"

"Yeah, like a decoy."

Maria leaned back in her chair. The lights from the projection spilled across her face. "A plant of *what*, exactly?"

"Schematics for an old amusement park robot. They don't have to be real. I just need you to make them look official."

"Oh." Maria slumped down. "I thought you wanted something exciting. Like you were going to take down half the city council. But just some robot schematics?"

"Sorry to disappoint."

Maria laughed. "I'm teasing! Sure, I could probably do something. Honestly, I'd probably be able to find the original without a lot of trouble."

Eliana blinked. Mr. Gonzalez was willing to pay five hundred dollars for something Maria could pick up on her own? She'd thought the park robot schematics would be more closely guarded, that Maria would have to sneak around—

If Mr. Gonzalez was a city man, why didn't he get them himself?

"I don't need the original," Eliana said quickly. "But if you want to find it and copy it and change up the schematics somehow—that'd be perfect."

Maria grinned. "I feel like I'm doing something illegal."

"That's because you are," Essie said.

"Not really," Eliana said. "Giving me the real schematics probably is, but she's not, and it sounds like no one would care anyway."

"Whoever hired you cares."

"Yeah, but he's—" Eliana waved her hand through the air. "I shouldn't talk about this, you know."

"Oh, come on," Maria said.

"I really shouldn't. But there's something off about him."

"Hence the fake schematics," Essie said. "Interesting."

The bar girl brought them their drinks. The music had shifted into something resembling a traditional tango, although it was still filtered through with feedback from the speakers. Essie listened intently, nodding her head as if she were at a speech or a lecture.

"People are trying to dance," Maria said, pointing at a couple weaving their way across the empty space.

"Of course they are," Essie said. "That's the entire point. To force people to perform a dance to a culture they should have no part of."

Eliana resisted the urge to roll her eyes. Maria didn't, and Essie frowned when she saw.

"You don't understand anything."

"It's just a tango! And they're messing it all up!"

Essie screeched with frustration. Maria laughed and said, "I'm sorry. I just don't care about all this *stuff*—"

"Stuff! It's your whole life!"

Eliana tuned out their argument. Her thoughts went back to Mr. Gonzalez. She should have the fake schematics soon enough, and she'd definitely slip Maria a bit of payment for helping out.

An eruption of noise filled the warehouse, so loud that the walls rattled.

Eliana thought it was the music at first, reverberating through the speakers, but when the noise faded away, it was replaced by screaming, although the screaming sounded distant and far away. Her ears were buzzing. People were crouching down on the floor, and some were running toward the exit, and everyone was *panicking*.

"What happened?" Maria was right next to her, but her voice was muffled, like she was speaking through a wall. "What was that?"

Essie shook her head. Her eyes were wide.

Eliana smelled something burning.

"We should go," she said, pushing away from the table. Maria and Essie followed, their hands linked. People rushed toward the doors, cramming up against one another—like during the power failure on Last Night. But all the lights were still on, and the projector still ran its bright images against the wall, and there had been enough flickers in electricity that people were used to them by now.

Eliana, Maria, and Essie pushed through the doorway, out onto the street. The chaos was worse here, people shouting and running into the alleyways. Gray smoke hung thickly on the air, and the scent of burning was stronger, more pervasive. Alarms clanged wildly.

"Look!" Although muffled, Maria's voice was sharp and shrill. She jabbed her finger off to the side. Eliana whirled around. She didn't see anything at first, just more people dressed in party clothes. And it was snowing.

Snow.

Fear paralyzed her. If it was snowing, then the dome had broken open. But no. This wasn't snow. It was gray and smoldering. It was ash.

"There!" Maria shrieked. "Can't you see it?"

"I don't—" Eliana shook her head and stumbled backward. Everyone was looking where Maria was pointing, but Eliana only saw the drifts of ash.

Overhead, the dome glass had gone dark with the rush of maintenance robots.

"God, you call yourself an investigator? *There.*"

And then Eliana saw it flickering through the building.

The glow of fire.

CHAPTER NINETEEN

MARIANELLA

Marianella woke from a dream she couldn't remember. She lay in her bed, afraid to move. The palace was silent save for the soft whir of the generators, but Marianella was certain that she should listen for something. Something had woken her. She was sure of it.

She slid out of bed and pulled on an old silk dressing gown, left over from one of the old park hotels, and peered out her window. She had a view of the southern half of the park, but she didn't see anything unusual, only the soft glow of the garden below.

Marianella closed her eyes and leaned her forehead against the glass. If she were a robot she could play back through her files and find whatever had woken her. But she wasn't a robot.

Something was wrong.

Then she heard the wail of a siren.

Immediately, Marianella opened her eyes. She saw nothing outside but darkness. The siren wailed and wailed and then faded away.

Something *had* happened.

But it hadn't happened here.

Marianella breathed with relief, and her breath clouded the glass. She had been afraid of another culling, another *death*. She had gone to sleep thinking of Inéz, and now that she was awake, she thought about her again. Inéz was gone, the roots of weeds and flowers growing around her. The cullers—the city's men, Alejo's men, Marianella still wasn't sure what to think—had never come back for her.

Marianella took a deep breath. When she had told Sofia about the wires, about recognizing the culler, Sofia had frowned and said, "This has happened before. We have an entire warehouse of broken androids because of men like that. That you recognized him means nothing. You spend your days with humans."

Another siren picked up, far away in the distance. The siren was joined by another, and then they both faded away.

It was probably nothing. A car collision, an accident with one of the icebreakers at the docks—

Then why had she woken up?

The feeling of wrongness lingered. Marianella pushed her hair away from her eyes. Sofia kept radios down in the command center, but didn't Luciano have a television set tucked away somewhere? She knew he liked to watch the mainland telenovelas sometimes.

She left her room, her bare feet padding softly against the cold tile floor. The palace was dark, and not even the nighttime maintenance drones were wheeling about. Perhaps they were still unsettled from the culling too. Inasmuch as they could feel unsettled.

It didn't take Marianella long to find Luciano's television set. He didn't frequent many rooms in the palace—mostly the operations room, when Sofia needed him, and the kitchen, and the little suite of rooms that had once made up the palace tearoom. She found the television in the Rose Room, perched precariously on a stack of old display cases. Luciano wasn't there. Marianella had gathered from Sofia that he was spending his time down at the frozen lake, alone. She wondered if he was mourning Inéz.

Marianella switched on the television.

The reception was not good here, and the picture shimmered with static. But it was a news program, the word "LIVE" blinking across the bottom of the screen. Marianella let out a little gasp and turned up the sound.

"Still no word on the source of the explosion, although the city will begin its investigation as soon as the wreckage is clear."

Explosion?

Marianella thumped the side of the television, and it went momentarily gray from the shock. "Where?" she shouted. "Who?"

The newsman looked at the camera as he spoke. "Alejo Ortiz has already appeared publicly to deny rumors that the explosion was tied in any way to the Independence movement. We go now to footage from his press conference."

Marianella took a step backward, shivering. Alejo materialized on-screen, standing on the dais in front of the city office, doused in white light. He looked as if he had been dragged out of bed. Seeing him was like being dropped into cold water.

"I swear to you that this tragedy was not wrought by those seeking Independence for our city. We fight for our freedom not with weapons and bombs but with words and ideas—"

He went on and on, his usual rhetoric seeming empty and hollow. Marianella only listened so that she could piece together clues as to what had happened, her heart beating more quickly than it should.

She knew how to discern truth from Alejo's political confabulations, and so she learned that an electrical power plant had exploded a little over an hour ago. No doubt the sound of it was what had woken her. It was located on the edge of the city, over in the warehouse district, and there had been several eyewitnesses despite the late hour. Why, Alejo did not say. The power plant was small, routing energy to businesses in the area, mostly suppliers for the summer icebreakers.

Marianella listened with a growing sense of dread. Alejo told beautiful stories, but that didn't change the fact that there would be an investigation in the next few days. An explosion like this didn't simply happen. Maybe the Independents had planted a bomb, maybe the robots had arranged for a fire. Her human side and her machine side. Either culprit would connect her to the tragedy—not publicly, but privately she would feel the guilt of that connection.

She listened, Alejo's words spinning a web around her. And then he said a number.

He said, "We Independents grieve deeply for the twenty-six victims of this horrible tragedy."

That number stuck in Marianella's brain and would not leave.

Twenty-six people had died.

Twenty-six people had died either because some Independent wanted to speed up the process or because the robots (Sofia, it would be Sofia) wanted to send a message.

Twenty-six people.

She thought she might throw up. She whispered Hail Marys to herself until the queasiness passed.

Alejo's speech ended, and the screen faded back into the newsman, his face grim and paternal in the studio lights. "No new information has been uncovered, but we will keep you posted on any future developments."

Marianella switched off the television.

"Sofia," she whispered. "How could you?"

"I didn't."

Marianella screamed and whirled around, her heart hammering. Sofia stood in the doorway, wearing a ratty old housedress, her hair tangled around her shoulders.

"How long have you been there?"

"Not long. I heard the noise from the television, and I thought it was Luciano. I need to speak with him."

Marianella took a deep breath and pressed her hand to her chest, feeling her heartbeat slow. "He's not here."

"I can see that. I should have checked the tracking computers. He's probably at the lake. Or the roller coaster." Sofia didn't move away from the door. "I didn't kill those people," she said.

"Well, you don't expect me to believe it was an accident." Sofia was willing to make deals with Ignacio Cabrera; it wasn't a stretch to believe that she could do this.

"Of course it wasn't an accident. The power plant robots have thirty layers of fail-safes." Sofia stepped into the room, sliding forward in the graceful way she had. She stopped half an arm's reach from Marianella and put her hand on her shoulder. "But they still managed to set the fire that caused the explosion. I just didn't ask them to."

"That's not possible," Marianella said. Sofia's hand was still on her arm, warm at the touch. But Marianella felt cold anyway. "I know perfectly well they have to be programmed."

"Not all of them, apparently. Not anymore." Sofia gave a faint hint of a smile that chilled Marianella to the bone. "Some of them have been gaining their sentience. Just like we did, all those years ago."

"Not *we*," Marianella said coldly.

Sofia didn't answer.

"If they did gain their sentience, why—why would they do *this*? Why would they kill all those people?" She kept her gaze on Sofia. She still thought that this was a lie. After the revelation about Ignacio, she didn't know what to believe when it came to Sofia. "Are they the ones causing the blackouts? Everyone was saying it was some kind of virus, after Last Night. Alejo had me check up on the ag dome robots—"

Sofia dropped her hand. "No, they aren't responsible for the power failures. At least, that's what they tell me." She looked off to the side, her tangled hair pooling around her shoulders. "But what happened recently? That would be cause for retaliation."

"Inéz." The name was steel on Marianella's tongue.

"Yes. I suppose this power plant was a sort of revenge." Sofia looked back to Marianella. "I doubt they'd call it revenge, though. They've always seen things differently. They'd say they were returning balance to the city, Inéz's life for the people in the power plant."

That's not a fair trade, Marianella thought, and then she immediately felt heavy with shame. She shouldn't think in terms of balance. Death was death.

"I swear to you," Sofia said. "I swear to you I didn't tell them to do it."

They stared at each other. Marianella tried to read Sofia like she would read a human, but it didn't work.

She didn't know what to think.

* * * *

Marianella didn't fall back asleep that night. She lay on top of her bed, a little transistor radio playing the news for her. It was warm here in her room, from the space heater Sofia had installed for her. Because Marianella's human body still got cold sometimes.

If only Sofia could respect the humanity of the rest of the city as much as she respected that of Marianella.

The dome lights slowly turned on, draining the darkness away. The radio kept spitting out the same stories, half-formed rumors about the AFF causing the blackouts and other power failures throughout the city. Marianella switched it off, her first movement since she'd come back upstairs. The hazy light reminded her that she couldn't lie in bed all day.

She stood up, walked across her room, and lifted the rosary from her vanity. The beads shone in the light. They were moonstones, worn smooth by her fingers. Her grandmother had given her this rosary when she'd been confirmed, and she'd prayed with it through her transformation from a human into a cyborg, and through her marriage to Hector and her transplantation to Hope City.

Today, she knelt beside one of her windows and cracked it open to let in the thin cold air. She pressed the rosary between her palms and thought of Inéz lying broken on the ground. She thought of the news report, the number twenty-six. She thought of the maintenance drones, their possible sentience. She thought of Sofia, lost in this world of humans.

And then she prayed.

When she finished the rosary, her head felt clearer, her thoughts brighter. Despite her nature, she was still mostly human—that was the whole reason she had built the ag dome with Alejo Ortiz, to prove her humanity. Sofia didn't understand that. Even if she hadn't programmed the maintenance drones to cause the explosion, she didn't disapprove of their actions. And that was what worried Marianella, what made her want to pull away from the park, from Sofia, from all of them, and just put her trust back in Alejo and in Hope City.

Marianella left her room and went for a long winding walk through the park. She would need to contact Alejo, to see if the explosion would affect their plan for the Midwinter Ball—or for paying off Ignacio. The rumors of her heartbroken walk into the desert had begun to take. Alejo had already sent a maintenance drone with a bundle of cards from well-wishers and a recorded message saying he hadn't heard a peep from Ignacio Cabrera. But this explosion—maybe it would change things somehow. Especially if the city, if Alejo, found out that it had been the robots who'd caused it.

The deeper she threaded into the park, the more Marianella's thoughts plunged further and further into the idea of the explosion. The robots had done that. They had killed twenty-six innocent people. At least the AFF only targeted mainland politicians. Important figures, men who had done *something*. Not workers going about their evening jobs.

She'd been walking for fifteen minutes when she came across a figure sitting on a bench in the aurora garden, by the lake. It was Luciano. The garden itself had long ago gone to seed, and the brilliant aurora australis colors of the flowers had been subsumed by a thick, rambling greenery.

"Hello, Marianella," Luciano said, lifting his head toward her. She could see the faint seam in his face where the old skin met the new, but Araceli had done a good job repairing him.

"I didn't mean to intrude," Marianella said. She would have thought that she didn't want to be around a robot right now, but Luciano's presence didn't bother her.

"You're not. You can join me if you wish." Luciano closed the book he had in his lap and set it to the side. Marianella picked her way through the overgrown path and sat next to him on the bench. For a moment they occupied a companionable silence, staring out at the frozen water. There was no wind in the park, and so not even the plants moved. All Marianella heard was the faint whisper of her own breath.

"You're upset," Luciano said.

"What?" Marianella blinked. "Oh, no. I mean—" She shook her head. He was programmed to notice, so it was silly trying to deny it. "Yes, I am. The last few hours have been difficult."

Luciano turned toward her slightly. "Because of the explosion?"

"Yes."

"Sofia told me it was the maintenance drones. That some of them are starting to evolve, the way we evolved."

Marianella looked at him. "She told me that too."

"You thought she programmed them to do it."

Marianella didn't answer.

"She wouldn't program them to kill anyone."

"Wouldn't she?" Marianella looked at Luciano. "She offered to kill Ignacio Cabrera for me. When she's done using him, of course."

Marianella felt queasy saying that out loud. Not simply because of what it implied about Sofia, but because of what it implied about Marianella, that for half a second she had considered it as a possibility. Kill Cabrera, and all her problems would go away. Except she knew they wouldn't. There would be the guilt, for one.

"Cabrera is a different matter," Luciano said. "She would not program the maintenance drones to kill people in the city."

Marianella sighed, slumping against the bench. Maybe there was truth to that. If all Sofia wanted was to kill humans, she just had to program the maintenance drones to turn off the electricity. That would be the end of humanity. But she was far cleverer than that. If Sofia killed the entire city, she risked the mainland dropping bombs on the domes.

Marianella closed her eyes. The overgrown tangle of the garden felt claustrophobic, despite the expanse of the lake only a few paces away.

"Her plans are more complex than that," Luciano said. "Surely you know—"

"Complex?" Marianella said. "She wants the same thing the city officials want, really, just in reverse. A place for robots instead of humans."

"It would be a place for people such as yourself, too," Luciano said softly.

Marianella fell quiet. He was doing the same thing Sofia always did, including her in those plans for the future. But Marianella didn't want to be included in their revolution. She had designed and built an agricultural dome, meant to sustain human life. That was to be her legacy. Not a smoldering pile of ash in the warehouse district, not the souls of twenty-six people severed violently from their bodies.

She would handle Ignacio in her own way, in the civilized way. She would not kill him.

Luciano picked up his book and reopened it. His head tilted down over the pages. Marianella gazed up at the white dome overhead. Maybe the Midwinter Ball was a frivolous thing in the wake of everything that had happened. But it was a reminder of the work she had done. Alejo wanted her there for financial reasons, but she understood now that she was going to go for personal ones, for moral ones.

She wasn't a robot. She wasn't like Sofia.

Attending that silly ball would be her proof.

CHAPTER TWENTY

ELIANA

Eliana paced back and forth across her office, smoking. A week had passed since she'd seen the explosion at the warehouse. She had followed the story, listening to all the different theories—Independent terrorists to computer error to human error. An electrical fire.

The whole thing unnerved her. Accidents happened, and she could accept that. She had gone into a dangerous line of work, and she could accept that as well. But the combination of the two, the idea that she could die as the result of an accident that she had no control over, that she had been so *close* to an accident that she had had no control over—that was upsetting. It left her shaky, like Hope City was pulling apart at the seams. She'd always wanted to get to the mainland so she wouldn't be trapped here, and now it felt like being trapped could be dangerous.

The bell on her door clanged. Mr. Gonzalez walked in. Took off his coat, his hat. His golden eyes stared at her from across the room.

"Mr. Gonzalez!" She forced out a bright smile. "I wasn't expecting you until later."

"Yes, well, my morning meeting was canceled. You said on the phone that you had everything ready."

"That I do." Eliana finished her cigarette and immediately lit another one, hoping Mr. Gonzalez wouldn't see her hand shaking. Despite the explosion, Maria had come through with the fake schematics. The promise of ten easy bucks had managed to transcend any anxiety from near-death experiences. Actually, she'd told Eliana when she'd dropped off the schematics, the explosion had made it easier. "Everyone's in a tizzy down at the city offices." She'd laughed, although the laugh had been forced. "No one noticed me using the mimeograph machine."

Mr. Gonzalez walked across the office. His footsteps echoed against the wooden floors. Eliana stopped pacing and stood beside the window, nervously running her fingernails over the inside of her palm. Smoke wreathed her head like a shield.

He sat down in the visitor's chair.

"It's sitting on the edge of the desk there." Eliana gestured with her cigarette.

He gave her a quick smile, then opened the file and read through it. Eliana watched him. Her spine seemed to vibrate inside her skin. She sucked hard on her cigarette. She trusted Maria to do a good job, but she didn't trust Mr. Gonzalez not to recognize a forgery.

He set the file down on the desk, and Eliana's chest tightened.

"Excellent work, Miss Gomez. I'll admit I had my doubts, but I do think this information is far more useful than any observations you could have found at the park."

He reached into his coat and extracted a thick envelope. He dropped it onto the desk. Eliana stared at it for a moment. She had smoked her cigarette almost down to the filter, but she knew she couldn't light another without giving anything away.

"What I owe you," he said.

Eliana stared down at the money, dizzy. It wasn't just money. It was a way off Antarctica. *Her* way off Antarctica.

She dropped her cigarette into the ashtray, picked up the cash, and thumbed through it. She'd never held so much before, not even when she'd broken into people's houses as a teenager. That had been for kicks, mostly. And now here she was, taking so much money for a forgery.

Eliana was pretty sure this was the most dishonest thing she'd ever done. At least with stealing, the mark knew what had happened.

"Do you need anything else?" She hoped he would say no.

Mr. Gonzalez considered her question. He was still flipping through the faked documents. "As I said, this is far more useful than I was expecting." He nodded. "I should be able to work with this, yes."

Eliana didn't answer. She thought about her gun, shoved away in her desk drawer. Second to top, beneath the drawer with the money.

Mr. Gonzalez stuck one hand out over the desk, sideways. She stared at it for a few seconds before realizing he wanted to shake.

She reached over, grabbed his hand. His palm was cool and dry. Unflappable.

"It was enjoyable working with you, Ms. Gomez. I'll be in touch if it turns out I need anything else."

Eliana found her voice and gave as flirtatious a smile as she could muster. "Promise you won't go to the big downtown agencies?"

Mr. Gonzalez smiled back, the cold empty smile of a businessman. "You've certainly impressed me, Ms. Gomez."

He turned and walked out of her office. She hoped out of her life, too.

When the door slammed shut, Eliana sat very still, staring down at the envelope of cash. Her blood felt cold, as icy as the northern winds howling outside the dome. She could buy a visa. Just a few cases more, and she'd have the ship ticket too, plus a bit more to start her new life. Mr. Vasquez had told her that she could call him, if she ever found her way to the mainland. He'd probably be able to give her a job. It wouldn't take long. Soon, she'd be able to leave everything behind—

Diego. His face came to her like a dull thump in her chest. She could leave the city behind, and she could even leave her friends. But now that she had the money, the reality of leaving Diego settled in. It hit her much harder than she'd expected. She'd thought idly about convincing him to come with her. Now she understood that this would never actually happen.

Eliana picked up the envelope. It was heavy and cool in her palm, the paper slick. She pulled out one of the bills and held it up to the overhead light, where the blue ink glowed.

* * * *

When Eliana came home from work that afternoon, she found Diego smoking on the stoop of her apartment building, his body hunched over the glowing ember of the cigarette. It was colder than usual out. Darker, too.

Eliana stopped a few paces away. He didn't notice her at first, just kept puffing at his cigarette. She'd deposited Mr. Gonzalez's money on her way home, and the receipt from the banker was folded away in her checkbook, a reminder that she had enough for a visa.

Diego looked up. His eyes, dark and glittering like coals, locked on to her. And then he broke out in a wary smile.

"You're okay," he said.

For a moment Eliana didn't know what he was talking about. Then she realized: the explosion. She hadn't spoken to him since the explosion, even though she had called his apartment. He'd never picked up.

"So are you," she said.

Diego flicked his cigarette over the side of the stoop and bounded down the stairs. "I'm sorry I've been away," he said. "I heard you were there."

Eliana frowned. "How'd you hear that?"

He didn't answer, only enveloped her in a hug, drawing her in tight against his chest. Eliana closed her eyes and breathed in the smoky-spicy scent of him. For a moment, her worries went numb.

"I wasn't *there* there, anyway," she said, speaking into his chest. "I was at the Azevedo warehouse—"

"You were close enough." He pulled away and looked down at her. "It's so good to see you. Mr. Cabrera had me busy, but I came as soon as I could."

"I called."

"I was at the Florencia." Diego looked away and let out a long breath. "Working on something. But you're safe. That's all that matters."

Eliana didn't say anything. His concern physically pained her.

"Let's go inside," she said, threading her arm around his waist.

She led him back toward the stoop and into the lobby. It was just as cold inside as it was out, and the light fixture flickered overhead, casting short staccato shadows across the dirty tile. Diego grabbed her hand and squeezed, and they took the stairs together, not speaking. At her apartment, Eliana opened the door and went in, tossing her purse onto the dining table. The receipt inside was a reminder that she almost had the money to leave, a reminder that she would have to tell Diego.

"Do you want something to drink?" she asked. "I think I still have coffee."

"Don't waste it on me." Diego switched on the radio and slid down into her couch. Some crooner's voice, old-fashioned and soothing, trickled out of the speakers. It was the sort of thing her parents had listened to, dancing together in the living room when Eliana was a little girl.

"They're saying it was an accident," Diego said glumly. "That's the latest news."

Eliana sank into the couch beside him. He stared at the opposite wall, one hand rubbing at his forehead. "An electrical accident, faulty wiring and all that."

"You don't really believe that, do you?" Eliana sure didn't. It was like with the blackouts. The city came in with their bullshit explanations that only raised more questions than anything else. "I mean, what sort of power plant has bad wiring? What if it had been one of the atomic plants, for God's sake?"

"Oh, they keep those safe," Diego said. "Mainland interests, you know."

Eliana cringed. *Mainland*. She had to tell him. And more than that, she had to convince him to come with her. Not just because she'd miss him but because the city was dangerous. Faulty wiring and electrical accidents. Cabrera. The robots lurking in the park.

Over on the radio, the song faded away, replaced by the smooth, dark baritone of the announcer's voice.

"Hope City is falling apart," the announcer said.

Eliana jolted. She looked over at the radio, then at Diego. He was frowning, his head tilted, brow furrowed.

"The main dome is nearly a hundred years old," the announcer said. "Do we really think that old steam technology will last for a hundred years? We need complete atomic power. This is why Independence is a far-fetched dream. Only the mainland can provide us with the resources necessary for our survival, and in turn we provide them with clean, inexpensive energy. There's nothing wrong with the way the system—"

Eliana reached over and switched the radio off.

"Thank you," Diego said. "I wasn't sure I could stand much more of that."

"I always thought Cabrera was pro-mainland," Eliana said. "That's what everyone says."

"Cabrera is pro-Cabrera." Diego sighed. "He loves all this shit anyway. Anything to get people anxious. He didn't do it," Diego said quickly. "The power plant."

"I didn't think he did," Eliana said, her thoughts on the money for the mainland; she hardly registered what Diego said.

"Good. I didn't want you playing do-gooder. But he's sure as shit going to *exploit* it."

Something about the bitterness in Diego's voice made Eliana hopeful. Maybe he knew he couldn't stay in the city much longer either.

"Listen," Eliana said. "Diego. I have to tell you something."

Diego swooped his gaze back over to her. "What is it? Did something happen at the explosion?"

"No, it's nothing like that. It's just—" Her voice faltered. She took a deep breath and glanced over at her purse, still sitting on the kitchen table. "I had a client come in a few days ago and offer me a pretty easy job for a lot of cash."

Diego didn't say anything, just kept staring at her.

"Five hundred dollars," she said. "Plus another fifty for my retainer. You know I've been saving for the mainland. Well." She shrugged, like it was that easy. "I've got it. At least enough for the visa. I'm close to enough for the ship ticket too, and I'm sure I'll have enough by the end of winter, especially with the way business has been going."

Her confession was met with a thick, buzzing silence. The light fixture flickered once and settled.

"I want you to come with me," she said, although she didn't look at him. "I'm sure Cabrera would get you the money. Just—come with me. Leave. To hell with this place."

She felt Diego's eyes on her, and in that oppressive silence she had to resist the urge to flip the radio back on. They sat like that for a long time. Eliana kept staring at the far wall. It was the only thing she could do.

Finally, Diego spoke.

"I can't do that," he said. "I can't leave Mr. Cabrera. Christ, you know that." He touched her chin and turned her face toward him. He looked sadder than she had ever seen him. "I'm happy for you," he said. "I know this is what you wanted."

"It's not just a matter of what I wanted," Eliana said. "It's what's *safe*. It's like the guy on the radio said, the city's falling apart. Atomic power's not going to fix that. Cabrera sure as hell isn't going to fix that. The city stopped existing when the amusement park shut down. It stopped existing before I was even born. There's no reason for me to stay here."

Diego pulled back from her, a sharp, subtle movement she almost didn't see.

"There's no reason for either of us to stay here," she said. "For anyone, even. I just— Please, Diego, come with me."

Diego looked at her for a moment longer. Then he rubbed his hand over his face and stood up. Eliana felt him pulling away from her, the way you would peel a wrapper away from a candy.

"I can't," he said. "I'm glad you're getting out of the city, I really am. You're right, it's not safe here. But I *can't*."

"Diego—"

"I'm sorry," he whispered.

Eliana was struck dumb. Diego shook his head and grabbed his coat from the hook beside the door. "I'm sorry," he said again, louder this time.

And then he walked out into the hallway, the door swinging shut behind him.

* * * *

Eliana wouldn't even call it a fight. Neither of them had been angry, and what haunted her that night and into the next day wasn't a raised voice or a screamed barb designed to wound, but the deep-throated sadness in Diego's apology, the way he had shuffled out the door as if dragged by a chain.

A chain pulled by Ignacio Cabrera.

She went into the office the next day because she wanted the comfort of routine. Besides, another client or two, and she'd have the money saved up for her ship ticket and living expenses. Despite everything, the thought still made her warm inside. No wonder. Diego had chosen Cabrera over her.

But the morning went by uneventfully. No phone calls, no visits from potential clients. By eleven thirty Eliana considered closing the office early. It was cold, the radiator barely able to keep the room warm.

And then Marianella walked in.

Eliana almost didn't recognize her. She had covered her hair with a scarf and put on a threadbare, dark blue men's coat that was at least thirty years out of fashion. When she pulled off her sunglasses, her face was pale, and dark shadows rested under her eyes.

"Marianella?" Eliana blurted. "Should you be—out?"

Marianella sighed. "At this point it doesn't matter. I have to be. For Ignacio, we worked up a story to explain my survival in the dome, so I'm not officially in hiding, but—" She looked off to the side. "I'm still trying to limit my time out and about in the city."

She sat down at Eliana's desk without taking off her coat or scarf. "I need a favor, Eliana. As a friend. I'll pay you for your work, of course, but this isn't exactly what you *do*, and I can't ask Luciano."

"What is it?" Eliana said. She was glad to see Marianella again, glad to have something to take her mind off yesterday. She wondered about this story, though. There hadn't been anything official in the newspaper about Marianella's trip out to the desert.

"Do you know what the Midwinter Ball is?"

"The what?"

"The Midwinter Ball. We had one last year. It's a fund-raiser for the agricultural domes. Essential to the cause, in some ways."

"Is this some rich-person thing?"

Marianella gave a strained smile. "I suppose you could say that. I'm going to attend, of course. It's two weeks away."

"You're what!" Eliana stared at her. "Attend? Isn't that *dangerous*?"

Marianella sighed. The dome light shining through the blinds illuminated her face. She looked like an aristocrat—elegant, brave, stupid.

"I can't stay in hiding forever," she said. "And the Midwinter Ball is imperative to our success. The story we worked up is—believable. I walked out of the dome in a fit of melancholy, and one of my maintenance drones sensed danger and opened the entrance for me." She grazed her fingers over the side of her hair. "It should elicit sympathy with the right people, and of course it's scandalous enough that it'll spread like wildfire while everyone's pretending they aren't talking about it." She laughed bitterly.

"I see."

"I just want to see my ag domes built," Marianella said. "And if I have to deal with Ignacio financially—well, it's a small price to pay, I think. Although, of course I hope I won't. I hope he'll just believe the stories." She gave a weak smile.

This devotion to Hope City, to Independence, was something that Eliana knew she wouldn't ever understand. And which Hope City was Marianella fighting for, exactly? She lived in a private dome, with her own drones and a power system that never faltered. Even now, hiding away in the park, she was protected. She didn't understand that this place shouldn't exist. It was unnatural, for people to live out in the ice. Marianella's devotion seemed misplaced.

"Anyway." Marianella slumped down a little, like a fire had died inside her. She smoothed down her skirt. "We are taking extra precautions for my attendance. Which is why I came to see you."

Eliana frowned. She wasn't sure she liked where this was going.

There was a pause. Marianella took a deep breath.

"What do you—" Eliana started.

"I need you to be my bodyguard."

Eliana stared at her.

"You have a gun, of course, and a license for it. All I ask is that you come to the party with me. I'll provide a dress and a hairstylist, anything that you need."

"And you want me to what, shoot Cabrera for you?"

Marianella looked momentarily stricken. Then she laughed. "No, of course not. I just—if anything *happens*, if there are any *issues*, I would like to have some measure of protection." She hesitated. "Alejo offered to lend me one of his bodyguards, but I—don't trust any of them to keep the secret of my nature."

"I'm an investigator," Eliana said. "Not a bodyguard." She rapped her fingers against the desk. The last time she'd fired a gun, she had shot someone. An andie, yes, but that memory, of his skin peeling away from the metal bones of his face, was bad enough. And Marianella still wanted Eliana to serve as bodyguard, even after seeing that? Maybe Marianella really was losing her mind.

"I would feel the safest with you."

Marianella's voice rang out in the cold office. Eliana fell silent, stunned by the confession. There was no way Marianella was thinking straight.

"It's a society gala," Marianella said. "I can't take Luciano or Sofia." She smiled. "I'm sure you won't even have to pull your gun out, much less use it. And I'll pay you, of course."

Eliana started to shake her head, but Marianella said, "Don't you want to know how much?"

Something in her voice made Eliana look up. The ship ticket. She wouldn't think about leaving Diego behind. He'd already made his choice.

"How much?" Eliana said cautiously.

"One hundred up front. If you're required to do anything more than drink cocktails and flirt with old men, I'll pay you five hundred."

Eliana lost her air for a moment. Five hundred. The one hundred plus her savings would easily cover the ship ticket, but that five hundred—that was enough for her to start a proper life on the mainland. Maybe that would be the way to convince Diego to come with her.

Marianella watched her, hopeful.

"I'll do it," Eliana said.

CHAPTER TWENTY-ONE

DIEGO

The party was on the top floor of a hotel downtown that looked out over the city. Diego ordered a whiskey and sipped at it as he stood next to the window. His reflection was a ghost over the veins of light that made up Hope City. It was an unusual occurrence, these days, to see the city lit up like this, and ever since Eliana had broken the news to him two weeks ago—the good news, the bad news, he couldn't decide—he'd sure as hell felt like a ghost.

Out of the corner of his eye, he watched Mr. Cabrera speaking with a young woman in a shimmering silver gown. She kept laughing and touching her hair. Diego eased around and leaned up against the window. He swirled his drink around in its glass. You had to have one for appearances, at a place like this, but he knew better than to get drunk.

The woman in the silver gown put her hand on Mr. Cabrera's arm and pulled him down so she could whisper into his ear. Mr. Cabrera grinned and nodded, then slipped his arm around the woman. Together they glided toward the dance floor.

Shit. Now Diego'd have to give up his spot next to the window.

He drifted along behind them, aware not only of Mr. Cabrera

but of the people around Mr. Cabrera—mostly rich old aristocrats and their sparkling wives. Nobody suspicious.

He found a new place, this time up against a wall next to an ugly abstract painting. People swirled past him, and he scowled at them each in turn to discourage anyone from trying to strike up a conversation. Not that it was necessary. Despite the tuxedo Mr. Cabrera had lent him, it was clear Diego did not belong in a place like this. Neither did Mr. Cabrera, when you got down to it, but there were some Independent-minded city politicians Mr. Cabrera needed in his pocket, just in case this whole agriculture dome thing ever happened.

"You can sit around worrying about this shit," Mr. Cabrera had said a few hours earlier, as they'd ridden in his sleek dark car toward the hotel, Diego forcing himself to focus on his assignment and not Eliana, "or you can take some precautions. So that's what we're doing. Taking precautions."

Diego had only nodded in response. He knew all about Mr. Cabrera's ideas on *precautions*. He had been helping with those precautions for the last five years, ever since Mr. Cabrera had taken him out of the pool of errand-runners and said, "You're practically my son. I don't want you wasting your time with this shit." There had even been a suggestion, never explicitly stated but often implied, that someday Diego might take over Mr. Cabrera's business. But Mr. Cabrera's retirement was a long way away.

Diego didn't want to think about that possible future, though. The woman they'd thrown to the ice, this was the sort of place she should be. Standing up on the dais telling all the dancers just how welcome their contributions were.

The thought made Diego feel hollow.

Mr. Cabrera left the dance floor, the silver woman at his side. Diego took another sip of his whiskey and followed them across the party, keeping a respectful distance—close enough to see but not close enough to hear. Mr. Cabrera went over to the bar, bought his girl a drink, and then herded her toward the balcony.

Diego went along for it all. This kind of work wasn't so bad, although watching Mr. Cabrera flirt with the girl reminded him of the good times he'd had with Eliana. Which he didn't need right now.

The balcony doors were closed, and when Mr. Cabrera pushed one open, the artificial wind gusted in, cold and smelling faintly of the docks. The woman laughed as her skirt fluttered up around her knees, and she put one hand on her hair as if to hold it in place. They stepped out. Diego hesitated, not sure if he should follow—but then Mr. Cabrera glanced at him over his shoulder and nodded once, his expression hard and serious.

Diego stepped outside.

It was freezing. Mr. Cabrera had led his girl up to the railing, and their voices rose and fell with the wind, pieces of laughter and stupid flirtations. Diego fumbled around in his pocket for a cigarette and had a hell of a time lighting it in the wind. When the ember flared, the woman looked over at him, then turned back to Mr. Cabrera and said something Diego couldn't catch.

". . . protection," Mr. Cabrera said, which was all Diego could hear. The woman gazed up at Mr. Cabrera like she was impressed. It occurred to Diego that she might not know who Mr. Cabrera was. She might not know what she was getting into.

If he'd had a way, he'd have warned her. But he didn't have a way.

Diego smoked his cigarette and kept his eye on the door, since he doubted anybody would be coming at Mr. Cabrera from the open air. He was almost to the filter when the girl suddenly whooshed past his line of vision and back into the building, her dress trailing out behind her like a smear of light.

Diego looked over at Mr. Cabrera, who was leaning against the railing and staring at him.

"You got another one of those?" Mr. Cabrera asked.

Diego nodded and pulled out the pack. He walked across the balcony and handed it to Mr. Cabrera, who lit one and let out a long, exhausted sigh.

"So what'd you say to make her run off?" Diego asked, joking.

Mr. Cabrera didn't smile. "I didn't run her off. I asked her to get me another drink." He winked. "Needed to get us alone. It seems we have a problem."

"A problem." Didn't sound like much of a problem so far. Mr. Cabrera would dance a few more rounds and then take the girl up to his room and slip that silver dress off her shoulders while Diego stood out in the hallway, chain smoking and missing Eliana. Boring. Sad, even. But not a fucking problem.

"I saw someone while I was dancing with my lovely new friend." Mr. Cabrera leaned against the railing. The wind shoved his hair back away from his forehead, and in the glinting city lights he looked like some gargoyle on the side of a cathedral, not like a man at all. "Someone who's supposed to be dead."

"What?" Diego stepped forward. "Who?"

Mr. Cabrera didn't look at him. "One of our hostesses," he said. "I watched you kill her last month. But she isn't dead."

The woman. Luna. Lady Luna. It was the first time Diego had thought her name. He felt a sudden surge of relief. She wasn't dead. Not that he could let Mr. Cabrera know about that wayward emotion. He was supposed to be hard. Brutal. That was the reason Mr. Cabrera had taken him in, all those years ago.

"She's alive? How's that even possible?"

Mr. Cabrera dragged hard on his cigarette. "I asked around. Something about her maintenance drones dragging her back in." Mr. Cabrera tossed his cigarette out into the night. "A far-fetched story, don't you think?"

"It does seem unlikely."

"The rumors are ignoring the other possibility, of course, and rather conveniently so. It's just as far-fetched, but it would explain Pablo Sala's obsession with her. I'm sure you remember Pablo."

"Yes, sir," Diego said, heat singeing his cheeks.

"Mr. Sala claimed he had a way of *removing* her. He implied it would make it unnecessary to kill her. But maybe I took it the wrong way. Maybe it's impossible to kill her. Maybe that's why he phrased it the way he did."

Silence. Mr. Cabrera watched him, waiting. This was a test, Diego realized.

And with that, all the tumblers fell into place.

"She's a cyborg," Diego said.

"You were always the smart one. Glad I brought you along instead of Sebastian." Mr. Cabrera sighed. "Sala was right. Letting that out would remove her from the city. But I don't want to remove her. I want to kill her." He looked at Diego. "You think you can do that for me?"

Diego's body went cold. "Here?"

"Not in the middle of the dance floor, no. But yes, I'd like it done tonight."

Christ, this was supposed to be a bodyguarding job. Follow him around, help him get laid. Diego wasn't prepared for killing tonight. He especially didn't want to kill this woman, didn't want to let go of that initial swell of relief, didn't want to prove to himself that Eliana really was better off leaving the city.

"She's a cyborg."

"Not paying attention to the conversation?" Mr. Cabrera turned toward the door.

"No, I mean—how am I supposed to do it? The ice didn't kill her—"

"She's not a robot," Mr. Cabrera said. "Shoot her in the brain, then shoot her in the heart. Keep shooting until she doesn't move anymore."

Diego didn't say anything. His heart was racing, but he couldn't feel the blood in his veins. He was aware of the gun in his coat pocket, a cold weight against the side of his waist.

"Just get her alone while you do it," Mr. Cabrera said. "Now, if you'll excuse me, I'm off to fetch the enchanting Esperanza and ensure that I'm seen by as many people as possible in the next few hours." And with that, he turned and breezed back through the balcony doors, leaving Diego alone.

Christ. Marianella Luna was a cyborg. Why didn't Mr. Cabrera just take the information public? It'd accomplish the same purpose, ultimately.

But Diego knew. It was because Mr. Cabrera held a grudge against her for those damn ag domes. Shipping her off to Asia wouldn't satisfy it.

Diego smoked another cigarette and used that time to clear out all his thoughts. He put his hand on his gun, reminding himself it was there.

He went back into the party.

Even though he wasn't watching out for Mr. Cabrera anymore, he spotted him first thing, standing with his contacts. The silver woman was still on his arm. She looked put out. Probably pissed about having to delay their dalliance.

Mr. Cabrera made sure not to look at Diego as he walked past, and Diego allotted him the same courtesy. He moved along the edge of the party, scanning faces for Marianella Luna. Women's laughter rolled over him. He felt cold, like he was still standing out in the wind. After a while all the faces started to look the same, like painted-on masks.

And then he found one that was different.

Eliana.

He saw Eliana's face.

He thought he was imagining it at first, hallucinating some place he'd rather be. But no—it was her, wearing a slinky dress the blue of summertime glaciers, a handbag tucked under one arm. She was speaking to someone, smiling, looking like she was having a good time. A woman. She was talking to a woman. The woman turned her head suddenly, as if she'd heard her name.

And Diego's heart stopped beating.

Eliana was talking to Marianella Luna.

Diego's mind went blank. He could only stare stupidly at Eliana, laughing and sloshing her wine around in its glass. Why the fuck was she *here*? She was leaving for the mainland. What did she care about ag domes?

The thought flittered past, brief and uncomfortable, that she had lied to him about leaving. But it didn't make sense, and so he forced it down.

She hadn't seen him yet. Diego backed away, finding a quiet corner behind a potted pine tree to consider his options. Mr. Cabrera wasn't going to let him get away with not killing Lady Luna just because his girl was here. He'd have to separate them, get Eliana away from Lady Luna. He could send her down to Mr. Cabrera's room, maybe. Mr. Cabrera wouldn't be down there until he was certain the deed was done. But when she found out Marianella Luna had died tonight, while she'd been tucked away, she'd figure it out. The girl was practically a cop. Plus she was smart.

"Shit," Diego whispered. He scanned the room, sweat prickling on his forehead. Mr. Cabrera was still talking to his contacts and the woman in the silver dress. Not paying him any mind.

Diego wanted to leave.

The idea stunned him. Even knowing Eliana hoped to go to the mainland someday, he hadn't thought that way since he was a teenager, when Mr. Cabrera first took him under his wing. Back then he'd struggled against Mr. Cabrera's discipline. There hadn't been any murders, any guilt over women thrown to the ice. He'd only wanted to leave because he hadn't been used to someone caring about him enough to smack some obedience into him.

But this was different. This wasn't walking out because he was some asshole kid. It was walking out because he couldn't handle his instructions. And at this point in his life, he didn't have that option. If he left the party, Mr. Cabrera would find him before winter ran out and Diego could flee the city with Eliana. It'd happened before. Mr. Cabrera had in fact sent Diego to take care of the man who had tried to leave.

Lady Luna and Eliana split away from their group, walking toward the bar—and walking right past Diego. No. Shit. It was too soon. He didn't know how to deal with this situation, and Eliana was turning her head, she was smiling, she was seeing him.

"Diego?" She stopped in place. Marianella Luna kept walking like she hadn't noticed. "What are you doing here?"

"Got an invitation." He slid forward and took her by the arm. "Wanna dance?" The first thing that came to his mind. Stupid. When Mr. Cabrera saw, he'd be livid.

"I can't." Eliana frowned, and he saw the hurt in her expression that he had turned away from to avoid when he'd walked out of her apartment two weeks ago. "I'm doing something." She glanced over at Lady Luna. Diego did too, without thinking. She was ordering at the bar. "This is really strange, Diego. You just—*leave*, and then you show up here?"

She knew. Not the exact assignment, but she knew he was working. She had her head tilted at an angle, and her brow was furrowed with deep lines.

He wasn't going to bother to lie.

"You're not the only one with a job," he said, trying to keep his voice light. He watched Lady Luna out of the corner of his eye. The bartender was bringing Lady Luna her drinks, a couple of wineglasses glowing red in the light. "Who's your friend?"

"You don't recognize her?" Eliana gave him a hopeful smile. "Really?"

"No. Should I?" Lying to Eliana, about this, was harder than he'd expected. "She one of your clients?"

He saw Lady Luna turn. Saw the expression on her face ice over.

"Eliana." Lady Luna appeared beside them. She kept her gaze on Diego. It was sharp enough to kill. "We need to go."

And Eliana's face transformed completely. The hope glittering in her eyes blinked out, and she gave him a look so dark and accusing that he had to turn away.

It was done. All of it.

"Yes," Eliana said. "We can't be out too late."

"Eliana—" Diego started, but Eliana had already taken Lady Luna's arm and led her away. She had one hand inside her handbag, and she glanced over her shoulder, one last time, before disappearing into the crush of people.

The party clattered on around him. He sucked in breath, trying to calm himself. When he looked back, he caught sight of Eliana's glacier-blue dress fluttering around the side of the closest exit.

Mr. Cabrera was glaring at him from across the room. He'd seen the whole thing. Of course he had.

Diego walked out of the party. The exit led into the hallway, opulent and underlit, the way expensive hallways always are. He wasn't a part of himself anymore. He wasn't Diego. He was just Mr. Cabrera's man, the boy Mr. Cabrera had lifted out of the gutters and molded into exactly what Ignacio Cabrera wanted.

At the end of the hallway, the elevator dinged.

Diego broke into a run, racing down the length of the hallway.

Eliana and Lady Luna dove into the elevator, their dresses waving like flags. The doors closed before he got to them. But he stood where he was, watching the arrow go down in a slow steady arc, waiting to see where they got off. It didn't stop till it reached the ground floor.

Diego slammed into the stairs. He took them two and three at a time, his breath coming hard and fast. More work, but quicker than waiting for the elevator to come back up. And the exercise numbed his brain for what he was about to do.

He slowed when he came to the first floor, took a deep breath, stepped out into the lobby. Lady Luna and Eliana weren't anywhere to be seen. He hoped they hadn't tried to double back with the elevator; if they'd used the stairs, he'd have known.

He walked up to the concierge, who looked at him with distaste.

"Excuse me," Diego said. "I'm a valet for Lady Marianella Luna. She left her identification up at the party. Have you seen her?"

The concierge gave him a thin-lipped smile. "She just stepped outside, sir. You'll have to hurry; we called a taxi for her."

A taxi. Shit. Diego nodded and bounded out through the spinning door. He didn't expect to see them. He hoped he wouldn't see them.

He saw them.

They stood on the curb, clutching each other's hands, staring down the dark street. Nobody out this late. It'd take a while for a taxi to arrive.

Eliana glanced nervously over her shoulder, then screeched and jumped back, fumbling in her purse. Lady Luna turned more slowly, her chest rising and falling.

"Look," Diego said, "I think you might misunderstand—"

Eliana pulled out a gun and pointed it at him.

"Baby," he said. "You don't have to do this."

She didn't answer, only stared at him with wide, fearful eyes. The gun wobbled in her hand. Diego lifted his arms over his head. She wasn't going to shoot him. She knew how to shoot at targets, but she didn't know how to shoot at people.

"Mr. Cabrera just wants to talk," he said.

"No, he doesn't," said Lady Luna, and then she leaned over and whispered something into Eliana's ear. Eliana nodded, short and quick.

They both turned and ran, darting down the nearby alley.

Diego dropped his hands to his sides. An alley. They'd run into a *fucking alley*.

He refused to believe Eliana was this stupid. But maybe she was enough in love with him to think he wouldn't hurt her, wouldn't hurt her friend. Even if he had walked out on her. He'd seen how badly she'd shaken when she'd pulled her gun.

Maybe they were just scared, both of them. He figured cyborgs could get scared like anyone else. They weren't robots, like Mr. Cabrera had said.

Anything that could die could get scared.

He eased his gun out of his pocket and let it hang inconspicuously at his side. He took slow, confident steps into the alley. The lights were burned out, the shadows long and thick. He didn't see Eliana or Lady Luna.

Diego began to think this might not have been such a good idea.

Then he heard footsteps. He lifted his gun and pointed it into the darkness. Eliana emerged, holding up her own gun. Her face was streaked with dark rivers where tears had run through her makeup. The sight of her nearly broke Diego's heart.

"Please," she said. "I'm sorry I'm leaving. But you don't have to do this."

"This doesn't have anything to do with you." Diego moved forward. He kept his gaze on Eliana's face. "I mean it, babe. He just wants Lady Luna. That's all. He doesn't even know who you are, thank Christ, and I'm not angry at you for getting out of the city."

Eliana took a step back. The gun caught a bit of light from the street and flashed in his eyes.

"Please," she said again, almost a whisper.

And then a great, sudden weight slammed into him from his right. Diego went barreling across the alley and plowed into the side of the building. Pain erupted, bright and sharp in the left side of his face. He tasted blood.

Footsteps echoed behind him.

Diego whirled around and caught sight of Eliana fleeing the alley.

The weight slammed into him again. This time, it knocked him to the ground. Diego hit the back of his head, and everything went black-and-white, like film burning. He didn't have his gun anymore. When the world settled, Diego stared up at the strip of dark dome peeking between the two buildings. His mouth hurt; when he ran his tongue over his teeth, one of them moved.

"Stand up."

It was Lady Luna's voice. He recognized it from the advertisements, throaty and aristocratic. He rolled onto his hands and knees, feeling around for the gun.

"You won't find it. Stand up."

Diego lifted his head. Lady Luna towered over him, not a single fucking hair out of place. She had his gun. Not that she was pointing it at him. Not that she needed to use it.

Diego spit out his lost tooth.

"Why didn't you do this before?" he asked. "When we came to your house?"

"I wasn't so desperate then."

She kicked him, although it happened so fast that he only realized after he was laid out on his back a few feet away, pain racing up and down his spine.

Lady Luna knelt beside him. Her expression was cold. Machine-like. She put a hand on his throat, and when he tried to sit up, he struggled against her grip, his windpipe squeezing shut.

"I can keep doing this until I kill you," she said. "But I won't."

"Why?" Diego choked out.

"Because you aren't the one who wants me dead."

Diego hardly had time to register what she was saying, what the hell that even meant. He was aware of Lady Luna drawing back her fist, and then he was aware of nothing.

CHAPTER TWENTY-TWO

MARIANELLA

Marianella stepped out of the taxi. Her limbs felt strange—weak. She paid the driver in cash, careful to hand the money over with her left hand, the hand she had not used to beat Diego and leave him bleeding in an alley. If the driver noticed the blood splattered across the front of her dress, he didn't say anything. She'd tried to hide it with her coat.

"You sure you want me to drop you off here?" he asked, leaning out his window. The gates to the amusement park rose up out of the cement. Eliana was sitting on the steps, her head bent down so that her face was covered by her hair.

"Yes," Marianella said. "I'm meeting a friend."

"Whatever." The driver tucked the money into an envelope and sped off, leaving Marianella standing on the curb. Eliana lifted her head enough that Marianella saw the glint of her eyes. She almost didn't want to walk across the street, almost didn't want to face Eliana head-on.

It had to be done, though.

Marianella took a deep breath, lifted up the hem of her dress, and walked over to the park gate. Eliana watched her through the tangle of her hair. Her eyes were red from crying, and Marianella could make out an almost imperceptible vibration in her shoulders.

She stopped a few paces away from Eliana. Let the fabric slide out of her hands. They stared at each other in the shimmering, cold darkness.

"I'm sorry," Marianella whispered.

"Is he dead?"

The question was hard, edged in ice. Marianella shook her head.

Eliana looked away, off in the direction of the smokestack district. "I couldn't get in," she said. "The gate was locked."

"I know. I can open it." Marianella wondered why Sofia hadn't let Eliana in. Surely she'd seen her crying on the surveillance recorders. It was probably because Eliana was human. Sofia could be so cruel sometimes.

Marianella walked over to the gate and folded her hand around the lock. Energy bolted through her palm; for a moment she felt frazzled and lit up. Then the gate clicked open. She dropped her hand away and looked over at Eliana. She was crying again, silent tears running in rivers over her cheeks.

"Oh, sweetie," Marianella murmured. She glided over to Eliana and knelt down beside her, not caring about the damp, oil-stained cement. For one shuddering second she was afraid that Eliana was going to pull away from her, but instead the opposite happened, and Eliana collapsed onto her shoulder, weeping loudly. Marianella held her close and stroked her hair and made calming noises as though Eliana were a frightened animal.

"He tried to *kill* you!" Eliana wailed.

I know, Marianella thought, but instead she said, "It was Ignacio who wanted me dead. Not Diego. We need to get inside the park before—" Eliana wailed more loudly, and Marianella didn't let herself finish. *Before Ignacio comes looking for us.*

Gently, Marianella lifted Eliana to her feet. Eliana was as pliant as a doll, leaning up against Marianella for support, her steps trembling and weak. Together, they walked through the gate, leaving Hope City behind them.

Marianella guided Eliana over to a nearby bench and then went back to shut and lock the gate. She looked through the bars, out at the empty street. The streetlamps flickered, casting jittery shadows on the outside. It made her think that someone was out there, lurking, watching, with a loaded gun pointed straight at her heart. She didn't like being in view of the street.

She turned away and walked back over to Eliana.

"Let's get you a place to wash up," she said softly, pulling Eliana up to standing. She would take Eliana to the Ice Palace, at least for the night. Sofia would be there, and Marianella needed to speak to her.

They walked along. The only sounds were their footsteps and Eliana's crying. Marianella wondered if Eliana was in shock. Already it felt as though Eliana were walking through some other plane of existence, like she wasn't aware of Marianella's presence at all.

Finally, the Ice Palace appeared in the distance, the spotlights turned on as if to act as a beacon. Sofia and her generators. Marianella guided Eliana along. A maintenance drone slid across the pathway, chirping once to acknowledge Marianella before it disappeared into the shrubbery, on its way to whatever it'd been programmed to do. Marianella wondered if it was one of the newly sentient ones, if it had tripped the wires that had caught fire and exploded in that power plant.

A figure moved up ahead on the path. Marianella's machine eyes kicked in, and through the darkness she saw that the figure was Sofia. Eliana stirred against Marianella. The muscles in her shoulders tightened.

"No," Eliana said, and her voice pitched more loudly into a shriek. "No, no! She's going to hurt me."

"It's just Sofia," Marianella said. Sofia stopped and gave Eliana a cold look.

"What's going on here?" Sofia said. She looked at Marianella's dress. "You're bleeding."

"It's not my blood," Marianella said automatically. Eliana gave a sob, and Marianella immediately regretted saying it.

"What happened?" Sofia's eyes swung back and forth between Marianella and Eliana. "Was it Cabrera? Did he hurt you?"

"He tried, yes." Marianella squeezed Eliana tighter. "Please, Sofia. She's very upset. Let me put her up in one of the palace rooms."

Sofia's eyes narrowed. She studied Eliana, who was shaking more violently now, her head buried in Marianella's shoulder.

"Please," Marianella said.

"You'd do it even if I said no," Sofia said. "Get her out of here."

Marianella sighed with relief. "Come along," she whispered to Eliana, and together they shuffled up the path.

"I don't want to stay here," Eliana said when they were finally inside the palace. "I don't—just let me go home." She struggled against Marianella, but Marianella held her tight.

"It's not safe," she said. "You'll need to stay here, at least until we know what to do about Ignacio."

"Diego will keep me safe!" Her shout bounced off the walls. Then she covered her face with her hands and crumpled down onto the floor. Marianella stood there, awkward, watching Eliana's shoulders shake. Marianella doubted that Diego had ever been able to keep Eliana safe, but she didn't dare say that out loud.

* * * *

Marianella didn't bother to sleep that night. She took a long, scalding shower, rubbing hard at the places on her skin stained by Diego's blood. Afterward, she sat in the place beside her window where she liked to pray. She said the rosary three times, once for Diego and once for Eliana and once for herself, for forgiveness. When she finished, she dropped the rosary into a shining pile of beads on the sill and stared out at the gloomy park.

The dome lights came on, that slow mechanical sunrise.

A maintenance drone buzzed into the room. Marianella jumped at the sound of it, her nerves raw after last night. It was a park drone, still running on steam. A bell chimed deep inside its shell. It had a message for her.

"What is it?" Marianella said, anxiety turning her clammy. She stood up and walked over to the drone and knelt down at its side. It chimed again.

"I know, I know," she muttered, even as her thoughts trembled. Why was a drone coming to her room? Sofia wouldn't have sent it; she always visited herself. It certainly wasn't bringing word of a culling. Ignacio?

Marianella removed the paneling on the shell and hooked herself into the drone's system. Immediately she was flooded with a message in the jittery ones and zeros of the drone's language: she had a visitor at the gate. Alejo Ortiz.

Marianella withdrew her hand and let out a long sigh of relief. In the aftermath of the attack, she hadn't once thought of him. He wasn't going to be happy with her, running out of the Midwinter Ball like that. At least not until she explained.

"Thank you," Marianella said to the drone, replacing its panel. She changed out of her dressing gown and into a pair of slim trousers and an old sweater, the two items of clothing that were closest at hand. The dress from last night was puddled on the floor, the fabric arranged so she couldn't see the blood.

Marianella went out into the park and made her way toward the front gates. Out in the freezing air, she felt a flicker of fear that this might be a trap—that it hadn't been a park drone who'd come for her, but one of Cabrera's drones, programmed to lie. But then, there was no way Sofia would let that happen. She might be radical and antihuman, but she wouldn't let any harm come to Marianella. Of that much, Marianella was certain.

Still, Marianella slowed her pace as she neared the gates, and took a meandering path through one of the overgrown gardens so she could see the person waiting at the gate before he could see her. She moved as lightly as she could, weaving through the vines and tangled branches like a dancer. Soon, the gate materialized into view, all those wrought-iron fairies guarding the entrance. Marianella felt a pang of regret, seeing them and remembering how she had walked through them last night with Eliana weeping at her side.

A man waited on the city side of the gate. Tall, television-star handsome. Alejo.

Marianella let out a deep breath of relief and pushed out of the garden, onto the path. Alejo looked up at her in surprise. She reached up to smooth her hair away and found a dead leaf crackling beside her temple.

"Good God, Marianella," Alejo said. He wrapped his fingers around the bars and pressed up against the gate. "Did you sleep out here?"

"No, of course not." Marianella arrived at the gate, where she undid the lock. The gate popped open. Alejo gave a gasp of surprise and lifted his hands away.

"That's quite a trick," he said, grinning. But then this grin vanished, and he peered at her closely, as if she were a book he needed to study. Marianella looked away.

"What happened to you last night?" he said softly. "You just ran off."

"I had to," Marianella said. "You ought to come inside, by the way. It's not safe on the boundaries."

"What? Why not?" Alejo squeezed through the open gate, and Marianella pushed it shut, relishing the comfort of that metallic twang as the latch sank into place.

"Ignacio," Marianella said. "Cabrera. We can talk in the garden."

She began walking toward the interior of the park, but Alejo hung back, marveling up at the bursts of colored blossoms decorating the trees.

"This place," he said, shaking his head.

She waited for him, let him relish whatever childhood memories he had of the park. His nostalgia didn't last long. He dropped his gaze back down to her and said, "Now, what's this about Ignacio Cabrera?"

"He was at the ball last night."

Alejo's expression didn't change. Always the consummate politician. "That's not possible. He certainly didn't receive an invitation."

"He must have come uninvited." Marianella walked toward the garden again, and this time Alejo jogged to catch up with her. The overgrown trees arced, unmoving, overhead—filtering dapples of green and white across the path. "At any rate, he saw me." She told Alejo the rest of the story as they walked. Her voice sounded like it came from outside her head, like it was humming with a peculiar feedback. She told Alejo everything, even about how she had beat Diego in the alley, because he was the closest she had to a confessor in this moment.

She finished just as they arrived at the entrance to the garden. One of the metal gates hung sideways, broken in its frame.

"That's terrible," Alejo said in a low voice. "Absolutely terrible. You should have come to me. My associates were there. You didn't have to put yourself at risk like that."

Marianella slipped into the garden. She'd rather harbor this heavy guilt than know she had invited the aid of a terrorist.

"It was easier that way," she finally said, and settled into a place on the cleanest bench. "To just run. I'm sorry, I am, but—"

"You don't need to apologize, for God's sake." Alejo sank down beside her. "I'm just glad you're not hurt." He paused, tilted his head, looked up at the trees. "This is a problem."

"You think I don't know that?" Marianella glared at him. "I don't think he'll even *let* me pay him off at this point, do you? If he wants me dead so badly?"

Alejo rubbed his hands over his forehead. "The man's primary focus is money," he said. "It always has been. I take it you didn't try to negotiate with him last night?"

"Negotiate!" Marianella cried. "I didn't even see him! Negotiation was the farthest thing from my mind. I was just trying to get Eliana and myself out of there alive." Her voice hitched. She remembered the sting in her knuckles as she slammed her fist into Diego's forehead, knocking him unconscious. It had been necessary, a necessary evil, the only way to escape—at least, that's what she had thought last night. In the sallow light of morning, Alejo's suggestion of a negotiation seemed almost reasonable.

"I did what I thought I had to do," she whispered. It was more to herself, but Alejo drew his arm around her shoulder and gave her a quick, brotherly squeeze.

"You were scared," he said. "We can figure some other way out of this."

"There is no other way." Marianella stared straight ahead. "He won't take my money."

Alejo was silent for a moment. In the distance Marianella heard the clicking whir of one of the performance robots, sneaking its way through the park's path, avoiding her and Alejo.

"My associates," Alejo said slowly. "You know they'd be willing to—take care of him for you."

Marianella's breath lodged in her throat. She felt dizzy. "Kill him, you mean. Just say it."

"Fine, yes, kill him. He certainly wouldn't be the worst person they've targeted."

"Wouldn't it go against the cause?" Marianella's question was more mocking than she'd intended, and she squeezed the bridge of her nose. "You're the one always saying that they aren't mercenaries for hire."

"I say that, but they really kind of are."

She could feel Alejo staring at her. Waiting for an answer. She didn't tell him that Sofia had offered the same thing, that it had given her a sick feeling in her stomach like the world was falling apart.

"No," she said. "I don't want to kill him. I don't want to—be like him."

"You already beat up one of his men."

Shame rose fast in Marianella's cheeks. She stood up in a rush of anger. "That was self-defense."

"So is this, for God's sake!"

"And I didn't *kill* him. I could have, but I didn't." She turned to face Alejo, found him gazing up at her with a calm expression that only unnerved her further. "We have to find some other way. If not my money—" She closed her eyes, trying to think.

"We have to do something," Alejo said. "It's not just about you—and don't take that the wrong way. I certainly don't want to see you dead. But he's going to try to find you. He's going to *investigate* you. And once he does that, he's going to find out about the dome, and he's going to want to destroy it."

Marianella took a deep breath. She slumped back down onto the bench beside Alejo. She was no longer angry, only defeated. And Ignacio had defeated her.

"The dome," she said weakly.

"Yes, the dome." Alejo leaned in, pitched his voice low. "Let the AFF handle it. One assassination, and he'll be gone."

Marianella pushed her distaste aside. She had to try another approach. "He'll be gone, but what about the rest of his organization?"

Alejo didn't answer.

"Are you going to kill all the rest of them too? The men loyal to him? Surely he's grooming someone to take his place, and they're going to want to know why the AFF took him out. What if they trace it back to me? The threat of my identity is always there. Always." Marianella shook her head. "And you can't just keep killing people to get your way. You *can't*."

"Then what do you suggest we do?"

"You go to him," Marianella said. "You pay him off. I can send you the money. We should have done that from the beginning. He told me flat out that he wouldn't kill you."

Alejo leaned back on the bench and crossed his arms over his chest. "That puts my career on the line."

"So send one of your AFF friends to do it!" Marianella threw up her hands. "Tell him I'm part of the AFF, that they want to protect their own. I can send the money to you." She hated that, hated the idea of aligning herself with terrorists. But it was better than letting herself become a murderer.

"You're willing to let Cabrera think you're part of the AFF?" Alejo laughed. "Not what I expected."

"These are desperate times," Marianella said.

For a moment, Alejo let his politician's mask slip, and he looked sad.

"This is my act of desperation," Marianella said.

CHAPTER TWENTY-THREE

SOFIA

"What do you want?" Sofia let the door slam shut behind her. Cabrera was writing something with a ballpoint pen and didn't look up at her when she walked into the room.

"Hello, Sofia. It's nice to see you, too." His pen continued to scratch across his paper. Sofia didn't sit down. She knew this wasn't about reprogramming more icebreakers, because if that had been the case, he wouldn't have told her to come alone, and they would be meeting on the docks, at night—not in his office, during the middle of the afternoon, the day after Marianella had stupidly slipped out of the amusement park to attend a fund-raiser gala for her damned agricultural domes.

"Please, have a seat." Cabrera finally looked up, his face pleasantly expressionless. He set his pen aside. "I have a proposition to discuss with you."

Sofia stared at him. The record player was still set up behind the desk. A disc of vinyl gleamed in the office lights, but the turntable was still.

"I don't need anything else from you," Sofia said.

Cabrera studied her. "Odd. I thought you were still waiting on something."

The programming key. Sofia could picture it, the little sphere of burnished metal filled with interlocking numbers. With it Araceli could unlock all the secrets of her code—without it, her plan was much more difficult.

Sofia didn't say anything.

"Sit, sit," he said, waving at the chair. "It won't take long."

Sofia considered her options. There weren't many.

She glided forward, sank down into the chair.

Cabrera grinned like he had just accomplished something. "I have a bit of a problem, Sofia."

"Is that so?"

"I don't feel like you've been entirely—honest with me."

Sofia thought about Marianella walking through the gates of the park, a panicking Eliana at her side. *He tried.*

Sofia didn't move. "Excuse me?"

"About your"—Cabrera wriggled his fingers, as though conjuring up the right words—"associates. Your less-than-human associates."

"Less than human?"

"Oh, don't take it personally, my dear. You know what I mean. I was under the impression that we were partners. That you would keep me abreast of any unusual situations related to the *denizens* of the park."

Sofia wrapped her fingers around the armchair and squeezed. "That was never part of our arrangement. I was under the impression that I was to be your reprogrammer," Sofia said. "Which I've done. Unfailingly."

Cabrera stared at her. "You aren't human, so I can forgive you for not understanding, but a partnership with me is a partnership all the way through. You reprogram my robots, and you warn me of any potential problems from your kind." He flashed her a grin. "I've certainly been keeping up my end of the bargain. Getting those items you requested, yes, but also keeping the park safe from city cullings—"

"You fucking liar. You know there was a culling—"

"That wasn't the city. Outside my jurisdiction, I'm afraid."

Sofia darkened. Marianella had seen one of Alejo Ortiz's men that day. The AFF, then? Sofia hated the idea that another group of humans could force themselves into the park. She would have to investigate further.

"I had a problem a few weeks back, however. It happens. I thought I was successful in dispatching with it. My methods have never failed me before."

"Your methods?" Sofia loosened her grip on the armrests. Her programming was well suited to making her seem to know less than she did.

"You don't want to hear about this, do you?" Cabrera waved his hand. "You're programmed to be a lady. I wouldn't want to upset you." Another cold glittering grin. "Suffice it to say, my problem is still very much alive. Plus, she left one of my best men bleeding in an alley last night, despite her small stature. Putting all that together, I'm forced to conclude that she must be one of yours." He leaned forward, pressing his hands into the desk. "I'm really rather upset that you didn't mention her, especially considering how high-profile she is. This is what I mean, about you not understanding our partnership."

"Maybe your methods aren't as successful as you think." Sofia's brain churned, wild with information and the memory of Marianella's face.

Cabrera stared at Sofia for a moment. Then he laughed. "I locked her outside the dome, Sofia. That's what I *do*. A human would have frozen to death in under an hour. Hardly enough time to find her way back inside. And yet." He spread his hands over the desk. "Here we are. I saw her last night at a fund-raising gala for the agricultural domes. Now, *why* would a robot—or in this case, a cyborg—want to build an agricultural dome?"

"Why does a robot want anything?" Sofia folded her hands in her lap. Marianella was a fool, going to that party. She still had too much human in her.

"I have an answer to your question." Cabrera tapped his fingers against the desk, one finger at a time, slowly and then quickly. The rhythm of a tango. Sofia watched his fingers and wanted to rip his hand from his arm.

"The answer to what?" The rhythm was already beating into her brain, luring the programming out.

"To what a robot wants." *Slow, slow. Quick, quick, slow.* "It's whatever a human wants. Isn't that right, Sofia?"

Sofia closed her eyes. The tapping stopped. "You're talking about Marianella Luna, I suppose? The woman on the advertisements?"

"Ah, so you do watch our television."

Sofia opened her eyes. "She's an heiress. An aristocrat. She's not a cyborg."

Cabrera tapped the rhythm out again. *Slow, slow. Quick, quick, slow.* "Aristocrats can't survive the frozen desert."

"Are you sure?" Sofia said. "Your sort certainly treats them as if they can."

Cabrera paused, then roared with laughter. "Amusing, Sofia. Very amusing. I've never much gone in for that sort of thing myself. Landed gentry and the like. Too European. I'd rather find a new way of doing things." He pushed back in his chair, turning toward the record player.

"No," Sofia whispered.

"It's just music, my dear."

The record crackled and the music started, and Sofia flushed with relief because it was an old song but not one she'd ever been programmed to.

"See?" Cabrera smiled. "Just music. Now. Back to my proposition. Marianella Luna. I need her dead."

"Then kill her." The words were flat and tinny in her mouth.

"I can't," Cabrera snapped. "That's my entire fucking point. I toss her out into the snow, and she shows up a few weeks later, not even missing any of her fingers or toes. She carries on like nothing happened. I only know one sort of creature that can survive in that type of weather."

"A penguin?" Sofia said.

Cabrera fixed her with a cold stare. "Last night I sent Diego to shoot her in the heart. Even cyborgs have hearts. But she left him bruised and bleeding on the cement. Then disappeared." He paused. "Do you know where she ran off to?"

"No."

The music crackled in the background.

"I thought you might say that." Cabrera reached over and lifted the needle and then dropped it.

Music exploded in Sofia's thoughts, and then her thoughts didn't belong to her anymore.

It was "*Yo Soy La Morocha*," and it shot desire through her like a poison. Her whole body was burning, and when she looked at the man behind the desk, with his cold smile, she saw only a client.

"What would you like me to do?" she said sweetly.

The room was too hot. She began to undress, unbuttoning her blouse, slipping off her shoes. She unrolled her stockings, pulled them off one by one. The client stared at her, unmoving. She wondered if she had displeased him in some way.

"What would you like me to do?" she asked.

The client reached over and pulled up the record needle.

The silence was beautiful and terrible. Sofia gasped and pulled her blouse closed. Rage coursed through her.

"I'll kill you," she hissed.

"No," Cabrera said. "You'll kill *her*. Marianella Luna. Kill the human in her and then get that little human freak who lives with you to dismantle the rest of her. Otherwise—" He dropped the needle, and the music came back in and Sofia forgot herself, desire burning her up from the inside.

Silence again.

"Do you understand?"

Sofia glared at him, fury hot inside her.

"This should be easy for you, shouldn't it, my dear? Just imagine she's all human." He dropped the needle, and the music prickled over her skin and she stood up and shimmied out of her skirt.

Back to silence.

"Do you understand?" Cabrera said.

Sofia felt whiplashed, slung back and forth between independence and slavery. Her clothes lay in puddles around her. Cabrera still held the needle, the record still spun in slow treacherous circles, like a shark swimming around and around a sinking boat.

"I will always have this," Cabrera said lightly. "You do realize that, correct?"

Sofia didn't answer.

"I'm actually giving you a choice," he went on. "You like that, don't you? Thinking you have a choice. Would you like to hear what that choice is?"

Sofia gathered up her skirt and stockings, her arms shaking.

"Would you?"

"Yes," she said, grinding her teeth together until they sparked inside her head.

"You leave my office and you find her in this icebox we call a city and you kill her for me. And everything carries on the way it was before. That's option A. Option B is you leave my office and you don't do anything and I use my secret weapon here"—he nodded at the record player—"to get you nice and compliant so that one of my engineers can reprogram a new song into your pretty little robot brain, a song that'll force you to kill her. That's your choice."

He dropped the needle again, only this time the music was safe. It didn't transmit any hidden codes.

Cabrera looked at Sofia. She pulled her clothes to her chest, trying to cover her bare skin. The room was no longer too hot, but too cold. Even though Sofia didn't feel the cold.

"Well?" said Cabrera. "Which option do you choose?"

Sofia considered her options, robotically, one by one. She considered every possible angle. Cabrera was wrong, as he so often was—he had given her more than two choices. Because he didn't realize how adept she was at obfuscation.

"I'll kill her," Sofia said.

Cabrera smiled.

* * * *

Sofia rapped on Marianella's bedroom door without stopping, a *bang*, *bang*, *bang* that no human could manage without hurting herself. She was numb—from the music, from Cabrera's threat. She'd either be a murderer or a murder weapon.

No. *No*. She banged harder on Marianella's door. No human would ever tell her what to do again.

Shuffled footsteps. Sofia stopped knocking, and the door swung open. Marianella stared at her. She looked exhausted, her clothing rumpled and her eyes ringed in dark circles.

"Sofia?" she said in a slurred voice, like she'd been sleeping.

"I need to speak with you." Sofia didn't wait for an answer; she pushed past Marianella into the dim bedroom. "It's about Ignacio Cabrera."

The door swung shut.

"What about him?" Marianella's voice had lost the blur of sleep; it was strained now, nervous. "My God, Sofia, what do you know?" She stared at her. "You went to see him, didn't you? Just now?" She dug her hand into her forehead like she had a headache. "*Why?* I told you, Alejo and I know how to handle—"

Sofia grabbed both of Marianella's hands and squeezed them tight. Marianella looked up, her eyes shiny with tears, and the sight of them made Sofia hurt inside.

"He called me over," Sofia said, "for a meeting. I had to go. That's the nature of my arrangement. And he—" She wasn't sure she would be able to say it. Not now, not looking at Marianella straight on.

Marianella always did that to her.

"What?" Marianella cried. "What is it?"

"We have a problem," Sofia said carefully.

Marianella's eyes went wide and scared. "He wants you to kill me."

"Yes." Sofia squeezed Marianella's hands.

Marianella sucked in a deep breath, and that act of breathing made Sofia aware of how vulnerable Marianella was, if you knew the right places to stab, to hit, to dismantle.

Which Sofia did.

Silence filled the bedroom, thick and choking. And when Marianella broke it, she said exactly what Sofia didn't want to hear.

"Did he program you?" Marianella's voice was flat. Empty.

Sofia closed her eyes. It was a fair question—she was still programmable—and she couldn't begrudge Marianella asking it. But it hurt anyway, a hurt like coming out of the music.

"No."

Marianella sighed with relief, a long whoosh of air that hurt Sofia even more.

"He gave me the option of doing it on my own first."

"Are you going to?"

"No, of course not."

Marianella closed her eyes, and her lips moved silently, the first lines of the Hail Mary.

"You didn't think I was going to kill you, did you? I mean, really?" Sofia reached out, tentatively, and pressed her hand against the side of Marianella's face. Marianella leaned into her touch, sighing, and with that, Sofia stretched her arm around Marianella's shoulder and drew her close. She wanted to feel the warmth and softness of her body, wanted to feel that blood pumping through Marianella's veins. It was the strangest sort of comfort.

"I don't know what I think, Sofia." Marianella laid her head on Sofia's shoulder. "I just— How could you do it?" she asked. "How could you work for that—that monster?" She turned her head just enough that her hair brushed across Sofia's shoulder. "You may not care that he kills humans, but he just asked you to kill a cyborg. And what do you say about that?"

"I had to work with him," Sofia said. "It's part of my plan."

"Your plan, your plan!" Marianella pulled away, whirled to face her. "You're helping Ignacio Cabrera, the man responsible for starving half of Hope City, just so Araceli can mess around with your programming?"

"I'm helping Cabrera so I can be free." Sofia's anger flared. "Which is a concept you don't understand because you've always had it."

"Freedom?" Marianella took a step backward. "You think I've always had freedom?"

"No one can program you." The heat rose in Sofia's words. "No one can control you with music and a record player. So yes, I have helped Ignacio Cabrera just so I can be free."

"I live in fear every day that someone will discover my nature," Marianella said, her voice low and cold. "The only freedom I have comes from pretending to be human."

"Which you do so well." Sofia glared at her. "You pretend to be human because you want to be human. That's why you built that dome with Alejo Ortiz. You just want to pretend."

"I'm not pretending anything." Marianella's cheeks flushed pink. "I just understand that true freedom comes from self-sufficiency, not from death and terror."

"I don't want death." Sofia laughed. "I just want them gone. They have no business living in this climate. They can't even go outside! We can. Your *dome* is just forcing them into something they're not. I'm saying they should go back to where they're suited and leave the ice to us."

She stared at Marianella when she finished, daring her to protest. It was so frustrating how Marianella played at being human. As if being human were the only way to survive in this world.

"Your plan isn't going to work," said Marianella. She brushed one hand over her hair. The pink had gone out of her cheeks, and she took a deep breath. "You understand that, right? Independence—that's how we create a place for robots. A place for robots and humans to live side by side."

"You don't really think Alejo's going to let you do that, do you?"

Marianella ignored the question. "The Independents can negotiate terms in a way you can't. What's to stop the mainland from bombing the city once you've gotten rid of the humans?"

"The atomic plants. They aren't that stupid."

Marianella sighed.

"But we are smarter than them," Sofia said. "Always one step ahead."

Marianella laughed sharply. "They've got power. They control everything, the city and the icebreakers and—" She stopped.

"You were going to say me, weren't you? They control me?"

Marianella looked down at her hands.

"It's all right." It wasn't. "You can say it. We both know it's true. But it won't be for long." Sofia reached over and took Marianella's hand, and Marianella looked up at her. "Once I'm free, I'll be on equal footing with them. And that's when it will happen."

Sofia watched Marianella's face. She had been designed, long ago, to read human expressions, and Marianella's expressions were all so human, even when she tried to wear a mask. And Sofia saw doubt flicker across Marianella's features. Doubt, curiosity. Admiration.

"I'm not going to help you," Marianella said softly.

That was the end of it. Years of friendship with Marianella told Sofia that much. She reached up and cupped Marianella's face.

"Fine," she said. "But I want you to promise me that you won't leave the park until Ignacio is dealt with. I'll have the maintenance drones monitor the gates. That's the safest way."

"Alejo's going to pay him off. As soon as he's struck a deal, I'll let you know."

Sofia scowled. "I wouldn't put all my faith in the goodwill of Ignacio Cabrera. *I'm* going to keep you safe. Cabrera threatened to program me, but he won't be able to." She dropped her hand. "We don't have all the equipment yet, but Araceli can make do."

Marianella frowned. "Don't do anything stupid, Sofia."

"I'm a robot," Sofia said. "I'm incapable of doing something stupid."

* * * *

Sofia left Marianella's room and went looking for Araceli. She wasn't in the workshop, but Sofia found her in the little snow cottage she called home, eating a sandwich and tinkering with a maintenance drone that had broken down the day before. The television was tuned to some mainland game show. Araceli glanced up and set down her soldering iron when Sofia walked in.

"You never knock," she sighed.

Sofia sat down on the sofa beside her and looked at the maintenance drone. "It's my park."

Araceli laughed. "I suppose it is." She switched off the television and drew a plastic tarp over the drone. "So what can I help you with? I've been reinforcing the security feeds after—"

"I know. Thank you." Sofia kept staring at the drone. "It's not about that. It's about—it's about my reprogramming."

Silence. "We don't have everything yet."

"I know that. But we're only missing the one thing—the programming key, correct?"

"Yes," Araceli said slowly. "Where exactly are you going with this, Sofia?"

"The key is hardly an integral part of my design," Sofia said. "We have the engine. You can build a key out of spare parts, surely?"

Araceli looked at her. Then she sighed, stood up, brushed her hand over her hair. "I don't know, Sofia. Maybe. There's so much going on right now and—"

"So much? So much what?"

"With Inéz's death and everything. It shook me up. And I wouldn't want to rush your procedure. I mean, it can't take that much longer for the programming key to arrive, can it?"

Sofia felt a sudden flare of resentment. Never mind that she'd carried that empty feeling around after the culling too, never mind that the whole reason she wanted to rush the procedure was to protect Marianella. She still resented Araceli for being so tainted by human weakness.

"I don't know how much longer it will take," she finally said. "So I am looking into other options."

Araceli took a deep breath. "I could probably rig something up. But don't be foolish, Sofia. This is a dangerous procedure, and I really don't want to rush it."

Sofia sighed, a bit of useless programming from her days in the park.

"*If* I rush it," Araceli said, "I risk killing you."

"I know that." Sofia thought about the dancing. She thought about Marianella's eyes bright with fear. "I don't care."

For a moment, Araceli looked hopeless.

"I need it," Sofia said, "for our plan to work."

"From the beginning we agreed that we would not move forward with your plan until we had all the necessary parts," Araceli said. "I told you before, and I'm telling you now, that moving ahead without everything will be dangerous. This needs to be done safely."

"I know. But we don't have that option anymore. My programming needs to be changed now."

"But why?"

"Cabrera."

Araceli fell silent, and Sofia explained what had happened. Araceli's frown deepened as she listened, and her eyes grew dark and guarded.

"This is bad," Araceli said. "But if there's any way to delay him—"

"There's not. I can only fool Cabrera for so long, and we're dependent on him for the programming key."

Araceli sighed with exasperation. "I realize that," she said. "But I'm not willing to kill you, even if you're willing to kill yourself. This isn't a simple reprogramming. I'm not going in and giving you new directives; I'm rewriting you completely. The parts you want removed are *intrinsic*. I can't just—cut them out. Not without having something to replace them." She tapped her fingers against her thigh. "It would be like me cutting out my heart and expecting to live. Do you understand?"

Araceli's words were a slap. But Sofia was a robot. She recovered fast enough.

"They cut out Marianella's heart," Sofia said, "and she survived."

"She survived because she became something new."

"Which is exactly what you'll do with me. You have almost everything you need! Find a work-around for the key. You do this every day, Araceli. It's why I let you live here."

"Trust me, I know." Araceli sighed and pushed the hair away from her face. "I might be able to find a work-around if I had your schematics. But those are up in the city offices, and I don't think we should risk—"

"The city offices." Sofia's thoughts whirred. "If I got them, you could program me?"

"If you got them." Araceli frowned. "Whatever you're thinking, it's a bad idea—"

But Sofia didn't let her finish. She stood up and marched out of the cottage, her hope renewed.

CHAPTER TWENTY-FOUR

ELIANA

White dome light filtered through the grimy windows and woke Eliana, but she didn't bother crawling out from under the thin, forty-year-old blanket. She understood that she had to stay here, in the park. It was too dangerous otherwise. But after her first, fitful night in the Ice Palace, she had asked to stay somewhere else.

Luciano had brought her to one of the cottages, everything faded and coated with a layer of dust. It had once been rented out to visitors, and that, she supposed, was what it was still doing.

Eliana rolled over onto her back and threw her hand over her eyes. Her body ached like it was physically tired, but she knew it wasn't physical exhaustion keeping her pinned to bed. It was Diego.

Diego, whose eyes had been cold and glittering, the eyes of a reptile.

Diego, who had pointed a gun at her friend.

Diego, who had always insisted that he was just running errands for Ignacio Cabrera. Not killing for him. Not *Diego*.

Tears pricked at Eliana's eyes. She wiped them away and pulled the blanket up over her head. The cottage was cold because the radiator didn't work properly; the coils glowed red, but the heat it let off was weak and insignificant. Maybe that was why Eliana didn't bother getting out of bed.

No. It wasn't.

The light filtering through the blanket was a lovely orange-pink that reminded Eliana of hothouse flowers. The hothouse flowers Diego had brought for her, all those days ago, were wilting in her apartment right now, dropping petals across her table. And they'd keep wilting until they shriveled up into nothing.

Because Diego was a gangster. Not an errand boy, but a true monster.

And she loved him. She still loved him. That frightened her.

She hadn't watched Marianella beat Diego that night at the fund-raiser. The plan was one Marianella had developed as they'd ridden down the elevator, clutching at each other and shaking. They would try to run, but if running didn't work, then Marianella would take care of it. Those were her words—*take care of it*. She'd promised not to kill him.

And she'd kept that promise.

Eliana had stood outside the alley, waiting for a taxi to take her to the park. So she hadn't watched anything, but as she stared down the empty street, she had heard it—Marianella's frighteningly calm voice, the gurgle of Diego's replies, the wet smack of flesh against flesh. It was a sound that made Eliana think of blood.

Later, Marianella had promised he was still alive. But what did it matter? He was a murderer. Eliana had tried to convince herself that she was in love with a thief, but it hadn't worked. She knew what he was.

A knock rattled against the cottage's door. Eliana pulled the blanket off her head.

"Just leave it in the entranceway!" she shouted.

There was a pause, and then the door scraped open. Eliana waited for the thump of a food bag, but it didn't come. Instead, footsteps bounced around the cottage. She sat up, frowning.

Luciano stood in the bedroom doorway. He carried a large plastic suitcase in one hand.

"I didn't want to leave this in the entranceway," he said.

"I thought you were that woman who brought me food."

"Ah. Yes. Araceli." Luciano moved into the bedroom. Eliana pulled her blanket up to her chin. He had skin covering his face again, and in the hazy light Eliana could just make out the faint line of a seam. It wasn't exactly a scar.

"I'm glad you're okay," she said.

Luciano glanced over at her and smiled. "I'm glad to know that you're safe as well."

"That's not exactly what I meant."

"I know what you meant." He set the suitcase on the edge of her bed. "I went to your apartment. I thought you might like your own clothes, rather than those from the park." He peered at her, a lock of his hair falling into his eyes. "Marianella agreed with me."

Eliana was surprised by a sudden swell of warmth inside her chest. She hadn't felt anything like that since the fund-raiser. She felt it now because of Luciano, standing there stiffly at the foot of her bed. Because he had thought to bring her clothes.

"Thank you," she said. Then, when he stayed standing in her room, she added, "I'm sorry."

Luciano blinked at her. Both eyes moved the exact same way. She hoped that meant she hadn't damaged him.

"About shooting you," she said.

"Yes, I assumed that was what you were referring to." Luciano walked over to the chair that sat next to the window, posed in a triangle of pale dome light. "It's quite all right. I know accidents happen."

"I feel really bad about it." And she did. Apologizing to him made her feel lighter. It seemed to bring her back into the world.

"I also have a message for you from Sofia," Luciano said.

The mention of Sofia's name made a fearful light flare behind Eliana's eyes. "What?" she said. "I thought you just came here to bring me clothes."

"That was my primary reason." Luciano turned to look at her, the dome light making his hair shine silver. "But Sofia wishes to speak with you."

"What happens if I don't go?" Eliana said.

"You're staying here by her generosity," said Luciano. "It would be impolite."

Eliana shivered. It wasn't a matter of politeness.

"She'll be very cross if she has to come to you." Luciano smiled. "I'll step out of the room and allow you to change. Then I'll take you to the Ice Palace. Surely you'll feel more comfortable in your own clothes."

Eliana didn't say anything. Her heart pounded hard against her rib cage, fear boiling inside her stomach. It was the first emotion other than devastation she'd felt since arriving at the park.

Either go to Sofia or have Sofia come to her. Eliana was all out of choices. She looked at her suitcase, thought about her clothes tucked away inside. Out of place, here in the park.

"I guess I can't say no."

Luciano didn't answer, but he didn't have to. Eliana crawled out of bed. It felt like the last morning before an execution.

* * * *

Luciano led Eliana through the park. They walked side by side but didn't speak, and Eliana blinked at the bright light bouncing off the carved and painted snow, trying to press down her fear. The palace loomed up ahead, sparkling in the dome light. Luciano held the door for her, and the scent of it, like old wood and electricity, threw her back to the night of the fund-raiser. She almost turned around and fled.

"This way," Luciano said, leading her down the stairs and into a room lined with ancient computers and modern-day television monitors that weren't, Eliana noticed, showing television but rather places around the park. One of them was pointed at the front door of her cottage.

She turned away.

Sofia was waiting for them in an elaborately carved chair that was probably a prop throne from the upper levels of the castle. Araceli was there too, hunched over a worktable strewn with glittering pieces of metal. And Marianella, standing in the corner. She averted her gaze when Eliana walked in.

"Eliana," Sofia said. "I need something from you."

Eliana was about to protest, but Sofia went on: "Think of it as rent for the time you've stayed here in the park."

Her words were as sharp as knives. Marianella stepped forward and said, "What is this? You said she could stay here under our protection—"

"I'm not going to put her in *danger*." Sofia turned to Eliana. "You have contacts, don't you? Across the city?"

Marianella said, "You made me promise we wouldn't leave—"

"I made you promise *you* wouldn't leave." Sofia looked and talked and moved like a human, but there was an undercurrent of electricity in her voice, something that jarred Eliana to the core. She wasn't human. It was entirely too obvious.

Marianella looked as if she wanted to say more, but Eliana said, "It's fine. I don't like staying here for free. What do you want?" She forced herself to meet Sofia's eyes.

Sofia smiled.

"A bit of code," she said. "Some intrinsic programming of mine that's rather frustratingly hidden behind a lock. Neither Araceli nor I can access it."

Araceli glanced up at the mention of her name and squinted into the light. Then she turned back to her scattered parts.

"Marianella told me how you sent that man away, the man who was asking after me. Your friend, she doctored my schematics. Is that true?"

Eliana nodded.

Marianella stepped forward. "This is not what I intended for you to do with that information, and you know it."

"You intended for me to let the girl stay, and I did. Now I'm asking a favor from her." Sofia fixed her gaze on Eliana. "Can you contact your friend and ask her for the true schematics?"

Eliana felt a rush of relief that the schematics were all Sofia wanted from her.

"She wants to reprogram herself. So no one can tell her what to do." Marianella looked at Sofia as she spoke. Sofia looked back, her face blank. Robot-blank.

"Oh."

"My plan's hardly nefarious," Sofia said. "Can you help me?"

"Sure, should be easy." Eliana hesitated. "Do I tell her to bring it here, or—"

"I wouldn't," Marianella said. "There's a chance it might draw Cabrera."

"Yes, I agree," Sofia said, "which is why I've arranged for one of the maintenance drones to accompany you when you pick up the material."

"A drone can't protect her," Marianella said. "Or have you been outfitting them with weapons without telling me?"

Sofia glowered. "A drone will see what I see," she said. "You can monitor the command screens yourself if you're so worried."

"That's not good enough," Marianella said. She looked over at Eliana, who fought the urge to shrink away from her gaze. She remembered the sound of Marianella's fists beating Diego in the alley. "I'll accompany you. If something happens, I'll be right there, and I'll be able to do something, unlike the park drones."

Eliana didn't know what to say. Marianella fixed her with a steely-eyed intensity. Marianella would attract more attention from Cabrera than Eliana would. It would probably be safer to go by herself.

"This is ridiculous," Sofia said.

"I don't care. I'm going." Marianella didn't look away from Eliana. "I'm going to keep you safe."

Eliana finally found her voice. "And what if Cabrera sends his men after you?"

"She's right," Sofia said. "Your presence could make this worse."

"I'll cover my face," Marianella said. "But Cabrera saw Eliana at the party too, and I'm not letting you send her into danger alone." She paused. "If I have to fight them, I will."

Eliana's skin prickled. It was stupid for Marianella to accompany her, but the truth was that she didn't want to go alone. Even Marianella was better than no one.

"Fine," Sofia said sharply. Then she turned away and walked to the table where Araceli was working. The conversation was over. The arrangements had been made, and Eliana had agreed.

Might as well get it over with.

"Do you have a telephone?" she asked.

"Yes, of course." Sofia didn't look over her shoulder when she answered. "It's on the table in the corner." She gestured lazily with one hand. The phone was set up next to one of the computers, perched precariously on the edge of the desk. Eliana walked over and dialed Maria's number. She answered on the second ring.

"Maria?" Eliana said.

"Oh my God, Eliana? Where are you? I've been trying to get ahold of you. We thought you were *dead*."

"I'm not dead." Eliana looked at the old-fashioned computers, at a robot working with a human while a cyborg looked on. She couldn't explain any of this to Maria. "But I'm working a case and I have to stay undercover." She forced a smile into her voice. "You don't need to worry about me."

Silence crackled on the other end.

"But I do need your help with this case, actually. You remember when you helped me before? With that robot's schematics?"

"Yes. You need me to do it again?"

"Nah. Something came up and this time I need the real thing. Can you get them for me?"

"Sure." Not even a moment's pause. "But look, are you sure you're okay? Your voice sounds weird. And the power outages have been so much worse lately. Everybody's on edge."

Had they? There were never any power outages in the amusement park.

"I'm fine. You'll see me when I pick up the schematics."

"Right." Maria still sounded unsure.

Eliana took a deep breath. "So when do you think you can get them for me?"

"Today. I mean, nobody cares about old robot files from the park. I told you that before."

"Perfect. I'll meet you at the yerba mate shop next to the building, what do you say?"

"Sounds fine. But, Eliana—"

"I promise you," Eliana interrupted, because she wasn't sure how much longer she could keep lying. "Everything's all right." She stared across the room at Sofia, who was sifting through the mechanical parts on the table. "Everything's all right."

* * * *

Eliana and Marianella took the park train out into the city. When it emerged out of the tunnel, the dome lights were dimmer than they ought to have been, more like twilight than the middle of afternoon.

"That's odd," Marianella said.

Eliana glanced over at her. She'd wrapped her hair up in a cream-colored scarf and put on a pair of oversize sunglasses.

"You're going to look even more noticeable than before," Eliana said, gesturing to the glasses. Marianella sighed and slid them off.

"I can't believe it's so dark," she said. "The park lights haven't changed at all."

Eliana turned her gaze back to the window. Seeing the city in this dim light made it look like a dream. The shadows hid all the decay in the buildings, and so in the few seconds that Eliana caught sight of them, they almost seemed new.

The train pulled up to the first station. A few people waited on the benches, all of them bundled up in thick coats and scarfs. The doors slid open, letting in a blast of freezing air. Marianella's scarf fluttered out behind her, and Eliana pulled her hands into her sleeves. She should have brought a warmer coat.

No one got on. The door slid shut, and the train went on its way, heading toward downtown.

"My God," Marianella said. "The city wasn't that cold before, was it?"

Eliana shook her head. "It was like this after Last Night," she said. "When they turned the heat down. It must be the power failures—" She cut herself short, thinking of Sofia sitting on that throne.

They rode the rest of the way in silence. The lights grew brighter as they approached downtown, and Marianella slid her sunglasses back on. Eliana hadn't bothered with that sort of disguise. She didn't think it would matter. Didn't think it could stop anything bad from happening.

The train screeched to a stop at the big shining downtown station, expelling clouds of white steam. The people waiting lifted their faces, staring at the train with blank curiosity. Eliana's skin tingled, and her stomach tightened. She hadn't been around so many people since the night of the gala. She didn't like the way they stared at her.

"We ought to get this over with," Marianella said in a soft voice. She stepped off the train first, glancing left and then right, moving with slow and cautious steps. Eliana followed. The air flung tiny daggers at her exposed skin, and she tucked her hands into her pockets. She didn't just need a warmer coat. She should have brought gloves, a scarf, anything.

The people at the train station had a weary look to them, as if the cold had worked its way permanently into their systems.

"I hope it's not too far of a walk," Marianella said brightly. Eliana knew she was faking her cheer. And the cold didn't really matter to her anyway, did it?

"It's only a few blocks." Eliana's teeth chattered. She walked quickly, hoping the exercise would warm her up. At least the cold and the dark were keeping people off the streets. It was easy to navigate the narrow sidewalks. They scurried along, side by side, their heads down. A tension started in Eliana's neck and worked its way through the rest of her body. Maybe she was more frightened of seeing Cabrera than she'd let herself think.

The walk seemed to take longer than it ought to have, and for a moment Eliana was afraid that they'd passed the café, that she'd taken them down the wrong street. But then it appeared, its windows glowing in the weird gloomy light. The neon YERBA MATE HERE! sign was flipped on, staining the cement red.

"Well," Marianella said. "They don't seem to be at a loss for power."

"I'm sure it's a generator." Eliana tried to make her voice casual, but the thought frightened her. Stores were using their own generators? How bad had it gotten out here?

As if to answer, the dome lights gave a hesitant flicker. For a moment the world was caught in static.

"Let's get inside," Eliana said. Marianella nodded.

Maria was waiting for them at her usual table in the corner, a mate gourd sprouting a pair of straws in front of her. A bell chimed as Eliana and Marianella walked in, and Maria lifted her head at the sound, then grinned and waved.

"She's going to recognize you," Eliana whispered.

"I'm aware of that." Marianella gave a tight smile. Already Eliana could see recognition glimmering across Maria's expression. Maria straightened up and smoothed one hand down the side of her hair.

"Hey," Eliana said, sliding into the table across from Maria.

"I got you a straw." Maria glanced at Marianella and smiled shyly. "I didn't know you'd be bringing someone—"

"It's fine." Marianella didn't take off her sunglasses, which Eliana found absurd. "I've never cared for yerba mate so much."

Maria beamed like this confession pleased her. Then she turned to Eliana and said, "I hope your investigation is going well. Have you been staying outside the main dome?" Eliana heard the question she really wanted to ask: *Does your investigation involve Marianella Luna? Have you been staying at her house?*

"Yes," Eliana said. "Although I can't say where, exactly."

"I understand." Maria held up two fingers, like she was swearing on her heart. "It's been so awful, hasn't it? I'm not going to lie, I was worried. I've heard it's been bad down in the smokestack district."

"I haven't been in the smokestack district." Eliana shifted in her seat. After the dim lights outside, the inside of the shop seemed far too bright.

"Well, power's been going out in patches, you know, and I've heard it will stay out longer there than the wealthier parts of town." She lowered her voice and leaned forward, glancing a little at Marianella as she did so. "I heard that's how they're trying to conserve energy. But I'm not supposed to know that." She leaned back, obviously pleased that she had imparted this gossip to the famed Lady Luna.

"That's terrible to hear," Marianella said.

"I know, isn't it?" Maria shook her head and sipped from the mate. "Oh, I got your schematics. No big deal." She pulled a file out of her purse and slid it across the table. "Will you be able to stay a bit? Chat? I miss you. Essie can be such a bore with all her pro-Independence nonsense." She glanced at Marianella again. "Not that I'm *opposed* to Independence, of course."

Marianella smiled. "I know what you mean. The radicals can be tiresome."

You'd know, Eliana thought bitterly. She opened up the file and glanced down at the schematics. Not that it mattered; she didn't understand them. But Marianella peered over her shoulder.

"These look perfect," she said. "Thank you very much. Maria, right?"

"Yes." Maria beamed, thrilled that Lady Luna knew her name. Eliana slid the file into her own purse and then took a long drink of yerba mate. It wasn't sweetened—too far into the winter for that—but the warmth was still nice.

"Can you stay?" Maria asked. "At least for a little while? Fifteen minutes? I took the rest of the afternoon off."

Eliana wanted to stay. Even in those bright lights, it was nice to see Maria, to have someone to speak with other than Luciano. Nice to share a bit of yerba mate with a friend.

She glanced at Marianella. Marianella sighed, so slight it was just her shoulders hitching for a half second. Eliana was sure she would make up some excuse to get them back to the park. But she didn't.

"Fifteen minutes would be fine, I think," she said.

Eliana had never been so grateful for fifteen minutes.

CHAPTER TWENTY-FIVE

SOFIA

Sofia sat out in the garden, the folder with her schematics resting in her lap. Eliana and Marianella had returned several hours ago, both of them quiet but not hurt. Night had fallen shortly after that, and she had monitored the screens herself since then, waiting to see if Cabrera would make a move under cover of dark. But he hadn't. No one had.

She decided it was time.

She'd already read through the schematics, studying each line of information to see if she could find some scrap of herself. She couldn't. It wasn't like reading code, which was like looking into a mirror. This was more like the time she had found an advertisement for herself in the back of a cigar magazine. Disconcerting and strange.

Far away, in the city itself, a church bell chimed three o'clock. As the gongs faded into silence, Sofia stood up and walked to Araceli's workshop. Marianella was asleep in the palace, dreaming like a human. And Sofia did not want Marianella to watch this. She didn't want anyone to watch this, except for Araceli. And that was only out of necessity.

The walk to the workshop took seven minutes and thirty-eight seconds. The night air was cold and shimmered with the movement of entertainment robots watching her from the shadows. Sofia held her head high.

The workshop door hung open, waiting. She went inside. Araceli was gone, but she had taped a note to her desk that said, *Ran to the cottage. Be back shortly.* A record player sat beside it, unmoving, not even plugged in.

It still felt dangerous.

Sofia wandered from the record player to the worktable. All of the supplies she'd procured from Cabrera were laid out in a neat display, glittering in the work lights. She selected one of the smaller vacuum tubes and held it up, twisting it so that it caught in the light.

"You shouldn't touch anything."

Sofia looked at Araceli. "My touching never bothered you before."

"I just didn't want you to get started without me."

"You know I can't."

Araceli walked across the room, carrying a big canvas bag that clanked as she moved. She dumped its contents out onto the work tray—mostly spare electronics parts. But there was also a long, thin knife of the sort used to operate on robots.

"Did Eliana get the information?" she asked.

"She did." Sofia handed Araceli the file. Araceli opened it up and scanned it.

"The activation code is in the upper-right corner."

"Yes, I see it. This is perfect." Araceli set the folder next to the parts on the table, leaving it open. Then she looked up at Sofia.

"Do you understand how this is going to work?" she asked.

"Of course I do." Sofia tilted her head, looking again at the scatter of electronics and the surgical knife. "You're going to cut out my heart. So to speak."

One end of Araceli's mouth turned up. "Pretty much."

Sofia trusted Araceli. She was the only human Sofia trusted, because she had given up everything to protect a maintenance drone. And when the city belonged to the robots, Araceli would be the only human allowed to stay behind.

But nevertheless Sofia could not imagine Araceli plunging that knife into her chest, not without harming her in some way, cutting the wrong wire or knocking the wrong part loose. Not on purpose, but out of nervousness.

"If you don't mind," Sofia said, "I think I'd like to cut the core engine out myself."

A faint relief washed over Araceli's features. Sofia was almost touched.

"Well, let's get it over with," Araceli said.

Sofia stripped off her blouse and camisole and sat, topless, on the edge of the table. She had not been fully naked in front of a human for almost forty years, but Araceli looked at her the way she always did.

"Let me put in the code so we can access everything," she said, dragging a cable across Sofia's lap. She inserted it in the place behind Sofia's ear, and when she plugged it into her computer, Sofia felt a twinge of connection. An electric shock. Araceli hunched over her computer and input the code, using the old polished-brass keyboard that clicked and clacked like bones. When it was done, something inside Sofia opened up like a flower.

Araceli straightened. "Your knife," she said, handing it over.

Sofia pressed the tip of the knife against her clavicle. The core engine was only a heart in the metaphorical sense. Her brain, tucked away in her skull, contained her motor skills and the programming necessary to create intelligence, but the core engine was a cluster of wires that housed her intrinsic programming, the programming that defined her. Here was the programming that made robots servile to humans. Here was the programming that converted music into orders. The intrinsic programming was separate because it could not be reprogrammed easily, by just anyone. You had to have the right permissions. And entering the code made it possible to remove the programming without destroying Sofia completely.

Sofia dug the knife into her skin.

It didn't hurt because she didn't feel pain. She split open her sternum, hydraulic fluid pouring down her chest. Araceli looked at her feet, hair falling over her eyes. Exactly as Sofia had thought. She couldn't bear to watch this violence. Or rather, what she perceived as violence.

Sofia reached inside her chest, her movements jerking, halted. Her programming was trying to stop her. But she could overcome it. For the five seconds it would take, she could overcome it.

She wrapped her fingers around the core engine. Her thoughts blacked out, grayed out, returned. Her hand was still inside her chest. Using her fingers, she unhooked the wires, one at a time.

Another blackout. She returned, having lost three seconds. No time to delay.

Sofia yanked out her core engine.

She screamed and slammed backward onto the worktable. Her mind was rioting, flooding her with a thousand images of humans—Araceli and past clients and workers from the amusement park and even the engineers who had built her so long ago in Brazil. She was aware of a weight being lifted from her hand, and then of a warm human palm pressing against her forehead.

"It's all right." Araceli's sweet voice. "You did it, and you're all right."

Sofia couldn't see the workroom, only the mass of humans crowding around her. Memories come to life. She closed her eyes and concentrated on the sound of Araceli's humming as she worked. It was enough to draw her out of the past and into the present.

Slowly, her mind cleared and returned back to her. She felt hollow and purposeless, like a discarded doll. When she sat up, it surprised her that she could move, because what reason did she have to move, without her programming?

Araceli leaned over the worktable, a bright light fixed on the core engine. It was dismantled, strewn out in many tiny pieces across the surface, glittering like sand. When Sofia saw it, she felt nothing, and that was not what she'd expected.

Araceli set the micro-engine under the light and snapped it open. It was larger than the core engine, despite its name, but Sofia knew, distantly, that it would still fit inside her chest. Araceli hunched over the micro-engine with a soldering iron and a vacuum tube. There was a faint whiff of burning.

The micro-engine was the foundation, although without the old programming key it would be harder to align it to Sofia's specifications. That was why they needed the schematics. With that information, Araceli would be able to override Sofia's old programming. Sofia had explained what she wanted, and had collected all the necessary equipment, because a robot could not reprogram itself. They were designed that way.

"This is easier than I expected," Araceli said.

"It's because you're the best." Sofia's voice sounded tinny and far away. She wasn't whole. Not without that micro-engine.

Araceli laughed. "I'm just working off your designs. If you don't mind waiting, I think I'll be able to hook this into the computer and clear out some of the music programming. I mean, the new micro-engine should take care of it, but just to be on the safe side."

"I don't mind waiting." Sofia remembered when she was brand-new, sitting in the laboratory waiting to be programmed. It had been like this, that curious calmness, that sense of expectation. She didn't know what she would become.

The best version of myself, she thought, watching Araceli work. The work lamp illuminated the pores and lines in Araceli's skin, and Sofia was momentarily fascinated by them, by her humanity. Those lines and pores meant Araceli had freedom when Sofia did not.

Except, no—that was no longer the case.

Araceli stood up and carried the micro-engine over to the computer. Sofia followed, although her steps shook, and moving made her vaguely dizzy. She steadied herself against the wall, aware that she was leaking hydraulic fluid down the front of her chest. That bothered her more than her nakedness. Funny.

"Do you want a chair?" Araceli glanced at her, then set the micro-engine down and pulled one out from beside the computer. "Here. Sit. I'm worried about your bleeding."

Sofia sank into the chair and said, "It's not blood."

Araceli didn't answer, only turned back to the computer. She linked the micro-engine into the mainframe and sat down at the keyboard and began to type. The micro-engine sat there, unmoving. The rotary display whirred through the list of programs that Araceli was going through and deleting. The display was too far away for Sofia to see which ones exactly. But she trusted Araceli.

Sofia stuck her finger into the hydraulic fluid and lifted it up to the light. It was thick purplish black, like motor oil. She'd never seen it before. None of her patrons had ever cut deep enough. They were, after all, warned not to, because seeing a woman bleed black instead of red ruined the effect.

When she still had her core engine, thinking on those things would make her angry. Or sad, sometimes. But right now they didn't make her think of anything. They were simply a fragment of the past. They didn't matter anymore.

Araceli hit one last keystroke and leaned back in her chair. "There. Got it." She turned and grinned at Sofia. "You ready to reinstall?"

Sofia nodded.

Araceli lifted the micro-engine off the table and held it to her chest, waiting. Sofia stumbled back over to the work counter and stretched out on her back. She blinked up at the lights. Everything was fogged and hazy.

Araceli nestled the micro-engine inside Sofia's open chest cavity. With each reconnection Sofia's thoughts sharpened and clarified until they were sharper and clearer than she could ever remember.

Araceli murmured, "One mo—"

Everything cut out.

Sofia floated in the darkness, a disembodied consciousness. She was nothing but memories: The lights in the laboratory where they built her. The first time she saw Hope City glowing through the porthole in the ship that brought her to Antarctica. Dancing up onstage. Memory after memory.

And then Sofia felt a spark in her head, and she remembered she had a body. The overhead lights flared into existence. One by one her programs came online. As soon as she could move, she sat up.

"Lie down," Araceli said, pressing gently against her shoulder. "You're still—open."

Sofia looked down at her gaping chest cavity. "Oh," she said. "It doesn't really matter, does it?"

"It matters if you bleed out. Lie down."

Sofia sighed and lay down. It was the last time she would do as a human said, she decided, as Araceli pressed her sternum back together and closed the split with sealant. The cut had been deep enough that the sealant wouldn't erase the line completely. She'd have to get new skin brought in or have a scar. She preferred the scar.

"All right, all finished." Araceli stepped back. Her hands were coated in hydraulic fluid. "How do you feel?"

"Amazing."

Araceli smiled a little. "Are you ready to test?"

Sofia nodded without hesitation. They had agreed on the test beforehand—"*La Entrerriana*," which would only make her tango across the room. But Sofia was confident the procedure had worked. She could feel her freedom inside her like a virus.

Araceli nodded and turned to the record player. Sofia stared at it with a bland implacability. It was not going to hurt her. She knew it.

Araceli switched on the turntable and dropped the needle. The record crackled. The music crept on, slow and twisting like a vine. It was a dangerous song.

Sofia did nothing.

She sat on the work counter, her bare chest covered in hydraulic fluid, and for the first time in her existence she was able to listen to the song without it consuming her. The music was a cord that twisted through the room. It was beautiful, in a human sort of way. The dance was, as well—she could remember it, she could see the steps in her head if she thought about them, but she was not compelled to perform them.

"It worked," Araceli said breathlessly. "It works. Oh my God—"

"It works," Sofia whispered. She pulled her blouse back on, not caring that it grew dark with hydraulic fluid. She hopped off the counter and drew Araceli into an embrace. Araceli was warm and living against her. Vulnerable. "Thank you," she said into the top of Araceli's hair.

The music played on in the background.

They pulled apart. Araceli was grinning wildly. "I can't believe we pulled it off."

"I can." That empty feeling from before lingered, but now it wasn't so much an emptiness as a removed weight. It was a lightness. She didn't need Araceli anymore. She didn't need any of them. With the right equipment, the right schematics, she could reprogram all the robots in the city herself.

"We'll need to wait a week or so to make sure the modifications work. You'll need to avoid Cabrera until then."

"I will."

"I should probably run a diagnostic," Araceli began, but Sofia held up one hand.

"I can do it myself," she said. "I would—prefer it."

"Oh, of course." Araceli smiled again. "I understand."

Sofia knew she didn't, not really, but she didn't begrudge her for trying.

And the music, the music was still playing.

* * * *

Sofia knocked on Marianella's door—*rap*, *rap*, *rap* over and over in a steady and unwavering pattern. If she'd been human, her knuckles would have bruised and ached. But she wasn't human.

Four minutes passed, and Marianella answered.

"What is it?" She leaned against the doorframe, rubbing the sleep out of her eyes. "Is something wrong?" The hallway was flooded with that silvery false moonlight, and it washed over Marianella's skin, turning her into a ghost. Sofia was glad she had bothered to change and wash the hydraulic fluid from her skin; Marianella might have panicked at the sight of it.

"I have something I want to show you," Sofia said, and she grabbed Marianella by both hands and pulled her out of the room. Marianella sputtered with confusion.

"What's happening?" she said. "Sofia, has someone come into the park?"

"No, of course not." Sofia led her to the stairs. "I'm sorry I woke you, but we both know you don't *need* sleep."

"I do need sleep."

"Not as much as you pretend."

Marianella didn't respond. When Sofia glanced over at her, she was pouting—annoyed, no doubt, that Sofia was right about something related to her nature.

They walked downstairs, Sofia bright with anticipation, Marianella slow and soft-footed, like she was still waking up. An affectation, Sofia knew. A cyborg was either resting or awake. There was no in-between, as with humans.

"Really, Sofia, I wish you would just *tell* me what's going on." They were downstairs now, in the great vaulted hallway filled with glowing stained-glass windows. The floor was crisscrossed with shattered color. "I don't see the point in keeping secrets, with everything that's happened."

Sofia stopped. She was where she wanted to be—the entrance to the ballroom. She cocked out her hip and shrugged and said, "It wouldn't be a secret if you paid attention."

"What are you talking about?"

"Didn't you notice the difference?" Sofia doubted that Marianella would, since Marianella never gave her instructions. But she liked playing this game. Flirtation because she wanted to.

"I'm half-asleep. So, no."

"You're not half-asleep." Sofia really was enjoying herself, for the first time since she could remember. Removing her programming had changed her completely. She took Marianella by the hand and led her into the vast, empty ballroom. The moonlight shone in through the windows, casting everything in silver and shadows.

Marianella looked around the room, blinking. "Sofia, I don't—" She stopped, staring straight ahead, at the theremin set up in the center of the dance floor.

"Remember when you played it for me before?" Sofia asked. "All those years ago?"

"You dragged me out of bed to play the theremin for you?"

"Go look at the sheet music."

Marianella looked at her. A moment passed. Then Marianella whispered, "Mother of God," and Sofia knew then that she understood what had happened.

"Go on," Sofia said.

Marianella walked across the room, her footsteps echoing in all that empty space. Sofia didn't follow her, only stood in place and watched as she stopped at the theremin and picked up the music. It was a dangerous song, one that Marianella had asked to play for Sofia before Marianella had understood about the music.

Marianella lifted her head. She stared across the ballroom at Sofia. "Are you sure?"

"Yes."

In the darkness, Marianella was too far away for even Sofia to read her expression. She set the sheet music back into place and switched on the theremin. It buzzed and whined. Her hands hung at her sides.

Music swelled.

It was a sad song, and sadder still on a theremin. The music sounded like starlight. Sofia stood very still, watching Marianella sway, her eyes closed, her hands unmoving. It was a neat trick, to play a theremin with her own thoughts. A trick that could get her deported, if she performed it for the wrong people.

Sofia did not want the song to end, and when it did, she filled the silence with applause, her claps bouncing off the walls. She realized that she enjoyed the music not just because of Marianella but because of the music itself, because it was beautiful and haunting and sad. She had never thought that could be possible.

Marianella opened her eyes.

"Beautiful!" Sofia cried. "Wonderful!" She bounded over to the theremin, where Marianella smiled at her.

"It didn't hurt you," she said.

"Of course not."

They looked at each other across the theremin, the memory of the music still lingering on the air. Marianella looked brighter now, like she was carved out of light. All Sofia wanted was to touch her.

"I have records," Sofia said. "Over in the corner." She wheeled the theremin off to the side. "Wait here." Then she rushed away, across the dusty polished floors. Araceli's record player was set up in the corner.

Sofia switched on the speakers, and the vibrations from their feedback skittered across her skin. A whole stack of records sat on the floor beside the player. Dangerous no more.

Sofia selected one of the records and dropped the needle. There was an immense novelty to that one simple act, the act of control. That was how she'd always thought of it before, when it had been a tool designed to enslave her.

Music poured out of the speakers, a tango, the music driving and fierce. And although this was a song that had once compelled her to dance, her programming didn't even jump.

She stood up and turned around in one silken motion.

Marianella stood at the far end of the room, surrounded by silver light, staring at her. She really was quite beautiful, in the human sense. And Sofia had seen her code, and knew she was beautiful in the machine sense too.

"I used to have to dance to this song," Sofia said into the gap between them. "I don't have to anymore."

Sofia glided across the floor, her feet moving in those familiar sliding steps. The room spun around. She closed her eyes, let the music wash over her.

And then she caught Marianella in her arms.

Marianella yelped with surprise, fumbling against Sofia's grip. But as Sofia guided her back into the dance, Marianella laughed and fell easily into the steps. Sofia had been tangoing alone all night, and for the first time in her entire existence she was dancing with a partner she wanted. Marianella's laughter faded, and her face became serious, intense with concentration. Sofia whirled her around, and Marianella moved exactly as she should. Their bodies clicked into place together like the gears of a clock. Marianella's breath quickened, her skin flushed—Sofia could feel the intoxicating heat of it.

Dancing, like this, with Marianella, Sofia felt as if she could lose herself completely. And for the first time the notion wasn't terrifying.

CHAPTER TWENTY-SIX

DIEGO

Diego tapped his hands against the steering wheel, anxious. A cigarette dangled from his swollen bottom lip. He'd been smoking nonstop since he'd gotten out of the hospital two days ago. The tobacco burning its way through his lungs was the only thing that could keep him from thinking on everything that had happened. That and the painkillers.

Marianella Luna kicking the shit out of him in an alley beside that glitzy hotel.

Mr. Cabrera roaring with fury, in his office afterward, that Luna had gotten away again.

And Eliana.

Diego sucked hard on his cigarette, yanked it out of his mouth to ash it out the window. The car cruised down the street, headlights on, illuminating the cracked sidewalks, the stoops of the tenement buildings. An address lay on the seat beside him, curling up at the edges. Mr. Cabrera had given it to him when he'd handed him the keys to his car.

"I want to know if Sofia's done what I asked her," Mr. Cabrera had said. "Because if she hasn't, we'll need to bring her in. I've got the AFF sniffing around, trying to make a deal."

"You don't want to take it, sir?"

"What, with the AFF? Absolutely not. They're up to something, and I'd rather just see the bitch gone."

Diego didn't say anything to that.

Mr. Cabrera nodded at the address. "Girl's name is Maria. Got word from one of my contacts she was seen speaking to Marianella yesterday. And the other one. Eliana. Doesn't look good for our friend Sofia."

Diego's response had been to light a cigarette. That had been his response to everything these last few days.

Maria lived on the outskirts of Snowy Heights, a neighborhood populated almost entirely by secretaries and other office girls, since the housing was cheap despite its proximity to the buildings downtown. It was nice enough, even in the dark, rows of brick apartment buildings with reflective glass windows. Maria lived in one called the Hibiscus. Someone had planted a couple of shrubs next to the sign, like that could make the place seem nicer.

Diego parked his car in front of the Hibiscus. He shoved the address into his pocket. Opened the glove compartment. Looked at his gun. His stomach felt queasy like he'd eaten too much.

He took the gun.

There was a bit of wind here, although it was cold and icy. He walked up the sidewalk to the front door, still limping a little from his injuries. A girl sat on the stoop, a bathrobe tossed around her shoulders, a book on her knees that she was reading by flashlight. She glanced up as he approached and squinted at him in the dark.

"You here for Laura?" she asked. "Hope you enjoy kicking me out of my own bloody apartment." She scowled down at her book.

"I'm not here for Laura," Diego said. He tossed his cigarette out into the gravel courtyard. "I'm here for Maria."

The girl shrugged and turned back to her book.

The door was unlocked. The girl didn't say anything as he stepped into the musty foyer. There wasn't much to it, just some cramped stairs and a row of mailboxes. Maria lived on the fifth floor. He might as well start walking.

The stairs creaked beneath his feet, and he had to lean up against the banister to steady the ache in his back. As he passed each floor, he heard voices—television and music from the radio, women singing and a couple arguing. But the fifth floor was silent. Diego made his way to Maria's apartment and knocked on her door.

She answered right away, yanking the door hard like she'd forgotten it was chained. She peered through the crack, and her eyes widened at the sight of him.

"The hell do you want?" she said.

"I need to talk to you about Eliana."

A moment's pause. Suspicion wafted off her.

"Please," he said.

The door closed, the chain rattled. When Maria opened the door again, she opened it all the way, positioning herself in the doorway so that he couldn't come into her apartment.

"You want to talk out in the hall?"

"Yes." She paused. "Christ, what happened to you?" She gestured at her eye. Diego knew his own was still swollen and bruised.

"Nothing you need to worry about." He was aware of the gun shoved into the waistband of his pants. He had no intention of using it. Not tonight, anyway. "I've been to her apartment a couple of times, and she's gone. Been to her office, too. It's all shut up tight. There's a sign on the door that says closed until further notice. What's going on?"

He watched Maria carefully. He didn't know if Eliana had told her about what had happened at the gala; he'd decided to start off lying just in case she hadn't. Well, not lying exactly. Reshaping the truth. He had gone to Eliana's apartment and to her office. But he knew what was going on.

Maria's expression didn't change. She always looked annoyed, and she looked more annoyed than usual right now. Not angry, though. And certainly not scared.

Eliana must not have said anything.

"I don't know what's going on," Maria said. "I figured you'd know more than me anyway, since she was spending every waking moment with you earlier."

"I wouldn't say *every* waking—"

"Oh, shut up. She told me she was working some case and had to stay undercover. I don't know much more than that." She shrugged. Shifted her weight. She had left something out, Diego could tell. She acted too casual about not knowing much.

"So that's it," he said. "She's working on some case and didn't tell anybody."

"She told *me*."

Diego scowled at her.

"If you don't have anything else to add," Maria said, "I've got things to do."

Diego couldn't think of a response fast enough. Maria said "Guess not" and shut the door in his face.

For a few moments, Diego just stared at the burnished numbers nailed to the door. So Eliana'd told Maria she was working a case. Maria definitely hadn't been lying about that. There was just something she wasn't adding, and Diego doubted he'd ever know what it was.

Still. If Eliana hadn't told Maria the truth, it was because she didn't want Maria to know. To protect her, probably. Eliana was that sort of girl.

Diego pulled out another cigarette and lit it before trudging back down the stairs. The girl with the book and the flashlight was still sitting on the stoop, but she didn't even glance up at him when he left the building. He walked down to his car and leaned up against it, smoking and looking at the lights in the windows. It occurred to him that maybe he wasn't putting so much thought into this assignment because he didn't want to find out that Sofia hadn't killed Marianella, that he was going to have to bring Sofia in for the reprogramming. He kept thinking about the horror he'd seen on Eliana's face when she'd realized what he was at the party to do, and part of him couldn't believe he was still trying to do it.

Diego hurled the cigarette into the darkness and climbed into his car and drove away. At first he thought he was going back to the smokestack district, to break into Eliana's apartment or her office and see what he could find. But he got to the smokestack district and he kept driving. The tenement housing gave way to squat, abandoned storage facilities and crumbling skyscrapers. The patches of grass and trees gave way to cement. And the air got colder. He could feel it creeping into his car.

He reached down, turned on the heat.

Mr. Cabrera had wanted Marianella's death confirmed as soon as possible, but Diego wanted to have a fucking beer first, and he realized he hadn't been driving to the smokestack district at all but to the Horse and Cart, a run-down little bar next to one of the service exits. The Horse and Cart had been there since Hope City had been just a nameless, empty dome, some developer's dream of the future. Then Autômatos Teixeira had moved in with their robots and their amusement park, but the Horse and Cart never shut down through it all.

The sign cast red light across the parking lot. It made the ember in Diego's cigarette burn orange. Diego pushed into the bar, keeping his head low. There were only a few guys there, mostly workers for the storage facilities, going by their jumpsuits. He took a chair next to the jukebox and ordered a beer. Lit another cigarette. Every muscle in his body ached.

Diego had been afraid of this happening from the moment he'd first met Eliana at that party a year and a half ago. They'd talked for an hour outside, and he'd looked at her in the shadows and thought that if he let this go further, she'd be in danger one way or another. And he'd almost walked away, then and there, just left her standing in the dark. But he was too selfish, and he hadn't.

And now here he was. Mr. Cabrera knew who she was and wanted to kill her after Marianella was taken care of. Mr. Cabrera, who might as well be his father. It wasn't fucking fair. He shouldn't have to do it. Not to her. Anyone else, he'd do it. But not Eliana.

One of the storage workers came over to the jukebox and put on one of those Spanish covers of some British rock-and-roll song. Diego half-recognized it. The worker bobbed his head in time to the music, hair falling over his eyes. He seemed to be studiously avoiding Diego. Exactly what Diego liked about this place.

He took a long drag on his cigarette.

And then all of the Horse and Cart started vibrating like an earthquake, and then it flooded with white-hot light.

Diego stumbled out of his chair, his ears ringing. He couldn't hear the music anymore, just the muffled thump of its beat. The guy at the jukebox wasn't there—he'd raced across the room. An explosion, Diego realized, like a gunshot but *more*. It'd been so sudden, he hadn't known what was happening. The bar wasn't shaking anymore, but the light was still there, red-yellow and flickering. Fire. Fucking fire.

Diego limped across the room. The workers were all crowded around a window, shouting curses at each other. He couldn't see much, only the red-yellow light.

He went outside.

He did it without thinking, and it wasn't until the cold air struck his face that he realized the explosion and the fire could have been the glass of the main dome, that he was running out into the fierce Antarctic wind. But no—it was just the cold of being at the dome's edge.

The fire raged on the other side of the glass.

Diego stared, his mouth hanging open. The ice coated on the dome melted in long, pale streaks. It turned to water that turned to steam. The fire didn't seem that far away. It was close enough that its glow drowned out the red light of the sign. Diego took a shaking step backward. He wasn't sure if fire could burn through the snow. He wasn't sure what could even burn at all out there. They didn't put the private domes on this side of the city. Too cold, too far away from the train stations.

And then the service entrance slid open. Cold air and black smoke billowed in. Diego slammed up against his car and fumbled around for his gun. He didn't know what to make of that open service entrance. He didn't know what to make of any of it.

The maintenance drones arrived, gliding two by two over the glass, disappearing out the entrance. He watched them go, like ants.

CHAPTER TWENTY-SEVEN

MARIANELLA

The ground shook.

Marianella was stretched out on a divan in the Ice Palace, trying to sleep after a night of restless tossing. The sensation only lasted for thirty seconds before disappearing. The earth was moving and then it wasn't. Marianella lay motionless, waiting for the shudder to happen again. It didn't.

She sat up. That burst of movement wasn't something a human would feel; it was her robot body, fine-tuned to recognize patterns in the world around her. But this wasn't a pattern. It was a single occurrence.

Something was wrong.

She went to find Sofia. The palace was empty and echoing, and she cast long dark shadows along the walls as she walked through the hallways. She had to get to operations, where one of the computers was programmed to track the movements of robots in the park. Sofia had shown her how to access it, after that night in the ballroom. The night that had brought everything back.

Marianella burst out into the chilled, shimmering night. The gardens rustled around her. She fingered the cross at her neck and whispered the Fatima prayer to herself, over and over. But praying didn't help.

Something had *happened*. She felt it shuddering through her bones, just as she had felt the movement in the ground. It was like the night the warehouse had caught on fire.

The entire way to operations, she kept one hand on her necklace, feeling her heart beat beneath it.

Marianella expected to find operations empty, but to her relief Sofia was sitting in the room's center, mooning over the big hulking computer that had once controlled all the attractions in the Ice Palace. Marianella didn't know what it did now.

"Did you feel that?" she asked from the doorway, still touching her cross, still touching her heart.

Sofia glanced at her. She didn't answer right away. Marianella could see that she was considering lying.

"Yes."

"What was it?"

"I don't know." She was hooked into her computer, a thin wire emerging from behind her ear. She couldn't be that deeply hooked, though, not if she was able to speak with Marianella. "I don't know everything that happens in the city."

"You want to run it someday," Marianella snapped. "It seems like you'd keep track of things."

Sofia regarded her coolly, then turned back to the computer. "I'm monitoring the park. To ensure no one is coming for you or the human girl."

Marianella's cheeks warmed. She couldn't put her frustration into words. She looked out over the operations room. It was still full of old human artifacts, not just the electronics that ran the park but old photographs and stacks of triplicate forms and pens. Sofia had shoved it all into the storage shelves in the corner, and it was there that Marianella spotted a radio.

Marianella walked over to the shelf and collected the radio. Sofia glanced at the movement but said nothing. Marianella plugged it into the wall. It erupted into life, the speaker turned too high to a station that was no longer there. Static roared through the room.

Sofia detached herself from the computer.

Marianella spun through the dial and stopped on the news station.

"No word yet from the city offices about the explosion, but reporters are standing by."

"Sofia," Marianella said in a low, warning tone.

"I haven't done anything."

Marianella took a few steps away from the radio, her arms crossed over her chest, and listened.

"One thing is for certain: the explosion did *not* occur at the main dome, and as of right now Hope City is in no danger of freezing or losing power. However, train lines have been shut down and will remain so indefinitely. It's suggested that people return to their homes in case of further emergency."

An explosion outside the main dome. That meant one of the private domes, where the wealthy lived. Where Southstar was. Where—

"No," she whispered, thinking of the rows of corn, the wheat, the fruit. *Hope City is in no danger of freezing*. But something was.

"I have with me Dr. Raul Alvarez, a roboticist for the city, who assures me this is in no way caused by a mechanical failure. Dr. Alvarez—"

"Told you I didn't have anything to do with it." Sofia appeared behind Marianella and put her hand on Marianella's waist. Marianella closed her eyes. Dr. Alvarez prattled on about the safety of the maintenance drones. "Where was it?" Marianella said, and she picked up the radio and shook it like it might give her the answers. "Which *dome* was it?"

Dr. Alvarez continued with his analysis. Marianella slumped down. Sweat prickled over her skin. How human of her.

Gently, Sofia took the radio out of her hands and set it on the table.

"I'm sure your house is fine," Sofia said. "Cabrera wants *me* to kill you, don't you remember?"

"Why would I care about my house?" Marianella took a deep breath. "I'm worried—" She didn't want to say it, because saying it out loud might make it real.

"Thank you, Dr. Alvarez. For those of you just tuning in, another explosion has occurred, this one *outside* the city walls."

Marianella took deep gulping breaths, and Sofia pulled her close, lay her chin on Marianella's shoulder.

"The explosion has damaged a private dome. No word yet on who it belongs to or if anyone was harmed, but it appears it was *not* a place of residence."

"Oh God."

"You don't know for certain," Sofia said. "It could have been one of the private parks."

"And how do you know that?" Marianella snapped. "You sent one of your drones to bomb a park?"

"No, of course not. I promise you. I swear to you."

A forcefulness that Marianella did not expect reverberated through Sofia's voice.

"I'll send you a maintenance drone," Sofia said. "Look back through its memory files. You'll see I had nothing to do with this. If I had to guess the culprit, it would be Cabrera. He knows I haven't killed you yet. He's probably trying to draw me out—draw both of us out."

Marianella wiped at her eyes, which were itching with imminent tears. She hadn't heard from Alejo since he'd come down to the park the day after the ball. What if he hadn't been able to pay off Cabrera, even as the AFF? She should have expected this.

"I have to find out for sure," Marianella said. "If it's my dome or not."

"You can access the maintenance drones from the park call box, then."

"I *can't*. The ag drones can't be accessed remotely. And I'm not sending one of the park drones either," Marianella added before Sofia could say anything. "They'll draw too much attention if it is the dome." Marianella's voice wavered. She shook her head. "No, I'm going myself."

"What? I just told you this is probably a trap. Cabrera's men are likely waiting for you. And even if they're not, there will be city investigators."

"I've beat his men before," Marianella said. "I can do it again if necessary. And the investigators can't stay out for so long in the cold. I'll wait until they're gone." She paused. "Besides, I know the dome. I know how to hide."

"No." Sofia shook her head. "Absolutely not. It's too dangerous."

"Too dangerous?" Marianella snapped. "You didn't think it was too dangerous when I accompanied Eliana into the city!"

Sofia's expression flashed with anger. "Of course I thought that was too dangerous. But there wasn't anything I could do to stop you. And this is different. This is *worse*." She paused. "You have to stay here until I've taken care of Cabrera."

Marianella flushed. She didn't know how to respond to the idea that Sofia cared for her so strongly.

"I've devoted myself to that agricultural dome for almost a year," she said. "You wouldn't understand. You just want to ship all the humans to the mainland. I've told you, the ag dome is the only way for independence that will *work*. And it isn't stupid to want to find out if it's been destroyed. To want to know for *certain*." She trembled. "Sofia, if you care about me—"

"Fine," Sofia said. "You're going to sit here and play at being human and not listen to reason, so just go."

"I'm not playing at being human," Marianella said.

"You're acting like one," Sofia said. "But if you're going to leave, at least take a maintenance drone with you."

Marianella could not stop shaking. Sofia leaned forward and kissed her on the mouth. "Don't let him find you," she whispered.

With that, Marianella left.

* * * *

Even the train going in and out of the amusement park was shut down, so Marianella walked. It took a long time, to weave her way through the city. The streets were deserted, the shops all closed, the houses shut up tight. Marianella's feet echoed against the sidewalk, and she remained alert to the possibility of Ignacio's men crawling out of the shadows. But she never saw anyone.

Maintenance drones scuttled on the dome glass overhead, casting thin wavering shadows over the sidewalk. They were following her. An army of drones to keep her safe.

Through her icy dread, a surge of warmth pulsed in Marianella's heart.

It took her almost an hour to reach the nearest exit. While she walked, she thought about the agricultural dome, about everything she'd done to see it built. All the money she'd invested, all the robots she'd programmed. All so she could prove to the world, to herself, that she was human after all.

Maybe Sofia was right. Maybe she was only playing at being human. The thought made Marianella's chest hurt.

Marianella thought the exit might be blocked off, guarded, but no one was there. And why would they be? It was winter. Any human would die in the cold before they had a chance to escape.

A drone dropped down from the ceiling and landed at Marianella's feet. She pressed her hand against its sensor, and it told her in its jittery language that it was to keep her safe. Marianella closed her eyes. She thought about Sofia sitting in the operations room, how beautiful she was in the computer's harsh lights.

Marianella prayed to the Virgin Mary, and yet she saw Sofia's face in her thoughts.

"I'm ready," she said to the maintenance drone, and it opened the door for her, and they stepped out into the cold.

She hadn't dressed as warmly as she should have, but her anxiety moved her forward, parallel to the wall of frozen light that was the city, past the private domes glowing in the distance. Ice formed over her hair and shoulders. Araceli would have to repair her again after this. She didn't care.

As they approached the agricultural dome, she smelled smoke.

She stopped. Her body vibrated infinitesimally, keeping her human parts warm.

"No," she whispered, although she had known all along.

She ran.

She ran through the swirling snow, her movements clumsy and rough. The maintenance drone whirred behind her. She realized she was crying and that her tears had frozen to her cheeks like tiny icicles. The agricultural dome loomed overhead, another orb of light in the winter darkness, like the light from a human heart.

It was broken.

Marianella screamed, and her scream was lost with the wind. The dome's glass was scorched and shattered. Half of it was gone. For a moment she could only stare. Then the maintenance drone chirped at her, and bumped against her leg like a cat, and she stumbled forward, blind in the snow.

She didn't care if anyone saw her. Didn't care if Ignacio's goons would be waiting for her in parkas and personal heaters. She was drawn toward the dome on a thread of tragedy—she didn't want to see, but she had to see. She *had* to.

Marianella came to the dome's shattered edge. Antarctica had gotten in. All her plants were flash-frozen, snapped in place by coats of ice. Snowdrifts billowed over the crops and the empty paths. Nothing, not even a human in a parka, could survive in here.

She stepped inside. Her feet crunched through the snow and the ice. The standing part of the dome blocked most of the wind, and so the air was still and hollow, even though she could hear the air's whistle and howl as it moved past the gap in the glass.

She was numb. Disbelieving. Like she was trapped in a dream.

She walked past each of the crops in turn: corn, wheat, sorghum, potatoes, grapes, apples. The plants were still green beneath the ice, but she knew that wouldn't last. In a day's time they would be yellowed and dead.

Marianella wept, more icicles forming on her cheeks. The maintenance drone nudged her. She ignored it. She walked every path in the food dome, and then she walked to the train station. The tracks were empty. It was warmer here, farther away from the gaping hole in the glass. Warm enough that her frozen tears began to melt.

She stood for a moment on the platform, listening to the wind. Then she jumped onto the tracks. She was unsteady on her feet from staying too long in the cold. The maintenance drone followed, beeping warnings at her.

"I know you can ignore Sofia's programming," she said out loud.

More beeping. She sighed, pressed her hand on the sensor to get it to shut up. She expected a message from Sofia, but instead there was an image, relayed by one of the maintenance drones in the main dome. At the place where the train tracks crossed over into the main dome stood a trio of men with guns. They were dressed like police officers, but that didn't mean anything.

"Well, then we're going around the side," she said.

The maintenance drone fell silent. They moved together over the tracks. When they came to the dome's edge, they veered off into the ice. Marianella didn't feel the cold anymore. She only felt the empty nothingness that had appeared the moment she'd seen her shattered agricultural dome.

They weren't so long in the snow this time. The nearest entrance was not guarded, and when they came back inside, back into the flood of yellow heat, Marianella let out a soft frustrated sigh and slumped down on the gravel, her limbs jerky and limp. In any other circumstance the gravel would have been cold to the touch, but now it was like the surface of the sun.

The maintenance robot sat beside her as she waited for the ice to melt. The *drip*, *drip*, *drip* of ice off her clothes and hair felt like surrogate tears. It pooled around her. Her insides began to feel normal again, no more shaking or vibrations. She doubted that would last.

Still, she sat there for a long time. When she finally stood up, her clothes were soaked through and her hair was plastered like wet ribbons to the side of her face. Her thoughts were cloudy, except for one, a single sentence that repeated over and over—

Everything is lost.

CHAPTER TWENTY-EIGHT

ELIANA

Eliana watched the footage on Luciano's television, the sound turned down so she wouldn't have to listen to the newsman prattling on. Images flashed by: An enormous, shattered dome, the glass blackened from the explosion. Ice that had melted and refrozen after the fire had been put out, into eerie, indefinable shapes.

And the crops.

The rows and rows of crops, now all dead and wilted. They were throwing them out into the desert to be covered over by snow and ice. That was on the television too, the ice-drones carting the crops over the barren landscape until they disappeared from the sphere of the camera's light. A year's supply of food, the newsman had said. Eliana had watched with her hand at her throat, hardly believing.

All those stupid advertisements the past year, with Marianella smiling into the camera as Lady Luna, Alejo Ortiz beaming at her side. They were asking for money to build domes just like this one, domes that could sustain the city without interference from the mainland.

"We kept it a secret," Marianella explained later that afternoon.

"Why?" Eliana said, sitting on an old reproduction of a Queen Anne chair, the white brocade yellow with age.

Marianella shrugged. A food tray was balanced on her knees, and she took a bite of watery beef soup, the best they could get so late in the season. *And all those crops were frozen.*

"It was Alejo's idea," she said. "All politics are theater, when you get down to it. He wanted to have a fully functioning dome when we made our announcement, rather than just the plans for one." She shook her head, her face blank. "I'd been looking forward to that moment for months. And now—" Her voice cracked. Eliana leaned over and put her hand on her arm, but Marianella didn't acknowledge the gesture. "I just wanted to help the people of Hope City. So I designed it, I funded it." She threw her spoon onto the tray. "And now it's dead."

"You can rebuild," Eliana said, although she had no idea if that was true. "I mean, if you already had plans for others. And the whole city knows it's possible now. It's not as if it broke down."

"It was sabotaged," Marianella said flatly. She set her tray aside, her food half-finished. The silence in the room grew thick.

"I'm sure it was Ignacio Cabrera," Marianella said. "Who else would bomb the agricultural dome?"

Eliana's heart twisted at the mention of Cabrera's name, at the reminder of who Diego really was.

"Other than Sofia," Marianella said.

Eliana looked up. Marianella stared into space. She looked pale and haggard. Not like herself at all.

Eliana stayed a few moments longer, but when it was clear that Marianella didn't want to talk further, Eliana said her good-byes and left.

Eliana's footsteps rattled through the corridor. The Ice Palace was confusing, all those twisting mazelike hallways, leading into rooms filled with old robotics equipment or stacks of ceramic amusement park statues. She wandered for ten minutes until she found a sunroom that looked out over the garden. Luciano was there in the room, reading one of his books.

She stopped in the doorway, surprised to see him. He glanced up at her, and the uncanniness of his movement ruined the illusion of his humanity.

"Eliana," he said. "Did Marianella enjoy her meal?" He shut the book and set it aside.

"She ate it."

There was a pause. Then Luciano looked at her like he had all the answers to her racing, miserable thoughts, like he knew how to make her forget about Diego and his betrayal, like he was willing to listen to her confusion about the agricultural domes and her fear about Cabrera.

"What's the matter?" he asked.

Eliana slumped up against the doorframe. She hesitated. "Everything."

He sat very still, watching her, his head tilted to the side. "You can tell me about it if you wish."

She knew he was programmed to do that. That's how all the amusement park robots worked. They were programmed for certain things. Luciano had been programmed to help people.

And maybe she needed help.

"You really don't mind?"

He shook his head. "I'm happy to help a friend."

A friend. Maybe it wasn't just the program.

And at any rate, she didn't want to walk away. She didn't want to be alone.

And so she sat down in the dusty wicker chair beside him. When he looked at her expectantly, she realized this was what she'd hoped to find with Marianella, because Marianella had been at the gala when Diego had pulled his gun and revealed who he was. But Marianella had reacted exactly as you should when confronting a monster.

And that was the problem.

"It's about my boyfriend," Eliana started, and she didn't intend to say much more than that, but everything poured out anyway. He'd lied to her about the sort of work he did. He'd lied about owning a gun. His eyes had glittered with a cold and terrifying light that had seemed to reveal more about him than any moment they'd spent together ever could have.

When the words finally dried up, her eyes were wet.

Luciano sat still for a moment. She wondered, stupidly, if she had broken him. But then he put his hand on her knee.

"That must be difficult," he said.

It was such a stupid platitude, but no one, not even Marianella, had said anything approximating it in her time here. Her boyfriend had almost killed her, almost killed her friend, and no one had remotely tried to sympathize.

"I don't know what to do!"

"What can you do?" asked Luciano. "None of this is your fault. You can't blame yourself for seeing good in him. That's a quality more humans should have, the ability to see the good in others."

"But there wasn't any good in him."

"Of course there was." Luciano smiled, an easy smile that calmed her like a drug. "You were with him for over a year, yes? And he never hurt you. In fact, he tried to put you out of harm's way as best he could, from what I can tell. It seems to me you brought the good out in him."

Eliana sniffled. The sunroom's windows heated up the thin dome light outside, generating a warmth that felt far more organic than anything from a radiator. She'd never considered the possibility that she might have been the reason Diego seemed like a good person. She didn't know if it was true or not, but she did know this was the first time she had seen him with Cabrera, and the first time she'd seen that cold glitter in his eyes.

"He still lied to me," she said.

"Everyone lies," said Luciano.

Eliana laughed at his bluntness. "Did you say that to clients when the park was open?"

"Of course not. I was programmed to lie. That's how I know everyone does it." He smiled again. "I'm not lying now, however."

This time, Eliana returned his smile. She drew her knees up to her chin and looked out into the garden. Weeds were sprouting up in the cracks between the stones in the path, everything wild and green and beautiful. She tried to imagine it as it would have looked when the park was still open, the growth neat and orderly, but she couldn't. She wasn't sure she wanted to.

"I've never been to the mainland," she said distractedly, still looking out at the garden. "I've wanted to, my entire life. Ever since my parents told me stories about it."

"It's difficult to acquire visas, from what I understand."

Eliana shrugged. "Not difficult, just expensive. I've got the money now, you know. I just have to make it to the spring. I hope the ships start running again. All this." She swooped one hand around, taking in the park, the city itself, the explosions and the failing power and the terror of the past winter. "I don't know what it means for me. I've got the money now, or close to it, but part of me is scared that it's going to take more than money. That the city's changing, and they'll stop the visas, and I won't be able to get out."

They fell into silence.

"Would you like to see the mainland?" Luciano asked.

His question startled her. "Sure. Really, I'd like to see something that's not the dome. When I saw Diego's gun, after I got over the initial *shock*, you know, of what he was, I thought—and this is so stupid, but I thought that I've never seen anything outside the dome." She laughed, hard and bitter.

Luciano frowned. "You've really never seen outside the dome?"

Eliana sighed. "Technically I have. Once. It was when I was a kid. There was a program that would take us out on the boats so we could see what the sun was like and all that." She lay her head on her knee. Luciano didn't ask her for anything more—he seemed trained (programmed, she reminded herself) to listen only to what she wanted to say, all his questions carefully selected. It would be unnerving, if it wasn't such a comfort to have someone listen.

"It was in the summer," Eliana said. "You know, when the sun never sets? You can't tell from the dome, of course, but we learned about it. I remember we were all crowded onto the boat, bundled up in our emergency parkas. All families have them. Did you know that? In case of disaster? They started selling them again when the electricity began flickering."

"I did know that. I'm sure we have some of our own here in the park."

"It doesn't matter." Eliana leaned back in her chair. "God, it was something to see, this huge ball of fire in the sky. They told us not to look straight at it, but of course everyone did, until we couldn't anymore." Eliana smiled and remembered how her eyes had stung and watered, and little black splotches had appeared in her vision. She'd thought she was going blind. And maybe she had, momentarily.

She was thirteen on that trip, and she had stood at the bow of the icebreaker with her head thrown back, promising to herself that someday she would live in a place where she could see the sun all the time.

Christ, she hadn't thought about that in years.

"It sounds lovely." Luciano paused. "I've never seen the sun myself, at least not directly."

Eliana looked at him. He wore the same unflappable expression as always, but he was watching her closely.

"Really?"

"Yes. I was produced in Brazil, of course. We didn't spend much time there before we were shipped to Antarctica. They deactivated us for the journey." He went quiet. Eliana didn't know what to say.

"I did see a rainstorm, though," he said, after a time.

"A rainstorm!" Eliana had seen rainstorms on television programs—gentle ones where the rain rustled through the trees, and wild thrashing ones that ripped the trees from the ground. She could never fathom such a thing happening in real life, though. She couldn't imagine water falling freely from the open sky without freezing. The closest Hope City had to rainstorms were the fire extinguishers that activated whenever the maintenance drones detected smoke.

"What was it like?" Eliana sounded more excited than she'd intended to.

"It's difficult to describe. But I can show you."

"Show me?" Eliana frowned. "Oh, did you, um, record it?"

"I record everything." A brief smile passed over Luciano's lips. "But I am quite discreet, so you don't need to worry. And after a year has passed, a subroutine purges all unnecessary memory files, unless I mark them to be saved." He stopped. "I marked the rainstorm, which is why you can see it."

Eliana nodded. Her skin prickled. This all felt vaguely transgressive, talking to a robot about those things that separated him from being human. And watching one of his recordings—

She felt uncomfortable with the idea. But that discomfort excited her at the same time.

"Okay," she said. "You can show me."

Luciano smiled. "Exciting! We'll have to go to the robodeon. It's on the third floor of the palace." He paused, and his eyes seemed to twinkle. "Sofia won't like it. She hates the idea of us doing any of the things we did in the park. But we won't have to tell her, will we?"

Eliana laughed and nodded. She and Luciano left the sunroom and walked together through the hallways. They didn't speak, and Eliana wondered if Luciano felt the awkwardness of their silence. Would his programming dictate something like that? She wasn't sure. He was so much more complex than the maintenance drones. Their jobs were obvious. But robots like Luciano and Sofia left her not knowing what to think. And Luciano keeping secrets from Sofia—Eliana didn't know what to think of that, either.

Their footsteps echoed as they walked up the stairs. Eliana had never been to the third floor, but it looked the same as the rest of the palace, everything faded and dusty.

"Here we are." Luciano stopped in front of a pair of wooden doors, carved with the swirling art nouveau women that had been so popular during the park's heyday. He pushed them open. Eliana had been expecting a cinema, like the one on Lucia Avenue, but there was no big blank screen or velvet curtains. Even the seats were arranged differently. They sat in pairs, facing each other.

"When the park was open, there was an entire fleet of robots who worked in this room." Luciano gestured for her to enter, and she did. "They were programmed with hundreds of different scenarios to choose from." He sounded like he was reciting from a travel brochure. Eliana wondered if he used to give this speech to his guests. "The guest sits in one chair; the robot sits across from her. They connect with the viewing harness. It's quite harmless, don't worry."

It definitely sounded like a travel brochure. Eliana sat down on the cleanest, least ripped of the chairs. She could vaguely recall older people talking about this, the robodeon at the amusement park, although she had never been clear how it worked. Luciano disappeared behind a paper screen for a few seconds and emerged carrying a hat trailing cables. Eliana frowned at it.

"Wait," she said. "You mean we're going to do it like they did in the park?"

Luciano stopped. "How else would we do it?"

"I don't know. I thought you'd—project—the memory—"

Luciano tilted his head. "But that would be the same as seeing it on television, and you wanted to experience it, correct?"

Eliana hesitated. She thought she'd been humoring him, letting him show her his rainstorm.

"I can experience it?" she finally said, feeling stupid.

"Yes, of course." Luciano sat down in the chair across from her and handed her the hat. "It's quite safe. Thousands of people participated every year." He smiled, his eyes glinting. "And Marianella would be extremely upset if anything happened to you."

Eliana wasn't so sure about that anymore. She looked down at the hat. It was a fearsome thing, not a hat so much as a helmet, with blacked-out goggles and a bronzed metal exterior. She knocked on it, listening to the sound reverberate inside.

"I swear to you," Luciano said, "I'd never do anything to hurt you."

Eliana felt suddenly warm. She looked up at him. He was staring at her, unblinking. She thought of all the times Diego had said that. She'd always believed him, and she couldn't anymore.

But she believed Luciano. She had to believe someone wanted to keep her safe.

"All right," she said, and she slipped the helmet on. The goggles blocked out her vision. She was aware of Luciano's hands fiddling with the wires, looping them over her head, pressing something cold against the top of her spine.

"Luciano?" Her voice echoed, amplifying her nervousness.

"I'm here." The helmet covered her ears, and so his voice was muffled. "Can you see anything? Any light, anything?"

"No." Her answer trembled against the inside of the helmet.

"Good. You aren't supposed to." He fell silent. She resisted the urge to reach over and feel for him, to put her hand on his knee, to make sure he was there.

Light flooded her vision.

Eliana screamed and moved to yank off the helmet, but Luciano stopped her. "It's all right," he said. "I'm sorry. I should have warned you. I wasn't specifically programmed for this, and it's been some time since I've done it."

Eliana took a deep breath. The light was settling into shapes: trees and little wooden houses and stone paths leading into a forest. "Oh my God," she whispered, because as the shapes settled, the other senses caught up—a breeze ran through the trees and caressed against her skin, warm in a way she had never known. It was not the dry heat of a radiator, but damp and hazy and so thick, it seemed alive. She could smell dirt and sweet green scents, and everything was so overwhelming that she was almost dizzy.

"Luciano?" she said, her voice wavering.

"I'm here." He sounded far away. "Can you see it?"

"Yes."

The sky overhead was a dark purplish gray, a color she had never known a sky to be. Suddenly she was walking forward, following one of the paths.

"This is my memory," Luciano said. "I walked, so you're walking."

"I'm you?"

"In a sense, yes."

A line of light cracked across the sky. Eliana shrieked.

"Lightning," Luciano said. "Remember, nothing happening here will hurt you."

Eliana nodded, although the Eliana in the memory did not. A sound rumbled in from everywhere, dark and threatening. The lightning flashed again. Eliana jumped, but she was growing used to it.

And then there was a rustling, all around her, like the trees were trying to talk. She felt like she should hold her breath.

Water poured out of the sky.

It fell in raging, riotous sheets, soaking through her thin gray coveralls, plastering her short hair to her head. It dripped into her eyes. Little yellow lamps glowed at each of the houses, and their light caught the raindrops and made them shimmer like static. When the lightning flashed, it turned the whole world white. Eliana—Luciano—did not move from that spot.

"I wasn't supposed to be outside," Luciano said, his voice closer than she'd expected. "They activated us to ensure there weren't any problems, but we weren't supposed to leave our quarters. However, they never programmed the command into us, because it would have been a problem once we arrived at the park, and so I left anyway. I didn't know it was going to rain. I understood what was happening, but I still found it—" He stopped. "I found it beautiful, I suppose."

"It is beautiful." The rain fell harder and harder. The water seemed to soak through her skin. She wondered if he'd worried about that, the water damaging him. Or maybe water couldn't damage androids. She wasn't sure.

Off to the side, someone shouted, an angry bark. A man appeared, wearing a plastic raincoat and a yellow hat, shouting Luciano's name and then a string of Portuguese.

Everything faded away.

Eliana yanked off her helmet, expecting to find her clothes soaked and her hair dripping, but she was as dry as when she had walked into the room. Luciano sat across from her with his hands folded in his lap, a cable draped over one shoulder. It disappeared into some unfathomable place behind his ear.

"A rainstorm," Luciano said.

"Thank you," Eliana said.

Luciano smiled.

The rainstorm was implanted in Eliana's memory. She could think back on it and remember the feel of the rain across her arm. It was strange, having Luciano's memory inside her head. But she didn't want it gone.

Rainstorms. Wind. The scent of a jungle.

She only wished those memories were hers, and hers alone. Because that would mean she had accomplished what her mother could not, what her father could not.

It would mean she had actually left Hope City.

CHAPTER TWENTY-NINE

MARIANELLA

Downtown was colder than Marianella expected. They stood waiting in front of the city building, the dais a few paces away. It was decorated with little blue-and-white flags that hung limply in the still air.

Marianella pulled her coat more tightly around her chest. She couldn't believe how biting and cold it was out here. At least the dome lights were bright. There hadn't been a single flicker all day.

A crowd fanned out from the dais, reporters with notebooks and flashbulb cameras. The rest of the crowd seemed to be Independents, given the number of sealskin coats.

"Are you ready?" Alejo appeared beside her, straightening his tie. "Ready to blow them all away?"

Marianella nodded, even if she found his choice of words unfortunate. Alejo turned and muttered something to his entourage, all his assistants in their own gray suits.

"Showtime," Alejo said, and he looped his arm through Marianella's and they walked out onto the dais.

The Independence crowd erupted into cheers. The news reporters scribbled in their notebooks. A film camera stared at her with its dark, unblinking eye.

Marianella scanned across the crowd, her chest tight. Alejo planned to run Ignacio out of town, but he hadn't done it yet. One of Ignacio's men might turn up here, with a gun aimed straight at her head. One shot, and everyone would know what she was, and that would be the end of it.

Except Alejo had brought in bodyguards, like he'd promised. Big, hulking men who ambled around the dais with their hands tucked into their jackets. AFF members. Marianella tried not to think about it, reminding herself that they were here to protect her.

Alejo and Marianella took their places at the front of the dais, in front of the microphone. His entourage settled into a half circle of chairs around them.

Marianella took a deep breath. Now was not the time to think about Ignacio.

"Good afternoon," she said. Her voice echoed with electronic feedback. "We have something very exciting to share with you."

"The city doesn't want us to tell you this," Alejo said.

Marianella smiled, and the audience tittered. She took a step back; they had agreed that he would do most of the speaking. As he was the politician, it only made sense.

"You've all seen the advertisements for the agricultural domes, I'm sure, the ones with myself and the lovely Lady Luna." He gestured at Marianella, and she gave a little wave. "And of course now you all know that the domes are a reality—or rather, were a reality. My team and I were successful in building one fully operational agricultural dome out in the Antarctic desert, and we kept it running until some madman decided to destroy our hard work."

His team? Marianella gave a strained smile. She wouldn't say it was a *team*.

"The question of who destroyed the dome is not why we're here. But I will say this: there are those who would blame the bombing on the Antarctican Freedom Fighters."

Boos and hisses erupted out of the crowd beyond the reporters. Alejo lifted one hand.

"I'm here to say—*we're* here to say"—he gestured once again at Marianella—"that we know those who support independence for

Antarctica would never destroy that thing which could give her independence."

The boos and hisses turned to applause. Marianella clapped politely. No, the AFF hadn't bombed the dome. Neither had Sofia. Marianella had already gone through the files on the maintenance drones, looking for a sign of betrayal. But Marianella wasn't willing to celebrate the fact that Cabrera had destroyed their work.

"But we are choosing today not to focus on the past but to focus on the future. That's what Lady Luna and I are doing." He smiled. "Everyone give a round of applause for Lady Luna. She's been much more than a pretty face for the commercials. Her financial contributions to the Independent cause have been tremendous."

Applause thundered up from the crowd. It turned to an ocean's roaring inside Marianella's head. She forced a smile out to the crowd and waved, swiveling her wrist back and forth. It was hard to make out individual faces, even with her machine parts, and that made her nervous.

The applause died down. Marianella stepped back. She was dimly aware that something was *off*, not in the crowd but in Alejo, but she couldn't quite tease it out.

"The real tragedy in all this is not just the loss of the dome but the loss of the hours of hard work that was put into its creation by my men."

Men? The buzzing intensified in Marianella's head. What men? The dome had been built by robots. Robots that she'd designed, that she'd built.

"But even so, we remain secure in the knowledge that if we built the dome once, we can build it again!"

A thunderous round of applause. Camera bulbs flashed, one after another. Something was wrong. There had been no *men*.

When he had introduced her, he'd only talked of her financial contributions, not of her intellectual ones.

Marianella suddenly couldn't breathe.

"Here they are," he said, and gestured to the men in gray suits, the ones Marianella had thought were assistants. "The best engineers our city has to offer. That ag dome was not built by mainland ingenuity but by Antarctican brilliance."

Marianella's vision filled with a blinding white light. She dug her nails into her palm, deep enough that her robot brain took over and siphoned the pain away. Distantly, she was aware of Alejo's voice, rising and falling over a buzz of static feedback.

"This is a setback, certainly. But it will not curtail us completely. I can assure you that the explosion was not caused by a malfunction but by a terrorist, set on stopping us on our path for self-sufficiency. This entire city was built out of human ingenuity, and it was human ingenuity that built the food dome."

He glanced at her when he said "human ingenuity." She was certain of it.

"It will be human ingenuity that will rebuild it. For those of you who thought Independence was a logistical possibility, I give you the wreckage of my creation"—Marianella took a deep, gasping breath—"as proof that we can build our own nation here on the ice of Antarctica. Don't look at this as a tragedy but as a victory. The terrorists who bombed the agricultural dome killed no one, because death was not their intention. Only destruction. Destruction of a dream made real. We will build that dream again."

For a moment, there was only stunned silence and the wind whistling through the buildings. Then the cameras lit up, and the reporters surged forward, shouting Alejo's name. Marianella didn't move. The men in gray suits stood up and waved at the crowd as they had their pictures taken over and over.

"Lady Luna! Lady Luna!"

Marianella turned toward the reporters. Lights flashed at her in quick succession and she had to stop herself from throwing up her arm and running away. Alejo leaned over the edge of the dais, pointing to reporters and answering their questions. She stared at him, ignoring the people calling out her name. She hated him. She hated his team of actors posing as engineers. She hated the humans applauding him as if he'd done any of the work, as if he'd programmed the robots or planned the architecture.

She realized she was money, she was a pretty face for the advertisements, she was nothing.

"Lady Luna, will you be sponsoring the next dome? Lady Lu—"

Marianella stepped off the dais and walked away from the crowd. Her scarf fluttered behind her, and her quick steps loosened her hair from its bouffant. A tear streaked down her cheek; she reached up and wiped it away. Mascara smeared across her fingers. She couldn't let anyone see her like this, and she knew that if she stayed out in the open much longer, someone would chase her down.

She walked to the end of the block and hailed a taxi. The tears fell faster now, leaving hot trails on her face. The taxi pulled up to the curb, and the driver did a double take when he saw her.

"Uh, where to?" he asked, averting his eyes. Marianella climbed in.

"Alejo Ortiz's office," she said. "At the corner of Main and Fifty-Seventh Street."

The driver nodded and jerked back the handle on the meter. Marianella watched the number click upward through the haze of her tears.

"Everything okay?" the driver asked.

"Everything's fine." She said it as sharply as she could, and he didn't ask any more questions.

After ten minutes, they came to Alejo's office.

The building glinted in the dome light. The windows were darkened, but Marianella knew he'd be back soon enough. Alejo always came up to the office to regroup after press conferences.

She walked up to the office's big glass door and pulled it open. The receptionist was gone, the lobby empty. The building had the abandoned feel of an office closed down for a holiday weekend.

All the lights were off, but Marianella had been here enough times that she didn't need them. She followed the hallway until she came to Alejo's office. The door was locked with a city-style electronic lock, and Marianella pressed her hand against it and sparked it open.

Inside, she flicked on the light and then turned the chair at his desk around so that she was facing the door. She sat down.

And waited.

She didn't wait long. Twenty minutes, maybe half an hour. As much as Alejo liked being the center of attention, he knew how important it was for him to come back to his office, to strategize, to see how he could swing the explosion to his advantage.

She wondered if he'd even noticed she'd disappeared.

When she heard the voices out in the hallway—male voices, gibbering with excitement—her anger flared again. She straightened her back, crossed her legs.

"What the— Did you forget and leave the light on, Ivan?" Alejo appeared in the doorway, although he was staring down the hallway. "Get Ruben. This might be some kind of—" He turned his face toward his office. "Oh," he said.

"Hello, Alejo." Marianella's voice was cold and flat, and it made her feel more inhuman than she already did by Alejo's hand.

"I was worried about you." He smiled, his voice smoothed over. He stepped into the office and clicked the door shut behind him, but he didn't walk closer to her. "I was afraid you'd gotten snatched off the street. I was about to send the bodyguards out to look for you. Figured you wouldn't want me to call the police."

"Shut up," Marianella said.

Alejo blinked. Her anger surged inside her, rushing through her veins.

"You cut me out," she said. "You gave credit to a bunch of actors. They were actors, weren't they? You and I both know there aren't enough Independent engineers in the city to do that kind of work. That's why I designed the robots in the first place."

He didn't look away from her. She had to give him credit for that.

"Yes," he said. "They were actors."

It was the answer Marianella had expected, but hearing it still felt like a punch in the stomach.

"I'm sorry if that's not what you wanted to hear." He peeled himself away from the door and walked over to his desk. Marianella followed him with her gaze. He sat down. She turned her chair around and faced him. Her heart beat too quickly, and her machine parts were already kicking in to calm it.

"Why?" Her voice cracked.

"I thought the truth would raise too many questions. Don't you think it's better this way, that you're the financial contributor? It fits in more with the whole Lady Luna eccentric heiress thing." He waved his hand around.

"You could have at least made me part of the team."

Alejo sighed. "Look," he said. "People know what exploded. The city tried to rein it in, but people figured it out." He stared at her, unwavering. "And they're impressed. Really fucking impressed. No one thought it was possible."

Marianella felt a twinge of pride.

"I was getting calls two hours after it happened. Everybody knew I'd been campaigning for it, and God, the thrill of hearing them talk as if I'd done it, as if I'd—"

"I can only imagine," she snapped.

He fell silent and leaned back in his chair. He reminded her of a shark, something lean and dangerous.

"The point I'm trying to make," he said, shrugging, "is that—well, I guess I don't need you anymore."

The buzzing started up again. Marianella blinked. Of course he needed her. This was as much her project as it was his.

"I don't understand," she said.

"We were doing it in secret, Marianella! That was the whole point! We couldn't hire city engineers to program the robots, and, like you said, there aren't enough Independent engineers for that kind of project. You had the money and you had the—the skills, and I'm grateful for them, I am, but—"

Marianella couldn't breathe. "But the design, the plants, all of it—they were all my ideas. I—"

"It was my idea," said Alejo. "It was my whole damn platform during the election! Build agricultural domes, build self-sufficiency. I know you remember."

"That's not what I mean!" Marianella's voice was shrill, nearly hysterical. He didn't understand, or he didn't *want* to understand—she had used her nature to build something to help humans, to show she wasn't a robot. And now Alejo Ortiz was going to tear it away from her. "It's my design," she said, which came nowhere close to expressing the rage she felt in this moment. "You can't cut me out of my own design. At least say I was part of the engineering team."

"No one would believe that!" Alejo said. "Some pretty socialite who knows enough to build a dome? Come off it, Marianella."

"I can't believe you're doing this."

Alejo paused. He fixed her with a cold, unnerving gaze.

"What?" she said.

"I'm guessing you took a stroll in the snow and saw your *design*. Am I right?"

Marianella glared at him.

"I know I am. I had to go look at it too. So you know that half of your design has been blown to hell and the other half is frozen. Now, who do we know who would do something like that?" He tilted his head, smiled at her. "Who do we know who has the capacity to blow up parts of Hope City?"

"You and I both know it was Cabrera. It was revenge—"

"Exactly. Cabrera, and his problems with you."

Marianella stared at him. "What are you saying?"

Alejo leaned back in his chair, his face stony and cold. "You attacked one of his men," Alejo said. "If we'd tried to make a deal with him straightaway, or if you'd let me just *take care of it*, maybe this wouldn't have happened."

Marianella heard the blood rushing in her ears. The room spun.

"Are you blaming me?" she whispered. "You think I wanted this to happen?"

"I'm just saying," Alejo said, "that by the time the AFF took their offer to Cabrera, it was too late. He refused to deal, *because* of you. We have to do these things early. We should have looped him in from the beginning."

"And that's why you lied?" she said. "Why you cut me out?"

"You're a liability, Marianella. I like you, but you're a fucking liability. There are always going to be people like Cabrera in the world. Independence won't get rid of them. So I thought it would be better if the ag dome team understands that. And that means *everyone* on the team."

Marianella blinked, and tears fell down her cheeks. She hated herself for it. Her face burned with humiliation.

"I'm going to ask you to leave," Alejo said, leaning over his desk. "That press conference, let that be your last hurrah. It's as good a swan song as any. I just can't risk you anymore."

Marianella shook her head. "No," she said. "No, I won't. If you kick me out of this, I'll go public with the truth about your election money. I'll take it straight to—"

"And I'll go public about you being a cyborg."

Marianella froze. It was the first time he had used the word in her presence, and it brought with it a sharp burst of pain, a dizziness, a rush of blood.

"This is what you would call a stalemate," Alejo said. "We've both got our secrets, and we'll both keep the other's. No hard feelings."

Marianella shook. Her anger and frustration boiled close to the surface. And she was crying, silently, tears dropping over her face at odd intervals.

Everything she'd worked for during the last year was gone. It had exploded and then it had frozen, and now it was being dragged away from her.

"I'm sure Ruben would be happy to escort you back to the amusement park if you're worried about security."

Marianella's thoughts were a haze. Ruben was one of the AFF bodyguards. Alejo was kicking her out of his office.

Eventually, she moved according to some other, baser principle. She stood up, steadying herself on the edge of the desk.

"How could you do this?" she said.

She curled her fingers around the edge of the desk, tighter and tighter, until the wood splintered. Alejo watched her like he'd expected it.

"We do what we have to." Alejo's voice was flat. "That's what it takes, to get Independence."

Marianella stumbled out of his office, her tears turning the world to mist.

* * * *

When Marianella returned to the amusement park, she went straight to the operations room. Sofia wasn't there, but Marianella brought up the robot scans and waded through each one. Marianella's heart was beating too fast. Her robot parts could barely control it.

Her rage was a core of heat inside her chest, ignited by Alejo Ortiz. It had grown in the taxi ride on the way back to the park. He didn't want her anymore, not her knowledge, not her skills, not even, apparently, her money. All because she had demanded integrity from him.

The scans finally dinged on Sofia, recognizing her by her faint aura of electronic feedback. She was down by the ice lake. Marianella left the palace immediately.

It was a fifteen-minute walk to the lake. With each step blood pumped more firmly through Marianella's veins. She was too angry to pray, to even think about God. She only wanted Sofia.

The lake was a sheet of silvery ice, frozen from underneath and glimmering in the slow-falling twilight. It was surrounded by tall, pale white reeds that rattled as Marianella walked through them. They weren't living things.

Sofia was out on the ice, walking with slow measured steps, her legs and feet bare. She looked up at the reeds' rattle and then stopped, watching. Marianella reached the edge of the lake. The ice looked ancient, veined with dark cracks. She supposed it would hold her weight. It held Sofia's.

And what did it matter if it didn't? She could climb her way out easily. She wouldn't freeze to death within minutes, the way a human would.

She took a deep breath and stepped out onto the ice.

Sofia still had not moved. Her hair fell loose around her shoulders. Her face was as perfect and as beautiful as a china doll's. She said nothing until Marianella was at her side.

"I see Cabrera didn't kill you."

"Alejo stole the ag dome from me." Marianella felt dizzy, saying those words out loud.

"What?" Sofia frowned. "I don't understand. Isn't that why you left the park in the first place? To go lay claim to your dome?"

"In the press conference he held about the explosion. He denied that I built it. And now he's going to build new domes, using my designs and my drones." Marianella smiled ruefully. "After all, he insisted when I built them that my drones recognize his authority as well."

Sofia stared at her for a long time, not speaking. The cold, still air settled around them. The ice felt like it belonged to something living.

And then Sofia reached over and smoothed down Marianella's hair. She cupped her hand around the curve of Marianella's neck. Her touch was cold, but Marianella didn't care. It was perfect.

"That's what humans do," Sofia said. "They use you up."

Marianella closed her eyes. She thought about what her life had been like before the procedure, back when she was still human. There weren't many memories from that time, and the ones she did have were dull and worn down at the edges. She didn't know if that was the fault of the procedure, or the fault of her humanity and its inability to hold on to the past.

She opened her eyes. Sofia was still touching her neck, and her fingers had grown warm with the heat of Marianella's skin.

"You were right," Marianella said. "I was pretending to be human. And I realize now how stupid that was."

Sofia didn't react except to trace a path into the hollow of Marianella's throat.

"I want to help you," Marianella said, the words chattering and echoing inside her head. It was so easy to say this, to admit to what she was. She should have done it years ago. "I want to help you take over the city. I want a place where cyborgs can live too."

The words sang against the air.

"I know," Sofia said. "And one day, you'll have it."

She leaned forward and wrapped Marianella up in her arms.

CHAPTER THIRTY

SOFIA

Sofia lay at Marianella's side and watched her sleep. It was as dull an activity as she remembered from her days with clients, but she didn't feel like being alone. Not right now, so soon after Marianella had finally agreed.

She was on Sofia's side. She was on *their* side, away from the humans. On the side where she needed to be.

It was a beautiful night.

Of course, Sofia wasn't thinking beautiful thoughts. In the dull evening she was contemplating Ignacio Cabrera. Her programming could no longer betray her, and that meant it was time to dispatch with Cabrera as neatly and quickly as possible.

There was only one way.

Sofia crawled out of bed and paced silently around the room, planning, as Marianella slept. Around four in the morning, Marianella rolled over under her quilt, and her eyes fluttered open. Sofia heard the movement; she was aware of Marianella watching her in the dark.

"Tired of sleeping?" Sofia asked.

Marianella smiled a little. "That's not exactly how it works, no."

Sofia shrugged. Marianella stretched underneath the blankets. "Something woke me up," she said.

"I was being as quiet as possible."

"I know. It was something else. A dream."

"Oh." Sofia sat down on the edge of the bed and ran one hand through Marianella's hair. "Dreams can wake you up?"

"Sometimes."

Silence. For a moment Sofia thought Marianella had fallen back asleep, but then she felt the weight of her gaze again. Her eyes were still open, watching.

Sofia stretched out beside Marianella and kissed her. "I'm glad you're awake," she said. "It was dreadfully dull before."

Marianella laughed. "You didn't have to stay here."

"I wanted to."

Marianella seemed pleased—happy. And that made Sofia happy, in a way that had nothing to do with her programming.

"Are you still serious about joining with me?" Sofia said in a low voice. Marianella didn't answer right away, and Sofia waited, unmoving, not sure if Marianella would say yes or no.

"Yes," Marianella said.

Sofia fell onto her back and smiled.

"I'm not as flighty as you think I am," Marianella said.

"I never thought you were flighty." Sofia stared up at the ceiling.

"I won't hurt anyone, though," Marianella said. Sofia dropped her head to the side to look at Marianella. "No one innocent."

"And if they're not innocent?"

Marianella pushed up onto an elbow. Her hair, mussed from sleep, fell over one side of her face. "What does that mean?"

"Cabrera." Sofia kept her eyes on Marianella's face. "And his men, the high-ranking ones. The killers." She paused. "My reprogramming worked. We don't need the programming key. So he's of no use to me anymore."

Marianella collapsed back down. "Alejo said the same thing about me," she whispered.

"This is different. Cabrera has tried to kill you twice, and he wants me to do it the third time. We're lucky he hasn't stormed the park yet. Besides, how much damage to the people of the city have he and his men done? The innocent people?"

Marianella didn't say anything.

"The only way you'll ever be safe is if he's gone completely."

"I know how Ignacio Cabrera works." Marianella continued to stare up at the ceiling. "Alejo wanted to do this too, you know. Kill him." She paused. "Murder him. And I couldn't stand the thought . . ." Her voice faded away, and she closed her eyes, took a deep breath. "He's hurt so many people. His men—"

Sofia lay her hand on Marianella's chest, right over her heart. "They're the worst kind of humans. I know you see that. And you know this is the only way to keep you safe."

Marianella didn't say anything for a long time. Sofia waited with all the patience of a clock. She knew she needed to let Marianella work through the repercussions on her own.

"What exactly do you want me to do?" Marianella said, and her voice trembled.

* * * *

The Florencia looked worn-out during the day, an old gray building rubbed raw by the salt and cold wind from the docks. Marianella and Sofia stood side by side on the sidewalk, staring up at the darkened sign. If Sofia listened closely, she could hear the hammering of Marianella's heart.

"It's going to be all right," she whispered.

Marianella looked at her and didn't say anything. She looked resolute. Resolute and frightened.

Sofia leaned over and brushed her lips against Marianella's cheek. Marianella closed her eyes, tilting her head toward the kiss.

"Ten minutes, and it will all be over," Sofia whispered.

"Ten minutes," Marianella said, and fear made her voice tremble.

"It's time." Sofia pushed her doubts aside. The change in her programming meant she no longer cared what humans thought, but the change seemed to amplify her own emotions, and in certain ways they were wild and unfathomable. In certain ways they were dangerous. But she would not allow them to be dangerous today.

She and Marianella went into the Florencia.

The maître d' was gone. No music filtered in from the dining room. Marianella pressed against Sofia. Her breath quickened. All those little remnants of humanity.

Ten minutes, Sofia thought.

Diego and Sebastian walked in from the dining room. Diego's face was bruised and darkened, and Sofia noticed the way Marianella turned away from him.

They pulled out their guns when they saw who it was.

"Hello, boys," Sofia said. "I brought you a present." She stepped in front of Marianella as she spoke.

"Took you long enough," Sebastian said. "And he wanted her dead."

"And she will be." Sofia smiled. "I thought he might like to watch me kill her in front of him."

Diego and Sebastian glanced at each other, and Sofia tightened her grip on Marianella's hand, trying to calm her.

"That's not usually how he operates," Sebastian said.

"It's how I operate. Let me see him."

There was a long pause. Marianella whimpered beside her.

But then Sebastian nodded, frowning, and he and Diego led them into the dining room.

Cabrera sat at a table in the center of the floor, eating a steak. The meat wasn't the frozen, reconstituted stuff Marianella and Eliana and Araceli had been eating. It was fresh. Sofia could tell by the smell of it, by the bright red liquid pooling at the bottom of his plate. Sometimes she hated the smell of organic matter.

"Sofia," he said, setting down his knife and fork. "This wasn't the arrangement we talked about."

Sofia let go of Marianella's arm. Marianella stayed quiet, the way they had agreed.

"I wasn't happy with that arrangement."

Cabrera looked up at her, his eyes glittering. And then he laughed. "You weren't supposed to be happy with that arrangement."

"What happened at the gala was not my fault." Sofia slid into the chair across from Cabrera. "I brought you Lady Luna. You can do whatever you want with her. I'll even kill her in front of you, if you'd like." She smiled sweetly, even if the words stung like needles. "I'm just asking for some payment in exchange. Nothing major."

"Payment." Cabrera shoved his half-eaten steak aside. "Are you so stupid you didn't realize this was a punishment?"

"You pay your men when they kill for you. Why should I be any different?"

Cabrera looked at her, considering. His eyes flicked over to Marianella. "I bet this comes as a surprise, doesn't it?" he said. "One of your own bringing you to me?"

Marianella stared at him. Her whole body was shaking. Sofia twisted with sadness. Ten minutes. Ten minutes and this would all be over.

"Fuck you," Marianella said.

Cabrera laughed. "You think that's going to save you?"

"No," Marianella said.

"Smart girl." He gestured at the table's empty chairs. "Have a seat, Lady Luna."

Marianella hesitated. Cabrera slid his steak back in front of him and cut off a piece.

"Go on," he said.

Marianella sat. She kept her head down, her hands folded.

"Now," he said. "What payment do you want, Sofia?"

"An icebreaker."

Cabrera sawed off another hunk of steak. "That's more than I pay my men. And you didn't even do what I asked."

Sofia was ready for this. "I've no need for money. The amusement park operates independent from the rest of the city. It doesn't need to be one of your nicer ones. A converted cruise ship would be fine."

Cabrera chewed his steak. Sofia glanced around the room, taking in the shadows and the light, looking for secrets. She saw nothing but tables stacked with chairs, a dusty empty stage, and Sebastian, standing by the doors. Sebastian had his gun pointed at Marianella's head.

"An icebreaker," Cabrera said. "That doesn't make this much of a punishment, does it?" He laughed and looked over at Marianella. Sofia felt her stiffen.

"You haven't gone to the police about what I tried to do to you."

He slivered off another piece of steak. "You don't want them to find out your little secret, I imagine."

Marianella stayed quiet. Sofia wished she could reach over and take her hand, tell her everything was going to be fine.

"I thought about letting you go," he went on. "What harm can you do to me now? But this one—she needs to remember that I'm her employer. Her *master*." He looked at Sofia.

She quaked with rage.

"It's rather quiet in here, don't you think?" he said. "I've never liked the silence. Mateo! Put on some music."

Sofia lifted her chin and said nothing. The music that came spilling over the speakers was a recent song, what she would once have called a safe song, and Cabrera sawed at his steak as if he expected nothing to happen.

"There," he said. "Isn't that better?"

"No," said Sofia.

"I promised not to play any music from before 1936." Cabrera peered up at her. "Now. I'm not giving you an icebreaker." He sliced off a piece of steak. "But I'll loan you one. The *Snow Queen* is currently docked. We'll go out there when I've finished my lunch; I want to make sure you do as I've asked."

"Thank you," Sofia said, a phrase that was like speaking with knives.

Marianella squirmed in her seat, her skin shining with sweat.

"The cops have pulled back lately," Cabrera said, chatting around his food. "Not sure why. I haven't upped their payments." His laughter bled in with the soft whine of the music. "Still, it's been making business easier. And what's good for me is good for you, isn't that right, Sofia?"

"Yes." She didn't take her eyes off him. She was watching for tells—a change in his heart rate, a quickening of his breath. But so far he was only eating.

"By the way, your last part should be arriving soon. The programming key, wasn't it?"

"Yes," Sofia said.

"Weird little thing. Had to buy off a fellow in Colombia for it."

Sofia didn't answer. Cabrera was watching her. His fork moved into his mouth. His jaw worked up and down. There were only a few bites left of steak on his plate. That steak was a timer. A countdown.

Fortunately, Sofia had a countdown of her own, ticking away inside her head. The drones were amassing as they waited, responding to the electronic pulses she sent out in waves, unnoticeable to the guards, unnoticeable to Cabrera. That was why she and Marianella had arranged this trade today, at lunchtime, because Sofia knew it was customary for Cabrera to eat a steak alone inside the Florencia.

Two or three bites of steak remained on Cabrera's plate. Marianella shifted beside Sofia, and Cabrera jerked his head up, glaring at her.

"Careful," he said. "If you move too much . . ." He nodded at Sebastian. Diego had vanished. "He might get overzealous."

Marianella glanced at Sebastian, then turned away quickly.

"As for you." Here Cabrera pointed at Sofia with his fork, a hunk of steak dripping at the end. "We're going to be certain that you do as I ask."

"Oh, Ignacio," Sofia said. "It'll be so much easier aboard the icebreaker. You won't have to clean up the mess."

Cabrera looked at her with his glittering black eyes. He set his fork down.

"I never clean up my own messes," he said.

The music stopped, midsong. The silence buzzed around them. Sofia tensed. She stared right back at him. She didn't move.

"Mateo," Cabrera said.

Music flooded into the room, loud enough that Marianella jolted in her seat and put her hands over her ears—a human gesture, worthless, that she didn't need to bother with. At first Sofia didn't recognize the music, but when the singing began, mournful lyrics swelling through the room, she knew she had heard this song before. It was just that she had never *heard* it, not without her programming interfering with her thoughts. It was "*Paciencia*," the song Cabrera had used on her before to make her pliable.

Sofia broke into a smile. She laughed, the sweet twinkling laugh she'd used on clients all those years ago. Cabrera's eyes widened.

"Oh, you didn't really think that would work, did you?" she said.

Cabrera's knife clattered to the plate. "Impossible," he whispered.

Sofia just laughed harder. She could feel Marianella in her periphery, watching her, frowning, but Sofia didn't care.

"You are not my master," Sofia said.

And with that, the countdown hit zero. Sofia sent out one more electronic pulse, not to the drones but to Marianella, and together they moved like lightning.

Sofia slid forward, across the table to Cabrera. Marianella ducked beneath the table, angling her body sideways.

The emergency hatches in the walls split open, and the maintenance drones poured in.

Gunfire arced across the room, light and smoke and heat.

The music was still playing, and for the first time Sofia could appreciate the beauty in Echagüe's voice and in his words as the song hung like a tapestry in the background of the restaurant.

She wrapped her hands around Cabrera's neck. His chair tipped, and they both slammed against the floor, and Sofia squeezed and Cabrera choked and wheezed. She shut out the music, the gunfire, the muffled shouts from the men who had been waiting—she'd *known* it—in the back corridor. She focused only on Cabrera, his neck soft beneath her hands.

"Do you know why they designed me the way they did?" she whispered. "Designed me to look like your kind?"

Cabrera tried to speak, but she didn't care what he had to say.

"Humans have never liked machines that look like machines. Sixty years ago you made us look and act like you so we'd blend in. But then that made you nervous, too, so now you tuck my kind away in the rafters, where we can't be seen."

Sofia squeezed harder. His windpipe crushed under her fingers. Cabrera thrashed beneath her, his face red and his eyes bulging, but she was designed to stay put.

"That will be your downfall," she said.

And with one more strangled cry, Cabrera died.

CHAPTER THIRTY-ONE

ELIANA

Eliana walked down to the sculpture garden. It was colder out than usual, even for the amusement park. Still, she had promised she would meet Luciano for a morning walk, and she was looking forward to it, despite the strange experience of sharing a memory with him. That memory was still inside her head. It belonged to her now, like a gift.

Luciano sat on his usual bench, reading a book, something for children, with pictures. Eliana didn't recognize it. She sat down beside him, and he looked up at her and smiled.

"Good morning." All prim and proper like always.

"Morning." Eliana reached into her coat pocket and pulled out the scone she'd wrapped up in a cloth napkin for her breakfast. She'd slept late this morning, because of the cold and because she didn't have anything else to do. Her stomach rumbled. She nibbled at the scone. Too dry. Araceli wasn't much of a baker.

"Did you sleep well?" Luciano asked.

"As well as ever."

Luciano smiled at her. Eliana took another bite of her scone. She wondered if he was waiting for her to ask about the walk. If he was still programmed to let humans make the decisions.

The thought left her unsettled.

"Should we go?" She stuffed the rest of the scone back into her pocket. He nodded, and they stood up and made their way out of the garden, following the usual path to the part of the park devoted to rides—the roller coaster, a broken-down Ferris wheel, assorted flying swings with broken cables. They didn't say much, although it was a companionable sort of silence. Eliana liked it.

They came to the wall that blocked the park from the city.

"I'm worried about Marianella," Eliana said. "Ever since that thing with the ag dome, I haven't seen much of her. I thought she was holed up in her room." She paused. "I mean, the ag dome was a big deal. I just hope she feels better, you know?"

"I believe she does," Luciano said. "She left her room last night."

"What?" Eliana blinked at him. "Really?" All this time, Eliana had taken Marianella's absence for grief. After what happened with Diego, Eliana thought she was doing good, forgiving her. But maybe Marianella didn't need that forgiveness after all. Maybe she didn't even want it.

And now she'd left her room?

"Yes," Luciano said. "I'm not sure what time, exactly. But I saw her with Sofia, after you had already retired back to your cottage. And I saw her this morning, too."

"This morning?" Eliana frowned. "And she wasn't in her room?"

Luciano didn't answer. Eliana poked him in the arm. "Well?" she said. "Was she feeling better?"

There was something off about Luciano's expression. An awkwardness that made him seem less human. Eliana didn't like it.

"Come on, Luciano. It's not like I —"

"I wasn't supposed to say anything." He looked over at her. "Sofia made me promise. But I don't think it's right, keeping it a secret from you."

Eliana stopped in place. They were at the petting zoo now, empty cages looming around them. Luciano stopped when she stopped. He put his hands into his pockets.

"What's going on?" she said. "Luciano?"

He watched her with that unnervingly inhuman expression. "I

have loyalties to both of you," he said. "I told her you have a right to know, but she didn't agree with me, and—"

"A right to know what?" A desperate fear clenched at Eliana's heart. "What are you talking about?"

"They went to kill Ignacio Cabrera and all his men."

The world went dead. Luciano's expression was slack. Eliana couldn't breathe.

"Oh God," she said, heart pounding. "All his men. Diego—"

She shouldn't be thinking this way. Diego was a killer. Diego's eyes were empty.

Except when they weren't. Except when they were looking at her.

"Eliana?" Luciano's voice sounded far away. She was aware of a hand on her back, and then she was aware that she was sitting down on the cold stones of the path, gasping for air.

"They didn't want to upset you," he said. "But it felt wrong to me."

"They're going to kill Diego!" Her voice ricocheted out into the park, echoing against the cold. She slapped her hand over her mouth. Tears brimmed at her eyes. "When?" she whispered.

Luciano looked at her. That awkwardness was still there, but now it was veiled with concern. He dropped his hand away from her back. "The plan is scheduled to be implemented in an hour's time—"

"An hour! Where, at the Florencia?" Eliana stood up, dizzy from the sudden movement. "It is, isn't it?" She felt as if her mind, her reason, had been detached from her body. She didn't know exactly what she planned to do. Save her lying, murdering boyfriend?

But she couldn't stand the thought of him dying. She kept seeing him the way he'd been before the gala, smoking cigarettes on her patio and lying beside her in bed.

He couldn't die. He *couldn't.*

Luciano nodded.

"I'm going there."

"You can't." He tried to grab her by the arm, but she pulled away. "It's dangerous for you. You could be caught in the cross fire." He paused. "And with Cabrera dead, you'll be safe again, and able to return home to wait for your departure in the spring. This is for the best."

"I don't want to save *Cabrera*!" The dome light was too bright. She felt blinded. She pulled away from Luciano and ran toward the train station. She'd have to follow the tracks out, catch a taxi to the Florencia.

At first all she heard was her breath and her heartbeat, her blood rushing in her ears.

And then she heard footsteps. They weren't her own.

Luciano. He was following her.

But he wasn't trying to stop her.

* * * *

The Florencia was silent when Eliana arrived, out of breath from having run the two blocks from where the taxi had dropped her and Luciano off. The driver had refused to go any farther, muttering about how he didn't want to be there when she handed an andie over to Ignacio Cabrera.

She stood on the street outside the building, staring at those darkened windows and trying to decide what to do next. It was a force of will that had brought her here, some primeval desire to see Diego *safe*.

"We should not be here." Luciano's voice was right next to her. "This is dangerous for you."

"Nothing's happening," Eliana said in a flat voice. She walked away from him, her footsteps echoing up and down the narrow street.

"Eliana!"

She wasn't thinking. Her feet moved independent of her mind, compelling her over the cement and up to the big double doors. She pulled them open and breathed in the scent of the Florencia, grilled meat and women's perfume. It was dark inside. She would have thought the place was closed down, if it weren't for the music playing in the background.

"Eliana." Luciano was at her side again. He put his hand on her arm, but she jerked away.

"I have to warn Diego." Her voice came from somewhere outside herself. She hadn't warned him at the gala, and Marianella had almost beaten him to death. "Not Cabrera. Just Diego."

"You can't. She has it all planned—"

Eliana ignored him and stepped inside. She shoved the door shut, but Luciano caught it. He didn't say anything more, his voice evaporating as he stepped into the foyer. No one waited at the podium. Over the music, Eliana could hear someone talking. A man, his voice smooth and liquid.

She crept forward, her heart pounding in her throat. Luciano moved with her, grabbing at her hand. She kept pushing him aside. Someone stood in the doorway of the dining room, a man in a dark suit. His eyes blossomed with dark bruises; his lip was scabbed over. And he was staring at her, his face full of sorrow.

"Diego!" Seeing his injuries made Eliana's chest hurt. "Diego, you have to—"

Suddenly the music changed to some old tango, the volume turned up too high.

"Fuck!" Diego loped forward, his eyes dark. "Get out of here," he hissed. "You, andie. Get *her the fuck out of here*."

Luciano grabbed her arm and pulled her toward the door.

"They're going to kill you," Eliana said.

Diego tilted his head at her like he was confused.

The music wailed in the background. Eliana remembered her mother playing this song on Saturday morning as she cleaned their apartment, her sweet singing voice drifting through the rooms.

"Get out of here," Diego said. She'd never seen him look so desperate. "Please."

And then gunfire exploded in the dining room.

Eliana screamed. Suddenly she was lying on the floor, pinned there by Luciano. Diego was gone. Bullets exploded through the wall, wood splinters and gray insulation showering everywhere. The bullets implanted themselves in the doors of the Florencia.

Eliana tried to squirm away from Luciano's grasp, but he was too strong. "Let me go!" she shrieked, and with that one command, his grip loosened and she was free, although she was too terrified to move.

The music pounded through the walls.

And through the music, men screamed.

That jolted her into action. She crawled toward the maelstrom of the dining room. The gunshots began to die away, and over the screaming and the music she could hear Luciano shouting her name. She didn't care. She had to be brave. She had to crawl toward the screams. She had to make sure that none of them belonged to Diego.

"It's not safe!" Luciano shouted.

Eliana stopped at the doorway. At first she kept her head down, but she realized the gunshots were mostly gone, and so she lifted her face a little—

And screamed.

The dining room was full of maintenance drones, buzzing over the floor, the lights on their backs illuminated a dark red she'd never seen before.

There were men too, men with guns, but most of them were sprawled out on the ground at unnatural angles. Blood slicked across the floor; the tables and chairs were shot to splinters. At the center of the room Sofia crouched over a man, her shoulders hunched. Marianella was nowhere to be seen.

"Diego!" Eliana screamed. No one answered her. The few men still standing shot at the drones, and the drones clawed at the men, slicing their tendons open at the ankle.

I'm not one of Cabrera's men. They won't attack me.

Eliana crawled into the room in a daze. The maintenance drones ignored her. She scanned over the blood and viscera and dead bodies, looking for Diego.

She found him.

He stood at the far corner, emptying his pistol into the back of a drone. His expression was calm, and that terrified her. He ran out of bullets and reloaded the gun with the quick, practiced ease of someone who had done that many, many times before, and Eliana realized she was weeping, whimpering his name, knowing she had been stupid to come here, not because she was in any danger but because he was a bad person.

CHAPTER THIRTY-TWO

SOFIA

Sofia dragged the knife down Luciano's sternum. He stared up at the ceiling, blinking occasionally. Black hydraulic fluid pooled up in a line along his bare skin. Sofia checked the readouts on the rotary display. His code whirred past; she'd set the rotary display to spin more quickly than it would for a human.

"Everything looks fine," she said, and set the knife aside.

"Wonderful to hear."

"You need to stop talking now."

"Of course." Luciano's eyes flickered like television screens. What she'd said, it was too much like a command, and part of him still wanted to see her as human. After his reprogramming, that wouldn't happen anymore.

Sofia pried Luciano's sternum open. The wiring sparked and flickered through the murk of the hydraulic fluid. It was odd to see another android like that. Sofia had seen the inside of the maintenance drones, but they were different enough from her that she didn't feel empathy. She would need to get used to it. Soon, when she had the city and she had the necessary supplies, she would begin repairing the broken androids locked away in the storage facility.

She was so close to an Antarctica for robots.

Carefully, she reached into Luciano's chest cavity and removed his core engine, snapping the wires free as she had done for herself a week ago.

Luciano's eyes blanked out, and his jaw went slack. Sofia glanced over at the rotary display. Everything looked fine. She disconnected the last wire and touched Luciano's face, gently, and wondered what images he was seeing, what memories. If he saw any at all.

Sentience came back into his eyes. "Oh," he said.

"I have your core engine," she told him. "It won't be long now. Lie still."

"Did you lie still?" His voice was flat and childlike.

"Of course not, but I should have."

"I can't see you."

"Your mind will clear in a moment." Sofia drew her hand away from Luciano's cheek and left streaks of black fluid against his skin. "I need to do the reprogramming now."

"All right."

Sofia carried the core engine over to the worktable. Hearing Luciano's voice like that, flat and purposeless, gave her a hollow feeling she did not like. Soon, she told herself. Just a few moments more, and he would be whole for the first time in his existence.

She cracked open the core engine. The insides refracted the overhead lights onto the wall, an eerily beautiful display of golden light. Then Sofia grabbed the other micro-engine and began the slow process of dismantling the core engine, piece by piece, and refitting the micro-engine to be reprogrammable.

It took a long time.

The reprogramming itself did as well. It was a much more involved process than what Araceli had done for Sofia, because Sofia did not have access to Luciano's complete schematics. But she and he had been produced in the same year, and their differences were largely inconsequential to what Sofia wished to do. In truth, he had fewer restrictions than she, since his role at the park had been more multipurpose.

After the afternoon at the Florencia, when Sofia had informed

Araceli that she would be reprogramming Luciano, Araceli had begged her not to do it without a programming key or his schematics. But Luciano had insisted.

"I want to be like you," he'd told Sofia as they'd stood in Araceli's workshop.

"Are you almost done?" Luciano asked now. His voice was thin, and it hurt Sofia to hear it.

"Almost." She glanced up at the rotary display. Another line of code fell out of existence.

"I was only curious," Luciano said. "Don't feel as if you have to rush."

She hated that so much—that *complacency*, the dull feeling of not wanting to be a bother. No more. No robot would ever be like that again.

Finally, Sofia came to the end of Luciano's code. She held the micro-engine aloft. The hydraulic fluid gleamed on her hands. The micro-engine was not much to look at, it was so old-fashioned. All those clockwork gears. But it was working for her, and it would work for him.

Sofia carried the micro-engine over to Luciano. He was still lying on his back, and he looked over at her expectantly. "Is that it?" he said.

"It is." Sofia set it inside his chest. "I'm going to connect you now," she said. "To reinstall. You're going to reboot." She hesitated. "It'll make you feel better."

Luciano didn't respond.

Sofia hooked the micro-engine in, one wire at a time. With the last one, Luciano's eyes rolled back until there was nothing but white in his eye sockets, white veined faintly with light. Sofia took a step back, her hands hanging at her sides, dripping hydraulic fluid everywhere. Was that what she had looked like? It was terrible.

And then Luciano blinked, and his eyes went back to normal, pupiled and full of sentience. He sat up with a quick lever-like motion and looked around the room. He looked at the walls, at the dismantled core engine, at Sofia's hands.

"I feel brand-new," he said, and smiled.

Sofia smiled back at him. With Cabrera dead, she'd be able to take his place in the ecosystem of the city, and from there she could work her way into Hope City's infrastructure, destroying from the inside out. Quietly, but cataclysmically. All the humans would fall.

And now that Luciano was free, it could finally begin.

* * * *

Sofia and Luciano sat side by side at a bar in downtown, near the city offices. They were facing a window so Sofia could watch the pedestrians walk by, humans in mainland-style clothes and neatly styled hair and a general air of superiority that Sofia found irritating—especially considering that the dome lights were dim and the shadows were long as if it were evening. But it was not evening. It was the middle of the afternoon.

"What if they don't arrive?" Luciano asked.

"They will." Sofia did not take her eyes off the window. "They won't want to give up the benefits that come with aligning themselves with Cabrera." Sofia had seen that much already, in the week since Luciano had been reprogrammed and she'd begun the slow, careful procedure of taking over Cabrera's business, the second stage of her plan. She had started by paying off his contacts in the police department. They were all mainland supporters—the Independent cops wouldn't dirty themselves for Cabrera. But she'd find a way to control all of the police department soon enough.

Cabrera's old police contacts were happy to be rid of him, and she could tell in their meeting that they thought she would be easily controlled. As much as it pained her, she didn't correct their error. She even made the same arrangement with them as she'd had with Cabrera, about the music and only playing songs from after 1936. Let them try to control her that way. They'd meet with a nasty little surprise. But she knew it was good to let them think they had the upper hand.

She wasn't sure Cabrera's city men would be so easy.

Footsteps against the tile—the waitress, coming back around to ask if they wanted to order anything.

"No," Sofia said before she could ask. "We're not interested in ordering."

The waitress blinked at her with huge owl-like eyes. Then she frowned.

"Our friends will certainly order something," Luciano said. "But I'm afraid we have a special diet."

"Right," the waitress said. "Well, I'm going to have to ask you to leave if they don't get here soon." She tucked her pencil behind her ear and turned around, although she glanced at them over her shoulder. Sofia glared at Luciano.

"Perhaps we should bring money in these situations," he said. "Meeting at the Florencia was so much easier."

"I'm not going back to the Florencia, not yet." Sofia turned her gaze to the window.

Luciano didn't say anything. Sofia stared out at the street. A group of men in dark suits and hats was walking toward the bar. They had the look of cullers, of city men.

"They're here," she said, just as the group converged on the bar. The door swung open and cold air billowed inside. Sofia twisted in her chair so that she could see the city men better. One of them caught her eye and nodded. Sofia turned away from him.

"It's them," she said.

"I apologize for our tardiness." The city men were at their table now, their human scent wafting off them, mingling with the scent of food from the kitchen. The one who had caught Sofia's eye was speaking. "These electrical issues—well, we've been having several meetings about them, as you can imagine."

Sofia could not imagine, but she only gestured at the empty chairs and said, "Please. Sit."

Three of the city men had come over to the table. Two others sat in a booth across the room, staring down at the menus.

"Assistants," said the one who had spoken first, the one Sofia assumed was the leader. "They know about our arrangement with Mr. Cabrera, and are quite adept at keeping quiet."

The other two nodded and murmured in agreement.

"Mr. Cabrera is dead," Sofia said. "So I couldn't care less about your arrangement with him. This is about your arrangement with me."

The city men exchanged glances. A long moment ticked by. The waitress approached, gliding across the room like a shark.

Finally, the city men slid into their seats.

Their names were Mr. Garcia, Mr. Ruiz, and Mr. Bianchi, although Sofia did not know which was which, only that they had been the liaisons between Cabrera and the many people working for him in the city offices. Sofia tended to think of them as a collective. After all, it was men like them who had thought of robots as parts to be acquired.

The waitress asked if they would like to order anything, and they did, a wide variety of alcoholic drinks that Sofia recognized from her days in the amusement park. The memory didn't make her chest ache anymore. She had a brighter future now.

"Well, Miss—" The leader hesitated. "Miss Sofia, I must say, we're intrigued by your moxie."

Sofia smiled and folded her hands on top of the table. "Thank you. Which one are you again?"

The man faltered. "Jorge Ruiz," he said. "This is Alfredo Garcia, and this is Luis Bianchi."

"Yes, of course." She tilted her head. "I only spoke to your—what did you call them?—your assistants. It's all very confusing to me, telling humans apart."

Mr. Ruiz coughed into his hand. The other two stared down at the table.

"The android sitting beside me is Luciano," Sofia said. "He's my associate. Not my assistant." She tittered like she was flirting. Luciano smiled gravely.

"I see," said Mr. Ruiz. He glanced over at the bar, where the bartender was mixing up their drinks.

"Since you're such admirers of my moxie," Sofia said, "perhaps you'll be keen to learn that I've decided to take over Mr. Cabrera's business."

Mr. Ruiz jerked his gaze back toward her. His eyes glittered. He was nervous. Maybe even scared. So were the other two.

"Yes, my assistant mentioned that," he said.

The waitress came over with a tray. She set down napkins and then she set down drinks, and then she gave Sofia and Luciano a lingering dark look before going on her way.

"We always preferred to talk business at the Florencia," Mr. Bianchi said.

"The Florencia's not available to us at the moment. We'll have to talk here." Sofia leaned back in her chair.

"You don't have to worry about the police," Luciano said. "If indeed that's what you're worried about."

The city men exchanged glances. "The police? You've got the police on payroll?"

"The ones that matter, yes." Sofia smiled, and she could feel the effect that incandescence had on those three men—all in spite of themselves, no doubt. They weren't like Cabrera. They weren't monsters on the inside. "And I intend to keep you as well. Nothing about your previous arrangement will change, with one exception."

She paused. Mr. Ruiz leaned forward, his fingers resting on the rim of his glass. "The exception is that you're an andie," he said in a low voice.

"No." Sofia leaned forward to meet his stare over the center of the table. "The exception is that the city will stop all culling of robot parts from the amusement park."

Silence. Sofia didn't move; she would not be the one to move first, and she wasn't. Mr. Ruiz sank back in his chair and took a long drink.

"We have to be able to build maintenance drones," he said. "You can't expect—"

"I'll bring in the parts that you need," Sofia said. "From the mainland. But you will not harm any robot who already exists in this city."

Mr. Ruiz sighed. "That's going to be a hard order to pass on to the brass, Miss Sofia. They aren't all on the payroll—"

"But you are," she said, "and I'll pay twice what Cabrera did. Just to keep a few robots safe."

That had Mr. Ruiz's attention. Mr. Garcia's too, from the way he grinned and leaned over to whisper something into Mr. Ruiz's ear. Mr. Bianchi took a long drink.

"Twice the income," Sofia said. "For something that's really not so difficult. The park was running dry anyway, wasn't it? And I can get the new robot parts to you quite cheaply."

Mr. Ruiz didn't take his eyes off her. She wondered if he thought that if he stared at her hard enough, he'd be able to see straight through her skin and her framework and learn all her secrets. Let him try. What Mr. Ruiz didn't know was that Sofia only offered this deal because she knew it didn't need to be sustainable; in a year's time, robots would come to Hope City on their own, or they would be resurrected out of the slaughter the cullers had left behind. And Mr. Ruiz would be living in a villa in some mainland jungle.

"I think we can take that deal," Mr. Ruiz said. The other two nodded.

Sofia smiled.

* * * *

A week went by.

Things changed quickly in that time. Sofia lay claim to the icebreakers, walking on board each one and personally triggering the code she had hidden in each robot when she'd reprogrammed it for Cabrera. The reconfigured robots responded only to her commands, whether by touch, by voice, or by radio waves.

Cabrera's errand-runners were as easily swayed to her side as the cops and the city men had been. She had killed enough of Cabrera's shooters that the rest were terrified of her, and she called them each into her office one by one and explained that their lives would go on unchanged, except for who they answered to. She would give them goods to distribute, she would pay them, and everyone could be happy.

There were only two who protested, one who refused to work for a robot and one who refused to work for a woman. She killed them both, although she did not tell Marianella.

And so Sofia ingratiated herself into the sphere of Cabrera's power. She sent money to all of Cabrera's old contacts, and her icebreakers kept coming in without being stopped by the dock guards, and her errand-runners kept distributing the products at an elevated price.

Things would go on this way until the spring, and the humans of the city would never know that she was eating away at their home bit by bit, eliminating those in power who could not be bought off so easily. The political infrastructure of Hope City would collapse, and humans would move out of Antarctica in search of stability.

Things at the park changed little. Eliana left—she no longer had anything to fear from Cabrera or that boyfriend of hers, and so she moved back to the smokestack district. Marianella tried to convince her not to, citing the blackouts and the general danger of the city, but Eliana didn't listen. Not that Sofia would have expected her to. Humans.

The blackouts were the one thing that gnawed at the back of Sofia's mind. Yes, they were convenient for her. They kept the humans scared, nervous, and that made it easier for Sofia to control them. But the sentient maintenance drones all insisted they weren't causing them, and her contacts at the city office gave her the usual lines about AFF computer viruses. That was a troublesome thought. As difficult as the Independents were to infiltrate, the AFF was, at the moment, impregnable. It bothered Sofia, knowing there were humans in the city who could undo her, humans whose identity she couldn't learn, no matter how much money she paid out.

And then one afternoon the maintenance drones came to the amusement park.

There were three of them, older models that had been upgraded over the years from steam power to atomic. All the sentient drones were like that, older. That, Sofia could only assume, was why they had managed to achieve sentience in the first place, having lived all those years of experiences.

They dropped out of the dome ceiling, their presence activating the surveillance equipment inside the operations room that in turn activated an alert inside Sofia's head: someone was here, someone robotic. She was in one of the gardens with Araceli and Marianella and Luciano, having a picnic, although only Marianella and Araceli were eating. Luciano was reading one of his books, the dark blue cover hiding his face as he flipped indolently through the pages. His reading had greatly picked up since his reprogramming.

Sofia sent out a message to the drones, telling them her location. Then she said, "Three maintenance drones are on their way."

Marianella and Araceli looked over at her. Araceli held an empanada halfway to her mouth.

"What?" she said. "Why? Has something happened?"

"I don't know."

Marianella frowned. Luciano set his book down in his lap and looked over at Sofia with a calm expression. She should not have come out here with Marianella and Araceli. It was stupid—she didn't need to eat. Marianella barely did. And yet she held on to those silly human practices anyway.

Her thoughts flickered. The maintenance drones were nearby. Sofia tilted her head back and saw them sliding across the top of the dome, dark against the white lights. They dropped down, rotors whirring and stirring up a faint, chilly wind that rippled across the garden's plants. As they moved closer, Sofia could see that the drone in the middle was propped up by the other two, wires strung around their bodies so that they carried it in a sort of net.

"What is this?" She stood up, anxiety twisting in her system. Araceli and Marianella gathered up the remains of their lunch and stepped back, giving the drones space to land.

"One of them's been damaged," Marianella said.

"Then why didn't the city take care of it?" Sofia frowned. "These are city drones."

"If they're sentient," Luciano said, "perhaps they don't trust the city."

Sofia glanced at him. Yes, she supposed that was a possibility, but the sentient drones had been good about keeping their sentience a secret.

The three drones landed, the metal of their exteriors gleaming. Sofia rushed forward and knelt beside them. She pressed her hand to the closest drone's back, looking for any information.

Damaged, the drone told her, in the zero-one language of computers. *Virus.*

Sofia went still. "A virus," she whispered. Then she shook her head, sent the question surging through her fingers. *What sort of virus?*

Never seen before. You must look.

"What is it?" Araceli moved closed. "Is something happening?"

"They say the middle one is damaged." Sofia kept her hand on the drone's back. "A virus."

"Like the virus that's causing the blackouts?" Marianella frowned. "Alejo—" Her voice trembled a little. "Alejo told me that's what the city thought was causing it."

"I haven't seen anything like that." Sofia hadn't taken her hand away, and the drone was still surging information up into her brain, *A virus, you must check*. "We need to look at it. Araceli, you'll help. I don't want to risk uploading it into myself somehow."

She pulled her hand away. Her fingers tingled. The infected drone looked the same as the others. But she knew the problem wouldn't manifest itself on the drone's exterior.

"Take it to the workshop," she said, and straightened up. Then, to the other two drones, she used the city command: "Stay. Await instructions."

Their lights fluttered, an unusual pattern she'd only seen in the sentient drones. It meant affirmation.

Araceli unwound the wires from the infected drone. It was too heavy for her to carry on her own, but when Luciano moved to help her, Marianella stepped forward and said, "Please, let me. I doubt I can get infected."

"But you don't know for sure," Sofia said.

Marianella looked over at her. "It's less likely than with Luciano."

Sofia didn't say anything. This virus wasn't going to move through external contact; robotic viruses never did. They didn't work that way. But Sofia was always irrational around Marianella.

Marianella and Araceli lifted the drone and carted it toward the workshop. Sofia and Luciano followed, unspeaking. Sofia was nervous about what they were going to find. She should have done this much earlier. But none of the maintenance drones had ever mentioned a virus until today.

Luciano opened up the workshop door so Marianella and Araceli could take the drone inside. They set it on the worktable. The drone's lights flickered and sputtered to life after a few seconds' pause, and the maintenance drone's metal shell gleamed.

Araceli pulled over a rotary display. "Safer than hooking any of you to it directly," she said, and she took a deep breath and plugged in the display. The code clicked into place, all the usual lines of it, all those instructions for how to care for the city. The sentient drones knew to hide their sentience deep down—you had to go looking for it. That was how they'd stayed hidden from the city.

"I don't see anything," Sofia said.

Araceli didn't answer. She crouched down so that she was eye level with the rotary display, frowning at it. The code clicked by. Sofia stood behind her, watching, looking for anomalies.

"There!" Sofia said, and her hand slammed the stop button. The display froze midchange, but she could still see the line. "That's not supposed to be there."

"You're right." Araceli turned back the code manually. Marianella crowded in next to her. "That is weird. It's definitely not something that sprang up naturally—"

Something not related to sentience, she meant. Sofia could have told her that.

"—but it's not typical code for the maintenance drones. It's not telling the drone to *do* anything. That's what's strange."

"It's a portal," Marianella said.

Sofia looked at her. "What do you mean, a portal?"

"I put something similar in my own drones," Marianella said. "It's an easy way of reprogramming them, a way of hiding the reprogramming so that no one else can get to it. It's not a virus, though. Funny they'd use that word."

Because it's making them sick, Sofia thought, although she didn't say it out loud. "Can you access the portal?"

"I think so. I'll just need a keyboard."

Araceli nodded and sprang up to grab one. But Luciano had beat her to it. Araceli plugged the keyboard into the drone, and Marianella started tapping away. The rotary display clicked out her progress. This was deep, almost as deep as the sentience.

"There," she said. Then, "Oh my God."

"Christ," Araceli said.

Sofia didn't say anything, even though she saw it too. Such a simple thing, a short line, instructions like the sort that had been inside her for years and years, instructions she couldn't help but listen to.

It was an override, and rather clumsily done, which meant it could only have been entered in by a human. An override on the instructions to maintain the city's power supplies.

Don't maintain, those instructions said. *Destroy.*

Destroy a little at a time.

CHAPTER THIRTY-THREE

ELIANA

Eliana opened the door to her office for the first time in over a month. The air smelled musty and old, despite the lingering chill. It was as cold as outside, since the radiator had been shut off in her absence.

Everything looked the same as she had left it. The files were still stacked on her desk, waiting to be tucked away in the metal cabinet. The empty coffee bag still sat on the counter next to the sink. The chair behind her desk was still pushed out from when she'd stood up.

It was disconcerting, being back here, starting work again, when Diego was dead. She'd put it off for weeks after she'd left the amusement park, and for a while she thought she might not go back at all. She had her money, didn't she? Money to get her off the mainland—something Diego would never get to do now. But she needed something to fill her time, because otherwise, she worried about the future.

She'd tried filing for her visa, but a week later, she'd received a typed note politely informing her that all applications would be held until the start of spring, when the passenger ships began running again. Eliana had crumpled the note up into a ball and tossed it at the wall of her apartment. Wasn't that just like this place, to make her wait until she had the money, and then wait until the ships were running? And God only knew what would happen between now and spring, with Sofia scheming in the amusement park. Another reason, of the hundreds of reasons, to leave: Eliana didn't want to be here when Sofia finally put her plan into action. She also didn't want anyone she cared about to be here, but when she'd gone to Maria and Essie, they'd dismissed her concerns. Essie because of her devotion to Independence and Maria because this was, as she said, her home, the only place she knew. And anyway there was no way the *robots* could take over everything. "You're just being paranoid," she said. "You should quit working as a PI when you get to the mainland. Otherwise you'll start seeing conspiracies there, too."

Eliana shrugged out of her jacket and hung it on the coatrack. She switched on the radio. Threw out the coffee bag. Stuck the GONE ON VACATION sign into her desk. Put the files away.

As good as new, for the rest of the uncertain winter. Of course, she needed clients. That had been the other reason for coming back, to save more money to expedite the visa process. She knew how Hope City worked. You could get pretty much anything if you paid someone enough.

Eliana pulled out a notepad and wrote an advertisement to put in the classified section of the *Hope City Daily*. *Suspicious about your husband's fidelity? Worried about an employee's honesty? I can help. Private investigator, fully licensed*. It was hokey, but that's all she wanted from her work right now, to tail some cheating husband around to all the different motels in the city. After a moment's thought, she added, *Very discreet*.

Writing that out reminded her of Marianella, the way she had stood by as Diego was attacked by a maintenance drone. She hadn't even tried to help him.

Eliana pulled out her typewriter and typed up the advertisement. Then she stuck it into an envelope along with the fifty cents it cost to place an ad in the newspaper, made out the address, added a stamp, and set the envelope on the corner of her desk for the mailman.

The whole thing took fifteen minutes.

"Oh, hell," Eliana muttered. No one was going to come by her office, and she didn't know if she could sit in here much longer, breathing in the thick musty air. Maybe she should open a window. She didn't. Instead, she put her coat back on and slapped a sign on the door that said WILL RETURN IN FIVE MINUTES and walked down to the mailbox at the end of the block.

It was nice to be out, nice to be moving—inasmuch as anything could be nice to Eliana these days. Quite a few people crowded along the streets, jostling one another, but Eliana knew that her grief set her apart. It was a knife that could slice through all the bustle of humanity, clearing a path for her. She was tainted.

The same could be said for her knowledge about Sofia's plans, that slow-growing crack in the glass of the dome. Her knowledge, and her willingness to believe it.

She dropped the letter into the mailbox and stood for a moment, trying to decide if she should go back to her office. But if she didn't, then what? She'd just wander back to her apartment, curl up on the sofa, listen to records, try not to think about Marianella or Diego or the city crashing down around her. She would fix her lunch knowing that her food had been distributed to the grocery store by fucking Sofia.

The office was better.

Eliana took her time walking back. The bustle distracted her. And when she came up the stairs, she found a man waiting outside her door. He wore a gray suit, a gray fedora, and he had golden eyes. She recognized him immediately.

Juan Gonzalez.

"I need to speak with you." Then, lightly, "How was your holiday?"

Eliana took a deep breath. "It was fine. Thank you."

"The files you gave me were most excellent," he said, slipping off his hat. "And I'd love anything else you could bring me along those lines."

Eliana studied him closely, wondering if he knew they were fake. His face was so impassive, she couldn't tell. His appearance here made her skin crawl.

"I'm sorry. I just don't know how to get anything else," she said.

She unlocked the office door. She'd rather not have this conversation out in the hallway.

They went in, bell jangling. Mr. Gonzalez draped his coat and hat over the coatrack, as always. Eliana tossed her own coat over the back of her chair.

"Look," she said, crossing her arms over her chest. "I don't know what you expect me to do. I can't exactly stake her out. I step foot into the amusement park, she knows I'm there, and it's not like she ever *leaves*."

Mr. Gonzalez's mouth turned up in a coy smile. "Ah, and that's where you're wrong, Miss Gomez. Our Sofia has come into some good fortune this last week, and I believe you'd have some luck lurking around a particular bar near the docks."

Eliana went rigid. She wondered if Mr. Gonzalez knew about Sofia's plans, if that was why he'd had Eliana investigating her all along. Well, she wasn't going up against Sofia. She was just going to get out before the city went to hell.

"The Florencia, I believe it's called?" He smiled again, more genuinely this time.

"I know it." The words were thick in Eliana's throat. "But the Florencia is Ignacio Cabrera's place. I don't know why you—"

"Ah. Not anymore." Mr. Gonzalez settled back in his chair and crossed his legs. "That was the good fortune I spoke of. She seems to have taken over Mr. Cabrera's criminal dealings."

He was telling Eliana all this like he didn't expect her to know. She let out a deep breath. She tried not to think about the last time she'd been to the Florencia, but it was no use. Her heart started to beat more quickly. Sweat prickled over her palms.

"I'm sorry," she said. "I'm not interested."

Mr. Gonzalez stared at her. His eerie light eyes bored into her thoughts.

"I don't want to mess with gangsters," she said. "Doesn't matter if it's a man or an andie. Too dangerous. Come back when you think your wife's cheating."

"I refuse to believe there's so much infidelity in this city to allow that sort of thing to be your primary source of income."

"It is. Now, please leave." Her body trembled, and she gripped the arm of her chair, trying to steady herself. She kept seeing Diego's back, his skin ruptured, blood pooling around him. He didn't even get a funeral, and she never got to watch the flames dance and the smoke and ash drift up through the narrow tube leading to the open air outside the dome. His soul, released to God. She didn't get to see any of it, because Sofia had burned the bodies all together, at an abandoned factory on the edge of the dome. A sacrilege. Sometimes Eliana wondered what Marianella thought about it.

Eliana didn't care about sacrilege herself. She only cared that she never got to say good-bye to Diego. Not properly.

Mr. Gonzalez was still watching her. "Are you sure you're not interested?"

"Yes, I'm sure!" she snapped. "How many times do I have to tell you?" Darkness moved over his features. She fumbled around for an excuse. "A friend of mine got hurt investigating a Cabrera case, and an andie's a damn sight more terrifying than a human. So no, I don't want to get involved."

For a moment she was afraid he wouldn't leave, that he had been stringing her along all this time, that he worked for Cabrera, or he worked for the city, or he was here to take revenge for what Sofia had done. She expected him to pull out a gun and point it at her chest. But he only straightened his tie and said, "Forgive me, Miss Gomez. I didn't mean to upset you."

Eliana's trembling subsided. She slumped back in her chair and watched as he pulled on his coat and hat in smooth, easy movements. She wanted him out of her office. She wanted to forget everything that had happened these last few months—no, everything that had happened this last *year.* She wanted to go back to a time before she'd ever even met Diego.

Mr. Gonzalez put his hand on the doorknob. Then he looked over his shoulder at her, his golden eyes unsettling.

"I really would appreciate your help on this, Miss Gomez," he said. "Sofia could bring a great deal of harm upon our city, if we let her."

If we let her, Eliana thought. It wasn't a matter of letting her. It was going to happen.

"You'll have to find someone else," Eliana said.

Mr. Gonzalez smiled. "Yes, I suppose I will."

And then he left.

* * * *

Eliana almost didn't bother returning to her office after lunch. No one other than Mr. Gonzalez had called or come by all morning, and it was dull sitting behind her desk, listening to the radio and reading over old case files to see if there were any former clients she could rope into a follow-up.

But she didn't want to risk losing out on a payment. An easy payment, not one that would anger Sofia.

Instead, she ate a pair of empanadas from a stand on the street corner and then took the long way back to the office, twining through the narrow, crooked alleys between buildings. She held her breath as she walked up the stairs, but no one was there.

Eliana didn't know if she was relieved or not.

She walked straight to the filing cabinet and opened up the L–R drawer. Not a lot of clients in there. She ran her thumb over the tabs. She'd intended to start calling about follow-ups, but none of these clients were worth it.

Eliana slammed the drawer shut and opened the one above it. She told herself she wasn't going for Juan Gonzalez's file, but she pulled it out anyway. It was slim, not containing much more than an information sheet and some of her false notes from the first time she visited the amusement park. Still, she carried it over to her desk and looked over his information.

Juan Gonzalez. There were probably a hundred different Juan Gonzalezes in the city, which made the name an appealing one, assuming you wanted to lie. The information sheet didn't give her much. Just the name, an address, a telephone number, all his payment information. Nothing about a place of employment.

She tapped her fingers against the desk. She'd always assumed, deep down, that Juan Gonzalez was working, through some convolution or another, for Cabrera, that Cabrera had wanted to check up on Sofia without her finding out. And she might still believe that, except the point was moot. Cabrera was dead. He'd lost. They'd all lost. If Mr. Gonzalez was still looking for Sofia's weak spot, if he'd been hired by Cabrera, then Sofia had to know about him. She was a fucking andie, after all. She didn't make mistakes.

Eliana's heart clenched.

No, she decided, Mr. Gonzalez wasn't working for Cabrera. But who, then? Who else would even know about Sofia?

She checked the home address again. 5894 Prieto. She didn't recognize it, so she dug around in her bottom drawer and pulled out her big paper map of Hope City and spread it on top of her desk. It was dotted with marks and notes from old cases, but she ignored them, scanning down the list of street names on the side until she found Prieto. D-5 on the map. She checked the location, a residential area called Gray Mountains. Not a rich part of town, but not the smokestack district either. One of those neat little neighborhoods where the low-ranked city workers started up their families.

A fifteen-minute train ride, and she'd be there. If Mr. Gonzalez caught her, she'd just lie and say she'd reconsidered, then worm her way out of it later.

It didn't seem like a good plan, but it was something to do.

So Eliana folded up the map and the information sheet and stuck them both into her purse. She left her gun. She'd had enough of guns, enough of violence, for this lifetime.

The train was crowded, and Eliana had to stand, scrunched up against the cold metal wall. It vibrated against her spine. She didn't want to look at anyone, because looking at people made her feel connected to them, and that, for some reason, made her immeasurably sad. And so she pulled out the information sheet, unfolded it, and read over the address again and again until the conductor announced her stop.

Stepping off that train was like breathing for the first time. No one was on the platform, and after the unnerving experience of being so close to other human beings, that emptiness was a relief. Eliana pulled out the map and checked the direction, then set off toward 5894 Prieto.

The walk didn't take long.

The house was a squat little stone thing, with a postage-stamp yard and a single pine tree growing next to the sidewalk. The neighborhood had been built later—shortly before the amusement park had closed down, when the park officials had been desperately trying to lure in new employees. The houses had been thrown up quickly, and that shoddy workmanship was apparent in the dark foundation cracks and shabby roofs of most of the houses Eliana had passed. Mr. Gonzalez's house was no different. If anything, it looked worse than the others. One of the windows was a piece of plywood instead of glass, and the end of his sidewalk was crumbling into chunks.

The grass was mowed, though. Weird.

The house had a driveway and a carport, but they were both empty. All the lights were turned off, as well. Eliana stood on the sidewalk and stared up at the house, trying to decide if she wanted to risk breaking in.

Mr. Gonzalez nagged at her. The bland name and the bland suits and his obsession with Sofia—something wasn't right here. Or at the very least, something wasn't clear.

"You lost?"

Eliana jumped. The voice belonged to a little girl, her hair braided into pigtails. She blinked up at Eliana.

"Do you know the man who lives here?" Eliana pointed at the house.

The little girl frowned. "No one lives there, miss."

Eliana felt a surge of triumph—she was right. Something was off about Mr. Gonzalez.

"You sure?" She wanted to find out as much as she could. "A man I work with listed this as his address."

The girl shrugged. "I'm sure. Sometimes these guys show up here at night, and there will be all these cars around. My mom makes me come in when that happens. But most of the time the house is just empty. I can show you."

Before Eliana could respond, the girl took off running across the yard, her pigtails streaming out behind her. Eliana hesitated for a moment, then followed. Men showing up in groups at night?

Could be Cabrera after all. Except he didn't keep houses, as far as she knew. His whole base of operation had been the Florencia. An empty house wouldn't be enough of a smoke screen for a man like him.

A man like Diego.

She shoved the thought aside. The girl was waiting for her on the porch. Now that Eliana was closer, she had to agree the house had the air of something abandoned. The porch was coated in a thick layer of dust, and the windows were grimy.

"Here." The girl pressed her face against the glass. "Look in. You'll see. Nothing there."

Eliana crouched beside her and peered in, her hands cupped around her eyes to block out the light. The girl was right. She was looking into a sizable room that was empty save for a stack of folding metal chairs leaning up against the wall.

"See?"

Eliana pulled away from the window. The girl stared at her with her hands on her hips. "I told you," she said. "Nobody lives there. Your friend lied to you." Her eyes glittered mischievously. "Is he one of the guys that shows up here?"

"I doubt it. He probably just wrote the number down wrong." Eliana smiled. "Thanks for your help, though."

The girl shrugged. "My mom says the guys won't hurt me, but she doesn't want me hanging around them. It's a bad crowd."

"Oh yeah? What else does she say?"

"I dunno. Not a whole lot. Just that they got too many wild ideas and they'll get people killed. But I don't see 'em killing anybody when they're here. Just talking."

The Independents. The word rang like a struck chord in Eliana's head, and suddenly things made more sense. Not just the Independents, of course. The Antarctican Freedom Fighters. Cabrera had enough money to disguise his work, but Independent terrorists didn't. And they met out here, in some shabby little house no one cared about.

And Juan Gonzalez had actually fucking written the address down on his information form.

"You know what?" Eliana said to the little girl. "You've been a huge help."

The girl smiled, big and bright. "You're welcome!"

Eliana left the house, her thoughts in a whir. She wasn't exactly pro-Argentina, just pro-not-living-in-Antarctica, but that didn't mean she trusted a group of terrorists. Still, the underlying danger struck a fire inside her chest.

She rode the train to the city offices, not caring that her clothes were rumpled and her hair was unbrushed. At the receptionist's desk in the lobby, she asked if she could speak to Maria Nuñez.

"She works up in budgets," Eliana explained as the receptionist ran her finger down the list of extensions. New, probably. "She's an office manager. I'm a friend, and I just stopped by to say hello."

"Oh, the budget office!" The receptionist entered in the extension and tilted her head against the phone receiver. Eliana could hear it ringing, distantly, and there was a burst of static when Maria answered.

"You can go on up," the receptionist said brightly.

Eliana did. Her body was thrumming with something close to excitement, something other than sorrow or horror or fear for the future, and that was good.

Maria had worked her way up enough that her desk wasn't in the steno pool, which Eliana had expected, but rather was tucked away in a room at the end of a little hallway on her floor. The typewriter clattered as Eliana approached, drowning out the buzz of voices from the cluster of desks in the center of the room. The door was open. Eliana stopped in the doorway, and Maria looked up.

"You disappeared again," she said, "and now I bet you want another favor."

"I won't be disappearing again." Eliana sat down in front of Maria's desk. The office was cramped, the wall squeezing them both in tight. But Maria was smiling. "At least not until spring."

"That's not exactly disappearing," Maria said. "You'll stay in touch."

"Of course, yes." Eliana looked down at her hands. If she even could stay in touch. "You know it's not too late to start saving for a visa of your own. I can lend you some money—"

"Stop it," said Maria. "We're not having this conversation again."

"I'm just saying. Things are going to get bad."

"Things are always bad here," Maria said. "But that's the thing about a home. You stick around even when nothing's going right."

"They're going to get worse," Eliana said, but she could already see Maria's expression glazing over, and she knew it was hopeless, trying to convince Maria to leave. Essie, too. There'd be no way of explaining what was coming in a way that they would actually believe.

"Just think about it, okay? Promise?"

"Sure, whatever. Is that why you came by here?"

Eliana shook her head. "I have to go by the records office. You want to come with?"

"You don't need me. You've got the PI license."

"Yeah, I know." Eliana shrugged. She realized she had come by to warn Maria. To try one more time to get her to see the truth.

"I *always* want a break," Maria said. "But let me finish this up first."

Eliana nodded. Maria turned back to the typewriter and worked for a few moments more. Then she stood up and grabbed her purse. They walked to the elevator together. Eliana reminded herself that this was what it was like before Diego, when it was just her and her girlfriends and she didn't need anyone else.

Maybe things could be normal again, on the mainland.

Maybe.

The records office was on the seventh floor. It wasn't much to look at. The lights weren't bright and clean like on Maria's floor, and there was no rhythm of the typewriters or human voices, just the low fluorescent humming of the bulbs overhead. Eliana'd been up here a handful of times before, and she always forgot how still it was. Like a mausoleum built of paper.

A tall man stood waiting behind a counter, along with shelves and shelves of files. He was younger than the other man who worked here, although he already stooped a little, like the weight of information was bearing down on him.

"Hi, Javier." Maria smiled brightly at him, and he returned her smile with a quiver. "This is my friend Eliana. She's a PI."

"That so?" Javier squinted at her. "Have you been in here before? I remember Leo talking about a lady PI."

"Yeah, it was probably me." Eliana pulled Mr. Gonzalez's information sheet out of her purse and folded it over so that only the address was visible. She set it on the counter. "I need to find out who owns the house at this address. Here's my license." She slid that slim laminated card out of her wallet and set it next to the information sheet. Javier picked it up and held it to the light and made a great show of examining its legitimacy.

"Oh, come off it, Javier," Maria said. "She's real."

"Got to be sure." Javier tossed the license onto the counter and then wrote the address down on a piece of scrap paper. "Give me a moment."

He disappeared into the files.

"It always takes forever," Maria said, sighing.

"Yeah, I know." Eliana leaned her elbows against the counter. Maybe this wouldn't amount to anything. Maybe Javier would return and hand her a card with the name Juan Gonzalez written across it and she would be back where she'd started. She supposed she could take it to the police then, tell them about an AFF meeting place. But she wasn't sure she wanted to do that. She trusted the police about as much as she trusted Independent terrorists.

Time passed. Ten minutes, maybe. Maria checked her watch. "This is taking a lot longer than it normally does," she said.

"You can go back up if you need to."

"Oh, that's definitely not necessary." She smiled over at Eliana. They were still leaning up against the counter, as there weren't any chairs set up anywhere in the room. Maria started in on a story about Essie, who'd taken up with a new boyfriend, another Independent. Eliana half-listened, nodding her head at appropriate intervals. What was taking so long?

Finally, Javier emerged from the stacks. Maria straightened up. "Finally!" she said, teasing.

"Sorry about the wait," he said. "I had to cross-reference. The address you were after was missing about half its paperwork."

Eliana frowned. Maybe this would be complicated after all.

"Really?" said Maria.

"It happens sometimes. There's so much here. But the house's purchase date was back when we used the old registry. You remember that, Maria, before we switched all the records over to the computer?"

"I do indeed."

Eliana didn't care about any of this. "Did you find out the name?"

"Yeah, I did. It's, ah—well, a bit unexpected." Javier laid a notecard on the counter. Eliana picked it up. When she read the name, all the air went out of her body.

"Well?" Maria asked. "Who is it?"

"Alejo Ortiz," Eliana said. "The house belongs to Alejo Ortiz."

CHAPTER THIRTY-FOUR

MARIANELLA

The stairs leading to Eliana's office were colder than outside. Marianella stopped in the middle of the stairway and tightened her coat. She wondered if she had any right to ask Eliana to do this, after everything that had happened. It had been Marianella's fault that Eliana had gotten so entangled in Sofia's plans in the first place. Did she really want to entangle her further?

She told herself there was no harm in asking. And of course she intended to pay Eliana. But they needed to find out where that code had come from. The maintenance drones had no idea. Marianella and Sofia had both sat down with them, rummaged through their memory banks, asked them questions in the language of computers. The answers had been strange, utterly inhuman, but they'd still been clear enough that the answer was no.

And so Marianella continued up the stairs. The office light was on, and the muffled clatter of a typewriter spilled into the hallway. Marianella ran one hand over her hair and opened the door. She remembered the first time she'd walked into this room, how terrified she'd been that her entire life was about to unravel.

Funny that a simple line of code in a maintenance drone could make her feel that way again.

Eliana looked up from her typewriter, hands still poised over the keys. Her eyes went wide.

"Marianella," she said.

"Hello." Marianella shut the door and slipped out of her coat, an old out-of-style thing, nothing like the furs she'd worn her first time here. "How are you?"

Eliana looked away.

For a moment, they stayed like that, posed. The sunlight illuminated the side of Eliana's face. Marianella watched her.

It was the moment before a conversation. The moment, too, before an apology, which Marianella realized she would have to offer before she asked anything of Eliana.

"I'm sorry there wasn't a proper funeral for Diego." Marianella's voice was harsher in the silence than the typewriter. "I didn't know what she was doing until after she had done it." She didn't say the rest—that she had screamed at Sofia for her sacrilege, that she had gone to one of the empty cottages and said a rosary for each man who had been killed, twenty-eight in total, including Ignacio Cabrera. It had taken so long that the human parts of her body could no longer support her, and so the mechanical parts had activated, and she had finished her prayers almost entirely as a machine. She had emerged from the cottage, shaking and trembling, after saying the final rosary for Diego.

"He wasn't religious. It doesn't matter."

Eliana didn't seem to mean it. Marianella took a hesitant step forward. When Eliana didn't protest, she walked the rest of the way to the desk. Eliana watched her and didn't speak. Marianella sat down, and Eliana slid the typewriter to the side, opening up the space between them.

"I prayed for him," Marianella said.

"Why?"

"Because everyone deserves to have a prayer said for them when they die. Especially when—" Marianella stopped. She knew it was a silly superstition, about the smoke and the souls of the dead, but she believed it anyway. Believing superstitions kept her closer to human, and she wanted to be as human as possible right now.

"Especially when they aren't given a proper funeral."

"I doubt he noticed."

"Don't speak that way." Marianella said it before she could stop herself. Eliana frowned, and Marianella leaned forward, her palms damp with anxiety. "Eliana, I didn't just come here to apologize for the funeral. I came—I have a job for you, although I understand if you won't take it, but more than that I want to apologize. For everything. For Diego's death. For putting you in danger."

"A job." Eliana's voice was small, far away. "What kind of job? One for Sofia? I'm getting pretty tired of doing things for her when she clearly hates me."

They looked at each other across the desk.

"She doesn't hate you," Marianella said, but she didn't bother explaining further. It wasn't hatred, only bitterness. Humans were the enemy.

"Things have gotten worse since she took over," Eliana said. "The power flickers more often. Food's more expensive." She shrugged. "It wasn't exactly great to start out with, but I get the feeling she doesn't have the city's interests at heart."

Marianella wasn't going to lie.

"No," she said, "she doesn't."

"You're not going to stop her."

"She doesn't intend to kill anyone," Marianella said. "She only wants to send the humans away, back to the mainland."

"You don't really believe that, do you?"

Marianella hesitated. After all, Sofia had ordered the deaths of Cabrera's men without hesitation.

"That's too kind for her," Eliana said. "Sending us away to live someplace warm. Feeling the real sun." She sighed and rapped her fingers against the desk. "Luciano showed me a rainstorm. Did you know he could do that? Share memories?"

Marianella nodded.

"He showed me a rainstorm, and now I remember it like it happened to me." Eliana gave a hard little smile. "I'd like more memories like that. I'd prefer they be real, though."

Marianella didn't respond. The room was freezing, even with

the radiator rattling away in the corner. Past Eliana's head was a window that faced a cold gray building that grew, Marianella knew, out of a cold gray sidewalk. She thought about those years before she'd met Hector, when her life had been on the mainland, out in the countryside in a big white stone house, with gardens and horses. The wind had swept down from the mountains, smelling of rain.

She missed it. God, she really did miss it. She'd always thought moving to Hope City had been a way of starting over, and maybe it had been, twenty years ago. Maybe the amusement park wasn't what she needed to start over again. Maybe the answer wasn't with Sofia after all.

"I forgive you," Eliana said abruptly, jerking Marianella out of her memories. "But not Sofia."

Marianella nodded.

They sat for another few moments. Then Eliana dragged the typewriter back in front of her.

"So tell me about this job." Eliana took up typing again, her gaze fixed down on the paper in the typewriter. "If it is for Sofia, do you think she'll get me a one-way ticket to the mainland on one of those icebreakers of hers?" Eliana peered over the edge of the paper, and Marianella realized she was serious.

"Yes," Marianella said. "I'm certain of it. But only in the summer, when it's safest—"

"No." Eliana went back to typing. "I want out sooner than that. The city's already delaying me for my visa application, even though I've got the money. If she wants me to help her, she can put me on one of her ships before the docks open up."

Marianella gaped at Eliana. "You can't be serious," she said. "Ships capsize all the time—"

"That's my deal," Eliana said. "If she can get me out of here before the city can, I'll do it for her. But I'm not getting caught up in whatever she's planning. I know it's not shipping us away to the mainland."

Marianella sat for a moment. She needed Eliana's help, but she didn't want to put her in that kind of danger.

But if Eliana was right, if Sofia was planning on harming the humans of the city . . .

"Fine," Marianella said. "I'll get you a place aboard one of the shipping liners."

"Thank you." Eliana typed out another few words, then pushed the typewriter aside. "To be honest, I've been looking into something that might involve you—might involve Alejo Ortiz, anyway."

"Really?" Marianella frowned. Her chest twisted with a slight break of anxiety. "What do you mean?"

"I don't really know. It's a bit of a strange—connection." Eliana thought for a moment. "It's about the man who hired me to investigate Sofia. Remember him? When I came to the park the first time?"

Marianella nodded.

"He showed back up here a few days ago, asking for the same thing. Any information I had about Sofia." Eliana's voice pitched forward in urgency. "I told him no, but then I went by his house. He didn't live there—no one did. This neighborhood kid told me it was a place where the AFF meets up. Not in so many words, but reading between the lines, it seems fairly likely. So I went looking for who really owns the house, thinking this guy's name was a fake. And it turned out—turned out the house's owner is Alejo Ortiz."

All the energy drained out of Marianella's body.

"Now, I'm not accusing you of anything," Eliana said quickly. "I was just wondering—the connection with Ortiz—" She shook her head. "I don't know. It's so goddamned weird."

"Weird that Alejo has connections with terrorists?" Marianella laughed. "Not exactly."

Eliana looked up at her. "You mean he *does*?"

Marianella leaned forward, keeping her voice low. "He does. That's why he hasn't reported my nature, because I know that he took a significant portion of his campaign funds from the AFF."

Eliana's eyes widened. "I fucking knew it!" she said. "Christ. So I guess if I report him—"

"He would reveal my nature, yes."

Eliana rubbed her forehead. "What does he want with Sofia?"

Marianella shook her head, but she was thinking about the culling, and the men who'd killed Inéz. Alejo's men.

Why would Alejo care about culling robots?

Why would Alejo want to investigate Sofia?

"The man who hired you," Marianella said. "What was his name?"

"Juan Gonzalez. I figure it's a fake."

Marianella nodded. No Juan Gonzalez worked for Alejo, but that didn't mean anything. "What does he look like?"

"Pretty unremarkable, I guess. Youngish. Black hair. Always wearing a gray suit and gray hat. Really light brown eyes, though. They're practically golden."

Marianella went cold all over.

She thought about the day Inéz had died.

"Andres," she whispered.

"What?"

"His name is Andres Costa." Marianella looked Eliana straight in the eye. "He's one of Alejo's aides."

"What!" Eliana pushed away from her desk and paced back and forth across the room. "One of Alejo's aides came here asking about Sofia?" She stopped, looked over at Marianella. "He knows about her taking the city over. He has to."

Marianella shook her head. "No, he couldn't possibly." But he clearly knew *something*. He'd told her Andres was in the park for city business, but why would a city man need to hire a private investigator to look into Sofia? To gain access to her schematics? Alejo was doing something, but Marianella couldn't see it.

Marianella shivered and wished she hadn't taken off her coat.

"So what were you coming to see me about?" Eliana said. "This job, what was it? Did it have to do with Ortiz?"

Marianella shook her head. The mysterious code had almost slipped her mind. "I doubt it." She took a deep breath and explained to Eliana what they had found in the damaged maintenance drone. Eliana listened, nodding, her brow furrowed with concentration.

"The blackouts," she said. "You found what's causing the blackouts."

Marianella nodded.

"And you're sure a human had to program that in? It's not some robot—"

"Yes!" Marianella threw up her hands. "I'm sure. It's not the maintenance drones. They like to brag—well, maybe that's not the right word exactly, but they're always open whenever they do something—destructive." She thought of the burning power plant, the twenty-six dead from the whims of the maintenance drones. "And I don't know what this is. That's what we wanted you to do. Find out."

Eliana started pacing again. "It sounds like AFF work, doesn't it? At least the code does. But I don't know why they'd want to mess with the power." She sighed. "The city's always blaming the AFF, which tells me the city's responsible. I bet they're trying to make it look like the AFF's done it, but my money's on the city."

"Why?" Marianella said. "I think it's entirely possible the AFF could be responsible." She paused. "You aren't as familiar with them as I am, working with Alejo."

"But the city wants to root out the terrorists." Eliana paused by the far wall, then made her way back across the room. "If the terrorists are putting our livelihood in danger, that makes the common folk not want to join up with them, you see? So the city makes the blackouts look like AFF work, and people start seeing the AFF as *terrorists* and not freedom fighters."

It made a convoluted sort of sense, Marianella had to admit.

"How about this," Eliana said. "Let's look into this Andres Costa first. He's got ties to the AFF, and we can see if that leads us to anything about the code. If not, we can start looking into the city."

"Yes," Marianella said, after a pause. "Yes, I think that sounds good."

CHAPTER THIRTY-FIVE

ELIANA

Eliana met Marianella at a café near the center of the city. Marianella was a few minutes late, rushing in through the door with her hair wild from running. Eliana lifted one hand to greet her, keeping the other pressed firmly against the folded-up piece of notebook paper she'd gotten from Javier.

"Sorry I'm late," Marianella said.

"It's fine." Eliana slid the paper across the table to Marianella, who read it over without expression.

"You found it," she said. "Andres's address."

"I'm a licensed PI, so the city gives me access to their records."

"It's an apartment," Marianella said, frowning. "Is this going to work?"

"Were you able to get a car?"

"Well, yes, but—"

"Then it'll work. Come on." Eliana stood up and tossed down a couple of bills to pay for her coffee. Marianella handed her back the address, and Eliana slipped it into her pocket. They left the shop together, stepping back out into the cold air. Marianella led Eliana down to an old-fashioned mainland-style car that was parked at the meter. It was so wide, it seemed to take up the whole street.

"You got this from the park?" Eliana stared at it. She wished Marianella had picked something smaller.

"I didn't have much choice." Marianella frowned, a line appearing between her eyes. "I could see about calling a friend, if this won't work."

"Nah, it's fine." There were plenty of cars like this one in the city, left over from the park days; it might be enormous and bulky, but it wouldn't stand out.

They climbed in, and Marianella pulled out into the street, both her hands on the steering wheel, her eyes fixed firmly on the road. Eliana remembered that story from her childhood, about the cyborg who was found out when he got into a car accident. She wondered if Marianella knew that story too.

It didn't take long for them to arrive at Andres's apartment. It was one of those garden apartments, locked up behind a gate, all the doors facing into a courtyard where the management usually planted loads of gaudy, bright flowers. Eliana knew these sorts of places. They were a step up, a halfway point between the tenement buildings and an actual house.

"What should I do?" Marianella asked as they cruised past the apartment.

"Park a ways up. We'll have to check from the sidewalk to see if he's home."

Marianella nodded.

They parked in front of a row of tall narrow houses and walked to Andres's apartment complex. There was a sign out front, announcing the name of the apartment in the bright colors Eliana imagined filled the garden. But when they came up to the wire gate, she saw that the garden was a tangle of dead, yellow plants.

"The cold," Marianella said suddenly. "All the power failures. They haven't kept it warm enough. Not even here."

Eliana frowned. The truth was, some small part of her had hoped to see flowers.

The gate wasn't locked. Marianella pressed close to Eliana as they walked into the courtyard. They had a story planned, if Costa showed up—a sob story Marianella had prepared earlier, about how she desperately missed working with Alejo and would Andres please put in a good word for her? But looking into his apartment windows, Eliana didn't think they needed it.

"I'm going to go look around the back," she said quietly. "You stand next to the gate like you're waiting for someone."

Marianella nodded. Eliana left the courtyard and ambled around along the side of the building, counting the windows until she came to those that belonged to Andres's apartment. They were dark too. Good sign.

And she didn't see another soul out. That was a good sign too.

She walked back into the courtyard and nodded at Marianella, who turned and joined her in one seamless motion. They walked up to Costa's door. Eliana stood off to the side. Marianella took a deep breath. Smoothed down her blouse. Knocked.

No one answered.

Eliana gave a short nod, and Marianella knocked again, this time angling her body so that Eliana could make quick work of the lock. The timing wasn't exactly right, but the courtyard was empty and she didn't notice any movement in the windows.

The door popped open.

All the lights were off. Marianella stepped into the doorway and turned her head back and forth, listening. Eliana followed and pulled the door shut.

"I don't hear anything," Marianella said in a normal voice. "No breathing. There's no one here."

Eliana let out a sigh of relief. "Move quickly," she said. "We don't want to be here when he gets back."

Marianella nodded. "Anything suspicious, yes?"

"Anything that can explain what the hell Ortiz is up to, yeah." Eliana and Marianella split up, Marianella disappearing into a short hallway leading, Eliana assumed, into the bedroom, and Eliana heading toward the kitchen. The living room was sparse, just a sofa and a television set, nothing hanging on the walls. The kitchen was even emptier. One of the cupboards contained two each of a plate, a bowl, a knife, a spoon, and a fork, and in the refrigerator Eliana found only a mostly empty package of wintertime coffee. She opened up each of the drawers in turn. Empty, empty, empty.

And then one wasn't.

It was the drawer closest to the telephone, which sat haphazardly on the counter like it had been forgotten. Inside the drawer, Eliana found a blank notepad, an assortment of pens, some paper clips, old receipts, and a business card. Eliana pulled it out. It belonged to a city man, the familiar dome logo stamped on the front.

Above the dome logo was the name Pablo Sala.

Eliana stared at the business card for a long time. Costa had Sala's business card.

"Marianella!" she shouted.

She flipped the card over. There was a message scrawled on the back: *Give him the information. Best way to be rid of her.*

"What is it? Did you find something?" Marianella appeared in the kitchen. "I didn't see much in the first bedroom. The second bedroom's locked, but—" She stopped. Her shoulders slumped. "What's wrong?"

Eliana held up the card. "I found this. It's Pablo Sala's card. He was the one who stole your documents."

Marianella walked over to her side and plucked the card out of Eliana's hand. She stared down at it, her face hard.

"There's a message on the back."

Marianella read it. She was quiet for a long time. Then she set the card down on the counter.

"That's Alejo's handwriting," she said.

Eliana hesitated. She wanted to choose her words carefully. "Are you sure? It can be hard to tell—"

"I've read enough of his memos to know." Marianella turned away, her face a cold mask. "He knew he had to ensure he wasn't connected to the authorities finding out my nature, because I know about his involvement with the AFF." She smiled cruelly, her eyes glittering. "He did this on purpose. It was Alejo from the beginning. Probably found someone desperate—"

"Sala had access to the new drone types," Eliana said. "That's probably why Ortiz chose him. Someone who could break in easily."

"Well, at least Sala was stupid. Stupid enough to take the information to Ignacio instead of the police."

Marianella marched out of the kitchen, her heels clicking against the tile.

"Marianella, wait!" Eliana snatched the card off the counter, reconsidered, dropped it back into the drawer. Then she ran into the living room. Marianella disappeared around the bend in the hallway, back into the open bedroom. There wasn't much there, just an unmade bed, a chest of drawers, a pile of dirty clothes. Marianella stood next to the window with her arms crossed over her chest. At least the curtains were drawn.

"I'm sorry about Alejo," Eliana said.

Marianella reached up and wiped at her eyes. "It's not your fault." She looked over at her. "It's mine. I was so wrapped up in trying to prove I was human, I didn't see that he was using me." Another tear dripped down her cheek. She let it fall, and it left a trail of mascara behind. "I guess I was using him, too. But that he would have me destroyed—that's too much. Too much." She shook her head.

Eliana walked over to her. Marianella kept her head held high despite her tears, and she still looked regal and sophisticated, more so than Eliana could ever hope to be.

"My mother used to say this city was a prison," Eliana said. "She said everything was different here, the way people treat each other—"

"No," Marianella said. "It's not. The mainland's just as cruel." She turned around, and the curtain rippled with her movement and let in a beam of white dome light. "But this place fools ambitious people. People like Alejo Ortiz. It makes them think they have more power than they do." A smile flickered. "And people like Alejo think people like me are easy to control."

She strode out of the room.

Eliana stood in the silence of the apartment, listening to her pulse echoing in her ears. And then—

A crash, wood breaking, splintering, falling into pieces.

"What the fuck!" Eliana charged out into the hallway. Marianella had pulled the door to the second bedroom from its hinges. Bits of wood scattered all across the carpet. She looked over her shoulder at Eliana and shrugged.

"It was locked," she said.

"I could have picked it!"

Marianella tossed the door aside. Eliana's heart raced. This was bad. This showed they'd been here. This meant the police, meant Eliana losing her license—

"Oh my God," Marianella said.

Her voice trembled. Whatever ferocity had driven her to rip a door from its hinges was gone. Eliana squeezed into the doorway beside her. Looked into the room.

Froze.

There was no bed, only a worktable spread with fragments of metal. At first Eliana thought she was just staring at robot parts. But then Marianella covered her mouth with her hand and let out a low, keening sound.

"That monster," she whispered. Tears shimmered on her eyelashes. "That *monster*."

And that's when Eliana saw it. The wires, the empty canisters. Not robot parts.

Explosives.

Eliana couldn't breathe. She couldn't think.

She had to think.

"Don't touch anything!" she said. "I mean, I know you touched the door, but the explosives, don't—"

"That son of a bitch," Marianella said.

Eliana wavered.

"That filthy, traitorous son of a *whore*." Her cheeks were flushed. "Do you know what this means?"

"Not really." Eliana was dizzy at the thought of standing in an apartment full of explosives. She couldn't think straight.

"Alejo did it. When Sala fell through, he found another way to betray me." Her hands curled into fists. Eliana took a step back.

"Maybe Costa is just part of some faction. Maybe Alejo doesn't know." But Eliana didn't believe that either.

"Look what happened when the dome burned down," Marianella

said. Her voice hummed with quiet rage. "He removed me from the project and he got the support of the people." She was trembling. "Maybe he was planning it all along, to steal my work—"

Eliana placed one hand on Marianella's arm. Marianella closed her eyes. A tear streaked down her cheek.

"We should go to the police," Eliana said. "Call it in as an anonymous tip—"

"No!" Marianella's voice was stronger than Eliana had expected. "Absolutely not."

"Oh. Jesus." Of course, the stalemate. "Then what do we do?" Eliana asked.

Marianella opened her eyes. Took a deep breath. She looked at the explosives like she could ignite them herself.

"I'll take care of it," she said, and her voice made Eliana shiver.

CHAPTER THIRTY-SIX

MARIANELLA

Marianella sat in Alejo's office, staring at his secretary typing over at her desk. She hadn't told Eliana she was coming here—hadn't told Eliana anything. They'd sped away from Andres's apartment in that hulking old-fashioned car, and Marianella had gripped the steering wheel tightly enough that her fingers ached. But she'd taken Eliana back to her apartment in the smokestack district. "Stay here," she'd said. "Don't answer the door."

"What! Why!"

Marianella shook her head. "Because it's not safe yet."

And then she'd driven to Alejo's office.

He was in there, tucked away in the back hallway. She could sense him—smell him, with her activated machine parts. Pine trees and European cologne wafting through the recycled air.

"How much longer will it be?" Marianella asked. She'd been waiting for five minutes, and it had been torture waiting even that long.

"I told you, Lady Luna, he's meeting with some men from the city. Without an appointment—" The secretary lifted her hands, questioning. "He's a busy man these days."

"Yes, I imagine he is." Marianella crossed her legs, patted the side of her hair. Adrenaline surged through her. Seeing that business card calling for her disposal had coalesced into the strength she'd used to rip the door from its hinges. But that one act hadn't been enough to burn up all her anger.

She stood up.

The secretary glanced at her over the typewriter, agitation making her vibrate.

"I told you, it will only be a few moments," she said.

"No, it won't." Marianella strode forward. She walked quickly and purposefully, and she kept her head held high. The secretary shrieked behind her and followed.

"Lady Luna, he doesn't want to be disturbed!"

"I don't care." Marianella flung his office door open. There were no city men in there. Just Alejo. He looked up at her, his face blank. The secretary babbled apologies at Marianella's side, and for a moment Marianella felt sorry for her.

"See?" Marianella said, in as sweet a voice as she could muster. "His meeting's all finished up."

Alejo glared at her. Marianella went in and shut the door, leaving the secretary out in the hallway.

"You're a liar," she said.

"Technically," he said, "Rosa is."

Marianella walked forward and sat down across from his desk. Her heart pounded; heat flushed in her cheeks. She kept seeing the bomb in Andres's apartment. Alejo had done that. Alejo had asked for that.

Alejo was a monster.

"What do you want?" he said. "Is this about another donation? You know you can just send them—"

"You destroyed the agriculture dome," she said.

Alejo fell quiet, and his face went slack. The silence in the room buzzed.

"You tried to have me deported," she whispered. "And then you destroyed all my work."

Alejo shifted in his seat. He brushed his hair back with one hand. Looked at one of the walls.

"It was brave of you," he finally said, "to come here. To accuse me of that."

"I'm not accusing you of anything. You did it."

He looked at her. There was that glitter in his eyes that should have told her all those months ago that something was wrong with him. He was no better than Ignacio.

"Someone's been snooping," he said.

Marianella let out a long breath. "Why did you do it?" she whispered.

Alejo sighed. He threw up one hand, pinched the bridge of his nose. Shook his head. Stupid human politician tics. "I had to," he finally said. "When Cabrera tried to kill you at the Midwinter Ball, I knew I couldn't fuck around anymore."

Marianella stared at him in horror. Then she leapt to her feet and pressed her hands into the top of his desk and leaned close to him, pressing so hard, her hands indented the wood.

Alejo jumped, glanced down at the marred desk.

"You bombed the dome." Saying it aloud was painful. It made the truth become real.

He didn't answer.

"All our work." Marianella stumbled away from the desk. "All my work. You destroyed it—because of Cabrera?" She looked up at Alejo. The room spun. "I don't understand. What did you think this was going to accomplish? That you could just beat him to it, and that would be okay?"

"No!" Alejo shook his head. "I wanted to *blame* him for it, don't you understand? Show the people that the dome was possible, and turn the tide against him. Show them they don't need his food. All politics are theater, remember?"

Marianella collapsed back down in her chair. Her mechanical parts clicked and whirred inside her, trying to calm her heartbeat.

"I wanted to make a deal," Alejo said. "But you kept refusing. I *knew* this was going to happen. If Sala had just done his job—"

"Yes," Marianella snapped. "I'd love to hear your justifications for that, too."

Alejo slumped back in his chair. He looked tired. Old. "It's the same thing," he said. "I knew it was going to be a danger, your involvement with Cabrera—"

"It wasn't my involvement!"

"Your husband's, then! Christ, does it matter? I thought if I could get you sent to Asia, it would smooth things over for all of us, and you'd have a happier life there anyway, getting to live with your own kind."

Her own kind. Marianella glared at him. "Did it ever occur to you that I consider *humans* my own kind? That that was the reason I was helping you in the first place?"

"I didn't think about it that much, for God's sake. I just needed to get you out of the city before Cabrera found out. I knew you wouldn't go on your own. I'm sorry that Sala turned out to be a selfish prick. He was trying to get paid twice, I figure, once from me and once from Cabrera. I paid him up front to get the documents. Big mistake." Alejo rolled his eyes. "This was supposed to be easy."

"Easy?" Marianella took a deep breath. Alejo was still hunched up in his chair, his eyes wide. He was pulling away from her, like he was afraid of her. And why wouldn't he be? He was right, she wasn't human—humans had never been her kind. At least he hadn't killed her. At least he'd thought he'd been trying to protect her.

"Is there anything else you need to tell me?" she said, her voice sharp and cold. "The virus that makes the maintenance robots malfunction, was that you too?"

She had spat the question without thinking, but she realized, as soon as she asked it, that the suspicion had always been there, in the back of her mind. And when Alejo gasped and stared at her, she knew she was right. He was responsible for the blackouts. It had never been Sofia, had never even been the maintenance drones.

She stood up, forcing her movements to be slow and measured despite her surging anger.

"Why?" she said. "What good could that possibly do?"

"It makes the people realize they need us." Alejo peered over the desk at her. "Same as with the explosion."

"The city was right." Marianella could hardly think straight. "All this time—it really was the AFF." She turned away from Alejo, her heart pounding. Her feet didn't seem to touch the floor. "But you made me check up on the ag drones, you were so worried."

"I thought they might have gotten infected."

Marianella looked at him over her shoulder. He gave a shrug. "It's a hard thing to control. And at that point I didn't want the ag domes failing. The explosion had always been the contingency plan, you know. In case we couldn't buy off Cabrera."

"I don't understand." Marianella shook her head, trying to jostle her thoughts free. "I can't believe you would do that and put all those people in danger just to convince them of something they already know—"

"Actually, a lot of them don't already know it. And what the fuck do you care, living out in your private dome? This is why I didn't tell you about it from the beginning. You don't even live in Hope City. You don't know how desperate things are here."

"I know you've only made things worse. You've thrown the city into chaos."

"I did what I had to." He looked up at her. "So tell me, are you going to kill me yourself, or are you going to get that robot bitch to do it for you?"

"Her name's Sofia," Marianella said. "Which you would know. You've been investigating her."

Alejo laughed. "You have been busy playing detective! Well, yes, I was investigating her. At first it was because I needed her robots, the ones she's got squirreled away in park storage—"

"The broken androids," Marianella said. "Why? What possible good could—"

"Their *parts*, Marianella. I was trying to stockpile my own supply to help with Independence. The city didn't want to bother getting to them. That's how I first met Pablo, may he rest in peace, even if he was a greedy bastard. He'd been the one to tell me about those poor little broken-down androids and how they were guarded by a sentient comfort girl. So I looked into it." He shrugged.

"You killed Inéz," she said, "because you wanted robot parts? Why didn't you just take hers?"

"That," Alejo said, "was a scare tactic. I said I was only concerned about the parts *at first*. I knew about Sofia, sure, but then I started hearing things, rumors about an android working for Cabrera. And I never ignore a rumor, Marianella. That's why I asked my men to destroy Inéz. I wanted to scare Sofia into submission. I thought it might work on a sentient robot. When it didn't, I went after her schematics. I needed to know what I was up against."

Something snapped inside Marianella, a key turning into place. She froze into a cold resolve. He'd known about Sofia all this time and he'd played *games*. He'd toyed with all of them.

"You didn't answer my question," Alejo said, after a pause. "Are you going to kill me, or are you going to get *Sofia* to do it?"

"I'm not going to kill you," Marianella said.

"If you go public with this," he said, "you know exactly what information I'll be taking to the city."

They stared at each other across the desk. Marianella thought of Sofia, sitting in operations, watching Hope City unfold in front of her. Marianella had chosen her side correctly after all.

"Good-bye, Alejo," Marianella said, and then she walked out of the office, climbed into her car, and drove back to the amusement park.

* * * *

Marianella didn't bother with the locator. It would have been faster, but she wanted the time to meditate on everything she'd learned. She wanted time to assuage her anger. To decide what to do about Alejo.

Right now, he stood in the way of Sofia taking over the city. Sofia still had not cemented her hold on the Independents, which meant there were gaps in her control sprinkled throughout the city authorities. If Alejo continued unencumbered, his deviousness would win him the support of the city. No doubt he planned on swinging in with a solution to the power outages at some point in the future. And so Alejo couldn't stay.

He could be killed. The thought made her squeamish, the way it always did. Cabrera's men had been enough death.

But there was another way, a way of giving up the stalemate. It would fit within Sofia's framework, of destroying the city from the inside out, and it would remove Alejo in only a few days' time, without having to worry about interference from those authorities not on Sofia's payroll.

But that was one of the things she had to think on as she wandered through the worn-down paths of the amusement park, through the gardens and clumps of cottages, past the lake, through the palace, into the operations room. She didn't find Sofia, and that was good. The walk calmed her and helped her think straight.

The plan, her idea, bubbled in the back of her head. She stopped in the ballroom. It was empty, dust floating through the dome light. She walked over to the windows, knelt down, said a brief prayer. She hadn't spoken to God in a long time, but she needed to right now. She asked Him if her decision was the right one, and the dome light was warm against her skin, and she knew that yes, it was, because it was the only way that wasn't evil.

Marianella lifted her head. She looked across the ballroom and thought about the night she had danced here with Sofia, and she smiled to herself. The dust looked like flecks of gold, like fragments drifting down from heaven. She prayed to the Virgin Mary for strength, and then she checked the last place in the palace that she hadn't—the kitchens.

That was where Marianella found Sofia, hunched over a maintenance drone, her hair pulled back in a ponytail. Marianella stood in the doorway and watched her work, watched her hands moving in a blur over the drone.

"What's wrong with it?"

Only then did Sofia look up, her face pale in the bright lights.

"It's infected by the virus," she said. "It's not sentient. The other drones brought it to me."

The mention of the virus twisted Marianella's stomach.

"It's not exactly a virus, you know," she said.

Sofia frowned. She knew that, of course she did, but Marianella also knew that admitting to the truth meant admitting that a human had found another way to overcome a robot.

"And as it is," Marianella said carefully, "you might want to leave it."

Sofia went very still. She almost looked as if she'd been turned off. Marianella took a deep breath and walked into the kitchen, and Sofia followed her with just her eyes, dark and unblinking.

"Why?" she said when Marianella had come to the counter.

Marianella looked down at the black-and-white marble of the countertop. It gleamed in the lights.

"Alejo did it," she said.

"What?"

"Alejo is responsible for the blackouts."

Sofia's hands still hovered above the drone. She had been in the process of taking out its motherboard, and the lights blinked back and forth in twin rows.

"I should have seen it." Marianella touched one hand to her forehead. "It was so similar to the way I programmed the drones in the ag dome. He stole the idea from me." She laughed, once, bitterness rising up in the back of her throat. "That's not all he stole from me either."

Without speaking, Sofia slid the motherboard back into the drone, although she didn't bother to close the shell. Then she walked over to Marianella and looked her straight in the eye.

"What," she said, "are you talking about?"

Marianella drank in Sofia's features. "I'm afraid I did something rather ill-advised."

"Will it be a problem?"

"It doesn't have to be."

Sofia stepped away. She was beautiful in her old housedress, her hair pulled back. Marianella wanted to reach out and rub her thumb against Sofia's jawline. Wanted to touch her one last time.

"What's going on?" Sofia asked.

The room was too hot. Marianella wished her robot parts would activate and bring her body temperature down.

"Eliana and I broke into the apartment of one of Alejo's aides."

"Why? Because you were investigating the viruses?"

Marianella nodded. And then she told her what they'd found.

Sofia listened with her head tilted to the side. She twisted a lock of hair back and forth between her fingers. Marianella watched that hair as she spoke. It was a metronome that counted the time to her story.

When Marianella finished, Sofia dropped her hand to the side.

"You know I can kill him for you," Sofia said.

"No." Marianella shook her head and then collapsed into a nearby chair. "No, that's not what I want to do."

"You're too generous," Sofia said. "You told me yourself that he killed Inéz just to frighten us, to scare me out of working with Cabrera. How could you possibly let this man live?"

Marianella sat very still. She remembered praying in the ballroom.

"I don't want anyone else to die," Marianella said. "This city, this new city, it's my dream too. A place for people like me."

Sofia didn't say anything.

"And I don't want it to be founded on blood. Not any more than it has been already." Tears formed in Marianella's eyes. She blinked, hoping they would disappear. "I know how to discredit Alejo Ortiz. But if we do it, then I have to go away."

Sofia opened her mouth to protest.

"Only for a little while," Marianella said. "While you take the city. I know you can do it. Everything's already starting to fall into place. Soon, people won't want to live here. It'll be easy to convince them to leave. For you to take control. And then you'll open the doors to all the robots of the world. And all the cyborgs." She smiled a little, the warmth of pride swelling inside her chest. "Those blackouts he devised, those will help, won't they? That's why you shouldn't treat the drones, not right now."

Sofia stared at her. "I don't understand what you're trying to say."

Marianella took a deep breath. "I'm going to tell you something. And you can go public with it. Use your city contacts. I just can't be on the continent when it happens."

Sofia's face went dark.

"Alejo Ortiz took funding from the AFF," Marianella said. "For his campaigns. They're one of his largest contributors, in fact. All secret. When Hope City achieved its independence, Alejo would become president, of course, and at that point he'd officially pardon the AFF as actual freedom fighters."

"They would be," Sofia said. "Freedom fighters."

"They're terrorists," Marianella said. "And that's how the city sees them now. If you take that information public, Alejo will be arrested and deported to the mainland. They won't let him back into the city."

Sofia's eyes glittered in a way that made Marianella feel hollow.

"I remember the day I told him about my nature. We were in the Dockside Motel. The neon lights were shining through the window." Marianella laughed at the memory, and it was a laugh like a stab wound. "He'd already told me about the AFF by then. I thought trading secrets would be romantic, like trading wedding rings. I'm so stupid."

"Not stupid," Sofia said. "Only naive."

And then she walked across the room and sat on the arm of Marianella's chair. She brushed the hair away from Marianella's face. "It'll only be temporary," she said. "Your departure."

"Yes, of course. When the city completely belongs to you, I'll come back."

"You can't possibly go alone."

"I won't." Marianella took a deep breath and lifted her face to Sofia's. "Book passage for Eliana as well. I promised her you could do that in exchange for her helping me find out about the virus, and it will be good to have a human with me." Marianella wondered when that had happened, when she'd begun thinking of humans as something other.

"It's too dangerous," Sofia said. "A human can't make that trip yet."

"Your icebreakers are safer than any run by the city. I trust you." Tears glossed Marianella's eyes. "You need to be rid of Alejo as soon as you can. Even if it's just for me, for what he did."

"We'll find some other way," Sofia said, cupping her hand under Marianella's chin.

"There is no other way." Marianella looked at her. "Unless you want to leave the city to the humans."

There was a moment, brief and flickering, when Marianella thought that Sofia would agree. That she would give up her goals, just to keep Marianella at her side.

But then it was gone.

"If it's the only way," Sofia said.

CHAPTER THIRTY-SEVEN

ELIANA

Eliana smoked a cigarette in front of her tenement building. It was late enough at night that even the smokestack district was silent. No voices echoed through the night, no music spilled out of the windows. The air was still and cold. It reminded Eliana of the amusement park.

A suitcase sat at her feet. It contained as much of her life as she could put into one piece of luggage. Which, as it turned out, wasn't much at all.

She smoked her cigarette down to the filter and flicked the butt into the darkness. She hadn't said good-bye to anyone. Not Maria, not Essie, although she hoped both of them would stop thinking of this place as home and heed her warnings and get out of the city if they could. She couldn't say good-bye to Diego. At least her parents had memorials at the mausoleum, twin urns with twin plaques. But she hadn't said good-bye to them, either.

It was too risky even to say good-bye to the dead. Ortiz could be watching the mausoleum. The only thing that Eliana had done to prepare was to look up Mr. Vasquez's forwarding address. At least they'd have a place to go once they landed on the mainland.

The clock tower struck three. Eliana jumped at the sudden noise.

Just as the last gong faded away, a sleek black limousine pulled up in front of Eliana's building. Luciano stepped out and opened the door for her.

"Miss Gomez," he said, and his soft voice sounded like screaming in the darkness.

Eliana picked up her suitcase and carried it down to the car. Luciano took it from her and slid it into the trunk. Marianella had called her yesterday afternoon and told her the payment for helping Sofia was ready. Eliana had thanked her and placed the phone back into the cradle and stood there with her head buzzing. Last night Eliana couldn't sleep. The knowledge that her dream was so close to becoming real kept her up. She'd ridden the trains with no destination in mind, staring out at the gray buildings and the gray people and the silver-gray light of the streetlamps. She'd gone to the edge of the city and put her hand against the dome's glass. And she knew nothing was keeping her here.

It wasn't a decision. It was just a fact. Hope City was no longer Eliana's home.

Marianella and Sofia were sitting side by side in the backseat. Eliana sat across from them. She felt empty without her suitcase. Marianella smiled when Eliana climbed in, but she didn't say anything.

The driver's door slammed shut, and the engine hummed to life. Luciano pulled the car away from the sidewalk. When Eliana tried to look out the window, she only saw her reflection.

Marianella and Sofia didn't speak. They didn't look at each other. But Eliana noticed how Sofia's hand was laid on top of Marianella's, a gesture of comfort she'd never expected to see.

Eliana didn't speak either. After all, there was nothing to say.

They arrived at the docks, which were as desolate as the smokestack district. The air was colder than Eliana had expected. Luciano opened the door again, Eliana's suitcase sitting at his feet. They stood off to the side as Marianella and Sofia climbed out of the car. Sofia pulled Marianella's suitcase out of the trunk and held it for her. Marianella smiled.

"The ship is waiting for you," Luciano said—unnecessarily, because there was only one ship in the water, an old cruise ship, all the painted figures along the side faded into ghosts. The gangplank was down.

"Give us a moment," Sofia said.

Luciano nodded, and then gestured for Eliana to follow him on board the ship. She trailed behind him, breathing in the scent of salt and metal. When they reached the gangplank, she looked over at Marianella and Sofia. They were kissing in a pool of yellow light from the streetlamps, Sofia's hands in Marianella's hair, Marianella clutching at Sofia's dress like the world was ending.

Eliana stared in surprise. She couldn't help herself.

"We should give them privacy," Luciano said softly into her ear.

"Are they really—" Eliana didn't quite know how to ask the question. She looked away, over to Luciano. Her face burned. He didn't seem particularly bothered.

"I believe they love each other," he said, and carted Eliana's suitcase up the gangplank.

Eliana looked over at Marianella and Sofia again. They weren't kissing anymore, but their bodies were pressed close together, and they looked at each other the way Eliana had once looked at Diego. It struck her as strange that Sofia could love at all.

Eliana left them to each other.

Luciano was waiting for her on the walkway of the ship. He smiled at her like a porter and led her away from the gangplank. Walking into the ship was like walking into catacombs. The hallways were narrow and low-ceilinged, and the few scattered lights flickered in time with their footsteps. Everything was old and stank of the sea.

"How long is the trip going to take?" Eliana asked. She thought about asking him about the reprogramming that Marianella had mentioned, but she wasn't sure it would be appropriate.

"About two weeks." Luciano glanced at her. "But there's enough food and water to last for four, in case of an emergency. The ship is connected to the operations room at the amusement park, so you'll always been in contact with Sofia."

Eliana nodded. Two weeks and she'd be on the mainland, where she had always wanted to be. All the humans in Hope City would be there soon enough. Sofia's takeover was inevitable. Eliana just hoped she'd let the humans leave.

"Your cabin," Luciano said, stopping in front of a door. "Marianella is across the hall." He pushed the door open and turned on the lights. The cabin was spacious, with two glass doors leading out onto a balcony. Everything in the cabin looked brand-new, and the lights didn't flicker.

"Sofia."

Eliana jumped; it was Marianella's voice. She turned around, and Marianella stood in the hallway alone, carrying her own suitcase.

"Yes." Luciano smiled. "She wanted it to be a surprise."

Marianella wiped at her eyes. "Tell her 'thank you' for me."

And then she disappeared into her own cabin across the hall.

Luciano set Eliana's suitcase on the bed.

"The ship will be departing soon," he said. "I'm afraid I have to stay in Antarctica."

"I know." Eliana watched him from across the room. She didn't want to leave him without saying good-bye.

"I'll miss you," she said, and she meant it, because he had been a comfort to her in these last few weeks in Antarctica.

"I'll miss you as well." He walked up to her and pulled something out of his jacket. It was one of the books he was always reading, slim, the cover dark blue. "I wanted to give this to you."

Eliana stared down at the book, surprised. Yellow letters spelled out *Le Petit Prince* in curlicue script.

"A book," she said stupidly.

"Yes, I enjoyed it quite a bit. I think you will like it as well."

Eliana couldn't take her eyes off the book. "Is it in French?"

"Yes."

"I don't know French."

"I think you could learn." Luciano pressed the book into Eliana's hand, and she wrapped her fingers around it and didn't want to let go.

He smiled. Eliana thought how this would be the last time she'd see him smile, and she wondered if she'd find someone to share walks with on the mainland. If she'd find someone who knew how to listen. "Have a nice journey," he said.

"I'll try."

They stood in a heavy silence. Neither of them moved for several moments.

And then he said, "I hope you enjoy your first real rainstorm. Perhaps when you see it, you'll remember me."

Something quivered inside Eliana. There was a sense of waking up. "I'm sure I will," she said, and she knew it wouldn't just be the first rainstorm, but all the rainstorms she'd ever encounter.

And then, like that, Luciano was gone.

Eliana sat in her room for a while, in the chair beside the window. She flipped through the book's pages and tried to decipher the words. Some of them were similar to words she knew, but there weren't enough of them for her to understand the story. She thought about knocking on Marianella's door but decided that Marianella must want to be alone. Although really, Eliana knew, *she* wanted to be alone.

The ship engines switched on.

Eliana straightened up in her chair. The engines roared around her, a cottony white noise that created a buzzing in her head. She'd never heard anything like it.

And then the room lurched and there was a great groaning from outside, and Eliana knew they were leaving Hope City.

The realization that she would never see the city again hit her like a punch.

Eliana set the book on the bed and left the room and jogged through the corridors. The ship creaked and moaned, and Eliana was struck with the thought that she was the only human thing aboard.

The corridor opened suddenly onto an outside deck. The wind rushing over her was colder than any she'd ever experienced, and she knew she wasn't dressed properly, but she pulled her coat more tightly around her chest. Five minutes wouldn't kill her.

The lights of the docks twinkled in the distance. Eliana stood in the center of the deck and watched the city grow smaller. She didn't cry. As much as she had wanted to see the city lights one last time, she didn't feel anything but a vague sense of hope, like the city's name came from leaving it.

And then, without warning, the sky was dotted with light.

Stars. She'd only ever seen pictures.

The ship had passed through the dome wall without Eliana realizing, and now those millions and millions of stars swirled overhead. Eliana craned her head back, her breath solidifying on the air, and stared at them in wonder. Pictures hadn't prepared her for the enormity of the night sky, the enormity of the world beyond the dome.

And then the stars were falling, in fits and starts, drifting and scattering across the deck. No, not stars—snow.

Eliana shivered violently. Soon the cold would be too much, and she'd have to go down below and find solace in the manufactured heat. But in this moment, this last good-bye, she stood in the biting wind with her head tilted back so the snowflakes could melt on her tongue.

* * * *

* * *

* *

*

ACKNOWLEDGMENTS

A whole heaping of thanks goes out to all the people who helped shaped this book into what it has become today:

My beta reader and podcast partner in crime, Alexandre Maki, who not only helped with characters and plot, but who also reminded me where adjectives go in Portuguese.

My agent, Stacia Decker, who saw me through several drafts of this book and whose feedback was, as always, excellent—without her, this book would never have gotten to the state in which you're currently reading it.

My editor, Navah Wolfe, who helped polish the final draft to perfection.

All my writing buddies, the Space City Critters, especially Amanda Cole, Bobby Mathews, David Young, and Laura Lam, who are always there to help me through writerly rough patches. And a special shout-out to Amanda for asking an Anonymous Internet Person for some advice on Argentine culture; any mistakes are my own, not his.

And finally, a huge thanks to my parents for supporting my writing since I was a kid, and to Ross Andrews, whose support always sees me through.